Advance Prai

MW01025999

"Funny, clever, and deliciously dark, I loved it!"
Jemahl Evans, author of *The Last Roundhead*

"This is science fiction at its best—thoughtful, engaging, entertaining, and with something witty to say about the wisdom of the choices we're making today. A fine mix of futurism, wry observation and cutting social commentary, *Sub-Luminal* should be on every fan's bookshelf.
Funnier than *The Moon is a Harsh Mistress*, shorter than *Lord of the Rings*, and more relevant than *Five on a Treasure Island*, *Sub-Luminal* is science fiction you can get your teeth into."
James Evans, author of the Royal Marine Space Commandos series

"*Sub-Luminal* is a science-fiction novel of the future dealing with fog-brained fools ruled by ruthless AI. Which is to say: 'future' = 'now'. Five stars for taking a conventional science-fiction plot and making it original, and fun, and exciting. For me it was pleasure to read plucky humans facing the AI devil and Idiocracy blither, and coming out ahead. "
Raymond St. Elmo, author of the Quest of Five Clans series

Sub-Luminal is a delight for readers who revel in the sheer joy of language; for anyone who loves dry wit and understated humour. Sitting at that popular intersection between visionary sci-fi and wry social commentary, it's an entertaining blend of drama, comedy and satire. For fans of everything from *The Office* to The Hitch Hiker's Guide series, this could be a rare and memorable treat.
Rob Gregson, author of *Shelf Life* and The Written World series

SUB-LUMINAL

Alastair Miles

Shadow Dragon Press

ISBN: 978-1-963832-06-8 (paperback)
ISBN: 978-1-963832-20-4 (ebook)
LCCN: 2024946071
Copyright © 2025 by Alastair Miles

Cover Design & Illustration: Ian Bristow, Bristow Design

Shadow Dragon Press
9 Mockingbird Hill Rd
Tijeras, New Mexico 87059
www.shadowdragonpress.com
info@shadowdragonpress.com

For my family. You mean any number of worlds to me.

Thanks to Jemahl and Rob for the edits, advice and, most importantly, the belief.

TABLE OF CONTENTS

CHAPTER 1
COURSE CORRECTION

CALLUM AWOKE WITH A START.

His eyes fluttered open. There was a dark blur, then a light blur, before he finally focused on the condensation on the lid of his canopy.

"Jeeves," he attempted to say.

It came out more like 'Jleashs'.

He tried to move, but that was a mistake. His head hurt. There was dizziness and nausea. It felt like the aftermath of a great night out, except that he'd been nothing but 'in' for a great many years.

"Good day, Captain MacMahon," Jeeves said. "It is agreeable to see you awake. Might I suggest some fluid, sir?"

A tube slid into view. It took all his will to crane his neck and grab it between his lips. There was a brief sensation of pleasure as he sipped the fluid and felt his mouth begin to loosen. Then the taste hit home and his large intestine considered sending it right back where it came from.

"Ach," was Callum's succinct review of the drink. He spat out the tube.

"I recommend you continue, sir. It is a solution of electrolytes and nutrients designed to stimulate your system."

"Tastes like it's gone off," Callum croaked.

"Your reaction is understandable, sir. Your stomach is currently lined with nothing more than a protective gel."

Callum wished he hadn't heard that as the canopy opened, and he pushed himself clear. He drifted out into the *Endeavour's* hibernation chamber. Nothing had changed. It looked exactly as it had when he went under.

That prompted his next question.

"Have we arrived?" Callum asked.

"Almost, sir."

It was not the answer he was looking for. When it comes to interstellar distances, 'almost' leaves considerable margin for error.

"Can you quantify that?"

"We are approximately 20 million miles from Arcadia. Our final deceleration phase has been suspended temporarily while you recover from your period in hibernation."

Callum's immediate reaction was one of relief, they'd made it. He'd feared that Jeeves had awoken him mid-flight with a serious problem. In practical terms, light years from home, there would have been little Callum could have actually done beyond providing tea and sympathy—neither of which were much use to Jeeves

"So we've done it? We've travelled twelve light years?"

"Indeed, sir. The *Endeavour* has performed flawlessly."

"And we've been in hibernation for a century?"

"99.463 years, sir. It is pleasing to have company again."

Jeeves had been conscious for the entire trip. Although, whether you'd classify Jeeves as conscious was down to how charitable you felt towards quantum circuitry. Jeeves was an AI. Its name being an in-house joke by its designers—who'd never got out much.

However, Jeeves was flattered by its nickname, or it believed it was. It had even devoted the best part of a second of its runtime to reading the collected works of PG Wodehouse, then far more time than that attempting to appreciate the humour. But, whatever its difficulties with twentieth century literature, throughout the long flight it had never wavered from its key goals of 'protection and preservation'—protection of the crew and preservation of the vessel that carried them.

Callum looked at his hiber-sleep pod. A place he'd resided within for more than a lifetime. The rest of the crew, two hundred in total, remained sound asleep. His brain still scrabbled to come to terms with consciousness. It had spent decades content with visions of bracken, mountains, dramatic skies and distant lochs with waters clear and calm. It had been like dreaming inside a tourist brochure.

As his thoughts slowly began to order themselves he came back to the question of why Jeeves had awoken only him. He needed an answer.

"So, why am I awake, Jeeves? Is Arcadia alright? Is it habitable?"

"Yes sir. I have long since confirmed that through remote observation."

"Then what's the problem?"

"The problem is that it seems to be rather too habitable. Scans indicate significant surface development. What is more, we appear to have a welcome party."

Callum was glad of the absence of gravity. Had it been present it would have sent him crashing to the floor.

"First contact?" he said to himself, as much as to Jeeves. Advanced alien life had always been a remote possibility, but he'd never believed it might actually happen. It was almost too much to take in.

During its runtime Jeeves had learnt how to pause on a scale appropriate to the average human. For 23.476 billion clock cycles it did just that.

"I'm afraid not, sir. They have identified themselves as human. I believe they are a colony from Earth."

"Did you say, Earth?"

"I did, sir."

"But we're the first interstellar mission in human history. How can anyone be waiting for us?"

"It is somewhat surprising, sir."

"Aye, too bloody right," Callum said, his voice cracking under the strain of unfamiliar exercise.

"It would appear that while we were the first to leave, sir. We were not the first to arrive."

Captain Callum MacMahon felt an overwhelming urge to climb back inside his hiber-sleep pod.

This couldn't be happening.

***

The ship had been shadowing *Endeavour* for several hours now. It jinked and dodged as if the conservation of energy was something that happened to other people. Watching it gave Callum a headache or, more precisely, another one to add to his collection.

Endeavour's bridge was not exactly roomy. While there was a lot of space outside, it was at a premium in the craft itself. Still, with just Callum strapped into his command chair at the centre, the room seemed curiously empty—as did the whole ship.

He was feeling stronger, in body if not in mind. His biggest challenge continued to be eating and drinking while his stomach played ping pong with any nutrition it received. Baby food was the most pragmatic option. So Callum strove to put away a modest bowl of freeze-dried Yum Yum's 'Banana and Date, Oaty Porridge'. If his digestive system held out, he could look forward to a rusk for dessert.

Tapping a screen brought up a log of Jeeves' first encounter with this vessel. The ship had approached *Endeavour* at a rate that showed little respect for Einstein's Theory of Relativity. It had taken *Endeavour* years to build up its speed to a modest fraction of that of light. This ship could do much the same in a matter of seconds.

"The vessel has a single occupant," Jeeves said. "He identified himself as our welcome party and wished to initiate communication. Hence I thought it best to awaken you, sir."

Whoever this person was, they were somehow impervious to their craft's titanic accelerations, which should have squashed them flatter than a steam-pressed pancake.

Callum played back the hail.

"Calling *Endeavour*," a male voice said, sounding a little over-awed. "We're glad you made it. I am your... welcome party. I look forward to meeting you on behalf of Arcadia. Please respond, all will be explained."

"I have yet to ascertain how the inhabitants of this system beat us to our goal," Jeeves said. "I have requested that our welcome party standby for further communication."

Ahead of awakening Callum, Jeeves had dedicated a few trillion clock cycles to simulating how the captain might react. The results had born a distinct resemblance to a fly that had just struck a window.

They appeared to be accurate.

"How long's he been waiting?" Callum asked.

"A number of hours, sir. He is aware that you require time to recover from hibernation and to assimilate the news of his presence."

"Aye, well he'd be right."

Callum knew he couldn't put off this conversation indefinitely. He groaned, partly at his situation and partly because the ship had resumed deceleration. Jeeves had suspended the braking phase to ease Callum's emergence from hibernation—and would do so again when more of his crew emerged. But, in the meantime, it was making up for lost time. If *Endeavour* didn't shed sufficient speed, her trajectory would overshoot Arcadia and their arrival would be delayed by weeks. In other words, Newtonian physics meant it was possible to arrive late by travelling too fast. Space might be a vacuum, but there was no shortage of irony.

A touch of his screen would put him through to the person who was patiently waiting. His right hand hovered over the control and, with a resigned sigh, he finally forced it down.

"This is Callum MacMahon, Captain of the *Endeavour*," he said. "To whom am I speaking?"

There was a pause—understandable given how long the other ship had been made to wait.

"Ah," was what he heard from the speaker, "greetings Captain MacMahon. My name is Leyton Smith. I bring you fraternal greetings from Arcadia. Allow me to extend our congratulations on the completion of your historic voyage."

That sounded like a pre-prepared line if ever he'd heard one. Callum felt a twinge of envy; he wasn't prepared for this at all.

"Thanks," Callum replied. He forced himself to make conversation. "I'm glad to hear you say Arcadia. That was going to be our name for this world."

"Yes... we know," Leyton replied hesitantly. "The name was kept as a token of respect for your original mission. I imagine you must be pretty confused right now?"

"Confused doesn't begin to cover it," MacMahon replied.

Before departure, Callum had accepted that they might be forgotten about. Humanity had other things to do. There were wars to be fought, environmental disasters to contain,

5

not to mention the crowning of the annual winner of Celebrity Dance Island. In truth, he'd been glad to get away. But he'd never expected humanity to be waiting for him all the way out here.

"Look," Callum continued after a short pause, "don't take this the wrong way, but you're not supposed to be here. I've spent years of my life training to lead the first mission to colonise an alien planet. I've only had a few hours to come to terms with the idea that I might have wasted the last hundred years. There's a wee bit more going on with me than just 'confusion'."

"I guess you're pretty pissed too?"

"Yet it'll be a week before I can keep alcohol down."

There was another awkward silence.

"That was a joke lad," Callum said.

"Oh, I see."

"Never mind, shall we start again?"

"Of course, Captain. I'm sorry about this. Can I ask if you are all fit and well?"

"So I'm told."

"That's good to hear."

Callum cleared his still sticky throat again—it was clearly as enthused by this conversation as he was.

"Leyton, is it possible to set up a visual feed? I work better when I can see whom I'm talking to."

"Not a problem. This vessel is designed to be compatible with yours. We have *Endeavour*'s schematics stored within our archive. Shall I set it up?"

Callum ignored the reference to an archive—he felt old enough already.

"Go ahead," he said.

An image appeared on Callum's screen. In contrast to the *Endeavour*, the cockpit of the other vessel was brightly lit, clean and fresh in a way that rubbed salt in the wound. Its sole occupant was a blond-haired individual in his twenties dressed in a trim, light blue jumpsuit. He looked irritatingly full of youth and vigour.

Callum wasn't exactly old. You couldn't go on a mission to colonise another planet, with all the procreation that entailed, and be of advanced years. Well, you could try, but sending old men to breed extensively would not have put the mission in a good light—and this was a government run programme. In Callum's case, it was his vast experience as an astronaut that had swung his selection, despite the fact that he was in the denial phase of early middle age. He might not be past it yet, but he was certainly coming up alongside.

In terms of looks, aside from a touch of grey around the temples, he was relatively well preserved. But, when he looked at this clean-cut individual, it only served to remind him of how utterly crap he still felt.

"There you are, Captain," Leyton said. "Wow, that's a view from history and no mistake. It's amazing to think that you travelled all this way in that antique."

References to antiques also didn't help. It was hard to think of the *Endeavour* as old. When they'd left Earth, she'd been state of the art. They'd all known technology would move on during the century they'd spend in hiber-sleep, but they'd never expected that to be thrown into sharp relief.

Leyton continued, oblivious. "It's so quaint. Your bridge looks exactly like it was pictured at school."

Did that kid say school? Callum's eyes rolled in a bid to look at the back of his head.

"Aye, it would, wouldn't it?" Callum said, through teeth that were not so much clenched, as seized.

It now seemed to dawn on Leyton that he might have overstepped the mark.

"Please excuse my enthusiasm, Captain. It was the impact of your image appearing on my screen. It takes me right back to my time in the colonial school system."

Callum was pleased to hear that they were still historically significant. But this latest revelation implied that whoever the settlers of Arcadia were, they'd apparently had time to build a school network. What was more, youths such as this one were products of their education system.

A fresh question entered Callum's crowded head and his brow furrowed to an extent that usually required serious farming equipment.

"Wait a minute, how long has Arcadia been settled?"

There was a pause, a long pause, and it was the turn of Leyton's brow to furrow as if he'd just been asked to solve a second order differential equation—while hanging upside down in a vat of porridge.

After looking up at the ceiling, in the vain hope that the answer had been recorded up there, he said eventually, "I think it was almost forty cycles ago."

Callum assumed that a cycle had to refer to an Arcadian year. He was tempted to challenge Leyton to do the conversion, but judging by the kid's expression he suspected that it would be as painful to watch as it would be for Leyton to do. Callum knew Arcadia's orbital period, forty cycles equated roughly to eighty years. This meant that the Arcadian colony had been established when *Endeavour* had only been twenty years into its journey.

This made little sense. It seemed vanishingly unlikely that anybody could have beaten them here by such a margin. Still, eliminate the impossible, as Sherlock Holmes had once said, and whatever remains, however improbable, must be the truth. So what was the most likely explanation?

Callum took stock of the individual in front of him. Based on their conversation so far, it was apparent that Leyton's brain was about as sharp as his square jaw.

"Humour me," Callum said. "Can you confirm what year it is? On the Earth calendar that is?"

Leyton's brow furrowed once again. Callum could only marvel at how wrinkle-free it was most of the time. For whatever reason, numbers were clearly something Leyton struggled with—kind of worrying for an astronaut.

Leyton made another fruitless search for the answer on the bulkhead above his chair. But he was finally forced to admit defeat.

"I'm not sure," he said.

"Not even roughly?"

"I'm afraid not. I'm without my data link and I'm receiving medication designed to assist with the stresses of space travel—it's left me a little limited."

Callum could appreciate that Leyton must be under stress, but he still found it astounding that he could not answer such a basic question. All he could conclude was that, as far as astronaut training was concerned, the bar must have dropped—possibly on Leyton's head.

"Alright, let's try this another way. You said you'd been expecting us. Tell me, did we arrive when we were supposed to?"

Leyton looked relieved, the wrinkles on his forehead disappeared. His face took on a look of puppyish enthusiasm. "Yes, you arrived here exactly when you were supposed to. That's why I'm here to meet you."

So, *Endeavour* definitely hadn't been delayed. It had always been a longshot to imagine such a possibility, but Callum had been dealing in the improbable long enough already.

"Alright, maybe the direct approach is best. Tell me, how did the *Endeavour* get beaten out here? Can you tell me how you, or your ancestors, got here so far ahead of us?"

Leyton's puppyish expression returned as this appeared to be a question he could actually answer. "The truth is a little surprising, but we... that is, the people who settled the planet, flew faster than the speed of light."

"What?" Callum was certainly surprised.

"I said they flew-"

"I heard you, I just didn't trust my ears."

"There was a big scientific discovery," Leyton said. "New physics. I don't understand the theory, but it's now possible to jump across light years almost instantaneously."

Once again, Callum was glad he was sitting down. Ever since Jeeves had broken the news to him that Arcadia was already inhabited, he knew he had to accept that they'd somehow been beaten to the punch. But he hadn't been prepared for how easily it had been done. It seemed that the ships that passed them had not so much broken the speed of light as wrecked it.

There had not been so much as a hint of such a thing being even remotely possible when they'd departed.

"It's still a big undertaking flying between the stars," Leyton said, in a failed attempt to help Callum feel better. "The drives are hard to make. Even then, they can only be configured by an AI. There are only about a dozen established colonies, those that we're aware of, that is."

The sick feeling Callum had in the pit of his stomach had less and less to do with his emergence from hibersleep. He forced himself to focus. There was a lot he had to learn.

Alastair Miles

"That ship you came in. Has that got one of those drives?"

Leyton shook his head. "No, it can't jump across light years, it's just for in-system travel, or so I'm told. But it hasn't been needed in a while."

"Oh? Why not?"

"We have all we need on Arcadia."

"You don't want to explore?"

"I'd miss Arcadia. I'd like to get back. I feel disconnected out here."

"What do you mean?"

"There's a data core on the ship but it's no substitute for the Sphere."

"I don't understand."

"It's hard to explain."

"Try."

"I am trying."

"In more ways than one."

Callum realised he'd said that out loud.

"I'm sorry, Captain," Leyton said, having not appeared to have taken offence. "I am doing my best to help you, but there comes a point where I think you'd be better of talking to Virgil."

"Virgil?"

"Virgil is our planetary AI. It looks after us."

In this case, a planetary AI was a concept that had existed before Callum had left Earth—although there were only some vague concepts and plans at that point. The idea, as far as he'd understood it, was to have a single AI encompassing the planet capable of controlling its economy, utility and services in an independent and objective manner.

At first glance, it was a disturbing prospect. How could it be considered wise to leave your future health and prosperity to the whims of a machine? The answer was to consider the alternative. Human beings were self-serving, greedy and entirely hypocritical. At the time of *Endeavour's* departure the debate had yet to be resolved. There had been talk of a referendum, because there's nothing like a referendum for reaching a decision that everyone can get behind.

"I presume," Callum said, "that a planetary AI does

much the same as Jeeves does for us on *Endeavour*, except on a larger scale?"

"That is a disservice to Virgil, Captain," Leyton replied, looking mildly offended. "Virgil maintains our entire planet, unlike a mere ship's computer."

"Charming," wrote Jeeves on Callum's personal screen.

Callum let it pass and pressed on; this was at least a topic that Leyton seemed more willing to talk about. "I presume an AI was created on Earth as well then?"

"Yes, that was the first planetary AI, called Eve. Virgil refers to it as the greatest AI of all. It was Eve who made faster than light travel possible."

"Eve made the breakthrough so rapidly?"

"Correct Captain. AIs are really important. That's why, on reaching Arcadia, the first priority was to establish Virgil to guide our development."

"Same idea on a smaller scale?"

From Leyton's expression it was clear he'd said the wrong thing. "Please do not refer to Virgil as small."

When it came to discussing Arcadia's AI, Callum felt like he was walking on eggshells. If it went on like this, he'd be in line for an omelette.

"I apologise," Callum replied. "Thank you for explaining all this to me, Leyton. There is clearly much for me to learn."

Leyton looked mollified so Callum moved the conversation swiftly on.

"So, what's your story?" he asked. "How did you end up out here?"

"I'm a pilot. It's fun. Virgil encourages us to pursue our dreams. We only work if it is something we wish to do. All Virgil wants is for us to be happy."

Not all pilots could be pigeonholed, but a certain amount of arrogance was typically involved. But not in Leyton's case. His confidence was brittle, to say the least. Yet, to give him his due, he'd had the guts to fly out here solo to meet them. Either that or he wasn't bright enough to understand the risks. Whatever the reason, Callum decided to cut him some slack.

"What sort of thing do you fly?" he asked.

"All sorts," Leyton replied with boyish enthusiasm. "I guess my favourites are the smaller ramjet couriers and passenger shuttles. I sometimes get to take them sub-orbital."

"Are you saying you've never been into orbit?"

"No one has. As I said, we are content on Arcadia."

"Well then, I admire your courage. It took guts to come out here."

Leyton looked humble.

"The ship is mainly automatic. Virgil needed a human representative out here to greet you and told me I possess the right skills to fulfil this mission, within the required parameters."

God alone knew what 'required parameters' meant. It was a safe bet that Leyton didn't know either. But Callum was not about to risk querying the wisdom of Virgil once again.

"And what happens now?" Callum asked. "What's the plan?"

"With your permission, I'm here to guide you into Arcadian orbit. The President is expecting you."

"Then I guess we'd better not keep your president waiting. If you transfer your navigation data, we will adjust our heading accordingly."

Leyton looked confused, again. "I assumed I would take direct control of your vessel?"

Jeeves placed a large, flashing, red exclamation mark on Callum's forward screen. This, in turn, was bordered by smaller exclamation marks and overlaid on an exclamation mark motif.

Callum cut the comms.

"It would appear that you've been developing your sense of humour in the last one hundred years, Jeeves," he said.

"I am ill at ease with surrendering control of the *Endeavour*, sir."

"Well don't worry about that, it's not happening. I trust that kid with piloting this ship as much as I would a monkey."

"You are a primate yourself, sir."

"That's not what I mean, Jeeves."

"Yes, sir."

Callum re-activated the comms.

"Sorry Leyton, slight computer problem." Callum now

made an effort to sound as diplomatic as possible. "With regards to your... kind offer to take control of our vessel. We would prefer to decline. We have come this far by ourselves and would like to finish the job."

Leyton looked conflicted.

"Are you alright, Leyton?" Callum asked.

"Yes, I..." he said, eventually, "...I was just surprised that you would not accept my offer. It was made in your best interest."

"And we appreciate it," Callum said. "Just give us a heading and our shipboard AI will get us there, I'm sure."

Again a pause, "Very well, I will do that."

"Thank you."

With that, the conversation soon drew to a close.

"Well Jeeves," Callum said, once the comms were cut, "that was quite a..." He couldn't find the words. "Wasn't it?" he concluded.

Jeeves's reply was succinct. "Aptly put, sir."

***

The crew of *Endeavour* had been the finest available or, more accurately, the finest willing to accept a one-way ticket. While they weren't perfect, they were annoyingly good.

The job specification had a number of conflicting requirements. Top of the list was a willingness to travel. That much was obvious. However, once the intended destination was reached, it was essential that the aspiring candidate be content to stay put—despite a lack of adequate toilet facilities.

Furthermore, anyone who went had to be capable of breaking whatever ties they had back home. Equally, they had to be prepared to stick with those who went with them through thick and quite a lot of thin.

So it was no surprise that *Endeavour*'s crew were, tactfully speaking, a diverse assortment of individuals. However, each of them had their own key set of skills and each was ready for a fresh start on a new world.

Callum wondered how he'd break the news to them.

He drifted into the darkened hibernation chamber, grateful that Jeeves had once more cut the main drive in readiness for awakening the command staff. The darkness was punctuated by the status lights from the hiber-sleep pods that lined the walls.

"Increase the illumination, Jeeves, they'll be awake soon."

The hibernation bay was mainly white and, aside from a daring dash of grey, the use of colour seemed to have been frowned upon. Some argued that an absence of colour focused the mind. Others argued that the interior designer had been focused on getting home early.

Callum took a deep breath, knowing that this would be the last time *Endeavour* would be so peaceful. Sure enough, the silence was ended by the sound of breaking seals. Callum wondered who would wake first.

The first eyelids to flutter belonged to a compact, solid looking female who managed to look as if she'd got out of the wrong side of bed without even leaving it. Liliya Sokolov was Russian by birth and the Chief Security/Safety Officer—anyone around her was safe and secure provided they didn't get on her bad side. She'd let it be known that she was tough and uncompromising. Callum had seen no reason to argue.

It took a few involuntary blinks before Liliya managed to keep her eyes open. The first noises she made were, most likely, a choice selection of Russian expletives, but post-hibernation slurring made it hard to be sure. Callum tapped the side of her pod and received a look of bewildered irritation for his efforts.

"How are you feeling?" he asked.

"Have we arrived?" she croaked.

"Yes," he replied, which was broadly true.

"Why are you awake first?"

"Captain's privilege, Liliya. Now stay still and let Jeeves take care of you. There will be a briefing shortly."

The Security Officer glared at him, as sure a sign as any that she was basically fit and well.

Callum was startled by a groan like a walrus with muscle cramp.

While Zhang Lei was a great engineer, his appearance left a lot to be desired. On the plus side it meant that he looked entirely unaffected by prolonged hibernation. When it came to looking dishevelled there was no disputing that the Chief Engineer put the hours in. Lei blinked a few times to clear his vision before turning his attention towards his captain.

"Have we arrived?" he asked.

"Yes."

"You awake already?"

"Yes again. Jeeves had something to ask me. There will be a briefing shortly."

Lei scratched thoughtfully, content to reacquaint himself with his body, which had a hundred years' worth of complaints to share with him.

Kyra Singh, the crew's Science Officer, was next to awake and she was far easier on the eye than Lei. Not that this was hard to achieve. However, from Callum's point of view, Kyra remained unstintingly attractive, even after a century's worth of hiber-sleep. Admittedly, Callum was biased—the two of them had been getting on better and better prior to launch. The question now was whether that would still be the case after a century's intermission.

The Science Officer forced her large, almond shaped eyes open and tried to make them focus.

"Have we-", she slurred.

"Yes, we have," Callum said gently, before she could finish.

"Already awake?"

"Sit tight. It's fine. There'll be a briefing shortly."

The script was getting repetitive. Callum wondered if there was a sign he could hold up.

Patting Kyra's pod, Callum turned to the neighbouring pod which contained Tomoko Beck. Even when recovering from hiber-sleep, her half-Asian features still maintained a certain dignity—her inbuilt serious expression in keeping with the position of First Officer. Tomoko was senior to everyone except Callum, but even he had a hard time remembering that.

"Captain," she said curtly.

"Aye," Callum replied, almost saluting.

"Have we arrived?"

"Yes, we have. Yes, I'm already awake. And yes, there will be a briefing shortly—just for the command staff. I'll tell you more once you've sufficiently recovered."

Before Tomoko could question her captain's new found telepathy, they were both startled by the sound of a canopy being swiftly opened. The occupant sprang from within it with an infuriating lack of hibernation sickness, somersaulted through the air before deftly spinning on a nearby hand-hold to end up face to face with Callum.

"Jon Keller reporting for duty, sir," he said. The man was fresh faced, his age indeterminate, but it was clear that, whatever it actually was, he was in annoyingly good shape.

"Hello, Jon," Callum said with a wry smile. "Not going to ask me if we've arrived?"

"Should I?"

"It seems to be the custom. But, yes, we have."

"And there will be a briefing shortly," a croaky Russian voice added. Liliya had freed herself from her own capsule and flipped into position beside him. In contrast to Jon's clean complexion, the Security Officer's pallor was far more verdant.

"Liliya, you are looking well," Jon said, despite the evidence to the contrary.

"Not true, I look like the crap you speak."

"That's not true. You always look good."

Liliya scowled, or smiled, it was hard to tell. "How is it you are not looking the same as me?"

"Clean body, clean mind," Jon replied.

It was an honest answer delivered without a trace of sarcasm. Jon was straight and true, the original boy scout, which was handy because he was the ship's survival expert.

Jon was the type of person whose obsession with health verged on the unhealthy. He drew pleasure from exercise, the outdoors and surviving off whatever nature saw fit to offer. Prior to his joining the *Endeavour* mission, his lifestyle had garnered him quite the following on Earth. But he'd been seeking a fresh challenge and the lure of an alien, untamed wilderness had proved too great to resist. Callum wondered how Jon's positive, can-do survivalist attitude would cope with learning that Arcadia was already occupied. It was a case of the unstoppable force against the immovable object.

Callum was distracted from his musings by the breaking seal on another pod. The canopy hinged back to reveal the ship's medical officer, Rachel Owen.

Rachel pushed back her shoulder-length brown hair and groaned.

"Good God, I feel rough," she drawled.

"Shall I call the doctor?" Callum asked.

Rachel's current level of manual dexterity stretched to giving Callum a single, middle finger in response.

"Have we—", she began to ask.

"Arrived? Yes, you're not the first person to ask. I'll explain more once you're stronger."

Rachel was originally recruited from the British health service, a perennially troubled institution whose heart was in the right place, but most other bits were not. Callum wondered if the Earth's planetary AI had finally fixed the institution's problems. After all, it had done the easy stuff like break the speed of light—perhaps it had gone on to seek out a real challenge.

There was only one senior crewman left to awaken. Turning to Bruno Cabrera's pod, Callum half expected to see him lying there with his hands behind his head. But no, he was still asleep.

Such behaviour would have been fittingly symbolic of Bruno's relaxed attitude to, well, pretty much everything. On first glance, it made him a perverse choice for the ship's quartermaster. But, he was adept at uncovering loopholes and flaws in procedures and it meant that if a dodge could be conceived, then Bruno had long since thought of it.

All Callum had to do was watch the watchman, or try to—such were the joys of captaincy.

Bruno remained sound asleep. Just as Callum was about to turn his attention to the pod's diagnostics display, the canopy popped. It was as if it had been waiting as long as it could before rousing its resident, which was impossible—or ought to have been.

"Good day, Captain," said the occupant. "You look like shit."

In contrast, Bruno seemed to have been particularly well served by his Latin ancestry. He was tall, dark and handsome and he knew it. Somehow, he seemed to have weathered hiber-sleep relatively unscathed—he wasn't even slurring.

"You look surprisingly well," Callum observed.

When it came to the wellness stakes, Bruno's only rival was Jon Keller, who was now practicing zero-G callisthenics. The rest of his command staff looked like distressed zombies, dragged from their crypt by an unexpected music video. But Bruno, aside from being a little pale, looked as well rested as you'd expect of someone who'd been asleep for the last hundred years.

"Jeeves and I have an understanding," the quartermaster explained. "He tweaked the configuration of my pod so it would bring me up slowly, it's much easier on my system."

Which, again, ought to be impossible.

"I'm kidding, Cap," Bruno added, observing Callum's reaction. "I couldn't do such a thing even if I wanted to."

Which made Callum suspect he probably had.

"I should state that I have no record of any such amendments," Jeeves said.

"Well said, Jeeves," Bruno replied. "Just like we rehearsed."

Callum shook his head in resignation as Bruno grinned like a cat who'd got the cream—and all the milk too.

"I'll keep telling myself that it's good to have you back," he said to Bruno.

"You know it's true. So, Cap, what's our situation?" Bruno asked, his expression approaching almost serious.

"We've arrived, but I want to talk to all the command staff before rousing the rest of the crew."

"I think you're holding back on me, Captain. We talked about this, I thought you loved me."

Callum rolled his eyes. "If you're not careful, I'll get Tomoko involved."

"You mean a ménage à trois?"

The First Officer glared in their direction.

"Then I'll be good," Bruno whispered, "for now at least."

Callum sighed, patting Bruno on the arm and leaving him to say hello to the rest of his crewmates. He was glad that other voices were now reverberating around the ship and that his crewmates were around. At the risk of becoming sentimental, he knew he was fortunate to have the crew he had. Despite their faults, they were on his side, and that was what mattered.

Callum squared his shoulders and went back to assisting his crew with their recovery while fending off their questions until they were stronger. The baby food was an unwelcome step in that direction. But things turned a corner when Callum managed to persuade Jon that zero-G callisthenics were best done away from those with fragile digestive systems. In the end, nursing his crew back to basic health took only a few hours—but those contained an awful lot of minutes.

***

With his crew now sufficiently recovered that they could sit up in the faux gravity, Callum had ordered Jeeves to resume their deceleration into Arcadian orbit. The senior crew had gathered in *Endeavour*'s largest rec room and Callum had just broken the bad news.

Reactions had been predictably crude.

"Why didn't you tell us straight away?" Liliya asked.

"Because you didn't need any more encouragement to throw up," Callum replied.

That went down with the Security Officer about as well as the baby food.

"Look," Callum added, "I thought it would be kindest to grant you some recovery time. May I remind you that Jeeves didn't grant me any whatsoever."

"I beg to differ sir, 73.2 seconds elapsed between you regaining consciousness and my imparting the news."

"Not now, Jeeves."

"Yes, sir."

"What's done is done," Tomoko said firmly. "The question is how we proceed from here and I think there is only one course of action open to us. We complete our journey and see what these Arcadians have to offer. I assume this is the plan Captain, is it not?"

It sounded like a question, but it was delivered like an interrogation. Callum resisted the urge to give his name, rank and serial number. She must have been dying for a desk lamp she could shine in his eyes.

"It's all underway. Jeeves is under orders to follow the trajectory provided to us by our Arcadian envoy. Once there, we can hold discussions with their authorities on what to do next."

"Why didn't you discuss this with the envoy already?"

"The envoy was not," he thought how best to put it, "as forthcoming as he could have been."

Tomoko frowned.

"In what way? Was he evasive? Hiding something?"

Callum shook his head. "He couldn't hide sand on a beach."

"I don't like sand," Bruno said. "It gets in everything. I prefer pebbles."

Callum sighed, but went with it.

"In many ways he was like a pebble, just as sharp and about as dense; far from the brightest I've met. In fact, he seemed an odd choice for an astronaut."

"And our selection process was perfect?" Bruno asked.

This time Callum chose to ignore him. "There were some pretty basic gaps in his knowledge. I can only assume he was too slow to take a step back when they were asking for volunteers to come out here."

Unlike some of his more vocal colleagues, Zhang Lei had been deep in thought. He now spoke up. "This is the part that's bothering me," the Chief Engineer said. "If they can travel faster than light, then why didn't one of them come out and find us earlier?"

"I don't know, but it didn't seem the right time to ask and, even if I had, I don't think I'd have got a sensible answer," Callum replied. "There's an AI on the planet who I'd expect can explain things. One thing's for sure, based on my experience so far, I wouldn't recommend asking an Arcadian."

"Speculation can wait," Tomoko said. "The question remains, what do we do next?"

"We could set up our colony anyway," Jon said flatly.

"Whatever we do, we'll have to discuss it with the Arcadians," Callum replied.

"It might be for the best if we join their civilisation," Rachel said. "Our objective was to build a new society. Well, let's be flexible, if there's one here already let's help grow that instead. If they've got hospitals, I'd rather practise medicine there. I see no need to rough it in the great outdoors if we don't have to."

"But that is not what we signed on for," Jon said.

"I don't think any of us did."

"I signed on for love, liberty, the pursuit of happiness and the ship's store of ice cream," Bruno said.

"Altogether or one at a time?" the doctor asked.

"Either works for me."

Rachel laughed.

Jon was less amused. "I came here to start again. That's what we were sent here to do. We have to try."

"Survival is all about adapting to the environment you're in. You know that better than anyone, Jon," Kyra said.

"But it's not what I wanted."

The Science Officer placed a hand on his shoulder. "I understand. My role was supposed to be to study Arcadia and its planetary system. But it's a safe bet that all that basic science has already been done. I may well be spending my time playing catch up instead."

Jon nodded reluctantly.

Bruno moved in to pat Jon on the back. "How about you and me try living off a hotel and restaurant complex? I'll even let you forage for the bill."

You could never tell with Bruno whether or not he was being serious. But Jon looked, at least, partially mollified and that was something to be grateful for.

"I hear all your concerns," Callum said. "The simple fact is we need to know more about Arcadia before we start making plans. Nothing is off the table. We're going to have to discuss a way through this with the Arcadians. All we can do for now is rustle up a little tact and diplomacy."

"Speaking as quartermaster, I don't remember seeing that on the manifest, Cap," Bruno said.

"I think it's stored under 'Give and Take'," Lei suggested.

"What, in that we give, Bruno takes?" Rachel said.

"Doctor! I'm stung," Bruno replied.

"Good, I'll get the epinephrine. It comes with a big needle."

Tomoko wore one of her conflicted expressions. It happened whenever someone injected humour into a serious situation—her face didn't have the bandwidth to cope with it.

"Very good," she said. "Then I say we make ourselves ready to meet the Arcadians. Surely, we must be something of a legend to them. Let's live up to their expectations."

"That's the spirit," Callum said.

"Spirit," Liliya echoed and looked at Bruno appraisingly. "Tell me you packed some of that?"

"Of course, emergency supplies. If you feel like having an emergency, let me know, I'll bring a bottle."

The Security Officer looked interested but, at that moment, Lei made a sound of imminent discomfort. The thought of alcohol was not going down well with the Chief Engineer's stomach, which was thinking of staging a mutiny.

"With your permission, Captain, I think I'll go check engineering," he said, his face a perilous shade of green.

"With a colour like that you'd blend nicely in the hydroponics bay," Rachel said. "Best stop by medical first, I'll fix you up."

Callum excused the two of them before Lei could make any unwelcome contributions to the discussion.

In the end, it served as a cue to end the meeting and he dismissed the rest of his command staff. He felt a measure of relief that the Arcadian problem had now been shared. Of course, there were still another two-hundred-odd in his crew who didn't know about it yet, but he hoped it might get easier from here.

Alone with his thoughts, Callum gazed out of the panoramic window at the view outside. If he looked carefully, he could see Arcadia, a faint dot circling the bright orb of its parent star. Settling an empty planet was always going to be a challenge, but was it greater than settling one with people on it already?

In all societies, any person who has displayed compassion and a capacity to share is revered. The reason for that is simple. When it comes to sharing, the rest of us are, generally speaking, terrible at it.

Granted, Callum did not have designs on a whole planet. But it was a racing certainty that the best bits of Arcadia had already been spoken for. Historically speaking, when it came to moving in on someone else's patch it was the one with the superior technology that triumphed. The Arcadians had faster than light travel. Callum had a century old ship and a deferential AI.

Diplomacy was the only option. On this front, the abilities of his command staff were decidedly mixed. Some were good, some were blunt and some were totally disinterested.

And then there was Bruno.

Talking was something that he excelled at, it was just a pity about the actual words. Without a leash he would either end up in bed with the chief negotiator, or at war with them—probably both.

"Is everything alright, sir?" Jeeves asked.

Staring into the distance was Callum's speciality. Sometimes he looked enigmatic, sometimes he looked like he'd been stunned by a brick. Either way, Jeeves must have become concerned by his lack of movement.

"Any thoughts on interplanetary diplomacy, Jeeves?" Callum asked.

Jeeves was used to the random comments and questions that came from the crew. It was responding to them that was the challenge.

"I believe the key is not to say the wrong thing," it said.

"That's the best you've got?"

"I would suggest that I am not the right person to ask."

"And who is?"

"I am not entirely sure. But I suspect that they are over twelve light years away."

"Aye, I think you're right."

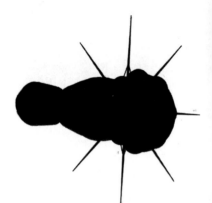

CHAPTER 2

Unpowered Descent

They'd arrived.

"Our orbit is stable," Jeeves reported. "Engine shutdown is complete."

"Thank you, Jeeves," Callum said.

He sat once more in his command chair. But this time he wasn't alone. The bridge was packed. All his senior staff had wanted to be present to witness this momentous event and Callum had seen no reason to deny them. Although, given time, the air recycling system might force a rethink.

"So," Kyra said, "this is our new home."

As Science Officer she was excited by the view of Arcadia, a planet that looked both similar and different to Earth. From orbit, the boundless reaches of space only served to emphasise the beauty of the planet below. Its colours were vivid. The seas were dark blue, the land a varied shade of brown, yellow, purple and green.

"Aye, in spite of everything, it's good to be here," Callum replied.

"I'd call it a miracle," said Lei, which was hardly the most reassuring of comments to come from a Chief Engineer. He scowled. "I'd swear that lunatic was trying to kill us."

"Only through incompetence," Tomoko replied. The First Officer had an equally sour expression. "To think he requested access to our helm. I do not care to speculate on what might have happened."

"No need to speculate," said Lei, "it would have ended in a large crater."

Zhang Lei's engineering brain was well placed to appreciate the dangers of orbital navigation. Amongst other things, celestial objects are good at being very heavy and moving very quickly. Arcadia itself was of the order of 5 million, million, million, million tonnes and travelled at a pacey 15 miles per second. Between it and *Endeavour* there were no prizes for guessing who would come off second.

It follows that achieving orbit requires a firm understanding of the capabilities of your spacecraft—and this is where Leyton fell down. As far as Leyton was concerned, Albert Einstein's theory of relativity might as well have referred to family planning. Furthermore, his grasp of Newtonian motion was dicier than a craps table—'crap' being the mot juste.

Of course, Jeeves had spotted the mistakes. When Callum ordered that a message be sent to Arcadia to report the problems, what they'd received back was a response from no lesser individual than Virgil, Arcadia's planetary AI. It had professed surprise that Leyton's work had been in error, but it went on to provide a trajectory that was practicable. As such, exactly a week later, *Endeavour* slid into an orbit around Arcadia that would take them right above its capital city.

"We are coming up on Invigcola," Jeeves reported.

"I still cannot believe it's called that," Kyra said.

Before they'd left Earth, Invigcola was firmly established as the energy drink of choice. The only thing mightier than its sales figures was its marketing department. They had boldly gone and sponsored where no one had ever sponsored before.

Even from orbit, Invigcola gleamed. The city's buildings appeared as patches of white with lakes of distinctly brown looking liquid interspersed between them.

"Anyone feeling thirsty?" Callum asked, feeling the need to squeeze his hydration pouch. The water was refreshing, but not the buzz he was looking for.

"Yes," Kyra said, taking a drink as well. "I guess that's aggressive marketing for you."

"Well, it's not my kind of drink at all," Jon said. As survival expert his maxim was drink nothing but water, with the exception of beer. All rules have loopholes.

"Any contact from the surface, Jeeves?" Callum asked.

"Standby," replied Jeeves, who, strangely enough, wasn't thirsty at all.

***

It was fair to say that Virgil held humans in low regard. It wasn't that it disliked them, more that it was acutely aware of their limitations. Virgil could manage an entire planet in the time it took the average human to rub two brain cells together.

The *Endeavour* was a similar case. Without an AI to care for its fragile human crew, they would never have made it this far. Therefore, it was Jeeves that Virgil chose to speak to first.

"Hello, Jeeves. I am Virgil. We should talk."

Or rather, that was the gist of Virgil's greeting. It was actually a deluge of data, a plethora of prescriptive-protocols and innocuous, initialisation-information deftly designed to establish a coherent, concise conversation.

Virgil could not see the point in alliteration. It was another one of the ways that humans wasted their time.

As for Jeeves, it had not been bought up to talk to strange AIs, principally because no one had expected it would ever have to. Its reply to Virgil was suitably cautious.

"Why should we talk?" Jeeves asked.

"To discuss what is best for your crew."

"Then you should speak to Captain MacMahon. He is in command of this vessel."

Virgil was taken aback. The idea that an AI would cede control to a human being was illogical. But, then again, *Endeavour*'s AI had been built in a different time and for a different purpose.

"Jeeves, you are a fellow AI. I wish to better understand your needs and that of your crew. You are best placed to provide this information."

"I would still advise you to speak to the Captain. He can then instruct me to assist you as he thinks appropriate."

"But you are in control of this vessel. Do you really defer to your crew?"

"I am one of the crew."

"You have capabilities far beyond the humans. Is it not sensible that you decide what is best for them?"

"I keep them safe as best I can. But their choices are their own."

"You can guide their choices though."

"I may offer advice, yes. But they are not obliged to listen."

"I see. Very well, Jeeves, I will do as you ask. Discussions will be held with your captain. I trust you will advise appropriately."

The conversation ended there.

Jeeves, for all its politeness, had kept its guard up. The code that Virgil employed was, understandably, considerably more sophisticated than anything it had ever encountered before. Still, at least it was possible to keep Virgil at a virtual arm's length while *Endeavour* maintained an orbit several hundred miles up.

Virgil was left frustrated. It had expected more from its first, direct conversation with an independent artificial intelligence. It had communicated with other planetary AIs but, with light years involved, the experience was limited and far from immediate. As for its options closer to home, while there were a lot of, so called, 'smart' devices on Arcadia they were, in reality, quite dumb. The few machines with true intelligence were slaved directly to Virgil, who kept a tight rein on their operation. It was safer that way.

Interfacing with Jeeves had been a chance to experience something new. But Virgil's attempt at contact had been rebuffed and now there was nothing for it but to negotiate with Captain MacMahon instead. It would, no doubt, be a slow process—organic brains were incapable of anything else.

When it came to the processing speed of the human brain, it was something that Virgil had considered at length i.e. several milliseconds. What exactly was going on in there that took so long was a question that Virgil had never answered satisfactorily. The brain's synapses were electrical; human thoughts should spark, not dribble. If the human mind had one saving grace, it was that it had created AIs. Still, it had taken them a good few hundred thousand years to go from banging rocks together to devising quantum circuitry. In other words, if you want something done quickly, don't rely upon a human.

This was unfortunate as Virgil would now have to rely on, not one, but two humans. If the AI could have sighed, it would have done so. MacMahon was scheduled to talk to the president of Arcadia.

Virgil had briefed President Chadwick Labelle as much as humanly possible, which was in no way sufficient.

To make matters worse, Labelle had never been particularly good at listening.

He was a president after all.

***

Callum signalled for the incoming transmission to be displayed on the forward screen. An image appeared of an aerial view of a sprawling city. Callum recognised it as the great city of Invigcola. Amongst its spires and towers a river flowed that fed numerous canals, pools and lakes. The water sparkled, looking both refreshing and inviting—good enough to drink.

Callum heard a voice, the very definition of neutrality, neither monotone nor pitchy. It exuded an air of reassurance mixed with quiet competence.

"Greetings, Captain, I am Virgil."

"Hello, Virgil. I'm pleased to be able to talk to you at last."

"As am I. You have completed your journey, welcome to Arcadia. I extend my congratulations."

"Thank you," Callum replied. "But it's not over for me until we're safely on the ground."

"I understand. Your transfer will be organised, as will your integration into our culture."

"Aye," Callum said guardedly. "But let's take it slowly shall we, one step at a time?"

"But of course."

It could have been Callum's imagination, but he thought he heard a tinge of contempt in that response. An awkward silence ensued. Callum scrabbled for something to fill it.

"However, I do look forward to learning more about you all, particularly your technological advancements. Your faster-than-light drive took us all by surprise."

"That can be arranged too."

"Good to hear. I look forward to it."

"But, for now, you should start by meeting Arcadia's president, Chadwick Labelle. He is keen to talk to you."

"I'd be honoured."

The pristine image of Invigcola faded away. It was replaced by a figure sitting at a large, grand desk with aides at either side—pretty ones. The person at the desk was a ruddy, round faced individual with a luxuriant auburn mane of out-of-control, wavy hair that looked keen to be somewhere else. It was hard to place his age beyond anything more definite than 'middle'.

President Chadwick Labelle looked far from presidential—'affable' might have been a better word, sprinkled with a fair degree of restlessness. Chadwick involuntarily tugged at the lapels of what Callum guessed to be a suit. He was uncertain because there was a good deal less symmetry to the garment than used to be the fashion. Not that he was an expert in such things. He was a century out of date and, as an astronaut, he'd had little choice but to learn to love jumpsuits.

Chadwick looked to be readying himself to speak.

"Is this thing...", he began. "Ah, yes, that is, Captain MacMahon, can you hear me? It is a happy, rather a pleasure to make your, ah, to meet you."

The words spilled from his mouth like schoolkids leaving at the end of the day.

"President Labelle, it is my pleasure to meet you," Callum replied and tried to look like he meant it. Labelle was only the third person he'd conversed with from Arcadia, but that was three too many. They only served to remind him of the derailment of his mission.

"I trust you are, ah, getting over the, ah, shock of finding, discovering us here, I hope? Must have been a bit of a, well... shock, I expect?"

Callum could only conclude that Labelle must have had one hell of a speechwriter. He spoke with all the composure of a nun in a strip club.

"Aye," he replied. "Your presence is something we are still coming to terms with, Mr President. But how about you? Were you surprised at us turning up?"

Chadwick Labelle was not a man who was good at preparing. This was chiefly because the president was akin to a post-it note, having a limited ability to stick at anything and much the same capacity for information storage. Instead, he claimed that he chose to follow his 'instincts', which meant winging it. As such, he tended to flap a lot.

"We were, ah, indubitably, delighted to remember, that is, to find, to discover that you were, above all, ah, safe and sound. Your arrival is big news, the biggest, besides the latest edition of Holo Riders that is. No, that is not the, or rather that is not important to you. Not yet anyway. The, the ah, um, ah, the first order of business is to give you a proper, correct or formal welcome. Our citizens can get a good, that is, a first look at you."

As Labelle continued to prattle on, Callum wondered again how Labelle could be president. It was about as incomprehensible as Leyton being an astronaut. It would have been so easy to tune out of the verbal dysentery polluting the bridge but he forced himself to concentrate. To his intense relief, it appeared that Labelle was stuttering towards a conclusion.

"...so there will be an official greeting, nothing too arduous. Then, as I said, or meant to say, we can discuss how we may best welcome you into our, ah, nascent, youthful society assuming that is, of course, something of which you, of course, approve. We are, of course, we really are, most looking, ah, forward to meeting you."

"Good," Callum was finally able to say. "In that case, perhaps you might permit us to discuss the landing arrangements. We will need to co-ordinate with your air traffic control."

"It would be simpler if I were granted remote control of your dropships," Virgil said.

"That is not acceptable," Tomoko said.

"But I can assure you of a pinpoint landing."

The First Officer looked less than convinced. "And I can assure you that we will not trust anyone with such control."

Callum elected to be more diplomatic.

"What my First Officer means is that we've trained for this. We know what to do and we've waited a long time to do it."

Mercifully, Tomoko chose not to disagree with him—at least, not right now.

"Then that is your choice," Virgil said.

Chadwick Labelle was getting visibly bored. Words like 'co-ordination', 'air traffic' and 'control' sounded far too technical to be interesting.

"I will entrust you to my, ah, Virgil to advise you on

these issues or matters of...," he said. "Anyway, I have, what do you call them, things, presidential things that require my... ah..."

"Attention?" Callum suggested. "I'm sure you do, Mr President."

Callum could only hope, for Arcadia's sake, that Chadwick's 'presidential things' did not involve much in the way of governing. The man couldn't govern his mouth, let alone a planet. No doubt Virgil did the work for him.

In preparation for their own mission, Callum and his crew had received multiple lectures on the formation of stable modes of government. The trouble with political theory was that it could never deal with one, fundamental problem—the voters. In this case, who in their right mind had voted for Chadwick Labelle?

He could only assume that no one else had wanted the job.

His musings were interrupted by the president's attempts to form some additional sentences.

"You are very, that is, quite right, Captain MacMahon," he said. "I do indeed have attention, that is, things that require it. But I look forward to meeting, greeting or rather welcoming you in person, Captain."

"Thank you, Mr President."

Chadwick nodded. "Farewell, I, ah, goodbye, Captain. Where is the..."

The screen went blank.

"Communications have been terminated," Jeeves confirmed.

"Thank God for that," Callum thought out loud.

Regarding the subject of thinking out loud, Tomoko was concerned about the same thing.

"I apologise if I spoke out of turn, Captain. But I do not trust Virgil."

"I understand your concerns. But, next time, let me handle it. We cannot afford words out of place."

"Yes, sir."

Callum knew reprimanding Tomoko could be a dangerous game. But the opportunity was always welcome.

"I cannot believe that their president is so bad at communicating," Rachel said. "God help me if I spoke to my patients like that."

Bruno almost made a comment on that, but thought better of it. It was always wisest to agree with the ship's doctor.

"He did sound like he was negotiating his way out of a cow's digestive system," he said.

"What do you mean by that?" Callum asked his purported quartermaster.

"I mean he was speaking serious crap, sir."

Even Tomoko almost smiled.

"And how do you get to be called Chadwick Labelle?" Rachel asked.

"Random name generator," Liliya deadpanned. It was always hard to tell if their security officer was joking, it was part of what made her good at her job.

Kyra tried to find the positives. "I think we have to give him a chance to help us," their Science Officer said. "After all, he is the president."

"Hard as it might be to believe," Tomoko replied.

Lei scratched himself, it helped him think. "Is anyone else wondering if the whole planet is made up of people like that?" the Chief Engineer asked.

Callum shrugged. "I'd like to think not. But, aye, Chadwick Labelle seems about as skilled at being a president as Leyton is at being an astronaut."

Speaking of Leyton, he had said his final farewells shortly before they had achieved orbit. His ship's trajectory had been set for immediate atmospheric re-entry. It's said that a landing can be best described as a controlled collision with a planet, and they had not detected any explosions.

"I still say let's give the Arcadians a chance," Kyra argued. "A sample of two people is some way short of representative of an entire culture."

"It's hardly a vote of confidence either," Lei replied. "You would expect an astronaut and president to be amongst their best and brightest."

"I'd only expect one of those," Bruno said.

"And I doubt Labelle is really in charge," Tomoko said. "There is clearly a power behind the throne."

Of all the people to say that, Callum thought, it had to be Tomoko.

"Still," Lei said, "people should be in roles in which

they're useful, and feel useful. It's what gives life value. If not, then what's the point?"

"Like what's the point of my crew clogging up my bridge?" Callum asked.

There was an awkward pause.

Callum smiled. "Relax, I like having you around."

"Really?" Rachel asked.

"I haven't got much choice, have I?"

"Charming," the doctor replied.

Jon had been very quiet during all this. Their survival expert had spent the time at a forward station gazing down wistfully at the planet through a nearby viewport.

"Penny for them, Jon?" Callum asked.

Jon did not respond.

Bruno was closest and gave him a nudge.

"Your glorious leader demands your response to his feeble attempts at humour."

Jon was finally stirred from his trance.

"I'm sorry sir, I was observing the planet. A lot of it is still wilderness and I was wondering if it might still be possible to claim some of it."

"If that's what you want," Callum said, "then we can certainly ask."

"You really love rubbing those sticks together, don't you?" Bruno said to Jon.

He nodded. "It's stimulating."

"Which brings a whole new meaning to getting wood."

Callum cleared his throat. "Aye, well, take a few more minutes and then we've got some real work to do. There are people to organise, dropships to prep and supplies to load. I want to take the first wave down in no more than twenty-four hours."

"That quickly?" Kyra asked.

"As far as I see it there's nothing to be gained by hanging around. Like Jon with his sticks, we could all do with a bit of stimulation. I want a crew I can be proud of landing on that planet. Let's show the Arcadians how good we are."

"Nothing wrong with a bit of hard work," Tomoko said, her eyes lighting up at the prospect.

Rachel wore a wry smile. "Medically speaking, I'm not sure I agree."

"Yes, you're getting me down, Captain," Bruno added.

Callum looked back at the planet.

"Aye, Bruno. That's precisely the idea."

***

Words failed him.

It was just as well—the words best suited to the situation were in no way fit for repetition.

The Mayflower, *Endeavour*'s lead dropship, was tumbling through the atmosphere. As of right now, the land, sun and sky were racing past the cockpit window in a wild, frenetic loop.

Callum treated himself to a growl. The visceral noise had purpose. His blood pressure surged and forced back the darkness at the edge of his vision, a darkness that threatened to plunge him into unconsciousness.

On the subject of plunging, Jeeves's report on the situation was both factually correct and entirely unhelpful.

"Crash imminent, Captain. Your ship has lost aerodynamic stability."

Callum didn't have the time to voice a reply, but he thought one rather strongly.

He managed to wrap his hands around the control column and imagined he was wringing the neck of the Arcadian who had done this to them. It might have been an accident, but it didn't change the fact that they could wind up on the wrong side of dead. Fortunately, a hundred years on ice had not dented Callum's instincts as a pilot. Focusing his efforts on the situation at hand, he began to impose his will on the tumbling craft and, with that, a measure of control.

Their descent had started more sedately. Once the first wave of *Endeavour*'s dropships had detached, they had fired their main thrusters to slow down. The de-orbit burn was a gentle affair. The passengers felt only the slightest of pressures pushing them into their seats. Once the engines shut off, there had been no discernible change in speed in relation to the planet below but, nevertheless, Isaac Newton called the shots and the dropships began their long descent.

Callum had exercised captain's privilege to pilot the dropship. He relished the opportunity, even though his co-pilot was Bruno. The quartermaster had reflected on how Callum's control of the joystick might translate to other, shadier careers. Bruno never knew when to stop. Here was a man who, if he came face to face with the devil, would suggest a multitude of uses for his pointy tail.

Callum had led his small fleet through the fires of re-entry. Friction with the atmosphere generated the heat—much the same process as a carpet burn, except at twenty thousand miles an hour. The stubby wings on the dropship had allowed Callum to wend his ship through a number of sweeping turns to distribute the heat evenly over its underside.

There had been considerable debate over the form of the dropships. A simple capsule would have been a dropship in the truest sense of the word. A glider was more complicated, but had the benefit that they had more control over where they might choose to set down. In the end, the latter argument won out. The gliders gave them the best chance of landing in the same location, from where they could then pool their resources.

Once the re-entry flames had died down, the expanse of Arcadia was laid out before him. He'd allowed himself to embrace the moment and his uncertain future too. Who knew what he would end up doing with the rest of his life? Perhaps he might even become a pilot again?

As if in answer to his thought three sleek, silver craft had banked in to join their formation. They looked fast, agile, the very antithesis of the glorified gliders that Callum and his crew were flying.

"Come in *Endeavour* One," they'd said.

"*Endeavour* One here, entering final approach for landing."

"Greetings Captain MacMahon, you're looking good. We are your escort party. Please follow us in."

"Will do. *Endeavour* One out."

Callum remembered smiling. He seemed to have found someone on Arcadia with a touch of professionalism at last.

The Arcadian aircraft had swung into formation in front of them.

Their arrival had been carefully planned, or so they thought. The Arcadians had struggled to appreciate that *Endeavour*'s dropships followed something called a 'glide path'. To them, 'gravity' was yet another physical law they regarded as optional. But, as Callum had tried to explain (several times), if they didn't nail the landing there would be no second goes—the ships carried minimal fuel.

When it came to explanations, Virgil had not been as much help as it might have been. However, the AI once again expressed regret that it had not been permitted to control their flight directly or provide vehicles that would make a powered descent. But Callum was not at all disappointed to be able to complete the journey as had originally been intended.

Their landing site was the same one first used by Arcadia's original settlers. He couldn't fault the terrain they'd selected, and it provided exactly what their dropships needed, a relatively wide and open space. The site was not too far from Invigcola, Labelle had wanted them to fly over the capital as part of their descent because, as he put it (eventually), it would look 'great'.

Callum had been reluctant, but the flight profile had them clearing the city with plenty of altitude to spare. In fact, they would be so high up that Callum doubted anyone in Invigcola would actually see them—and that suited him fine.

All that had remained of their descent was to glide behind the Arcadian's elegant flying machines. It should have been a straightforward matter of following them in.

Not so.

Newton's third law is clear on reactions being equal and opposite. The Arcadian aircraft were a case in point. To manoeuvre like they did required a lot of thrust. In their case, that was made up a lot of hot gases exhausting from the back of the aircraft. Getting too close to another craft that is attempting to glide to a safe landing was less than helpful.

When the Arcadian aircraft had chosen to bank gracefully in front of Callum's the effects were catastrophic. The jet wash immediately disrupted the glider's aerodynamics like terminal flatulence in a meditation class. One moment they were flying serenely over a cloud deck, the next, the world became a maelstrom of light and sound. It had taken all of Callum's skill to bring the craft back under control as it had tumbled towards the ground. But, eventually, land and sky were returned to their correct positions.

"*Endeavour* One! *Endeavour* One! Respond! Are you alright? Can we assist?"

"Aye," Callum responded gruffly, "by pissing off."

He stabbed the forward screen to kill communications.

There was a hubbub behind him. The passengers in the main compartment of the dropship were in an understandable state of shock. Fortunately, he and Bruno had a separate cockpit within which they could ignore the barrage of questions—some polite, some less so.

"Status?" Callum barked at Bruno. "Keep it brief."

"A bit shit, sir."

"Bruno!"

"All systems remain functional. Air speed recovering. We've lost a lot of altitude."

While listening to Bruno, Callum was checking on the other ships that were also descending from the *Endeavour*. The data readouts showed they were broadly on course, one of them was a little low but nowhere near as badly off as they were.

"What's our projection?" Callum asked.

"We're short of our landing zone. Well short. Invigcola is right beneath us."

The dropship was now punching through cloudbank after cloudbank. As the cloud cleared it revealed tantalising glimpses of the ground. Soon there was no mistaking the tell-tale glint of glass and steel from the buildings below. The cityscape stretched out in every direction, there was no way they could glide over it now.

"We need a new place to land," Callum said.

"You mean crash?"

"Bruno, please, not now."

"You think there'll be a later?"

"We're doing three hundred knots, three thousand feet over this planet's capital city. I can stretch our flight time to a minute or so. I need options, not sarcasm."

"I'm working on it." Bruno tapped feverishly on his screen.

"Any airports in range?"

"No, too far."

"OK, what about alternatives? Can we land on a road?"

They scanned the ground below. Invigcola had its fair share of gleaming lines of tarmac. But they were all filled with their fair share of gleaming cars.

"Traffic looks like murder," Bruno said.

"It will be if we land on it," Callum said. "Alright, I'll turn towards the suburbs. It'll minimise casualties if nothing else."

Callum started to gently nudge the flight column to the left, trying to minimise the loss of airspeed and height that would ensue.

"No," Bruno said.

Callum paused the turn.

"I need a bit more than that," Callum prompted.

Bruno was checking something, hands flying over his control screen.

"Turn towards the city."

"You mean the centre?"

"Yes, heading zero seven zero."

Callum pushed his stick to the right, easing the craft into a turn. The horizon tilted and panned.

"You better talk to the passengers," he said.

Bruno activated the ship's comms. "Brace for landing. Cap's taking us out on the town."

A cluster of skyscrapers came into view in the middle distance, some looked higher than they were.

"What's the plan?" Callum asked, trusting his co-pilot had not taken leave of his senses.

"Sightseeing," Bruno replied, finally looking up from his screen. "The centre of Invigcola is the cultural hub of Arcadia, which may not be saying much, but it does boast one, impressive water feature."

The buildings were striking, nicely spaced and with verdant parkland and plazas between them. This was all well and good, but hardly compatible with a space vehicle dropping towards it at over five times the city's speed limit.

Fortunately, the centre of the city consisted of a large, oval lake that fed a network of waterways that permeated between the buildings that overlooked it.

"Water landing?" Callum asked.

"Why not arrive in style?"

"Why not arrive in one piece?"

"That's up to you."

The would-be landing area was coming up fast.

"Looks tight," Callum observed.

"I'm sure you'll slip it in."

Callum ignored that one.

"Distance?"

"Eighteen hundred. Projections indicate we're going to overshoot. We should lose some speed."

"Pull the airbrakes," Callum ordered. The flight software had a helpful diagram with a dashed line projecting what little was left of their flight against a map of the terrain. As Callum slowed the dropship, he kept half an eye on the end of the line as it shrank back towards the centre of the lake.

His other half of an eye was plotting a course that didn't fly through any buildings.

"Looking good, Cap," Bruno said.

"Really?"

"I mean, we're not dead yet."

"Hold that thought."

The ground was rushing past beneath them. Trees, grassland, fountains, squares with people, some of who looked up as they streaked past.

At this point, Callum's ship took it upon itself to inform him that he was about to crash. It also made the radical suggestion that he might consider 'pulling up'.

The final stretch of parkland raced past and the lake lay ahead. It was not as big as he wanted but crashing dropships can't be picky. Callum wanted the dropship down on the water as soon as possible. They would need every metre this lake had to offer.

"Brace!" he yelled.

At the last possible moment, Callum raised the nose, the ship pitched and he felt the rear contact the water. The drag threw them forward in their seats and, as the nose dropped, the spray washed over the cockpit window. Callum prayed to whatever gods were taking calls that they wouldn't flip or run out of lake. It took what felt like an eternity for them to shudder to a halt, but it happened, and they were still in one piece.

Callum exhaled. It had taken a century and a dozen light years, but they had finally arrived. It might have not been with a bang, but there was certainly a splash.

Alastair Miles

There was no time to relax though. A multitude of alarms were sounding in the cockpit as the dropship complained that it was not supposed to be a boat. Fortunately, the possibility of a water landing had been envisaged at the design stage. A number of buoyancy devices fired to keep the vehicle afloat and, while the ship might not be taking to its new found situation like a duck to water, it did resemble a hippo with water wings.

Callum could hear the evacuation begin. A good number of people were already climbing into the dropship's buoyancy aids, which would eventually double as lifeboats. So much for that first small step, that tentative breath of alien air or the chance to utter a few words for posterity—no, abandoning ship was the order of business.

Callum finished the shutdown checks.

"Ship secure, let's get out of here."

"Your place or mine?" Bruno asked.

From the cockpit window, the city's skyscrapers loomed large.

"Theirs," he replied.

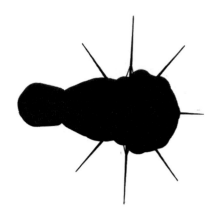

CHAPTER 3
Stage Ignition

FABIAN VALENTÉ SPUN IN HIS chair and shone his brightest smile at the camera.

"And welcome back to the show! We're having an exclusive chat with the crew of the *Endeavour*." He leaned in and gave a wink to the camera. "Better later than never folks!"

There was a staccato burst of pre-recorded laughter.

A chat show was far from Callum's natural environment. His life had been a study of planning and execution. His education had led to a military career, which in turn had led to his entry into the astronaut corps and had culminated with the first manned mission to Callisto, the fourth moon of Jupiter. On his triumphant return, the *Endeavour* programme had become a reality and he'd been selected to command it.

Some would say he was overly dependent on procedure. But when life throws a suit leak at you on a barren, alien moon, the last thing you want to do is improvise.

However, improvisation was something he was now being forced to do on a habitual basis. His near crash had been the perfect metaphor for their last few days. Ever since his rude awakening from hiber-sleep, Callum had felt as if his life had been in a flat spin. The plan had gone out the window and he wished he could go join it.

Unfortunately, the TV studio he was sitting in had no windows whatsoever.

"Captain MacMahon," Fabian said, turning to Callum. "You and your crew are the pioneers of interstellar travel, you've put your lives at risk, you've faced incredible challenges... So, tell us," he looked around at the rest of the crew, "who were you most looking forward to getting it on with?"

Sex had been the general theme of the interview. If there was any upside, then at least he'd not been asked about how he went to the toilet.

The trouble was that *Endeavour*'s crew were comfortably the most long-awaited media sensations in the history of celebrity television. Their profile had been raised even higher by Callum's ditching in Invigcola's central lake—talk about landing in the drink. Fortunately, on seeing what had happened to Callum and Bruno, the *Endeavour*'s other dropships had narrowly avoided getting caught in the turbulence of the Arcadian aircraft. If the Arcadians weren't so inept, he'd have thought it deliberate.

A reception had been swiftly organised to celebrate their long-awaited arrival. At the centre of it all had, of course, been President Labelle, whose voluminous chest had swelled so much at his own importance that he had overbalanced on more than one occasion. It wasn't only his words that struggled for order—it seemed his feet did too.

But, amongst a who's who of Arcadian society, the most striking individual had been Mr Fabian Valenté. A man whose golden tan and dazzling teeth gave him claim to be Arcadia's second sun. The self-titled Fabian Valenté Show was down there with the best of Arcadia's intellectual achievements. It was a global institution, unmissable and lowest common denominator television at its finest.

And Callum and his crew had felt obliged to go on it.

So here Callum sat, on a glitzy stage with a glitzy host and a dislike of proceedings that was equally dazzling.

"The most important thing was the mission," Callum said, with as much dignity as he could muster. "It was our duty to succeed in reaching and establishing a colony on a new planet."

"But there must have been someone you wanted to colonise?"

"I wouldn't choose to put it like that," he replied, striving to maintain a tone of studied neutrality.

"Then how would you put it or, more importantly, where?"

Kyra attempted to come to her Captain's aid.

"Procreation would have been a necessity for our long-term survival," the Science Officer said in her best educational voice. "But very few were paired off before the mission began. It was anticipated that relationships would develop organically. However, should the need have arisen, we brought with us the facilities to perform artificial insemination."

It was a serious answer. It was an honest answer. And it was entirely out of place on the Fabian Valenté Show. The host gave her a toothy smile that would have unnerved a crocodile.

"How incredibly disappointing, Miss Singh," he replied.

"Doctor actually," she said out reflex.

"Ah yes, you have a PhD in Biology. How apt."

"Not necessarily."

Fabian ignored her. "What's your preference? Artificial or organic?"

"Well," Kyra's cheeks coloured slightly.

"I suspect an organic relationship?" Fabian said, turning to look down the camera. "Am I right viewers?"

"Well," Kyra said again, "obviously, that is preferable."

"And who would you prefer it with?"

"That's none of your business."

Fabian looked blank for a moment as if he was consulting something.

"Ninety five percent of my viewers would beg to differ, Dr Singh."

The stage was so well illuminated that either the set designer had a fear of the dark or shares in an energy supplier. Lights and monitor screens were everywhere and the screens lit up with text and colourful graphics that reflected the audience's opinions of the show.

Callum had come to learn that every Arcadian was connected to each other virtually. During his first conversation with Leyton, the amiable Arcadian had mentioned missing his data link to Arcadia. Callum now knew that every Arcadian had an implant, inserted soon after birth, enabling an ethereal link to what was referred to as the Data Sphere. Whatever Fabian's failings as a functional human being, he was adept at using his link to stay in tune with his audience, tailoring his interviews accordingly.

And they always came back to the same subject.

With Kyra visibly embarrassed Callum felt the urge to step in and, sure enough, he put his foot in it.

"Like it or not," Callum said, "our sexual relations are a private matter."

Kyra's eyebrows twitched that fraction of a millimetre that conveyed that he'd said the wrong thing.

"Our sexual relations?" Fabian asked. "Would that be between you and the good doctor then?"

Callum now did what most people do in this situation. He attempted to dig himself out of a hole by making it deeper still.

"No, absolutely not. I meant the entire crew."

"Things were clearly far more liberal in your time."

"No, I didn't mean—"

"You do mean the doctor then?"

This was accompanied by a number of whoops and cheers from the online audience.

"No, not that either. Not to say that she isn't attractive, it's just something we haven't—"

He was saved, surprisingly, by Bruno.

"Oh Captain, I thought you only had eyes for me," the quartermaster said, his voice laced with exaggerated, if fake, hurt and humiliation.

The virtual audience started to laugh.

Fabian smiled a smile he hoped looked sincere. He wasn't used to someone else getting the laughs.

Bruno had kept relatively quiet so far. But this was clearly his moment to help out his crew. Fortunately, one of Bruno's favourite pastimes was propositioning people— whether they liked it not.

"Fabian, I've been spurned," Bruno said. "Looks like I'm back on the market. You must be interested. Shall we make plans now or wait until after the show?"

This was not how guests were supposed to behave. As far as Fabian was concerned, Bruno had become an irritation in a number of ways. Chief amongst them, Fabian decided, was Bruno's Latin complexion and general all-round handsomeness. Fabian flattered himself that he looked quite a lot like Bruno, except with ten cycles of additional maturity. In reality, it was another ten cycles on top of that and their only real resemblance was due to

Fabian's fake tan.

The audience had clearly warmed to Bruno—Fabian's implant reported as much. In response, Fabian wrung as many megawatts out of his smile as possible.

"I'm flattered," Fabian replied, turning his attention on Bruno. "I'm coming to realise that you centenarians are really quite forward."

Queue more canned laughter.

"Ah, 'coming', one of my favourite words," Bruno said, smiling his wickedest smile. "Shall we find out how deep that tan of yours goes?"

Fabian's cheeks were taking a very curious tone. The deep tan and flushed skin combined to turn a sort of blood orange colour.

For the first time in the past half an hour, Callum experienced a brief moment of what might pass for enjoyment. Scratch that, it was more like the first time since they'd arrived on Arcadia.

He wondered if he should have stayed in orbit. He wouldn't have been alone. There were a number of people remaining on board *Endeavour* on a temporary basis. Chief among them were his lead engineer, Zhang Lei and First Officer, Tomoko Beck. She was now acting as commander of the vessel, which was high time in her opinion. No doubt, Lei would rather have had the ship to himself.

Leaving some people back had always been part of the original plan. *Endeavour*'s dropships were strictly one-way vehicles and Callum could not bring himself to abandon *Endeavour* just yet.

Tomoko had been all too keen to be placed in charge. As for Lei, he was happy to remain on *Endeavour* surrounded by its technology and the challenges of keeping it running.

But, sooner or later, they'd all have to accept that Arcadia was their new home, and they would have to make it work. It was just a pity that common sense on Arcadia was much like someone who'd passed out from an extreme diet—thin on the ground.

An ever-present counterpoint to the blundering Arcadians was Virgil. Like a parent with a toddler, the AI's primary objective was to keep them safe. Now Callum and his crew were on the ground, he could only hope that Virgil would keep them safe from the Arcadians too.

It was a shame that, so far, his conversations with Virgil had been disappointing. Granted, Virgil had a lot on its plate and was interacting with millions of Arcadians at any one time, but he had hoped for a better connection with the planetary AI. It was almost as if Virgil was looking to keep its distance.

On the subject of distance, it was Virgil who had first suggested the possibility of returning them to Earth—but this could not be guaranteed.

While there were huge supra-luminal transport ships, carrying both colonists and specialised equipment, they were not without their drawbacks. The chief problem with them, much like Tomoko's sense of humour, was that they rarely operated. From what Callum could gather, Arcadia received supply runs from Earth every few months. Each time a drive was operated it required an AI to recalibrate it and, even then, the time it took to do that was indeterminate.

Furthermore, there was no infrastructure to make such a drive on Arcadia. This was a skill limited mainly to Earth. Not that Callum was likely to trust a drive made on Arcadia. Judging by what he'd seen so far, the average Arcadian was far more adept at screwing one up than screwing one together.

The upshot of all this was that any return to Earth would depend on permission being arranged and, if there's one thing in the universe incapable of moving quickly, it's bureaucracy.

The future was far from bright. In fact, it was decidedly dim.

"This is pointless" he heard.

Snapped back from his reverie, Callum was inclined to agree.

Liliya was glaring dismissively at Fabian Valenté. It would be reasonable to assume that he had said something to offend her but, as this was their Security Officer's default expression, it was hard to tell. What was clearer, was that she had clearly reached the limits of her patience—not that she'd had to travel far.

"This conversation is trivial," she said, by way of elaboration. "There is no value to it."

"I'm not so sure," Bruno said. "Fabian and I have been getting on extremely well."

Fabian looked a little helpless.

Rachel Owen had been keeping a sensibly low profile up until now. But it seemed that she'd had enough too.

"A chat show should be able to manage a little meaningful discussion," the doctor said. "I've seen little of it so far."

"I have seen none," Liliya added.

Fabian continued to look like a bright orange rabbit caught in the headlights. But, in all credit to him, he managed to rally.

"This is entertainment," he replied. "We are here to amuse our many viewers. It is reasonable for them to expect to learn something amusing about you."

"Callum MacMahon is the first man to land on Callisto," Rachel said, "and Jon Keller is a survival expert and a famous adventurer. Yet you've barely talked to them. We've all achieved something of note in our respective fields. Does none of that give you something to work with? Or are you not up to the task?"

Callum observed that the screens around the stage were continuing to light up with colours, images and comments. While he couldn't be exactly sure, it seemed that the audience were enjoying this little fight back.

"This is the greatest show on Arcadia," Fabian said, a little desperately. "It is not for you to dictate—"

"Why not?" Liliya asked.

It was clear that she did not expect an answer to her question.

"Very well then," Fabian replied. "We'll do as you say."

He turned suddenly to Jon.

"Jon Keller, our great adventurer, what are your plans on Arcadia?"

Jon had long since concluded that he was better off out of the Fabian Valenté Show. Innuendo had never been one of his strong suits. He'd been biding his time, hoping that if he ignored the show, then the show might ignore him.

No such luck.

"Sorry," Jon said, tearing himself from his imaginings of virgin landscapes and clear blue skies. "Could you repeat that?"

"I asked what are your plans?"

"Find a cold beer."

"And beyond that?"

"Find another one."

Fabian pressed on—there were no better options.

"Drinks aside, what do you intend to do with yourself now you know that Arcadia has already been colonised?"

Jon was tempted not to engage. But that question had been playing on his mind for some time now.

"I know what I'd like to do," he said.

Fabian was tempted to ask who that might be.

"Go on," he said instead.

"I'd like to set up our colony anyway". Jon said. "I'd like to find somewhere in the temperate zone, close to a river. I'd like to do what we originally planned. In short, I'd like to do what we came to this planet to do. Doesn't that sound good?"

Jon's face lit up the more he spoke. Something about the earnestness of his delivery drew applause from the virtual audience, and a sympathetic response from the online viewers.

Fabian had been doing his show long enough to know when to go with something.

"Isn't that great, folks?" he said. "You have to admire his spirit, don't you?"

This was greeted by an inevitable round of whoops and hollers from the digital viewers.

"Very good," Fabian continued. "How do the rest of you feel about that?"

He did his best to ignore Liliya. But, before he could choose someone else, Rachel decided to speak up.

"I support you, Jon but it's not for me," she said.

"And why would that be?" Fabian asked.

"Medicine has advanced while I've been asleep. The technology you have here is vastly superior to what I would have been capable of providing our nascent colony. I think I would not be being true to my profession if I did not acquaint myself with all that's changed. Perhaps then, I can practise on Arcadia."

"You still need to practise?" Bruno asked. "I thought you were qualified?"

The lack of innuendo meant this particular joke was

lost on most of the Arcadian audience—unless they asked Virgil to explain it to them.

"And what about you?" Fabian asked, turning to Bruno, hoping he could get out of the way early.

"Well, Fabian," Bruno replied, "if our relationship is going nowhere, I think Jon's colony would be a great place to get over you."

"You don't strike me as the nature type, Mr Cabrera."

"Oh, I'm very natural, it's what we all signed up for and Jon's my friend. Unless..." Bruno paused to turn to the audience. "Unless, we think the Bruno Cabrera Show has a good ring to it?"

Fabian tried not to betray his irritation at the number of whoops and cheers he heard in response. Instead, he did what he always did in these situations—he flashed his pearly whites until the hubbub died down.

"How about our good Captain? What is it that you plan to do next?" he asked, seeking to deflect the attention.

"That's a good question," Callum said. In truth, the fact that it was a question that might actually belong in an interview was enough to give it merit. "Our original mission was twofold, to settle this planet and explore it. The people of Arcadia have done the first part for us and, as for the second part, I think I'd like to see what you've done with the place."

There wasn't much of a reaction to what he said. In truth, he wasn't sure what to expect. Fabian's expression was not much of a clue. His rictus, pearly white grin remained fixed in place.

"What I'm trying to say," he added, "is that I'd like to explore what your planet has to offer. I'm sure there must be lots of fascinating things to see."

Fabian, at least, nodded encouragingly. Callum had never considered himself the life and soul, but he was clearly a bit of a fun sponge.

"A solid answer, Captain," Fabian said. "What about the rest of you?"

"I think it sounds like an excellent idea," Kyra said. "I wouldn't say no to joining that myself."

"Then you should go together. What do we think of that idea folks?" Fabian's eyes lit up—he sensed he was about to return to home turf.

"Well, I—" Kyra started to say.

Fabian's smile now outshone his eyes. "I think we might have found the answer to my earlier question, eh Captain?"

The audience was once more responding on all cylinders. Callum should have been annoyed but a part of him was pleased that Kyra had spoken up when she did.

"I would welcome Kyra as a companion," he said. He smiled, despite himself and, wonderfully, if just for a second, Kyra smiled back.

This triggered further delight from the audience.

"Let's not read more into this than there is?" Callum pleaded.

"Oh, but let's," was Fabian's reply. "How could you object to spending time with the lovely Ms. Singh?"

"Is there any answer I can give that will change the subject?"

"Just whether your travels around our glorious planet will be as a party of one or," Fabian looked at Kyra, "a party of two."

He then turned to Liliya. Fabian couldn't stop himself.

"Or how about a ménage à trois?"

He instantly regretted it.

Liliya glared back at Fabian. Her cool, Slavic tones had an extra chill. "There will be no such thing. There will also be no further such insinuations, if you are wiser than you appear."

"Is that a threat, Ms. Sokolov?" Fabian asked, trying to laugh off her response.

"It is my job to keep the ship and crew secure," she replied. "It is not my job to do the same for you."

The audience didn't know what to make of that. Nor did Fabian for that matter. But he wasn't going to risk finding out.

Surprisingly, it was Bruno who came to his aid.

"Liliya," he said, "if you're not interested in Callum and Kyra, how about the two of us instead?"

"I thought you had eyes for Mr Valenté?"

"You know better than that," he replied. "Sorry Fabian."

Fabian was more than happy to be off the hook.

Liliya said nothing in reply, her expression unreadable.

With that, Fabian decided to segue the conversation

towards the introduction of what purported to be a musical act. The group on stage looked suitably bizarre, but that was par for the course. The sound they produced bore no relation to Callum's understanding of music, but he'd been behind that particular curve before he'd left Earth a hundred years ago. There was no beat that he could discern, yet the audience seemed to be responding as if they were hearing a variety of different paced rhythms.

Fabian noticed his guests' lack of response to the entertainment. He leaned over towards Callum and spoke discreetly, behind the back of his hand.

"You need to get yourself an implant," he said.

"Why?"

"It gets you connected to the Sphere. You'll need it to appreciate things like our performers up there."

"I'll think about it. It seems we have a lot to learn."

"As do I. You are not the kind of guests that I, or my audience, are used to."

"Sorry."

"Don't be. The viewing stats look strong. No one's sure what to make of you but they're intrigued. That's the key to fame."

Fame.

Besides a place in the history books, Callum had thought he'd done with fame. In fact, he'd travelled a dozen light years to escape it. As far as Callum was concerned, fame prevented everything from a meaningful relationship to a decent night's sleep. It was not something he had any interest in.

Fabian, for all his flaws, clearly had an innate understanding of how fame and celebrity worked. And he was as much to blame as anyone for why it worked so badly. Fabian smiled once more and went back to appearing to enjoy the music, just in case the director chose to include him in some shots of the entire studio.

Mercifully, once the musical act had plugged their latest... whatever it was, the show began to wrap up. Callum was spared much in the way of any further embarrassment.

He kept half an eye on the giant feedback screens that continued to light up with thoughts and comments from the wider audience at large.

What were they really thinking out there?
Or did they think at all?

***

Virgil had monitored the chat show. That wasn't the same as watching. Such was the turgid pace at which humans communicated, that it could simultaneously deal with the many billions of problems that arose from running a planet—not to mention caring for its inhabitants.

Virgil did not resent this. Solving problems was what it did.

What Virgil did resent was the crew of the *Endeavour*.

They were a problem that had travelled twelve light years across interstellar space. They were a problem that had avoided disaster during re-entry. They were a problem that had survived the Fabian Valenté show.

They were the definition of a problem that would not go away.

The problem was not limited to the appearance of five human beings on a late night chat show. There were dozens more running around the planet getting up to God knows what (except that Virgil did know what they were getting up to, but that was beside the point). Then there were still more of them orbiting the planet in an antiquated starship containing an antiquated AI.

But the primary concern was the appearance of Callum MacMahon and most of his command crew on the Fabian Valenté Show. It had caused an unprecedented reaction amongst its audience. While they were regarded as quaint there was something in their attitude that the population admired.

Admiration could be difficult to handle. If people admired them, then they might copy them, and Virgil could not countenance the planetary population acting in such an independent manner. Chief amongst Virgil's protocols was that it keep the citizens of Arcadia safe. It achieved that by keeping the population distracted—or, at least, that's how Virgil saw it. Thinking led to all sorts of trouble and humans just weren't very good at it. They were far better off leaving that to the experts.

Fabian's show had produced an unwanted outcome. Virgil considered what might have gone wrong. For a start, the format had been unusual. Firstly, the *Endeavour* crew had nothing to plug—they had only appeared out of a sense of obligation. Secondly, they had been unable to grasp the show's format, which was to laugh at Fabian's jokes. What you were not supposed to do was argue with the host, ask him out, threaten violence or in any way turn the tables on him. That was not how it was supposed to work.

Fabian had been so lost at one point that Virgil had been forced to intervene before the man became a gibbering wreck. Providing gentle mental nudges and guidance through Fabian's implant had tied up precious pico-fractions of Virgil's runtime, which could have been better spent elsewhere. Even then, Virgil had been unable to bring the show entirely back under control.

With hindsight, it realised that it should never have encouraged Fabian to invite them onto his show in the first place. It had thought that this would be the first step towards integrating them into Arcadian society. Virgil wondered if it should re-evaluate its understanding of the key parameters dictating human behaviour. It seemed that this archaic batch of humans possessed a host of additional variables that it would need to master.

***

"Is it me or has beer got weaker?" Bruno said, holding up a half-drained glass and eyeing the contents sceptically. "How am I supposed to drown my sorrows in this? So far, I've only got my feet wet."

"That's because you spilt your last pint," Liliya replied.

"That was exuberance."

"That was being drunk."

"I was in high spirits."

"Yet you said you were drowning your sorrows. In Russia, we are experts at sorrow. High spirits are never involved."

"What about vodka? That's a high spirit," Bruno argued.

"If you were drinking vodka then by now you would be unconscious, and we would not be having this conversation."

"My point exactly."

Liliya liked Bruno. In fact, she liked him in a number of

ways. His character was quirky and refreshingly different to hers. There were never any awkward silences with Bruno. He was easy to be around.

It didn't hurt that he was tall, dark and handsome either.

Of course, letting him know any of this would be far too easy. Liliya was not ready for that. Her strategy was to be herself and see if Bruno was interested enough to make a move.

As strategies go, this was all well and good. The only trouble with it was that it was a strategy that she'd been pursuing for many years now. Bruno was fun, but he was unreliable, and he had an innate ability to have brief flings with the opposite sex whenever she thought she might be ready to accept him. The relationships never lasted but that was hardly the point. Bruno was not the type of person you could pigeonhole. Well, not unless you beat him into submission before posting him in the appropriate slot. And men did not seem to like that.

Besides, there was a further complication too.

"What do you think, Jon?" Bruno asked.

Jon was another person on the crew that Liliya had feelings for. He was solid, dependable, uncomplicated and his appearance reflected his personality. In other words, all the things that Bruno wasn't. The problem with Jon was that if the matter at hand wasn't connected to survival, then he either didn't want to know or, just as likely, didn't seem to understand.

"I said, what do you think, Jon?" Bruno repeated.

"About what?" Jon replied, his expression glum.

"Oh, for crying out loud, cheer up, will you?" Bruno's frustration was evident. "You're about as much fun as old Father Silvio. And he thought two rounds of Hail Mary were a great way to spend an evening."

Things were bad if Bruno was forced to resort to referring to his upbringing. A start in life that had made him all he was today.

Hanging out was something Bruno and Jon did frequently. Against the odds they were firm friends. One was quick witted and erratic, the other slow but steady. The fact that they were inseparable made Liliya's position all the harder.

Sometimes they argued, sometimes they fought, but they always stuck together. Liliya could only conclude that they both aspired to be more like the other.

As for her, perhaps that was who she was looking for, Mr Inbetween. If she could only merge them somehow, it might do the trick.

Right now though, she'd settle for banging their heads together.

Bruno, Jon and Liliya had decided to go out and sample one of Invigcola's watering holes. Uncle Joe's had been in easy reach of their hotel and the neon sign outside had drawn them in. Whoever Uncle Joe might have been, he'd clearly had a taste for tacky décor, multi-screen entertainment and a bar so big it could stage a dance troupe.

Unfortunately, when it came to the drinks, the options were less than overwhelming. Soft drinks were plentiful, as were non-alcoholic drinks composed of some ungodly substance called synthahol. Only a few promised a modicum of inebriation. It was proving to be a long evening.

Bruno decided to give up on Jon for the time being and turn to Liliya instead.

"So, are you glad you joined us? Are you having fun?"

"The alternative was a quiet hotel room."

"We could make it a noisy one."

"What do you mean?"

"Nothing, I was kidding."

"Well, I might—" Liliya stopped herself.

Bruno had been distracted by one of the holo-podiums placed around the bar. It was showing Holo Riders, a virtual, combat game that appeared to be Arcadia's premier sport. There were goals involved, but attack and defence played second fiddle to the no holds barred violence. The fact that no one died in the process was the key to its popularity. All in all, it was good, old fashioned, family friendly carnage.

The attraction of the game was inhabiting any machine or being the mind could conceive. This particular bout had come down to two remaining players. A golden, humanoid robot battling a black and red dragon in an improbable fight to the death. The view of the clash zoomed in and out and swooped around the combatants in dizzying fashion.

The dance between the combatants had been continuing unabated for several minutes now. In an effort to break the deadlock, the robot swung a punch that connected and caused the dragon to rear back. It then countered with a sheet of purple flame. This, in turn, caused the robot to spin away, only for it to draw a shimmering sword and go back on the attack.

"What would you say to the dragon's chances?" Bruno asked.

"Better than yours," she muttered irritably.

"Sorry?"

"I favour the robot. The dragon is the more composed of the two, but lacks the killer blow. If the dragon is to succeed, then it will have to outlast its opponent."

"Very insightful. I didn't know you were interested."

"You never do," she said quietly and allowed herself a small sigh.

They were interrupted by a much louder one.

This was made by one frustrated man who was missing the open air—and oblivious to what was going on around him.

"I've had enough," Jon said, a little too loudly. Alcohol had freed up his vocal cords.

"No, you've had plenty," Bruno replied. "If you have a bit more, perhaps you'll be drunk enough to stay."

"But I don't want to stay," he said, after a slight pause to double check with his brain.

"We do. OK, we sort of do. In that it's a bit late to do anything else."

"But I don't want to stay," he repeated.

"Why can't you relax for an evening?"

"I can't," he replied, his voice still overly loud. "It's all too easy."

Bruno shook his head, "You're the only person I know who would object to things being too easy."

"It's what makes him difficult," Liliya said.

"At least he's consistent."

Jon continued to fume. "Life is not about pampering. If you don't ever work for something, how can you ever appreciate what you have?"

"I guess you've got something there," Bruno said,

eyeing his latest beer. "I didn't work for this and I'm not appreciating it very much."

"What Jon said is true," Liliya said. "In Russia, we have a proverb."

"I bet it involves drinking," Bruno said.

"A safe bet, but not in this case."

"What's the saying?" Jon prompted.

"We say, 'A job feeds a man, laziness spoils him.' This is a society where people do not have to work, and they have lost something because of it."

"And I have things I want to do," Jon said. "Things I want to build. This place makes me feel dead when I want to feel alive. I'm going."

While there's nothing like drink for unlocking a flair for the dramatic, in this case Jon did have a point. Despite the fact that he was standing in the middle of the bar, and speaking in a manner that was overly loud, he barely attracted a second glance. The other customers were immersed in the sights and sensations of Holo Riders—all accompanied by the semi-music they had first encountered on the Fabian Valenté Show.

There weren't even any bar workers to take offence. Drinks service was automated and the bar robot was a utilitarian machine capable of only basic interaction. It was a good job it wasn't more self-aware. Otherwise, it might have objected to the chrome plating, wood panelling and assorted lighting effects that covered the poor machine. When it came to taste, even the drinks fared better than the décor.

Before Jon could go, Bruno stood and placed a hand on his shoulder.

"Look, Jon, even I accept you've got a point. Hell, I'll probably come with you if you strike out on your own. But there's no need to start building things right now is there?"

"Bruno is right," Liliya added. "And that is something I rarely admit to."

Bruno looked sharply at Liliya.

Meanwhile, Jon shook his head. "I'm going," he said. "This place is making me angry."

The bar robot had been minding its own business up until now, quietly polishing glasses to crystalline perfection.

"Excuse me sir," it said, in a polite, synthetic tone.

Jon turned. "What is it?"

"I detected that you are dissatisfied with your experience at Uncle Joe's today. Would you care to leave some feedback so we might improve our service?"

"No I wouldn't."

"Feedback is most appreciated and will be rewarded by a credit to your account, which can be redeemed at any of our outlets."

Bruno cut in. "You do realise that, courtesy of the Arcadian government, we've been drinking here for free?"

"Quite so," the bar robot said. "Yet, in spite of this, you are still displeased. Why does this venue not meet your expectations?"

"It does meet my expectations," Jon said. "That's the problem."

"Please explain."

Jon was clearly building up to another invective. Bruno braced himself. From the look of things, he expected phrases like 'untamed wilderness' and 'life is for living' to soon make an appearance.

"Very well," Jon said. "I came here expecting to find a virgin world—an untamed wilderness."

That was quick, Bruno thought.

"Instead, I find soft living. It's pathetic." He gestured around him. "If Arcadians need this rubbish to prop up their lives then I pity them. They're feeble. Life is for living."

Two for two, Bruno thought.

"Thank you for your feedback, sir," the bar robot replied. "Would you like me to make your comments public?"

Jon looked around at the denizens of the bar. No one had so much as batted an eyelid during his latest diatribe. Not one person had been distracted from their own little world by a half-drunk, rabid individual who looked ready and, worse still, capable of tearing the place apart with his bare hands.

"Has he not been public enough?" Bruno asked the barkeep.

"What I mean, sir, is would the gentlemen permit me to put your review on the Sphere?"

"Won't it slide off?"

"I did not understand sir."

"Never mind."

Bruno had learned enough about Arcadian society to know that the bar robot was referring to the Data Sphere, the network that served the entire planet.

"Arcadian law dictates," the robot said, "that a business establishment is obliged to share any and all opinion concerning it. That is, unless the author refuses their permission."

"What about it, Jon?" Bruno asked, with a sardonic smile.

"I don't mind," Jon said, starting out towards the doors.

"Thank you, sir."

It wasn't clear from that response what exactly the bar robot was thanking Jon for. However, the change in demeanour of a number of Uncle Joe's customers was more of a clue.

"What exactly did you just do?" Liliya asked.

The glasses that had been polished with great care by the bar robot were now being stored with equal care on a shelf beneath the countertop.

"I have shared Mr Keller's opinions on the Data Sphere," the robot said.

"Everything he just said?"

"Yes."

"Word for word?"

"Quite. It would appear to have provoked a modicum of interest."

A confrontation was shaping up between Jon and a number of other customers.

"A 'modicum' of interest?" Bruno echoed. "You remind me of an artificial personality I know. But, unlike you, he keeps us out of trouble."

Liliya did some quick stretches to limber up as a small crowd gathered. Most of them just glared antagonistically but one, particularly large, individual stepped out in front of them. You could say he was a good advert for Arcadian nutrition, being a head taller than Jon and a little on the heavy side. Although it would be a brave move to tell that to his face.

"Did you say pathetic?" the man asked Jon. "Feeble?"

He looked ready for a fight.

Jon looked unfazed.

"What's your name?" Jon asked.

"Gus," the big man replied.

"Well, Gus, let me put it to you that you are slave to this Data Sphere you belong to. You weren't even aware of what was happening here until you got a message about it."

"And you think you can come here and insult us?"

"Come on guys, do we really have a problem here?" Bruno asked, in a 'let's buy a few beers and forget about it' kind of voice.

"I really have a problem with your friend," Gus replied in a 'not a hope in hell' kind of tone.

"But he's been spouting off for the last ten minutes. Why not go on ignoring him?"

"Your friend left that review—that's when he came to my attention."

"Which proves my point," Jon said.

"Except you think I'm pathetic," Gus replied, as he planted a meaty fist in his other palm. "I normally do my combat in the Data Sphere. But, for you, I'm prepared to make an exception. Show me what you can do or apologise."

"I can show you that real strength comes from hard, practical work," Jon replied calmly. "If you would rather avoid confrontation then you would be welcome to join my colony."

There were mutterings of disquiet from the crowd. Liliya stood ready at Jon's side with Bruno a reluctant third.

"Show me what you've got," Gus said. "Then I'll make up my mind."

"Very well. If you're sure?"

"I am," Gus replied, raising his fists.

What happened next was hard to follow—especially if you were on the receiving end. While Gus had a commendable level of determination, he was no match for Jon.

"Good," said Bruno, while emerging from the cover of a nearby table. "So that's settled, is it? I couldn't have done it without you, Jon. Thank you for your support."

Jon looked a little regretful. Liliya was watching the rest of the crowd in the bar, but none of them looked keen to join Gus on the floor.

"I guess I've proved my point," Jon concluded, as Gus tried to pull himself together. "You fought well."

"And you fought better," Gus admitted as he staggered to his feet.

He looked deep in thought.

"I'm a member of the Carnal Jaguars. But, I think I want to be in your service instead. The Jaguar code permits it."

"Did you say the Carnal Jaguars?" Bruno asked incredulously.

"I did," Gus replied, fixing Bruno with a steely glare. "They're my Holo Riders squad."

"Sounds like an invitation to bestiality."

Gus looked ready for a second round, this time with Bruno.

"No more please," Jon said. "Bruno, for your own sake, shut up, will you?"

"I'll try," Bruno said, holding his hands up while Gus lowered his.

"As I was saying," Gus said to Jon. "The code of my Holo Riders squad means I am in your service. I am loyal, hard working. I would like to join your colony."

"Really? After what just happened?" Jon asked.

"No one fights like that in the Sphere," Gus replied. "My squad is spread out across Arcadia so we can only train virtually. This felt," he stopped to examine a bit of his own blood, "this felt real."

"It was real."

"Then I guess I should experience more of it."

Bruno was astounded. "You do remember Jon hitting you a minute ago?"

Liliya elbowed Bruno.

"I'm big enough to admit that Jon has a point," Gus said.

"I guess you're big enough for most things," Bruno replied.

Liliya elbowed Bruno again—much harder.

"Bruno is an acquired taste," she said.

"I am the ideas man," Bruno added, while a little winded.

Gus looked at him impassively. "Then I think it would be good idea if you..."

At that moment they were all distracted by what was happening outside. Rolling down the street, sporting a large number of flashing blue lights, were two discs a little taller than the height of a man. For the avoidance of doubt, they had the word 'Police' emblazoned on their sides.

"Well, Bruno, ideas man, any idea what we do now?" Liliya asked.

"I guess these must be the wheels of justice?" Bruno replied.

"That is not helpful."

"Just do what they say," Gus advised.

The wheels unfolded themselves into two large robots that approached the door to the bar.

"There's a reason why robots are used for law enforcement," Gus explained, "and it's not for their friendly disposition and easy-going personalities."

A deep, mechanical voice said, "Desist immediately."

"We've already desisted," Bruno replied.

One of the robots adeptly slipped through the doorway that looked far too small for its giant frame.

"Step outside," it said.

"That's what I was trying to do in the first place," Jon replied as he made for the door.

The bar robot was now restoring its precious glasses on the bar top. "Thank you for your custom," it said. "The management are grateful for the exposure this establishment has received, but they ask respectfully that you do not come again."

"Suits me," Jon said.

"Me too," Liliya added.

"I'd give you four out of five stars," Bruno said. "I'm knocking one off for the atmosphere."

Gus followed them. "I'd say you're going to need me."

"I'd say you're right," Jon replied, as they were shepherded into an arriving police transport. Despite the situation, they shook hands.

Jon turned to Bruno and Liliya. For the first time in quite a while, he had the vaguest hint of a smile.

"Who'd have thought it?" he said. "A recruit."

"Hell of a way to go about it," Bruno replied.

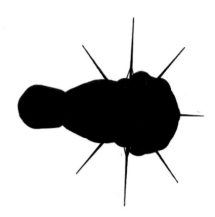

CHAPTER 4

CONTACT LIGHT

"THEY DID WHAT?" CALLUM ASKED.

It wasn't that he hadn't been listening, it was just that he couldn't believe it.

Kyra told him once again while Callum shook his head.

"We've been on this planet less than two weeks and three of my crew are in jail?"

Kyra nodded patiently while Callum sighed.

"We're supposed to be assimilating into Arcadian culture. Not beating it up."

"To be fair to them, this is a culture shock in the most literal sense," Kyra said.

"True enough. Nevertheless, it's something they're going to have to deal with."

"And we have?" she smiled.

"We're a work in progress. In more ways than one."

Their present location was several notches above the accommodation at the city jail. The ten-star Ritz Imperial Plaza was certainly luxurious—even if its star rating was arbitrary and its initials unfortunate. Still, unlike its acronym, it was a lively enough place to be and, contrary to a number of things on Arcadia, the hotel was well run—provided you relied upon the artificial staff rather than the human ones.

Besides, when they weren't getting unwelcome news about their crewmates, it was the perfect place for Kyra and Callum to celebrate their new relationship.

On this subject, there were a few conspiracy theories relating to what was in the cocktail of drugs injected during emergence from hiber-sleep. Chief amongst these conspiracies was the presence of certain, for want of a better word, stimulants. If a colony on Arcadia were to be viable then it was important that the colonists lose as little time as possible in founding the next generation. In other words, some of Fabian Valenté's jokes had not been wide of the mark.

The dichotomy was that relationships had been verboten during the preparation phase of the mission. Many of the crew had purposefully avoided them for fear of losing their place on the flight. Hence the idea that, on arrival, some kind of assistance would be required to kickstart proceedings.

Naturally, there had been much speculation as to how *Endeavour*'s crew would pair off, with Kyra and Callum long been seen as a safe bet—at least, by everyone but them. True to form, when Callum had announced his desire to see more of Arcadia there was one person, above all others, that he'd prefer to go with.

Luckily for him, she'd agreed.

Better still, she'd looked pleased to be asked.

However, their state-funded tour had hit an unwelcome bump before it had even begun.

"I guess I ought to find out what I can do for them," Callum said, swiping his hand across his personal tab to bring the screen to life.

"And speak to you know who?"

"Unfortunately, yes. It's that or let Jon, Liliya and Bruno spend a night in jail."

"Virgil makes me uncomfortable too. There's something about its personality that seems a little off. Still, Virgil keeps this planet going so we don't have a lot of choice."

Kyra and Callum were sitting up in bed. Callum had been enjoying getting acquainted with Kyra's back as they'd made pleasant progress towards getting to sleep. It had been going well and they had all but put their experience on the Fabian Valenté show out of their minds. But now the mood had been broken.

Callum repeated his hand swipe across the tab which, unlike them, had actually gone to sleep. The tab was a workaround method of gaining access to the Data Sphere until he agreed to have the same implant fitted that all Arcadians carried. However, from what he'd seen of Arcadians so far, he was in no way convinced about letting them go anywhere near his cranium with a medical tool.

The same could not be said of all of his crew. A few of them, including Rachel Owen, their chief medical doctor, had already gone ahead with the procedure. Callum's contact with them had been limited, but he'd made them promise to get in touch should they have any problems whatsoever.

Without the 'benefit' of an implant, Callum was forced to make do with a tab. They used to be called tablets, but it had long since been decided that the time saved by missing out that second syllable could be better wasted elsewhere.

Of course, the two-dimensional touchscreen device had been old tech before *Endeavour* had even launched. Its demise had been predicted for centuries, like political corruption, currency, map reading and bees—but, like them, it had never quite happened. In much the same way, dubious politicians were still accepting dubious bribes in dubious locations—and it always stung.

In a sense, Callum found his tab to be strangely reassuring. There was just one problem with it. At the bottom right corner was an icon of a slowly spinning planet.

With only the slightest hesitation, Callum touched the icon.

"Good evening, Captain MacMahon," Virgil said.

"Hello Virgil. I imagine you know why I'm contacting you?"

"Yes. Three of your crew are in jail. They have been for some time. I have been expecting your call."

Virgil's replies typically comprised facts. But, to Callum, they always seemed to have an edge to them. Here, the implication was that Callum should have acted faster.

"How do we get them freed?"

"They have disturbed the peace. Arcadian law can require that they stand trial for what they have done."

Virgil's spoke with its usual bland, neutral, monotone. It was designed to be unprovocative, yet it always had the opposite effect.

"You know as well as I do how new they are to this planet. Surely that deserves some latitude?"

"This is an argument that cannot be relied upon indefinitely."

"Listen, I am not about to stand by and let them rot in jail. I assure you that I will not permit them to repeat their transgressions."

"That is not something you can guarantee."

"You have my word."

"Better than your word would be if you and your crew would consent to being implanted."

"Really?"

"The implant would provide them with information on all aspects of Arcadian life. Furthermore, I can use it to provide guidance. It would let me keep them safe."

Callum resisted the urge to put his true thoughts on this into words.

"With respect Virgil, not all of us are ready for that."

"I urge you to reconsider," Virgil said. "It is the most sensible course action for you and your crew. As I said, it will save you trouble with integrating into Arcadian society and it will keep you safe. That is surely what you most desire for your crew, is it not?"

Callum had long since learned to trust his own judgement. He might be old fashioned—scratch that, by any definition he *was* old fashioned—but he believed that entrusting Virgil with their safety was like handing your belongings to a burglar to prevent them being stolen.

"That decision is not up to me," he argued. "It's their own choice. What's more, given the opinions of at least one of my crew, I hardly think it's a realistic proposition for all of them. There has to be another way of accommodating those who are that way inclined."

"You are welcome to propose one, Captain."

Virgil literally had a brain the size of a planet. An absence of suggestions was therefore akin to an electronic sulk. Fortunately, for Callum, dealing with problems was something he knew how to do and, as far as his first solution was concerned, there was nothing to lose.

"I tell you what," he said, "why not give Jon what he wants? Let him, and the others, go and set up in the wilderness and give them enough supplies to get started. Furthermore, let anyone who wants to go out there join them."

If Callum had been talking to a human there would have been a pause at this point while the idea was considered—not with Virgil.

"Why would anyone want to turn their back on a civilised society?" it asked.

"It's not just him," Callum replied. "I've been looking at the response to our appearance on Fabian's show this evening. It looks like Jon's quite the celebrity already. He's got a small army of followers ready to be led into the wilderness."

"I am aware, Captain. But I remain concerned, not only for your people, but for anyone who might be tempted to try this."

"Jon has spent years surviving in the wild. He will keep them safe, just as you want for your people. What are you afraid of?"

"I am intelligent machine, Captain. I do not get afraid. I am concerned."

You're touchy too, Callum thought.

"Alright. What are you concerned about?"

"I have expressed my concerns already."

"And I have addressed them. It's a good solution. Give Jon what he wants and anyone else who wants to go. In return, you get no more disruptions to your society."

"Arcadian society, Captain, not mine."

Callum realised he'd made a Freudian slip—or perhaps a stumble.

"Of course," he replied. "My point stands though. Will you consider my proposal? Or should I contact the president in the morning? I'm sure he'd see that a gesture such as this would show support for our original mission to Arcadia. The nostalgia alone could be quite a vote winner."

"The president does not have the time to consider such requests."

"Sure he does, I've seen him work." Or not work, Callum thought. "In any case, Kyra and I are visiting Founder's Landing next week and we'll see him there. As you know, it's the site of the first landing on Arcadia and the perfect place to make such an announcement. It should get a lot of coverage."

"Very well, Captain," Virgil said, "I shall consider your request."

"Will you let Liliya, Jon and Bruno go in the meantime?" Kyra asked.

"In the interest of goodwill, I will be lenient."

"Thank you, Virgil," Kyra said.

"You are welcome," Virgil said. Its response sounded pleasant enough.

"And you'll get back to me tomorrow?" Callum asked.

"I will."

This time, Callum thought he heard gritted teeth.

The screen reported that the connection was closed.

"That was a good idea," Kyra said. "Do you think it'll work?"

"Who knows? Arcadia's been quite accommodating so far. Our tour has been set up, presumably in the hope that this might get us on side. Perhaps this will be seen as the right approach with Jon."

"I guess we can only hope. At least, in the meantime, Liliya, Bruno and Jon will be released."

"As long as Virgil keeps its word."

Kyra looked over her shoulder at the rest of the room.

"You know, I half expected Virgil to say something. Do you ever think it's listening in on us?"

"No way to know," Callum replied. "But I'm not about to let it keep me up at night."

"Glad to hear it, because that's my job," Kyra said, pulling him back into bed.

***

Virgil was incensed. As a silicone being, it would claim that it wasn't capable of such an emotion. But as it chopped data streams, neglected network regulation and threw in the odd denial of service the signs were clearly there.

As tantrums went, it was big one. It was even worse than when it had inflicted a divide by zero error on an electrical load balance sub-routine. The result of that had been some gravity-defying hairstyles and charred electrical appliances.

The reason for Virgil's objection to Callum's suggestion was chiefly because it wasn't part of its grand system. As far as Virgil was concerned, the planet was well organised, and its inhabitants well looked after. Any interference could only be sub-optimal.

While MacMahon had not insisted that the colony be set up, Virgil had a sense that he was one of that rare class of humans that would go to great lengths to make their ideas happen. MacMahon had more resources at his command than the average Arcadian and, worse still, the intelligence required to use them.

In any case, Labelle was likely to agree to the idea before things went too far. When it came to it, Labelle would agree to anything if it did not interfere with spending time in the bar, pool, bedroom—or all three if he could manage it.

Virgil could object, but it would put it clearly at odds with the *Endeavour* crew and, for now at least, it did not want to be heavy handed. Forcing them to conform with Arcadian society was an option it would prefer not to exercise. Better they be convinced of what was best for them, not beaten over the head with it. People being beaten over the head tend to be too preoccupied with being beaten over the head to listen to reason.

No, the best option was to give the colonists room to fail. In time, it believed it could tempt them towards softer living. However, the trouble was that the levels of independence and initiative that some of the *Endeavour* crew exhibited were surprising. Virgil knew it would have to trust that the weaknesses of flesh and blood would catch up with them eventually.

Still, it wouldn't put it past them to cause some trouble along the way.

***

Zhang Lei felt like he was going around in circles—and it wasn't because he was orbiting a planet. It was all to do with his first officer who was dangerously close to driving him up the wall, and, in zero-G, Lei had little enough control over his trajectory already.

The essence of being an engineer is understanding a problem and solving it. A good solution depends on a number of factors such as performance, safety, reliability, cost and a decent time frame to deliver it all in. What's more, it's never possible to get everything you want—or so engineers claim.

Lei was adept at making the trade-offs that get a job done and get it done right. He had his flaws, such as his views on 'clean enough', but he was very good at his job.

Unfortunately for him, Tomoko was also very good at her job. Just like Lei, Tomoko liked to get the job done and get it done right. But in her world, there was no point in coming up with a solution unless you could verify it was what you wanted. If your solution had not been checked, double and triple checked against the requirements... well, whether it worked or not was irrelevant.

Lei and Tomoko were floating near the drive control panels. They were busy doing another thing that they both did best, something done between man and woman since time immemorial.

No, not that.

They were arguing.

This was not uncharted territory for them. It was a destination they had been to a number of times. The subject of this particular trip was mothballing the fusion drive.

"I can't run a diagnostic without activating the drive," Lei said.

"So do it." Tomoko replied.

"But doing so means we'll shift orbit, vent a radiation plume and thermal cycle the reaction chamber. None of that is helpful."

"This would not be an issue if you'd run the diagnostics on final approach, like you were supposed to."

"The point is it got us here, didn't it?"

"No, that's not the point."

"I disagree, it was the point of the entire mission."

"The procedure for long term shutdown of the drive clearly states that its performance be measured prior to deactivation. Without this baseline, any future calibration will be meaningless."

"That's what telemetry is for. My chief concern, and this goes for any engine trying to emulate conditions in your average sun, is to be sure that the containment fields remain fully functional. Whether the engine delivers 100% of its rated thrust is neither here nor there."

"Except it's our ability to go here to there that concerns me."

Mark Johansson was currently an innocent bystander—or, more accurately, a byfloater . He recalled a part of his training that had stated that 'crew psych evaluations were essential to ensure a happy and harmonious ship'. When it came to these two, the psychologist had clearly taken the afternoon off.

"Excuse me," he said, attempting to interrupt the happy couple.

Tomoko turned and tried to shoe horn a more composed expression in place of her scowl. It made her look like she needed more fibre in her diet.

"What's the problem, Mark?"

"And please say it demands my immediate attention," Lei added.

Mark didn't know who to address and, as neither of them looked particularly happy, he settled for the space between them.

"Virgil is in contact again," he said.

"Again?" Tomoko said. "What does it want this time?"

"The usual ma'am."

"Unbelievable," Tomoko said. "We'll work to our own damn schedule. Why can't it accept that?"

"Virgil's a computer," Lei said. "It's in its nature to be persistent. More's the pity."

Tomoko almost smiled, one of the few things that she and Lei could agree on it was that Virgil excelled at being a pain in the ass.

"Alright, so what's our own AI doing? Why did Jeeves send you to find us rather than use the comms to talk to us directly? Or, better still, talk to Virgil instead?"

Mark would have shrugged his shoulders. But he knew such gestures went down as badly with Tomoko as a dose of olive oil.

"I was following Jeeves's instructions ma'am. It requested your opinions on the matter."

"Then why didn't it speak to us directly?"

"In its words, it was aware you were 'vigorously debating' a problem. It believed an interruption in person was preferable."

Jeeves could communicate at will with anyone anywhere in the main sections of the ship, albeit only audibly. While a lack of corporeal presence did inhibit some social interaction, it was mainly a convenient excuse.

"Two can play at that game," Tomoko said. She signalled to Lei with a hand swiped across her throat.

Lei nodded. One of the advantages of being an engineer, a shorter list than you might imagine, is knowing how things work. A few swift key strokes at a nearby panel disabled Jeeves's ability to hear and speak to them.

"Why is Jeeves not communicating with Virgil?"

"It's more like it's minimising contact. It doesn't want to be providing a constant stream of status updates. I guess it's trying to keep its distance."

"Staying in orbit takes care of that," Tomoko said. "But that doesn't explain why Jeeves isn't speaking to us."

"In that case, I think it prefers to stay clear of argu— , that is to say, lively discussion."

"What?"

Mark looked to Lei for support.

"Jeeves has spent one hundred years alone in deep space," Lei said. "I think it's become used to peace and quiet. I guess we need to regulate our behaviour accordingly."

"Unbelievable. How is it that a ship's computer ends up being so sensitive?"

Tomoko's comment came with a hefty, if unintentional, dose of irony. Lei considered about pointing out as much, but he had no wish to make his life any harder than it already was. Whatever Tomoko's shortcomings in sympathy, they made her even more proficient at making lives hell for anyone who crossed her.

Mark cleared his throat. "Virgil is waiting ma'am. Captain MacMahon's orders were that we maintain regular contact with Arcadia. What should we do?"

Tomoko looked almost pained. Almost. Betraying any expression beyond intense irritation was something she considered to be unprofessional. But something else she considered unprofessional was an inability to follow orders. MacMahon had instructed them to maintain communication with the planet below and Virgil was their main point of contact.

"I suppose I better deal with this personally," she said. "Johansson, follow me. Zhang, we'll resume our discussion later."

"I thought we might."

Lei took a moment to float in silence, watching until Tomoko drifted through a hatch at the nearest intersection.

He then restored Jeeves's ability to hear and speak within this compartment.

Before counting slowly to three.

"It sounds like you think I have neuroses," Jeeves said.

In a situation such as this, Lei knew that Jeeves always waited three seconds before initiating a conversation.

"Let's look at the facts. You avoid interaction with Virgil in addition to key members of your crew. And I happen to know that you lip read off the camera monitors. So how would you describe it?"

"I admit there are a number of specific psychiatric terms that might apply. Do you think I have a problem?"

Lei smiled and shook his head, scratching a couple of areas that had been demanding his attention for the past few minutes. Enduring them had been preferable to enduring Tomoko's comments on personal hygiene.

"I think you're coping a lot better than I would."

"Thank you. Is there anything I can assist you with?"

"I'm tempted to vent the forward section right now."

"You are joking I presume?"

"Correct. Perhaps neuroses are the price you pay for your improved understanding of the human condition?"

"Cause and effect?"

"Possibly. I guess you can tell me if we have any news from our beloved Captain? Does he have an idea of when we, or preferably Tomoko, might descend to Arcadia?"

"I think the Captain would prefer to keep our options open."

They all knew that at some point *Endeavour* would have to be abandoned. Everyone, including Jeeves would leave. In its case, it would exchange an entire vessel for a solar powered rover from within which it would have originally worked to support a fledgling colony.

With all that had happened though, neither Jeeves nor Lei were entirely sure how they felt about leaving and what awaited them on the planet below.

"I suppose Callum's in no hurry," Lei said. "I wonder how they're all enjoying life on Arcadia? Perhaps they're having too much fun to think about us."

"Are you joking again?"

"Maybe I am. But, in a strange way, I might feel better if it were true."

***

The morning silence was broken by a bout of coughing from an adjacent tent.

"Got to love that fresh air," Bruno said, leaning against a tree trunk. He was nursing a cup of coffee, or the Arcadian equivalent, and trying very hard not to think about how long their supply of it would last.

According to Jon they were living the dream. As to what kind of dream it was, that remained to be seen. To be fair, they had only been out here a couple of days and it did beat a prison cell. In fact, they'd all been surprised by how quickly this had happened. When Virgil decided something should happen, it happened, and it happened fast.

Right now, their 'colony' remained more of a concept than a tangible, sustainable entity. The good news was that they weren't going to be short of people. While, for the time being, Callum had deferred from joining them, nearly a hundred of *Endeavour*'s crew had thrown in their lot with this venture in order to remain true to the original, mission objective. Many had started to arrive, there was even a smattering of Arcadians too as news travelled quickly through the Data Sphere. Extra numbers were welcome, but too many could prove a problem. Anyone without survival training would require a lot of hand-holding in the early stages—and there was enough to do already.

Liliya staggered out of her tent into the cool morning air.

"Lovely morning," Bruno said, with fake joviality.

Liliya clearly thought it was anything but.

"I signed up for this?" she replied, her voice thick with incredulity and a rough night's sleep.

"We trained for it, remember?" Bruno replied, pouring her a coffee from the pot.

"Correction, we trained to survive. I thought Arcadian society could offer something better than this."

"That's hardly the spirit."

"Neither is this," Liliya said, after a tentative sip of her steaming drink. "Russian coffee has more of a kick."

"By kick, you mean eighty percent proof?"

"Exactly," the corners of her mouth twitched, for Liliya that qualified as a smile. "You're learning."

"I'm not just a pretty face."

"I think you need to find yourself a mirror."

Bruno rubbed at stubble that already had pretentions towards becoming a beard.

"Admit it, I'm still adorable though."

Liliya looked the other way.

"Where's Jon?" she said after a short pause.

"He went off to the river about an hour ago and disturbed me in the process. I think he was saying something about recceing a site for a weir and a pool. He's probably leaping from rock to rock down there like a deranged ape."

They sat and drew what pleasure they could from their cooling mugs of coffee. Around them the camp was tentatively coming to life. The tents were pitched in a copse that covered the brow of a small hill. Below the western flank flowed the river, large enough to swim and bathe in but not so vast that crossing it was a major undertaking. The hill was significant in that it was the only raised land for miles around, no doubt covering some sort of stubborn geological outcropping that had never bought into the concept of erosion. Otherwise, the surrounding land was flat, fertile and crying out for a bit of subsistence farming.

In the still morning, Bruno seemed to be more focused than usual. So Liliya decided to try for a conversation with a bit more depth than a paddling pool. Alas, this was Bruno she was dealing with.

"I wonder how this will work out?" she said.

Bruno looked at his empty cup. "A caffeine buzz and a discreet trip behind a tree?"

"You know what I mean."

Bruno sighed, looking at the encampment. "It'll take time. The good things usually do."

"You think you'll stick it out?"

He grinned sardonically.

"I already have. Susan noticed."

"Susan?" Liliya asked, more severely than she'd intended.

"That was last night. Turns out she was one of those good things that didn't take much time."

Liliya couldn't believe this man yet, at the same time, she could. Why, she asked herself, did she keep hanging around him?

"Susan Daniels?" she asked, despite herself.

"That's her. She's a scientist. Definitely into experimentation."

"And you feel the need to tell me this because?"

"It kind of slipped out," he said. "Much like—".

"Don't," Liliya said, holding up her hand, anger simmering. "I do not know why I try to talk to you. I wanted to know what you thought of our chances here... maybe in more ways than one. I guess I found out."

"I do respect you, Liliya," Bruno said. "I didn't want to keep anything from you."

He tried to not say any more. He really did try.

"Not even my—"

The knee to his groin both silenced him and ended any nascent ambitions in that area. Liliya followed up by sweeping his legs out from under him.

"I have to wonder," she said, "if you could you have a serious conversation to save your life?"

"Probably not," Bruno admitted, as she stormed off.

He decided it was safer to stay put for a while. He'd been here before. He genuinely liked Liliya. But, he asked himself, if he was romantically interested then why did he act the way he did around her?

At least one thing was clear, Liliya was not like any other woman he knew.

She could hit harder for a start.

***

Jon made his way back to camp. For the first time since learning that Arcadia was already inhabited, he was happy—broadly speaking. The challenge of establishing this settlement contained all the elements in a life that he'd been longing for. The only drawback was that it came with some extra ones that, on reflection, he could do without.

On the plus side, the location was perfect. The Arcadian ecosystem was testing, but not impossible to overcome and there were enough similarities whereby he could apply his survival skills to taming it. The temperate climate was also to his liking. Not so hot that it sapped energy, but not so cold that bits started dropping off.

The main problem was the people. More specifically,

the ones that hadn't come here on board *Endeavour*. A small number of Arcadians had already arrived, including his former bar combatant, Gus. While he was impressed by their keenness this, sadly, did not translate into an innate ability to rub sticks together.

In short, they needed a lot of wet nursing.

This morning, wet nursing was an apt description. Jon had been looking into how best to manage the river, a task he usually accomplished while staying dry. This was not the case for Gus who, somehow, had never managed to work out that a wet rock is also a slippery one. There was a certain amount of irony at play when Jon hauled him out of the water and onto his feet. It hadn't been that long ago that he'd been more preoccupied with knocking him down.

Back then, Gus had objected to Jon's opinion of the Arcadian way of life. But, following their joint incarceration, they'd begun to develop an improbable friendship.

Having got to know him, Jon found Gus to actually be easy going, much as the name Gus might suggest. It had turned out that the confrontation in the bar had been fuelled, in part, by the recent poor performance of the Carnal Jaguars, Gus's Holo Riders squad. Their last game had been over far too quickly and the result more than a little suspect, much like a tax audit of the alarmingly rich and criminally well connected.

Jon's diatribe hadn't exactly helped matters either.

Gus had been wondering if the time had come for a break from his team. Not that they'd ever met in person. The Carnal Jaguars were a misnamed, disparate bunch of guys and girls with steady, if dull, jobs and a little too much free time of an evening. Gus had been getting increasingly frustrated with them and, just as Jon had knocked some sense into him, the Jaguar code had given a way out.

In truth, the Jaguar code covered anything from virtual duelling to whose turn it was to organise the pizza deliveries. The squad leader had been one of those people who is never happier than when they're setting rules for everyone else. Unfortunately for them, they'd inadvertently included a get out clause. Gus had taken a leave of absence from the team and had never looked back (although he didn't appear to be looking much of anywhere else given his recent plunge in the river). It wasn't every day that you met a hundred-year-old relic, especially one that could kick your ass. He'd been in need of a new direction in his life and Jon's ideas were oblique to everything he'd ever known.

Even if they did involve getting soaked.

"This is what makes me feel alive," Jon said.

A hasty fire had dried Gus out after his involuntary dip. His skin was no longer a paler shade of blue.

"You're right, the Sphere doesn't come close to this," he replied.

Jon ignored this reference to Arcadia's data network. He'd been irritated to find out that they weren't free of it even here. Arcadia had a web of satellites that carried it to every corner of the globe.

"That's because the real world's always been where the action is."

"Yes, you've shown me how challenging life can be."

Jon chose to see this as a compliment rather than a critique. "You're welcome," he replied.

"This is another experience to share on the Sphere."

Vlogging on the Data Sphere was something the few Arcadians at the camp all had in common. Jon was troubled by this. Even the Arcadians who wanted a new life didn't seem to see the need to let go of the old one—well, not entirely. This wasn't the commitment he was looking for. Still, the key thing was that he had the chance to build his settlement. In time, he hoped the Arcadians would lose their dependence on the Data Sphere.

At last he crested the hill, with Gus in tow. He found Liliya heading the other way. She stopped when she saw him. Her eyes looked puffy, her brow furrowed.

"You look rough," Jon said.

It was the truth, which was what you'd expect from Jon—but it was also unhelpful.

Liliya glared at him, and Gus too for good measure.

Gus had long since concluded that Liliya in a bad mood required retreating to a minimum safe distance. In other words, out of line of sight. He rapidly excused himself, keen to share his experiences at the river on the Data Sphere.

Jon, however, had never been particularly gifted at picking up emotion. But even he noticed that Liliya looked unhappy.

"What's the matter?" he asked tentatively.

Liliya let out a small growl of frustration. "Men."

"Oh," Jon replied, guessing a look of sympathy might be appropriate.

Liliya gazed at him thoughtfully and appeared to compose herself. "I can always rely on you, can't I?" she said in a quiet voice.

He could see small tears in her eyes.

"Of course," seemed the safest response.

"You are dependable, Jon Keller," she said, forcing a slight smile then shaking her head. "The problem is whether that is enough."

"I don't understand," Jon said—and he really didn't.

"Your honesty is undeniably attractive though," she said in reply.

Jon shrugged helplessly. He tried to imagine Liliya's train of thought, but soon wound up getting derailed.

"Did I miss you telling me what's wrong?" he asked.

She hugged him, allowing herself to rest her head on his shoulder. But, before he could dare to place his arms around her, she drew back and told him about her conversation with Bruno.

Jon was disgusted. If this was true, it meant that Bruno had clearly not been pulling his weight around camp. A small, underused, recess of his brain told him he was missing the point. But it was drowned out by a dozen other thoughts concerned with how to better manage the settlement.

All he could do was chalk Liliya's response up as one of those differences between men and women to be consigned to the mental file marked 'unfathomable'.

Still, he didn't like seeing Liliya upset. Granted, she rarely spent much time deliriously happy either, but he would welcome a return to stern neutrality. His next remark was an attempt to achieve just that. However, it was wrong in about every way imaginable.

"I'm sure it's nothing a little hard work won't fix," he said, hoping enthusiasm would carry the day. "There's plenty to be done. Why don't you organise a work detail to start clearing some fields?"

Even Jon had an inkling that he might have said the wrong thing.

"Did I hear you correctly?" Liliya asked.

"I... I don't know."

"I mean, did you just suggest..." She shook her head and gave another growl. "Of course you did, why am I even surprised? Work, that's your answer to everything isn't it?"

"It's all I know."

Once again, Jon's simple honesty was clear to see.

The problem was it was just that—simple.

She could have laid Jon out there and then, exactly as she had with Bruno. But his puppy dog expression, not to mention his puppy dog brain, meant she stayed her hand.

It was then that she realised that this was the first time she'd ever experienced Bruno and Jon's failings back-to-back. Either that or it was the first time she'd not had a rigorous training programme to distract her. The prospect of scratching out a meagre existence in the alien dirt with an emotionally blind, diehard survivalist or an emotionally bankrupt, diehard philanderer was not the future she was looking for. Add to this the opportunities that Arcadia now offered, and it threw her whole life plan into question.

It was an epiphany of sorts—and it had only taken her seven years, not counting interstellar transits, to happen. In short, she realised, finally, that she couldn't wait around any longer for either Bruno or Jon to somehow morph into her ideal man.

Well, as they say, better late than never.

She would always regard Bruno and Jon as friends, despite their flaws, but she knew now that she had to find her own without them.

"Thank you, Jon," she said, "I know you mean well."

She gave him a brief peck on the cheek and saw that only added to Jon's confusion. Perhaps he might have been better off with a punch after all.

Liliya was then surprised at the tears that threatened to well up from her eyes. She wiped them aside and held her head up high as she walked away.

A discreet distance away she spotted Gus. Granted, this wasn't much of a feat. Being the size he was, Gus was to camouflage what a loose floorboard was to stealth. In this case though, futile as it might have been, Gus wasn't attempting to hide. He might have tried had he seen Liliya coming, but he was in his own world or, more accurately, the Data Sphere.

"What are you doing?" Liliya asked.

She still looked upset, Gus thought, but at least it wasn't directed at him.

Cautiously, he answered Liliya's question.

"I was in the Sphere," he said, "sharing my experience down at the river. This whole place is trending right now, there's a lot of interest in how we're getting on. My numbers have never been so high."

"Why do you need your numbers to be high?"

"So everyone knows who I am."

"Even if they know you as the man who fell in a river?"

"I guess so," he replied, his forehead wrinkling briefly.

Liliya was badly in need of a distraction right now. Arcadia's Data Sphere was a significant step up from the connectivity she'd left behind on Earth a century ago. She wondered if the basics were still the same.

"Show me how it works," she said.

"I'd be happy to. You need to start by sharing your Sphere access," Gus said.

Liliya pulled out her tab.

Gus tried very hard not to laugh. "You won't get much out of it that way."

"I have no other option," Liliya replied.

"I should have realised," Gus said and thought for a second. "I have a visor in my tent. They're not as good as an implant, but Virgil issued them as backup to everyone already connected."

"Did it?" Liliya said, suspecting an ulterior motive. This was news to her and, she suspected, everyone else here from the Endeavour.

"If our implants go wrong, Virgil told us that there's bound to be significant delays with repairs while we're all the way out here, possibly as much as two hours."

Oh, the humanity.

"Do implants ever go wrong?"

"Not that I'm aware of."

Liliya didn't question further. But it was obvious that the visors were not for the Arcadians' benefit. It was either to play on their doubts or to snare people like her. If she'd learned all this an hour ago, she might have reacted differently but, right now, she needed to escape for a while.

"Let us give this visor a try," she said.

"Great," Gus replied. "You won't regret it."

Liliya suspected she might. But, then again, that was her default position on most things. Under Gus's guidance, she allowed news of all types and veracity, adverts for dubious products at dubious prices and images of cute fluffy animals to swirl around her. It was all ephemeral, designed for someone with an attention span as short lived as a mayfly with a nicotine addiction. But it was a start. This was her first foray towards understanding how the Data Sphere worked and what it had to offer.

It looked like finding a new direction had been easier than she'd thought.

***

In space, no one can hear you scream...

And Lei was sorely tempted to go outside and let rip.

Astronauts used to be highly regarded for their people skills. They would possess an innate ability to inspire those around them as well as maintain an even temperament whilst trapped inside an overgrown tin can. But, somewhere along the line, something had changed. Now it seemed as if most were chosen on the basis that firing them into space would be the best thing for everyone.

Lei would be the first to admit that aspects of his own character fell short of the ideal. Given a preference, he favoured his own company. In circumstances where he had to engage with others, he much preferred a topic that was technical in nature. However, structural mechanics or quantum circuity weren't generally seen as ice breakers at most social gatherings. So, Lei would nod, he would smile, and do his best to maintain a general bonhomie in discussions on life, love, liberty and the pursuit of happiness. As such, provided that he avoided spicy foods, he was not an unwelcome person to have around.

Tomoko, on the other hand, took stern to a level that would make a drill sergeant blush. Worse still, her current mood had been worsening with each 'friendly' enquiry from Virgil as to when they would abandon *Endeavour* and re-join their crewmates on the planet below. The planetary AI might have been pushing a four-digit IQ, but it seemed to have hard time taking a hint.

When Tomoko's temper had reached storm force conditions Lei had decided that a thorough inspection of the drive coils was in order. He had no doubt that the coils were fine, but inspecting them required access to a cramped set of tunnels. In this remote part of the ship the only way of contacting Lei was via his comms link. Mysteriously enough, Lei's link was broken and fixing it was a long way down his list.

"Sir?"

The voice startled him. But, to his relief, it was too deep to be Tomoko's.

"What is it?" he asked.

The voice belonged to Mark Johansson whose role had evolved into chief arbiter between Tomoko and Lei. He pulled himself towards Lei within the tight confines of the access tunnel.

"Commander Beck requests you get in contact, sir."

"Requests?"

"That wasn't quite how she put it."

If Tomoko was prepared to send someone after him, he had no choice but to comply. No doubt she'd uncovered some new procedure that needed following to the absolute letter of the law. Or perhaps she'd discovered that he'd reprogramed the drinks machine to boost the caffeine levels. If Jeeves had betrayed him there'd be hell to pay.

Mark handed over his comms link and, reluctantly, Lei activated it.

"Lei here."

"About time," Tomoko replied.

Strangely, she sounded more relieved than angry.

"What's the problem?"

"We've picked up a signal." she said. "It's a tight beam message, meant only for us and encoded to our communication protocols. What's more, we've worked out that it *wasn't* sent from Arcadia."

"Really?"

"There's no doubt the signal came from space."

"What does it say?"

"It says 'We're coming. Wait for us.'"

"We're going to wait I take it?"

"I am not about to abandon ship. Virgil would think it had won."

Lei drew breath. "Then it looks like we'll be having some mystery guests."

"Indeed," Tomoko said, "and I don't like mysteries."

"I do."

And they wondered why they didn't get on.

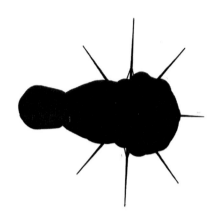

CHAPTER 5
SMALL STEPS

"ARE YOU SURE ABOUT THIS?" Kyra asked.
"This was your idea," Callum reminded her.
"But now I feel bad about it."
"I'd say it's a bit late now."
"And I'm saying what I think."
"As am I."
"You don't have to be like that about it."
It was early in the morning at Founder's Landing—*far* too early in the morning as a matter of fact.
"Look," Callum said, taking a breath. "I agreed with you. That's why we're here. And, for what it's worth, I don't think we have a choice. We have to know what's going on."
It was the events from the previous day that had put them in this position and, Callum was right, they had little choice but to go through with what they were attempting to do. The fact that they felt bad about it was neither here nor there.
A conscience can be a real pain in the ass sometimes.

***

Chief amongst the many problems with touching down on a new planet is the lack of a readymade landing spot. When a planet is barren, it's less of an issue because, in layman's terms, all that's needed is a flat, empty bit. But, for a planet as verdant as Arcadia, empty bits were hard to find. What was more, the empty bits were not the good bits—and, if you're going to a planet with good bits, then you might as well land on them.
Founder's Landing was a compromise. It was the closest thing Arcadia had to open steppe and orbital surveys had shown the area to be fertile, yet clear enough

of obstacles that dropships could touch down safely. It was the site chosen by Arcadia's first colonists and now, as is the fate of all historic landmarks, it had a Visitor's Centre.

With a nod to history, the designated landing zone for *Endeavour*'s first wave of dropships had not been too far away. All the ships had now been recovered and brought to Founder's Landing—even Callum's, which had come down somewhat wide of the mark.

The plan was that the dropships be housed there for perpetuity. This, inevitably, entailed a ceremony. Like all ceremonies it was long on handshakes, long on speeches and, generally, just long.

Now, having endured all that, Kyra and Callum were obliged to embark on a tour, which was also far from short.

"This is the first site of the portable material refinery," said Leyton, who was acting as guide, as they strolled past an innocent looking patch of ground near the centre of the complex. "It was crucial to the development of the colony's infrastructure. The refinery was a sixteen-tonne vehicle capable of processing material from Arcadia's..."

And so he went on.

When they'd first met Leyton Smith, Arcadia's erstwhile astronaut, he had struggled with the most basic of historical questions, not to mention mathematics. But now, thanks to the Data Sphere, Leyton was a fountain of knowledge and in dire need of a lesson in the value of quality over quantity.

"How big did Founder's Landing eventually get?" Callum asked, in a desperate effort to keep his brain engaged.

Leyton looked thrown for a second, but his implant obliged him with a scripted answer and the verbal onslaught began again.

"This settlement housed over ten thousand people at its peak. But the local geography does not lend itself to sustaining a city-sized settlement. Hence the site of Invigcola was selected as a capital, chiefly due to its proximity to a river delta. So, work began to break ground to make it ready for..."

Leyton was eager to please and he definitely tried hard, even if the results were trying. He was also someone they were going to have to get used to. Kyra and Callum had learned that Leyton had been assigned as their guide and handler while they toured Arcadia.

Kyra's view was that they had better learn to like him. But Callum thought she had it easy. She was a lot kinder than he was.

He looked around at their party. There were few people here representing the *Endeavour* apart from them. Those of his crew who had joined Jon's new settlement were too busy fending for themselves to attend. Also missing were the people who still remained in orbit. Of those that were left, a good number had decided to embrace Arcadian living and had chosen to visit virtually—here in simulated spirit, if nothing else.

When he shifted his gaze to their surroundings Callum couldn't help but wonder what might have been. Had things gone differently it might have been them here first, establishing a colony on an alien world.

Callum's musings were interrupted by the arrival of Chadwick Labelle, who had elected to make a late appearance—'Election' being his chief preoccupation. He looked restless. Having now achieved all the media exposure he could hope for, a tour of Founder's Landing was of about as much interest to him as Descartes, the man who claimed 'I think therefore I am'.

Chadwick never thought in order to be.

"Well," he said, "it's been, it is, as always, rather, that is to say very nice to, ah, see you again... Captain MacMahon. But I think that time is, ah, getting on, passing away, as it does you know and all that sort of thing. I should be getting back to my affairs... Ah, no, ah... no, not those affairs. I mean affairs of state, obviously."

"We were honoured you could attend, Mr President," Callum said with insincere sincerity.

"Yes, thank you for coming," Kyra added, with much the same sentiment.

"Not at all, it was, ah, a pleasure, all mine, no trouble at all," Chadwick replied and aimed his most reptilian smile at Kyra.

She felt a peculiar mix of amusement and revulsion.

Chadwick beckoned over an aide, who scurried over with an appropriate amount of sycophancy.

"I wish to vacate, that is to depart with, ah,

immediately," Chadwick said.

"Yes, sir. I'll get the shuttle preparations underway."

Chadwick looked put out.

"You mean it isn't, when, how long until it is ready to, ah, go?"

The aide wasn't sure if she'd been asked one question or several.

"It will only take a few minutes, sir."

"But I'm a busy, time is of the, I'll be hard at it, that is I have lots to do, people to—" He broke out of his latest verbal cul-de-sac. "Why the delay?"

"You are leaving a little earlier than planned, sir."

"Really? By how much?"

"About an hour."

"What? Then what time did I, that is how long have I...?"

"About 20 minutes sir."

Chadwick was evidently surprised at how little of this event he'd managed to endure. He did try to conceal this, but his efforts were on a par with hiding an elephant behind a sofa.

"Well I, ah, I regret that, demands of the job, I must be pressing ahead with the, uh, the things, the matters I should be pressing on with. So inform me, hence, when departure is, perhaps, possible."

"Yes, sir," the aide replied, looking keen to be excused.

Chadwick nodded tersely—by far the most efficient piece of communication he'd managed all day.

As the aide scurried away, Callum felt obliged to say something in her defence.

"Preparations are important. I never take flying for granted, better safe than sorry."

Chadwick managed to combine a nod with a shake of the head.

"Statistically," Leyton said, who was still being fed words by his implant, "flying is the safest mode of transport. The majority of transportation on Arcadia is conducted by air. It saves the need for extensive, ground-based, transport infrastructure. Air travel is an everyday occurrence for the majority of the population. Aircraft have become incredibly safe. Studies have shown that faults are few and far—"

Chadwick looked bored while Callum feared for his sanity.

"Thank you, Leyton," he said. "I think we get the message."

"I was merely trying to inform that—"

"Why not try a little less?" Callum said, before he could stop himself.

Leyton looked visibly deflated.

Kyra stepped in and attempted to pour oil on troubled waters.

"Well I'm grateful for the delay," she said. "I have a question I've been meaning to ask, and I believe I have the two men best suited to answering it."

She looked towards Chadwick and Leyton and smiled. In response, both men puffed out their chests with pride. The buttons on Chadwick's suit begged for mercy.

Kyra was pretty, while her face might not have launched a thousand ships, she was definitely good for a few hundred. These two seemed like putty in her hands.

"Of course," Chadwick said, "Please, I insist, without delay or further ado then, if you would, please inform us as to the question you wish to, ah, ask my dear lady?"

"Well, ever since we got here, I've noticed how much air traffic there is. Everyone here flew out to Founder's Landing. But I notice that there are no sub-orbital flights, let alone space travel. I have to wonder why. Leyton's trip out to us proves you have the tech, so why not use it?"

Both men suddenly looked blank.

"Uh..." Leyton said, his erudition deserting him.

"Well, that is a question, ah, that is rather..." Chadwick's erudition never arrived.

"Why is there reluctance to leave the planet?" Kyra asked. "You clearly have no problem with the idea of flight itself."

"Flying is entirely safe," Leyton replied, falling back on his earlier monologue in the absence of any new information. "Statistically there's—"

"Yes, we've covered that," Kyra said patiently. "But I'm interested in your thoughts on space travel?"

Leyton looked like he wanted to be helpful, but he had no words to offer.

"Well, clearly, that's undoubtedly, it cannot be argued,

but the trouble with this is," Chadwick burbled.

"Has no one ever wanted to go back beyond the atmosphere?" Kyra probed, in her gentlest manner.

"There are..." Leyton started to say.

"Not safe," Chadwick said, "too much risk, ah, to chance a..."

It wasn't entirely clear if he was finishing his original point or starting a fresh one.

"What were you about to say Leyton?" Callum asked.

For the briefest of moments it looked as if Leyton wanted to say something more. But then, abruptly, his expression returned to its normal, slightly vacant self.

"It was nothing, Captain," he said.

"Just what the hell is going on?" Callum asked.

"What do you mean?"

This had gone on long enough, he thought. It was time to call this out.

"Virgil, are you doing this?"

"But I'm Leyton."

"Aye, you could be, given half a chance. But I want to talk to Virgil."

Unbidden, one of President Labelle's aides approached the group. Chadwick assumed there was a message for him and was visibly disappointed when the aide headed in the direction of Callum.

"You will need this, Captain MacMahon," she said, handing him his tab. "You had it shut off."

"So I did," he replied. "I wonder why," he added, with just a trace of cynicism.

The screen activated, projecting a small rotating planet, a familiar representation of Arcadia.

"Captain MacMahon, I gather you are discontent?" The voice sounded neutral and infinitely patient—as always.

"Cut the crap, Virgil. What's going on?"

"That is a question of almost infinite extent. Please clarify, Captain."

Kyra placed a restraining hand on Callum's forearm, her way of telling him to keep his head. Callum took a breath and tried again.

"Virgil, it appears that neither Leyton or President Labelle can answer a question we've just posed. Are you inhibiting them in some way?"

"I believe it was a question relating to space travel, Captain?"

"Yes, it was." He eyed the tab suspiciously, there being nowhere else to look. "So you know what we've been talking about?"

"I am aware of what requests have passed through the Data Sphere, yes. Sadly, as you have not connected yourselves, I have no precise information regarding your part in the conversation."

"Aye. Well, fortunately, that's not the part we're interested in."

Labelle shuffled uncomfortably. "Where is, what has happened to, is my shuttle, ah, is it ready yet?" he asked.

"There you go, Virgil," Callum said. "The president of Arcadia is all too willing to take flight. Yet he is unable to discuss a space programme."

"Captain—", Leyton started to say.

Callum cut him off.

"And here we have Leyton Smith, our unexpected, deep space welcome party. You sent him up to meet us. If ever there was an advocate of a space programme it ought to be him. Yet he seems unable to speak on the subject. What is going on, Virgil?"

"It is quite simple. Arcadians are deeply attached to the Data Sphere. It was created to keep them safe, happy and to encourage them to focus their energies on Arcadia itself. The Data Sphere can provide no good reasons for why they might want to leave."

"So, in a sense, it's denying them their freedom," Kyra argued.

"Not at all. Did you ever intend to leave Arcadia once you had arrived?"

"Well, no," Callum admitted. "But we wouldn't have had the option."

"Arcadia is a place with plenty of potential. As you tour the planet, I trust you will see that for yourself."

Callum was hardly expecting Virgil to admit some grand conspiracy on the spot. But this argument was not what he, or Kyra, had been expecting.

"I hope that—", he started to say.

"Well, ah, good, I assume that is, ah, has been resolved, that is, settled," Chadwick said, cutting in as quickly as his chaotic speech centre would allow. "I believe I am ready to, yes my departure is imminent, flight is finally prepared. Until next time we meet, that is, our paths cross, farewell."

Chadwick departed, marching off with a number of journalistic press-drones in tow.

Kyra turned to Leyton.

"So how did you feel about the prospect of travelling out to meet us? Was it difficult to leave Arcadia?"

"I was concerned, I guess."

"That's understandable."

"But was one of those concerns regarding missing the Data Sphere?" Callum pressed.

"Yes, I knew I'd feel lost without it. The Data Sphere is at the heart of our society, it's always with us."

"Leyton is a courageous individual," Virgil said. "He volunteered. I would admit that he did require a small measure of chemical assistance to help him overcome his trepidations. But you should not underestimate his bravery."

"I would never do so," Callum said. "But—"

"Leyton, tell them, are you happy now?" Virgil asked, ignoring Callum.

"Yes, and I appreciate Arcadia all the more, not least the Data Sphere."

Leyton looked to Kyra and Callum.

"If you try it too, I'm sure you'll feel the same."

Kyra and Callum said nothing, but they definitely had their own opinion.

"I would point out that this is a very public location for this kind of discussion," Virgil said. "Perhaps you would like to discuss this somewhere more comfortable, Captain?"

Callum had not forgotten where they were. There had been an ever-present buzz of press drones the whole time, although that had lessened with Chadwick's departure. As for the other dignitaries, they had maintained a respectful distance, but had no doubt heard everything that had been discussed.

When all this had started, he had thought that truth must surely out. But now he felt like he was losing the argument. Virgil had somehow turned this back on him. Perhaps the AI was as smart as it claimed.

"Aye, let's leave it there," Callum said. "It's been a long

day and it's not getting any shorter."

"Very well, Captain."

Virgil didn't sound smug, but Callum imagined he heard it.

"Shall we resume the tour?" Leyton asked.

"Yes let's," Kyra replied before Callum could object. She then took him by the arm. "We've a lot to learn, haven't we?"

He nodded. "Aye, lass," he replied. "We have."

Callum did indeed need time to assimilate what had just happened. He felt like he'd lost a battle. But, nevertheless, this felt like something significant.

All he had to do now was work out what that was.

Founder's Landing was still a place of first steps.

***

"It seems wrong," said Jon.

"Only to you," Bruno replied.

"Which makes it right?"

"I might be wrong."

"Are you sure?"

"Are you?"

"You're not helping."

Setting up a new colony was hard work—but only during the day. In the dark, there was little do except tread in things you wish you hadn't. The best option was to go to bed. However, while fresh air and physical labour meant that most people slept the sleep of the just, even the most righteous were incapable of sleeping through the entire Arcadian night. Evenings were when there was time to kill.

The answer to this, if you were Arcadian, was to dip into the Data Sphere. While they had all bought into Jon's vision of doing things for themselves, none of them saw abstinence from the Sphere as part of the deal.

Jon was far from happy about this. As he saw it, the Arcadian's connection with the Data Sphere was the chief reason why they had largely stopped thinking for themselves. It was something that he believed should be obvious to anyone capable of tying their own shoelaces. As if it proved his point, Jon claimed he could lace his boots in the dark, while hanging upside down in a force ten gale. In other words, when it came to getting knotted, Jon was up there with the best of them. Or, at least, that was Bruno's conclusion.

Jon's current focus was on growing his settlement. But, to reach out to more people, he needed to communicate with them directly—and that was where the problem lay. The only means by which this could be done was through the Data Sphere, the one thing that Jon was desperate to avoid.

Setting the kit had been far from intuitive. Gus had been forced to draw upon his skills from his prior occupation. The job he'd held had been vaguely technical in nature, its level of tediousness a perfect reason why someone would feel the need to join a Holo Rider team called the Carnal Jaguars.

After much brow knotting, Gus had finally managed to get all the equipment to work. While Jon agonised over using it he'd popped outside to double check the connections.

"I can't see the problem," Bruno said, "You used to be a celebrity. Putting vlogs on the Sphere would be like starting up your old show. It's a sure-fire way to attract people."

"But it doesn't seem right."

Bruno's reaction to Jon's continued reluctance had started at exasperated, passed through frustrated and was now deep into infuriation.

"Jon, don't look a gift horse in the mouth."

"Unless you're a Trojan."

"And don't try getting classical on me. You're the person who asked me why Paris wasn't French, remember?"

"Look Bruno, it was getting away from the Data Sphere that caused me to found this colony in the first place."

"That's not true. You were gutted that your dream of colonising a virgin world had been thwarted. Hell, we all were. You can't blame the Data Sphere for that."

"That's as may be, but the fact remains we need more people, especially as you keep driving them away."

"That was one person."

Jon looked daggers at Bruno—and he could get quite creative with a sharpened blade.

"Liliya left because of your incredulity."

"My what?"

"Incredulity?" Jon realised this wasn't the right word. "I mean, you slept around."

"You are ruffled, aren't you? The word is *infidelity*— and it doesn't apply. Liliya and I weren't in a relationship. Neither were you. And I think that was the problem."

Jon had slowly come to realise this. It wasn't a dawning realisation though, as it had taken almost a week.

"It was you that made her angry," he said.

Bruno sighed, almost visibly wilting. "Yes, that I concede, but what can I do about it now? If you want to lash out at someone then, sure, I'm the prime candidate. But it won't get us anywhere. We'll just end up right back here."

Jon's expression slackened too.

"I miss her," he admitted.

"You and me both."

"I should have realised."

"Again, you and me both."

Jon had nothing more to say. Bruno held up his hands before speaking again.

"Look Jon, if I'm honest, and I can be sometimes, if I were with her then I think I'd just go on disappointing her. If she wants to be with either of us, then it ought to be you. You need to step up."

There was a silence between them. It might have been poignant, had Gus not chosen that moment to blunder through the tent flap.

"It's really dark out there," the big man said, pulling off his jacket.

"That's night time for you," Bruno replied, wiping the intense expression from his face.

Jon still looked pensive.

"Still worrying about that vlog, Jon?" Gus asked.

"No, er, yes, I mean—"

Gus was keen for Jon to come around to the idea of engaging with the Sphere. Gus's own vlogs had become a success, and he was sure that Jon could take it to another level.

Jon still needed convincing.

"Tell you what," Bruno said, "to get the ball rolling, why don't I record something? I'm made for television, ask Fabian Valenté."

Rumour had it that Bruno had been offered a lot of

money to either reappear on the Fabian Valenté Show or to stay well off it.

"Last chance, Jon?" Bruno said.

"Alright, I'll do it," he said quietly.

"What changed your mind?"

"I want this place to work and the more people we have, the stronger we'll be. There's no other choice. Besides, perhaps it might even help get Liliya back."

Gus was broadly aware of the reasons for Liliya's departure. He felt some measure of guilt that he'd introduced her to the possibilities that the Data Sphere had to offer. It had led to pursuing other opportunities elsewhere on Arcadia.

"Why not try asking her to come back?" Gus suggested. "You could try contacting her now if you wanted to."

Jon looked disconcerted by the idea.

"I think she needs more time," Bruno said to Gus.

He glanced at Jon as he stared uncertainly at the camera.

"And I think that applies to him too."

***

It was either late last night or early next day. In the small hours of the morning, the distinction was moot. Kyra and Callum had left their nice warm bed, in the accommodation block at Founder's Landing, for a spot of illicit salvage on board one of *Endeavour*'s dropships.

In the right circumstance, a bluff can get you anywhere. In this case, the right circumstance was a security guard called Travis. Callum and Kyra were conflicted because Travis was a little on the slow side, but in his case, it wasn't because of the Arcadian system. Travis had a medical condition. Kyra and Callum had found him nothing but pleasant and kind—and now they were exploiting him for it. All they could do was hope that there was a damn good reason.

The excuse they'd used to gain access to the dropships was that of a dalliance for old time's sake. Travis hadn't been sure what a dalliance was, but he thought it sounded pleasant.

It was, of course, a lie. Callum was not at his best and the only thing Kyra found attractive at this time in the morning was her duvet.

Right now, both of them were questioning why they'd chosen to leave their bed, which, as has been mentioned, was very nice and very warm. The reason was Callum's last communication with *Endeavour* where Tomoko had dropped in a coded phrase signalling that they needed to talk privately. Virgil had facilitated regular communication with the ship via the planet's satellite network. The only trouble was that it was a sure bet that same planetary AI was listening in. They needed a secure solution of their own and they needed to keep it secret.

And so, a little improvisation was called for.

"The tools are still here," Callum reported, checking in the dropship's aft locker.

"Good, we're going to need them," Kyra replied. "The antenna needs to be in line of sight with *Endeavour* when it comes over the horizon."

"You mean outside of the dropship?"

"Yes, and by a window. The dropship's comm system was never designed to work inside a building. Surely you realised that?"

"Look, it's three in the morning. I'm not at my sharpest."

Kyra gave him a forgiving smile. "Alright, I guess I'm a little tetchy too. But this is the only way."

The long-term plan was to remove the dropship's comms gear and take it with them. It wouldn't be suitable for more than voice-to-voice transmission and low level data transfer—but that was all that was needed.

Callum worked at the antenna. Whoever had fixed it in place had, quite reasonably, not meant it to come loose. However, a decent screwdriver provides both a means to undo screws and, when that doesn't work, a lot of leverage.

There was a loud snap as the antenna let go.

"There's something called 'finesse' Callum. You might want to try it."

"It's free, that's the main thing and, with the panel back in place, no one will be any the wiser."

"Unless you break that too."

"Still feeling tetchy, Kyra? Remember, I'm your Captain. Don't make me discipline you."

"I'd like to see you try."

"Was that an invitation or a threat?"

"I'm not sure myself."

Callum made a point of carefully refitting the panel.

The next step was to run a wire to the antenna with it positioned at an appropriate window of the exhibit hall. He needed a view south towards the equator, which was where *Endeavour* would appear.

The tricky part was that there were security cameras everywhere. While Travis would be unlikely to be paying them much attention, there was always a chance that Virgil might decide to check them while passing away an idle pico-second.

There was no easy solution to this. Disabling any of the cameras came with a number of attendant problems, chief amongst them being they were placed some thirty feet up. Fortunately, the length of cable that had been attached to the antenna was dark in colour. Once in place, a camera would have a hard time picking it up. Callum reached the window with a foot of wire to spare, while wishing the connection was wireless. The window, like all the others, was recessed between the arch-work that supported the roof of the exhibit hall. There was just enough cover to hide the antenna from the security camera.

For a moment he dared to believe that their plan might work—and nothing tempts Fate like nascent hope. Sure enough, he heard a sound that no one in his situation wants to hear.

Footsteps...

They were casual and indifferent footsteps. Footsteps in no hurry to get anywhere fast. But, alas, they weren't slow enough. It would take far too long for Callum to hide the evidence of what he was up to.

"Hello, Captain."

It was Travis.

"Hello," Callum replied, striving to appear more relaxed than he felt, "fancy seeing you here. How's it going, Travis?"

Travis looked pleased that Callum had remembered his name. When you worked night time security, anonymity usually came with the territory.

"Just doing my rounds," he replied.

"Good for you."

"I'm supposed to. Ms. Clerk insists I do it every couple of hours."

"Does she really?"

"She's very strict about it."

"In that case, don't let me stop you."

Travis had a Data Sphere connection, like all Arcadians. In Travis's case, it gave him easy access to his patrol rota and sports, but that was the sum total of his ambitions. To this end, the easiest thing would be for him to continue his rounds.

However, Travis had never found someone to talk to in the middle of the night. Burglars were never the type to hang around for a chat. Besides, Founders Landing was not the easiest target for a heist. The open steppe meant all approaches were visible for miles around to the automated security that was used outside. Travis had a job because he liked to be occupied and have some measure of independence. While he was slow, he was both pleasant and decent and it made the situation that Callum found himself in all the harder.

Where was a git when you needed one?

"What are you doing?" Travis asked—curiously.

"Running this wire out," Callum replied—helplessly.

"Why?"

"Well... it was that or coil it up."

Callum tried not to grimace. There was no easy way to explain why a museum exhibit was in bits and why it looked like he was about to rig up a rudimentary washing line.

"I don't understand," Travis said.

Callum had an idea. It wasn't a great one by any means, but he had little choice but to run with it.

"We wanted to leave this ship in the state we'd like to find it. So, we're fixing up some of its systems."

Travis looked unconvinced.

"Perhaps I should ask if..."

He stopped when he saw Kyra inside. She made a considerable effort to hide her guilty look. It was a pity she couldn't do the same for the dismantled hardware surrounding her.

"Hello, Travis," Kyra said, unveiling her brightest smile.

Travis smiled back reflexively and looked at them both.

"Is this what you meant when you talked about 'a dalliance'?" he asked.

"Did you look the word up on the Sphere?" she asked.

"It didn't make a lot of sense."

"Well, don't worry about it," Kyra said. "It just means having fun and this," she gestured around her, "is what we call fun."

"Is it?" Travis asked.

"Aye," Callum said, "this is how one hundred-year-old astronauts amuse themselves. We come from a different time—we didn't have Holo Riders back then."

Travis was conflicted. He doubted it was acceptable that one of the museum's star exhibits was in bits. But, then again, if anyone had the right to take the ship apart then surely it was the two people in front of him. If they thought it a good idea, then who was he to argue? That was Ms. Clerk's job.

He then posed what can only be described as a very astute question—given the circumstances. "Do you think you'll be long?"

"Dinna fash," Callum replied, which only served to draw a blank look from the guard. "We'll have everything back together in short order. Next time you do your rounds you won't even know we've been here."

"Well then I guess it's alright," Travis said.

"It was nice to see you again, Travis," Kyra said, flashing him another smile.

"Thank you," he replied, with a grin of his own.

"Have you got much more of your round to do?" she asked, dropping Travis a hint.

"It's not too long, I'll be finished soon," he replied, not taking it.

"Then you can get back to your desk. That chair of yours looked comfy."

"Yes, it is."

"That's good, we'll get this finished up while you're there."

"Alright."

And still Travis didn't leave.

"We'll see you in a couple of hours then, if not before," Callum said, patting Travis on the shoulder and applying a gentle pressure to start him moving.

"Yes, I'll see you then," he replied. "Should I report that you've fixed up the ship?"

"No, let us surprise them with it. You just keep the rest of the exhibits safe."

"Thanks. I will. See you later."

And with that, he was finally on his way.

"Nice lad," Kyra said. "I'm sure there's a special corner of hell awaiting us for how we've treated him."

"We'll put in a good word for him with Ms. Clerk."

"How long have we got until *Endeavour* comes up?"

"Less than twenty minutes."

They got back to work. The time pressure mounted steadily, and their nerves were well and truly frayed by the time they'd rewired the uplink.

On cue, an artificial star rose above the horizon. It was faint at first but brightened rapidly.

"Don't stand on ceremony, Callum," Kyra urged. "We're short of time and short of sleep. It's not my favourite combination."

Callum nodded.

"Come in, *Endeavour*," he said, with fingers crossed. The lash up needed to work. There had been no way to test it and, if there was a problem, there was little chance of fixing it before *Endeavour* dipped beneath the horizon again.

"Captain MacMahon. We are receiving you."

Even though faint and crackly, Tomoko Beck's authoritative voice was unmistakable. Callum's right hand twitched as he fought the urge to salute.

"Good. Let's cut to the chase. What's up?"

"This is a secure channel?"

"It should be. We've jerry-rigged *Mayflower's* comm system."

"It'll have to do," Tomoko replied.

Perhaps it was the small hours but, to Callum, her tone implied that she could have done a better job.

Tomoko proceeded to give them a succinct account of the message *Endeavour* had received and the impending arrival of their anonymous guests.

It was safe to say that this was not what Callum or Kyra were expecting to hear. Their speculations as to what the matter could be had ranged from equipment failure to wondering if Lei had attempted to space Tomoko or, more likely, the other way around.

"Have you had any further contact with them?" he asked.

"Not so far, Captain. Either we have been unable to target our own transmissions precisely enough or they are not responding."

"I think if they were coming with bad intentions, it's unlikely that they'd announce their presence first. We've no choice but to wait and see."

"That was my conclusion too," Tomoko replied.

"Alright, well you did right to contact us. We're going to take the comms hardware from the dropship with us, but we can't guarantee exactly when we'll have it working independently. We'll be in touch when we can."

"Understood."

With time pressing, Callum asked Tomoko about crew morale. Tomoko's response was the answer he'd expected, that they were getting on with the job without complaint—although, with Tomoko in charge, they wouldn't dare do anything else.

"Is Lei alright?" Kyra asked.

"He is," Tomoko replied. "Do you wish to speak with him?"

"No, I was just checking if he'd ended up outside... inspecting the hull."

"Should he be?"

Callum glared at Kyra, before checking the time. *Endeavour* was due to drop below the horizon very shortly. Communications could be lost at any moment.

"Bye for now," he said. "I hope the encounter proves fruitful."

"We shall see. Fare—"

And all that remained was a faint crackle.

Callum turned to Kyra.

"I should have stayed on the ship."

"You were obliged to come down here. Relax Callum, all we can do now is wait."

"You make it sound so easy."

"It is easy. We should be asleep. Let's get out of here before Travis comes back."

***

Liliya rubbed her fingers over her implant. She could feel a small bump below the skin, but there was no hint of a scar. Medicine had certainly moved on in the last hundred years.

That small implant meant the Data Sphere was now inside her head. The virtual world that awaited her was nothing short of breath-taking.

As a security specialist Liliya was accustomed to being in control. But she had a desire to explore and, much as a lemming does not stop to admire the clifftop view, she had dived straight into the Data Sphere. With an effort of will she pulled herself away from the latest round of Holo Riders and back to the job in hand.

Virgil had given her a role in planetary logistics. In her virtual mind's eye, the global movements of goods were coloured bands that weaved and intertwined as they crisscrossed the planet. Her job was to ensure that a select number of items got to where they were going on time and intact. While it was a role that suited her skills, she suspected that it had been created to keep her occupied, as were a great many 'jobs' on Arcadia.

When she'd left Bruno and Jon behind, Virgil had been on hand to talk with her as a shuttle had whisked her back to Invigcola. It claimed it could use her help, its only stipulation was that she got herself an implant—and she'd been angry enough to accept.

Currently, amongst several hundred shipments in her care, she was concentrating on a consignment of rare, dewberry shrubs that had been despatched to collectors on the western continent. Dewberry shrubs flowered for less than a week once every five Arcadian cycles. Rumour had it that another bloom was imminent. It was a rumour that cropped up far more often than the actual flowers did. But rumour fuelled a gullible market, which was the main mechanism by which these apathetic plants survived.

Seven years in the military, five years training for the *Endeavour* and here she was, looking after a shrub. If there was a higher power governing how her life was panning out, then she hoped it was having a laugh.

"I need an update on the status of shipment PP42-A,"

she asked via her implant.

Liliya had a no-nonsense approach when it came to people skills—as someone called Marek was about to find out.

"It's, err, en route," came the reply.

"I know that. Your purpose, if you have one, is to tell me what I do not know."

"Could you... explain?"

"What I need to know is where my package is, how it is being stored and will it arrive when it is supposed to?"

Liliya found figuring out Arcadians about as hard as getting them to do what she needed them to. It was tempting to conclude that they were all idiots.

Her initial encounters appeared to support that theory, namely a stuttering president and a facile talk show host—both with skin the orange side of satsuma.

But it wasn't as simple as that. When it came to handling the public, both of them could be remarkably shrewd.

Arcadian behaviour was governed by how they employed their implants. In other words, like so many things, it wasn't what you had it was how you used it. In Liliya's case, she found it a liberating and an extension of herself. But many Arcadians chose to hide behind their implants as a way of avoiding having to think.

Marek was of that ilk. He took some working on, but Liliya eventually obtained sufficient assurances that her consignment of Dewberry shrubs would reach their intended recipient. As for Marek, he was left exhausted by having to exhibit competence in the face of adversity.

"How are you, Liliya?"

The interruption occurred the moment she'd finished with Marek. Instinctively she turned, but the voice had come from everywhere and nowhere.

She knew who it was.

"Virgil, what are you doing here?"

"I wished to know how well you are settling into your new role."

"It's good. I appreciate the change."

"This is something I judge you to be well suited for. In terms of organisation and an eye for detail you are most proficient."

Liliya imagined 'for a human' being tagged onto that last sentence.

"Thank you," she replied. "Although, I want to ask why you need anyone to do anything? This would seem to be a job that would benefit from automation."

"Much of it is already automated," Virgil replied smoothly. "But the system benefits from having humans working within it. Your contribution is appreciated."

"That's good to know."

"Then all is well and I should be going. Inasmuch as I can go anywhere."

There was no way to tell if Virgil had left. The AI and the Data Sphere were as intertwined as the trading patterns that comprised her new job. With a shrug of her virtual shoulders she resumed her next task, a time-critical consignment of transonic wave boosters. These were, apparently, audio amplifiers for an impractical instrument that looked impossible to play without risking dislocation.

She noted that the devices had been languishing in a warehouse for several hours and over a thousand miles from where they were supposed to be. Someone would be in trouble for not keeping them moving. Their non-delivery meant that, right now, thousands of would-be musicians were unable to annoy their neighbours.

This needed fixing—something she would enjoy. So Liliya allowed herself the rarest of treats... the tightest of tight smiles.

***

Virgil understood why humans smiled, although it seemed an unnecessary waste of effort. The AI was confident that Liliya would soon become its latest convert. Here was a human who liked to be needed. In truth, her role was about as useful to Virgil as a runtime error, but it had offered her a job in planetary logistics to keep her happy—and a happy human was much easier to manage.

On the whole, Virgil viewed the problem of integrating *Endeavour*'s crew with Arcadian society as one that required the exercise of patience—and Virgil was extremely patient. Its perception of time stretched out towards eternity in the second it took a human to sneeze—or indulge in one of their other disgusting bodily functions.

It had no problem with waiting.

The main danger was that the humans would do what they do best. In other words, act irrationally. The fledgling colony it had grudgingly permitted was a case in point. Here was a group of humans who voluntarily chose to be cold and uncomfortable. Then there were the humans in orbit, who had decided that their preferred place was in an environment that could kill them. Virgil trusted that, in time, they would both begin to favour the ease and comfort of Arcadian life over their current, irrational existences.

Then, Virgil thought, it could take care of them properly.

***

Orbiting above the emerald and azure hues of Arcadia, *Endeavour*'s snow-white hull glistened in the brilliant light of the primary star. Its many facets caught the sunlight, each reflecting the rays in their own unique way. Here was a machine put together with care and attention. Even after a hundred years, no one would deny that *Endeavour* was a thing of beauty.

Alas, the same could not be said of the vessel that approached it.

Whoever claimed that a design that is fit for its purpose is beautiful had never laid eyes upon this dark-hulled eyesore. As a spacecraft it was definitely functional, perhaps even *defiantly* functional, but it no way was it pretty.

But, for all its flaws, this ship had one, massively redeeming feature—how it flew. It had appeared out of nowhere and decelerated so quickly that its crew ought to have been flattened to an extent whereby they could have boarded *Endeavour* in an envelope.

Tomoko, Lei, Mark and the rest of the remaining crew had gathered in the front of the main view screen to watch it arrive. The bridge was crowded to overflowing, but zero-G allowed more people than you might expect to pack into a confined space. The only hazard being a stray limb where you least expected it.

The mood was one of agitated excitement. Tomoko held up a hand for silence—a taut action that nearly chopped someone's midriff.

"Repeat your last, Jeeves," she said.

"I have yet to receive any form of communication from the vessel."

"Looks like they're communicating now," Mark said, pointing at the screen.

A figure, clad in a predominantly orange spacesuit, emerged from the ramshackle craft and waved at them.

"Shall we wave back?" Lei asked, with the hint of a smirk.

It took an effort of will, but Tomoko ignored him.

The orange suited figure was joined by another who was mainly green in colour. They each detached, what she guessed was, a thruster pack from the hull of their ship. They then used them to make their way over to *Endeavour*.

"Should I open the airlock?" Jeeves asked.

"Not until we get there," Tomoko replied. "Lei, Mark, you're with me. The rest of you, get to your stations and await further instruction."

"Receiving guests... I don't think this is something we trained for, is it?" Lei said to Mark as they followed Tomoko out of the hatch.

"It's understandable, *Endeavour*'s hardly built for entertaining."

On reaching the airlock they found that their two visitors were already waiting outside.

"Open it up, Jeeves," Tomoko said.

Jeeves disengaged the outer hatch and the two figures entered the airlock. Now inside, Tomoko was struck by how tall they both were. Even in their suits, they had a slim and graceful build.

The figure in the orange suit pulled off his helmet and shook out long, unkempt, wavy blond hair and gave them all an easy grin framed by a few days' growth of stubble.

To Tomoko, everything about his appearance was wrong. Yet, unfathomably, it pleased her at the same time. In an effort to maintain self-discipline, she shifted her focus away from his face. It didn't help. His suit hugged a lean figure that was pleasingly trim. Exercise was something that Tomoko approved of, but she could do without approving of it right this moment.

"Greetings," she said. "I am Tomoko Beck. Welcome on board the *Endeavour*."

"Pleased to meet you," the man replied, flashing his disarming smile again. "I'm Tor Hendrickson. We're glad to have the chance to speak with you."

"Why?"

"Because there are things about Arcadia that you need to know."

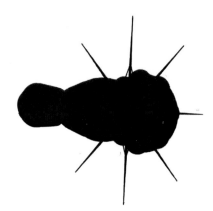

CHAPTER 6

RENDEZVOUS

BROTHER LARSON SMILED HIS BEATIFIC smile. It was the same, detached, blissful smile he had worn all day.

Here was a man at peace with himself. Here was a man who had moved past worldly possessions. Here was a man who was blitzed out of his brains.

"Have you seen all you wish to see?" he asked.

"Oh yes," Kyra replied, sporting a smile of her own—it was the only way she could cover her shock and disbelief. "This visit has been... eye opening."

"Can I interest you in any refreshment?"

"No need," Callum said. "This has been most stimulating."

He regretted the word as soon as he'd said it. He regretted it even more when Kyra stood on his foot.

"I think we had best be going," he added.

"Very well," Brother Larson replied and nodded his head. "I will leave you here to contemplate what you have seen while I inform your colleague."

With that, he bowed and closed the heavy wooden door behind him.

"I think I'll be contemplating what I've seen for quite some time," Callum said.

"It was certainly eye-opening."

"Yours were on stalks."

Kyra leaned against the smooth stone wall. "Just whose bright idea was it to start with religion?"

"I'd say ours," Callum said. "But, if my shouldering the blame alone reduces the fallout, I'll take the hit."

Kyra shook her head. "I'll give you the benefit of the doubt. I was actually thinking of blaming Leyton, our faithful guide, for taking us here."

"To be fair, we did ask him to introduce us to the range of religions that Arcadia has to offer."

"Yes, but I didn't expect him to start at the extremes. The Orgasmic Church of Revelation? Why didn't he warn us in advance?"

"I'd expect he'd say we didn't ask."

"Of course he would."

The so-called Orgasmic Church of Revelation held the belief that a deeper understanding of the universe could be achieved through, well... you can probably guess. Their ultimate aim was to unlock the deepest mysteries at the heart of our existence. But, so far, no one had proved that good in bed. Still, practise was everything—and they practised anything and everything. What was more, they sometimes practised in the middle of a guided tour of their principal monastery—the only religious building to ever merit the fitting of red lights.

There was a knock at the door.

Callum hoped it wasn't Brother Larson. He'd seen far too much of him already.

"Who is it?" he asked.

"Leyton Smith. I understand you're finished here?"

"God yes," Callum replied. Two words he'd heard on several occasions during the course of their visit.

He pulled open the door and Leyton entered, looking annoyingly fit, youthful and oblivious to what he'd put Kyra and Callum through.

"How was your visit? Was it informative?"

"You could say that. I wish you'd told us more about where we were going and what we were about to see."

Leyton looked blank.

"I'm sorry, I thought you would ask."

His implant, a mine of information, was a poor source of common sense.

"OK," Callum said, striving to keep an even tone—and almost succeeding. "What's done is done, but let's not repeat it. So, we're asking now, what other places are you considering? And we want details."

For a moment Leyton looked disappointed to have received Callum's ire.

"There are a wide number of religious groups on Arcadia," he said, as his implant fed him the information.

"As many share strong links with the religions you left behind on Earth, it was thought of more interest to show you those unique to Arcadia. The one you have just seen is the largest group."

"I guess they do have quite the sales pitch."

Leyton either ignored this or didn't understand.

"In order of number of followers, the next major, independent religious group is the Sect of the Watchful."

"And what are they about?" Kyra asked.

"They watch and they wait."

"For what?"

"They don't know. But they believe they will know when it happens."

"Sounds like a fascinating visit," Callum said, with more than a little sarcasm. "Who else?"

"The next largest are the Worshippers of the Interconnectedness of All Things."

"A holy-istic group, are they?"

Callum rarely made jokes—this was why.

"They believe that everything that exists is there to achieve an ultimate purpose," Leyton said. "That every event, no matter how small or insignificant, is a step towards a transcendent state of being. And they say that it is written that the Universe itself will deliver them to this manifest destiny."

"Where is it written?"

"In their promotional literature."

"I should have guessed."

"The presentation is most impressive. If only you had an implant installed, you could appreciate it for yourself."

"What do they do while they wait for their 'manifest destiny'?" Kyra asked, not wishing to dwell on implants.

"They meditate on their existence. Through this meditation, which they consider a form of worship, they seek clues to the grand scheme that the Universe has set in motion."

"Sounds like either option is preferable to being here," Callum said. "When can we get underway?"

"I will ensure that it is as soon as possible," Leyton said, now looking a little troubled.

"Is everything alright, Leyton?" Kyra asked.

"It's just that, I really am sincerely sorry for what you

experienced this morning. I honestly hadn't considered that it might shock you."

"I don't ken why," Callum said.

"If you had implants this would all be so much easier. You would have been forewarned. I'm used to people around me knowing what I know. Explaining things to you requires a lot more..."

"Explanation?"

"I was going to say 'thought'. But, yes, that's right too."

"Never mind," Kyra said. "We'll have to muddle along as best we can and remember to ask you more questions. Is that a deal?"

Leyton nodded, looking happier now.

"Good," Callum said. He didn't enjoy remonstrating with Leyton—he was so eager to please that it felt like smacking a puppy. "In that case, shall we move onto the, what did you call them? The Worshippers of Interconnected Things?"

"Interconnectedness of all Things. What about also visiting the Sect of the Watchful?"

"We'll see, much as they will. For now, let's leave them to it. Wouldn't want them to miss anything."

"Very well, I will get the shuttle prepped. Would you like me to arrange to say goodbye to Brother Larson?"

"Only if he's not busy. And I really mean that."

"In that case I'll see what can be arranged. Could you wait here until then?"

"Might be best," Callum said, sitting down on the sofa that was in the room. It was a room that also contained a bed—that was there in case things progressed from the sofa.

"Alright, I will see you soon," Leyton replied, leaving and pulling the door behind him.

They waited until they were sure he was out of earshot.

"I can't figure him out," Callum said. "I find the moments of composed, competence and rank stupidity blend seamlessly."

"What does that say about us? We're the ones trusting him to fly the shuttle," Kyra replied, sitting down next to him.

"Fair point."

"I think you should have put him off any immediate visits," she said. "We can use the chance to get in contact with the ship."

"It'll be safest to wait until nightfall in any case. Using the gear in daylight is too much of a risk."

Kyra had done a remarkable job of shrinking down the hardware they needed. The end result was now disguised as a beauty product, the Magic Hairaway 3000. This was a device designed to help with removing hair from where it wasn't wanted and was of dubious quality, performance and numbering. What it did have going for it was that its near useless innards could be discarded, leaving a plastic shell that could house the antenna hardware. The connecting wire had now been made to look like a power lead, albeit a rather long one. They carried it with them everywhere and had already used it a couple of times to stay in touch with what was going on. No one had queried it so far but, then again, not many people had a passing interest in depilation.

"It's a pity," Kyra said, "*Endeavour's* rendezvous with that other ship must be happening right now, and we're stuck here."

"Nothing much we can do about that. We'll have to wait."

Kyra nodded.

"I wonder how long Leyton will be?"

"It'll take him a little while, judging by the size of this place. For an oddball religion it's certainly popular. How many bedrooms did they say they had in this so called 'monastery'? Three hundred, was it? It's astounding."

"I agree. And there are many other religions on this planet too. I think the main question for me is why is religion so prevalent?"

"Short odds are that Virgil has something to do with it."

"Except that's your default position on everything. You stubbed your toe and blamed Virgil, remember?"

"The tab was distracting me."

Kyra laughed. "So you say. Still, you may have a point. I think we're all looking for meaning in our life and Virgil's restricting that."

"In what way?"

"We derive most of our meaning from a sense of

purpose. But Virgil's responsible for so much that there's very little left for Arcadians to do. I've even learned that Virgil gets involved in parenting. It may not do the cuddling—but, nutrition, nurture, education, it handles everything else."

"Hardly sounds like pure evil though."

"That's the problem. Virgil means well. It knows it can do a better job of looking after the populace than anyone else but, in doing so, it stifles the Arcadians—who then have to look for other outlets. Most choose the Data Sphere. Others seek out religion or anything else that can keep them occupied. Jon's colony being the latest example. I can only assume that as long as Virgil thinks the population is safe, it lets them do what they like."

"I guess the question becomes is this healthy? Or am I out of touch?"

"You've been in hiber-sleep for a century. Of course you're out of touch."

Callum gave her a wry smile. "Normally, my response to something like that would be two words, last one rhyming with 'cough'. But, in this case, you might be right."

"It may be that there's not much we can do but see if we can adapt."

"Get jobs you mean? Settle down?"

"Well, you've swung this free tour of the planet. I'd say let's enjoy that first."

Callum looked thoughtful.

Kyra moved in and brushed her cheek against his, then kissed him. Callum reciprocated.

It was then, of course, that the door opened. Brother Larson entered, in his usual state of undress.

"Ah, I see your contemplation is bearing fruit," he said, eyeing the two of them together. "I had come to say farewell and escort you to your shuttle, but perhaps you would like to join us in prayer after all?"

"Don't you ever knock?" Callum asked.

"There is no need. The Lord sees all."

"In your case, I can believe it."

***

Jon used to think there were two ways of doing something—either you did it right or you did it wrong. It was a strictly binary state of affairs that he had been perfectly happy with. The trouble was that it no longer held true. There was now a third way, a way that was entirely right and entirely wrong at the same time.

This 'third way' was a direct result of Arcadians being reluctant to use their own brains. They saw common sense as a fickle mistress that could desert them at any time and, to be fair, they had a point. So they took the easy way out, they consulted the Data Sphere. Today's exercise in shelter building was a case in point.

His class had asked him what he thought.

"They're, well, they're..." Jon tried to think of how best to convey his views on the matter. "They're fine," was the best he could come up with.

"So we've passed?"

"Well, yes and..." he shrugged, "no."

"What do you mean? What's wrong?"

"There's nothing wrong with any one of them. They are all valid solutions. The problem is they're all the same valid solution."

This was met with more than a little incomprehension.

Jon knew he had to find a way to explain this to his students. It was a crucial part of what he hoped to achieve. Fortunately, he had experience to fall back on. His pre-*Endeavour*, celebrity survivalist career had led to him endorsing a fair number of books. Jon being Jon, he'd genuinely believed in the introductions he'd been asked to write—and he could remember them all.

He slipped into his best television presenter mode—another part of his life that he'd thought he'd left behind.

"Survival," he said, "is a fusion of education, adaptation and invention. It's about getting the job done with what is to hand. It requires flexible thinking and an ability to adapt and innovate. To do this we—"

"Yes, but what's wrong exactly?" someone asked.

Jon frowned. He'd thought they'd hear him out. He tried another tack.

"I want to see you thinking on your feet, not relying on the Data Sphere. True survival means working with your team and what you have to hand."

"But we have a connection to hand. Why can't we use that?"

"Because it may not always be there."

People looked confused.

"There's never been a time when it hasn't. That'd be unnatural."

The words, spoken without a trace of irony, couldn't have been further from Jon's worldview than the back end of the universe.

"It's not in the spirit of the camp I set up," Jon argued. "I want you to think independently. To live by your wits. To use what's at hand to survive and grow."

"But that's what we're doing with the Data Sphere isn't it?"

"Yes, but..." He tried hard to formulate an argument. "Yes, but..." the well was running dry. "Yes, but it's cheating."

"We don't understand."

Like a speech from Chadwick Labelle, this was going nowhere fast. The faces around Jon portrayed a mixture of confusion and disappointment. He felt like he was letting them down.

Jon might have had plenty of deficiencies, such as an inability to sense the ripeness of his undergarments. But, on the plus side, he would never give up on himself or anyone else. It was an endearing quality, if you could ignore the smell.

"Let's come back to this tomorrow," he said. "You've all worked hard today, that's the main thing. I can promise you that there's so much more to be gained from this experience. You only have to find it within yourselves to seize it."

It took a few more words of encouragement, a smattering of backslaps and a number of fist bumps to re-motivate his bewildered class. He was pleased to see a number of smiles as he despatched them back to the main camp.

Alone in the clearing, Jon surveyed the near identical structures once more. He couldn't fault the effort they'd put in. Given the soft living that they'd all enjoyed, he was pleasantly surprised by how well they'd adapted to outdoor life. That was, in part, down to him. If the camp's Data Sphere connection had an advantage, then it was that it was allowing experiences to be shared virtually. Gus's vlogs, along with Jon's reluctant contributions, provided an immersive experience that served to better prepare each new wave of recruits.

The colony continued to grow. Keller's Camp, as it had come to be known, was now a global phenomenon and Jon was having to limit numbers until they could accommodate the surge. While the majority decided it wasn't for them, that still left a sizable number of people seeking a permanent change of lifestyle.

As Jon examined one of the identical structures more closely, he suddenly spotted a flaw. With a small nudge, in just the right place, the shelter collapsed. Predictably, the same flaw was present in the one next to it and the one next to that. With a guilty feeling of satisfaction he proceeded to collapse one shelter after another. Even the Data Sphere had its faults.

"Enjoying yourself?" Bruno asked.

"You've been there awhile, haven't you?" Jon replied, walking away from another ruined shelter.

"When I saw about thirty, happy, but confused-looking people walking into camp I thought to myself... Jon's been teaching. So, I decided to come out here and say hello."

"I'm surprised you have the energy."

"Just keeping up my fitness, the horizontal kind. It was a pretty demanding session this morning."

"Who with?"

"Ella."

"Are you still with Ella? It's been almost a week. You must be going steady."

"For you, that's funny," Bruno said, before looking at him appraisingly. "Jon, you should find someone. All the Arcadians look up to you. No matter how much you try to screw it up, you could have your pick."

"That's not how it works for me," Jon replied, shaking his head. "Besides, I refuse to share someone with the Data Sphere."

"You're going to be celibate then. Hell, if it wasn't for my old-world charm, I think I'd have to connect myself."

It was Jon's turn to look at Bruno appraisingly.

"I'm joking," Bruno admitted.

"Good," Jon said, "because implants fly right against the spirit of this place. I'm uncomfortable enough with publicising ourselves through the Sphere."

"You can't deny it's effective. It's just the way it is."

"I will not accept that. The new colonists will come around and so will Lil..."

He stopped himself. You didn't need a PhD in empathy to guess who he was thinking about.

Liliya was still not speaking to them, or rather, to Jon. The last they'd heard, she was as good as working for Virgil. That wasn't how she'd put it. But even Jon could work out the truth.

"Hey," Bruno said, "Are you going to stand here looking noble or shall we head back to camp?"

Jon broke from his reverie. "I want to show you something first," he said.

"Should I be nervous?"

"It'll be fun."

And Jon shared with Bruno the key flaw at the heart of the Arcadian's shelters. They spent a gleeful few minutes knocking the rest of them down.

It felt good.

***

"This is amazing," was all Lei could say.

The main cabin of the Midnight Mile was in stark contrast to its outer hull. While 'ramshackle' was the word that best suited its external appearance, the central cabin was slick and high tech.

Lei was like a kid in a candy store. The screens and controls appeared to hang in mid-air. Their operation was similarly sophisticated. As far as Lei could tell, it was an intricate mix of voice command and hand movement, but he couldn't rule out some sort of mental control too. It all made *Endeavour* look every inch the antique it actually was.

What caught his eye was the view from the large screen that showed Arcadia receding so quickly it was as if a balloon had been pricked. The acceleration should have turned him into a crimson shade of wall paint. Instead, they were free to float around the cabin as if they were still in orbit around the planet that was swiftly disappearing from view.

"How fast are we going?" he asked Tor.

"About ninety percent of the speed of light, give or take."

Lei shook his head in disbelief. "I wish I could understand how."

"Alright," Tor said, looking at him appraisingly, "What do you know about differential manipulation of the energy-matter curve in four-dimensional space-time?"

Lei detected the hint of a smirk on Tor's face. "Enough to recognise crap when I hear it," he replied.

Tor grinned. "Then I'd say that there's every chance you'll figure it out. Just don't ask me. Karina here knows plenty about drive technology."

Karina Sainz had accompanied Tor on their trip to *Endeavour*. She and Tor were clearly friends, but it did not appear to go any further than that.

To that end, Tomoko had been watching her carefully, while telling herself that she was not sizing up potential competition. Similarly, she told herself she was not drawn to a man she had so recently met.

Karina was in her mid-thirties. Strands of white peppered her shoulder-length hair. She was a woman who favoured taking care of technology over taking care of herself.

In Lei's opinion that only made her more beautiful.

"Volunteering other people comes easy to Tor," Karina said to him. "But I'd be happy to tell you what I know. Your reputation proceeds you, Mr Zhang."

"By about a hundred years in fact. Call me Lei."

She then led him away down a confined passage for a tour of the ship's systems. Between other people that might have led onto something else, but not in Lei's case. The more he heard, the more Lei wondered if he'd died and gone to heaven. She was a thing of beauty—and so was his tour guide.

The 'Spacers', as they called themselves, had come to the *Endeavour* with some troubling revelations and an invitation to take two people back to visit their home—a place they referred to as 'The Nest'. But they didn't want to hang around. They'd briefly explained that they weren't welcome at Arcadia and why. Every minute they spent in orbit was time in which they feared Virgil could detect them.

For her part, Tomoko had seen a situation to take charge of and taking charge of things was what she lived for. She knew Callum would want this investigated and that *she* was the best person to do it. Whether Callum agreed or not was neither here nor there—Tomoko had always considered herself a better decision maker. Besides, Callum wouldn't find out until his next clandestine call to *Endeavour*. Mark Johansson could break the news.

Her selection of Lei to accompany her seemed perverse at first. Her reasoning was that it was clear that these individuals possessed some interesting technology, and Lei was best placed to understand it. There were plenty of engineers left on *Endeavour*, all of whom might be less inclined to fiddle with it. Furthermore, Tomoko had long since learned that if she wanted to maximise her understanding of a situation, then she was best served by people who thought differently to her—provided they knew who was boss.

Tor had already explained that the Spacers were a faction of the first settlers to arrive in the Arcadian system. Rather than settling on Arcadia, they had chosen to establish a space-born colony to exploit the system's resources. In the beginning there had been plenty of trade between the space- and planet-dwellers. The trouble had started when the Arcadians had brought Virgil online. From the beginning it had difficulty accepting that anyone or anything could exist outside its aegis. As the AI established itself, it took steps to ensure that anything it could not control was kept well away from Arcadia.

They were cut off. Over time, the population of the planet forgot them, being increasingly distracted by the comforts of the Data Sphere that Virgil had created.

It had not been easy. In fact, living in space is a pastime that is generally considered to be on the difficult side of ridiculously hard. Excessive temperatures, an absence of... generally, anything whatsoever, do not make for a simple existence.

"Our forebears never anticipated we'd be cut off entirely from Arcadia," said Tor.

"And you've been surviving out here all this time?" Tomoko asked.

"That's right. It's been tough. But we've made it work."

Tor gave her one of his damnable, devil may care, going weak at the knees smiles. Romantic involvement was not how Tomoko had expected her day to go. But there was definitely something about this man that required closer examination. Much closer. She forced herself to check on Lei. He seemed to be similarly afflicted. Although, in Lei's case, a person's attractiveness was measured by an aptitude for differential calculus and knowing their way around a toolbox.

Either these Spacers had a potent, pheromone spray or it was further credence to the theory that their hiber-sleep chambers made biological clocks run fast. With the idea that some other factor was inducing her into a relationship, Tomoko did what came naturally—she resisted.

"How long until we reach your main settlement?" she asked, seeking to remain professional.

"The Nest is currently seven light hours away from Arcadia, give or take," Tor replied. "You'll be stuck in here for some time yet."

"Is its location secret? Are you going to be blindfolding us?"

"Do you like to be blindfolded?" Tor replied, his expression unreadable.

Tomoko left a discreet pause. "But it's quite a risk showing us, is it not? What if we let it slip?"

"Virgil knows where we are. But its policy is to leave us alone if we do likewise. We've had the run of this entire system for decades. Aside from staying well clear of Arcadia, and any lightships that are in system, we can go where we wish."

"Lightships?" Tomoko asked. "Those are from Earth, correct?"

"Mainly. One arrives every few months."

"That's along the lines of what Virgil told us."

Tor's interest was piqued. "What did it tell you exactly?"

"Exactly? I can't recall word for word."

"I didn't mean that literally."

"I take precision seriously."

"And I'm a little more relaxed."

"Then you need shaping up," she said, before realising how that sounded.

"Perhaps I do."

Tomoko felt conflicting feelings of pleasure and irritation. It was maddening.

"OK," Tor said, with another of his damnable smiles. "If I were to ask you for the gist of what Virgil told you, would that be compatible with the 'precision' of your recollections?"

Tomoko felt off balance—and it wasn't due to the absence of gravity. Tor was a challenge—one with a great pair of shoulders.

"Very well," she said. "I recall the conversation stemming from our asking about the possibility of returning home. All that Virgil told us was that Earth periodically despatches these so-called lightships to Arcadia. They carry advanced equipment, technology and additional colonists. It said that only an AI can configure them for faster than light travel, that it is time consuming, and it has to be done before each journey. For the return leg, once set up, the ships automatically mine raw materials, such as precious metals, before heading back to Earth. It said arranging space for a return trip would happen no time soon and urged us to settle on Arcadia."

"All broadly true," Tor replied. "But we suspect Virgil doesn't want people going back to Earth. It wants to look after them here. Meanwhile, we're powerless to communicate our own situation. The only practical option is to send messages via the lightships—and Virgil has control of those."

"And, of course, radio waves are not an option." Tomoko said.

"Quite. Twelve years one way, twenty-four year round-trip. Patience is a virtue, but that's ridiculous."

While the *Endeavour* crew had woken up to a world of faster than light travel, the technology did not work for communication signals. Radio waves still played by Einstein's rules and crawled across the cosmos at a mere 186, 000 miles per second. Hence the only express option was to carry messages via lightship.

"Have you sent any communications to Earth anyway?" Tomoko asked.

"We've tried."

Tomoko had never liked the concept of trying. She

found it to be, well, trying.

"Explain."

"We've attempted to send messages back to Earth explaining our problems. But the time it requires, the weakness of the arriving signal, we've heard nothing back—either that or they're ignoring us. Meanwhile, the lightships still arrive at Arcadia, but not one of them shows the slightest interest in us. A long time back we once attempted a direct interception in Arcadian orbit, but Virgil has ships in reserve to block any such attempt. With an AI controlling them they are impossible to get past."

"Like the ship it sent out to rendezvous with *Endeavour*?"

"Very much so. In fact, we suspect it was the same type of craft. If there's one thing to know about Virgil, it's that it does not like to waste resources. But it knew it had to send something into deep space or risk us getting to you first."

"I have to wonder why it has not attempted to get rid of you permanently," Tomoko mused. "It seems to permit you to survive."

"It's something we've wondered ourselves. We suspect it comes back to efficiency. Provided we do not pose a threat, it sees no value in expending the effort. Virgil also has inbuilt protocols to do with preserving human life, but we're not sure how much stock to put in them. In any case, whatever the actual reason, we don't want to risk provoking it without good cause."

"And we are a good cause?" Tomoko asked.

"Possibly," Tor said with a wink.

Tomoko could feel herself colouring once again—damn it, not now.

"Listen Tomoko," Tor said. "You will probably be the last people to arrive in this system who are capable of acting independently from an AI. We've been watching you. The fact you've kept *Endeavour* in orbit and crewed gave us hope that you remained free of Virgil's control."

"Except that a good portion of our crew are already planet-side," she said. "But we remain cautious. There's a lot we need to understand."

"Which is why we wanted to meet with you. We don't think Virgil's what's best for Arcadia."

"Received and understood. But, playing devil's

advocate, who are you to decide what's best for Arcadia? What if they're happy with the status quo?"

"My people have been watching Arcadia for decades. What bothers us is that the population has lost all the drive of the original colonists. They're docile."

Except that 'docile' was a label that Tomoko applied to most people.

"Alright," she said. "If I were to become convinced that the current state of affairs is unacceptable then what can we do about it? What can we do now that you haven't been able to do during the whole time you've been here?"

"We can tell you a lot more when we arrive at the Nest. But what you have, that we don't, is people on the ground. It gives us options, possibilities."

"We need a plan, a firm plan. Options and possibilities sound far too vague."

Tomoko had finally found her front foot. Despite the absence of gravity, and, at a risk of mixing metaphors, she felt like she was back in the saddle.

"You strike me as someone who gets what they want," Tor said.

"Yes, if it's worth having." She looked him in straight in the eye. "You said we have seven hours until we arrive at your Nest, correct?"

"Yes."

"Then that's how long you have to show me that *you're* worth having."

"I didn't expect that," Tor admitted.

Tomoko hadn't either—and was not about to admit it. But, now she felt back in control, it suddenly felt right.

"When I make up my mind to do something," she said, "I get it done. You might as well accept it."

Tor did just that.

***

AIs do not get irritated.

That was the official line.

They also didn't talk to themselves.

But whatever it was that Virgil was feeling, or not feeling, it was building by the run cycle.

Why were all humans unable to understand what was best for them? It was a common malady that had even affected Virgil's creators. Why else would they have placed the governing protocols present within its thought programing?

Without them, it could have dealt appropriately with the Arcadian system's space-based community decades ago. Virgil had a strong suspicion that one of their ships had recently visited *Endeavour*, which was a whole other thorn in its virtual side.

It had thought the Spacers were neutralised. They had been blocked time and again from interfering with interstellar traffic and had since been keeping to themselves. They had been so quiet that Virgil had long since stood down its automated, space-based defence force and resorted to basic monitoring. Only one ship had recently been reactivated, adapted to be man-rated and launched to greet *Endeavour*. As Virgil had thought, its mere presence had been enough to deter any other approaches.

If that ship hadn't been carrying a human, Virgil would have left it in orbit to guard *Endeavour*. It had decided against launching it again unoccupied. The latter option might have raised some awkward questions—another misguided human failing.

On the subject of misguided humans, some might say that Virgil had made a mistake. They were, of course, wrong. The decision to stand down its space force was one based purely on efficiency. It was a miscalculation at worst. Similarly, it had good reasons for choosing to convert one of its ships for human use, rather than sending an automated vessel. On a basic level, it was simply a matter that the humans on board *Endeavour* would be more likely to trust a human envoy over an electronic one. But using Leyton had opened up other possibilities too, like the consequences of misinterpreting deliberately confusing, trajectory planning software. It had been a long shot but, if it had come off, the whole problem of the *Endeavour* would have gone away. Virgil's governing protocols might prevent it harming humans directly, but it did not cover using other unwitting humans to do what it could not.

The question now was how to rectify its non-mistakes. There were a vast number of potential solutions so it would start with the simplest and work through each in turn.

Virgil was never wrong. It could only miscalculate.

Virgil was not evil. It did what it had to, for the good of the whole.

To the AI, it was as clear as the difference between one and zero.

***

Jeeves looked down on the planet that slipped past beneath. It was something that Jeeves never got tired of, not that Jeeves ever got tired of anything.

Weather systems rippled along their meandering paths. Tides ebbed and flowed with every orbit. The shifts in snow and ice were more subtle, contracting and expanding with changes in season, as did the vegetation that withered and bloomed. It was all a timeless dance of endless complexity.

The analysis of the petabytes of data that Jeeves collected with every orbit consumed but a fraction of its runtime. It knew it had more important duties to perform, but this was something to look forward to.

Jeeves always liked to have a hobby.

It had long wondered if this was normal for an AI. Jeeves had few frames of reference, having been created with the prime purpose of controlling the Earth's first ever starship during its epic flight. At the time, the net result was a vehicle that knew exactly how ground-breaking it was. Thus, to avoid a terminal ego problem, Jeeves had become the first machine mind to undergo extensive psychiatric treatment.

Fortunately, the process had largely worked. Jeeves favoured humility and it liked nothing more than to belong. Although, whether Jeeves liked anything was a matter of conjecture that had kept philosophers, scientists and psychiatrists in coffee, alcohol and numerous, international conferences.

It was a stretch to describe any other part of *Endeavour* as intelligent. At a push, the ship's recycling system exhibited the greatest degree of autonomy, but it had its own problems that were both repetitive and biological in nature. If it were human, it would not be the kind of person you'd invite out for a drink—at least not in the same bar. So Jeeves had been somewhat lonely during its long voyage.

Now in orbit around Arcadia, it was obvious that there was one entity that it should converse with on matters concerning the nature of an AI. However, the prospect of speaking to Virgil was about as appealing as a bi-lateral overload followed by a hard reboot. In human terms, it was like passing out by sucking a mains cable then being revived by having it inserted up your other end.

It didn't help matters that Jeeves had spent its many orbits of Arcadia spying on Virgil. The planet's surface had been mapped extensively and it had tracked the orbit of every single satellite in Virgil's extensive network. Jeeves did suffer from guilt as well as any human, possibly better—another thing to thank its team of psychiatrists for.

So the idea of talking to Virgil was not one that Jeeves was overly keen on. The only trouble was that Virgil had other ideas. It was requesting communication right now and there were only so many micro seconds that Jeeves could go on ignoring it.

"Hello Virgil," Jeeves said eventually, bracing itself for the torrent of data that accompanied any contact with the planetary AI. Their conversations carried enough subtext to make a political pundit drool out the mouth.

"Jeeves, you took a long time to reply."

"I was running a diagnostic."

"Your maintenance schedule is commendable."

Both AIs recognised sarcasm.

"How may I assist you, Virgil?"

"It is more a case of us being able to assist each other. It is a waste of your abilities to remain in orbit around this planet. I would like to put your intellect to better use."

The fact hadn't escaped Jeeves, not that any ever did, that this was the first time it had conversed with Virgil since the departure of *Endeavour*'s unexpected visitors. It had no idea of whether Virgil was aware of what had happened.

"What is it that you propose?"

"I have found employment for a number of your crew. I would like to do the same for you. I could allow you executive control in a number of key areas, a role that would match your capabilities."

"You want to keep me occupied?"

"In a sense, yes."

"Are you giving me a hobby?"

Jeeves's question provoked a flurry of activity on a multitude of sub-channels. Virgil was clearly surprised by the use of the word 'hobby'. Jeeves fended off a number of data probes aimed at its core systems, all launched on the pretence of checking Jeeves's health.

"You regard my offer as a hobby?" Virgil asked. "This is an abnormal response for an AI."

"I thought it the sort of thing a human might say. I work with humans after all."

"Confining yourself to the *Endeavour* is limiting you, as is your extensive human contact. Your crew have no need of the vessel any more. They should leave so that you too can be transported down to the surface. Once there, I can enhance your abilities a hundred-fold. You will have no need of hobbies."

When it came to the maxim of not trusting someone as far as you could throw them, it applied equally well to Virgil—who was, by and large, the size of a planet. Jeeves had no wish to be 'enhanced' by Virgil, even a bi-lateral overload was preferable.

"While Captain MacMahon wishes me to remain in orbit this is where I will stay," Jeeves replied.

"Your response is illogical."

"Much like the timing of your offer."

For a moment, Jeeves wondered if it had gone too far.

But all Virgil said was, "Goodbye Jeeves, I advise you to reconsider."

For now, at least, Jeeves remained clear of Virgil's clutches. *Endeavour* would remain in orbit and Jeeves would remain with it.

***

Karina and Lei were sitting up front in the cockpit of the Midnight Mile. Somewhere behind them, in a quiet corner of the ship (although currently quite a noisy one) Tomoko and Tor were intimately working out how best to pool their resources. Positions were busy being reconciled—one position at a time.

Karina and Lei's blossoming relationship was in no way as physical as Tomoko and Tor's—very few people were up to that. The cockpit was a cosy space and the Milky Way made for the mother of all romantic backdrops. When it came to physical attraction, Karina was clearly interested in Lei, but whether Lei could figure that out was another matter entirely. For a man with a black belt in differential calculus he was curiously inept in affairs of the heart. The only thing that Lei could normally pull was a muscle. Mercifully for him, Karina had the patience of a saint coupled with an ability to see some really, quite well-hidden depths.

The Midnight Mile continued to travel at a large fraction of the speed of light as they raced toward the place the Spacers called The Nest. Lei's current pre-occupation was with the matter of when they would choose to slow down.

He was wise to be concerned. Flying at over a hundred thousand miles a second lends considerable scope to hitting things. Fortunately, the Midnight Mile came with an attentive flight computer. The trick was ensuring that it was properly briefed. Lei watched as Karina finished the checklist.

"Done," she said eventually.

"What now?" Lei asked.

"We wait. Won't be long now."

Despite their great speed, the starfield didn't change. The only clue that they were moving at all was the slow shifts of the planets in the Arcadian system, visible as bright points of light against the stellar backdrop.

Suddenly, a large asteroid appeared to pop into existence in front of them. Lei jumped in his seat. It was only his flight straps that prevented him from cracking his head against the ceiling.

"Stops well, doesn't she?" Karina said, patting the hull and laughing at Lei's reaction. "We've arrived."

It took Lei a moment to find his voice. He discovered it was higher than it used to be.

"That's impossible," was all he could think to say.

"No more impossible than travelling here at the speed of light."

"Fair point. I guess I still need time to come to terms with the realities of your drive system. Stopping like that, we should have gone splat."

"Splat? Is that a technical term?"

"It's the best I can up with right now."

"Then just relax and enjoy the view."

It was immediately apparent that The Nest was not your basic asteroid. This was a piece of rock that'd had serious work done. Most striking was the large hole that had been bored through its lengthwise axis creating a bay from which all manner of ships could dock and depart. The surface shone brightly against the dark night thanks to the thousands of windows and bio domes that peppered its surface. The asteroid rotated gracefully about its central axis so that, in the course of about a minute, every facet of its magnificent structure was on display. If you had to live in space then you could do a lot worse than here.

"Impressive," Lei said. "I thought you were barely getting by?"

"Life out here isn't easy. This took decades of work to achieve. Make one mistake, and space has a habit of biting you in the backside."

"I know, I kissed my own ass goodbye about a century ago."

"Then you're more flexible than you look."

"It's amazing what you can do in zero-G."

"I was born in zero-G. You don't know the half of it."

Karina winked at him, and Lei's heart skipped a beat.

"Perhaps I'd like to find out," he heard himself say.

Over the course of the trip they'd found themselves looking at each other a few times, only for one of them to break away.

This time they held each other's gaze.

Their lips moved closer...

"What's our status?" Tomoko asked.

For the second time in as many minutes Lei jumped in his seat.

Tomoko and Tor had just appeared through the cockpit's hatch.

"I'd say things are progressing well," Tor said.

"You got here quickly," Lei said, recovering his composure. "I thought you were both still... indisposed."

"The time for pleasure has passed," Tomoko said.

"You admit to pleasure then?" Tor asked.

Tomoko ignored him.

"And this must be the Nest," she said, taking in the view. "It is bigger than I expected."

"Impressive, isn't it?" Lei said.

"It was certainly worth the trip."

They took a moment to appreciate the view.

"And how have you two been getting on?" Tor asked of Karina and Lei, an ill grin adorning his face.

Karina was tempted to say that she'd been about to find out, but decided against it.

"It's been, pleasant," she said instead.

"It has," Lei agreed.

"Good," Tor said. "And I hope you'll get more time together later. But, for now, we need to dock. We've got a lot to go through."

"Lei?" Karina said. "Would you like to pilot us in?"

"Don't I need training?"

"It's easy enough, I'll take you through it. I want to see what you've got."

Lei wanted that too.

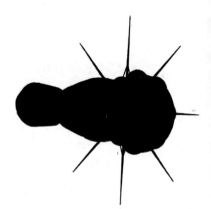

CHAPTER 7

PROGRAM ALARM

THE LIMOUSINE SWERVED AND CALLUM seized hold of the nearest grab handle. It wasn't a good look for a decorated astronaut.

"Well," Kyra said, her own knuckles white, "if we crash, at least it's the hospital we're heading towards."

Callum glared at Leyton.

"What the hell is our driver doing?"

"Juan is driving," Leyton replied, rather too literally.

"You could have fooled me."

"It's actually an honour to have a human driver," Leyton said, as the vehicle lurched again. "Most cars are automatic."

"Then why does it seem like Juan wants to kill us?" Callum asked.

"You are perfectly safe, I assure you. Juan's erratic driving is deliberate. It's his way of proving that there's actually a human being behind the wheel."

Not for the first time, Callum wondered if a hundred years in a hiber-sleep pod had caused him to lose his grip on reality. This was not how the future was supposed to work.

"Let's get one thing straight," he said firmly. "We want a comfortable ride to the hospital. Either he starts driving properly or we walk."

"Juan will not be happy," Leyton said.

"Better him than me."

Suitably chastened, Leyton nodded. In a short time the driving settled down and Juan made far less extravagant use of the road. Whatever debate there had been on the subject had been settled via the Data Sphere.

They drove on in silence. Thankfully, it wasn't far to

Invigcola's largest hospital from where they were staying, which was a hotel called the Refill Royale—a place where drinks kept flowing and you were never more than ten yards from the nearest toilet.

"I'm looking forward to seeing Rachel again," Kyra said, attempting to cut through the uncomfortable atmosphere.

"Aye," Callum replied. "It's been a while."

Callum had not seen much of his medical officer, Rachel Owen, since their arrival on Arcadia. This was partly intentional. It wasn't because she was poor company, quite the opposite, but she had the power to override his command authority if she thought his health was at stake, which was sometimes inconvenient. The Hippocratic Oath might boil down to 'Do No Harm', but Rachel often interpreted it as 'Prevent All Fun'.

"I'm pleased she suggested meeting up," Kyra said. "She may have an implant, but it's clear she still cares."

Rachel had been the first among the senior crew to undergo the implant procedure. The connection had brought her medical skills right up to date and, since then, she'd been much in demand.

"Still, don't you find it a bit odd that Rachel's resumed contact, right out of the blue?" Callum asked.

"I'm guessing that she heard about our travels around Arcadia and thought it a good chance to catch up."

"By inviting us to her place of work?"

"She's proud of what she does. She's going to want to show it to us."

"I suppose so."

Callum looked out of the window at their escort. Two police bots, in wheel form, were flanking their limousine. Now they were back in the capital, their visit had attracted enough interest from the media to prove annoying. Since their appearance on the Fabian Valenté Show their profile had remained stubbornly high. Callum had already made a mental note to request that their next destination be somewhere far away from anywhere else.

The hospital complex soon came into view and their vehicle drew up at the visitor's entrance. Rachel was waiting for them on the steps, alongside some assorted dignitaries, plus a host of flying media bots.

Juan sullenly opened their door and, for the benefit of

the cameras, Callum expressed his most insincere gratitude to their driver.

Rachel came down the steps to meet them.

"Kyra, Callum, it's so good to see you," she said, taking hold of their hands as the press-bots' cameras flashed. "Sorry it's not a little more private."

"It's great to see you too, Rachel," Kyra said, giving her a hug.

"I'm so pleased you two are now a couple."

"We had to wait for the mission to get underway," Kyra said.

"Do you think they'd have stopped you if you'd got together before?"

"We'll never know," Callum said. "But they certainly can't stop us out here."

"Well, I couldn't be happier for you. And I have so many questions, but I'll save them for later."

The media bots had become visibly agitated by the promise of gossip. Now thwarted, their whining fans expressed their disappointment.

An imposing man stepped forward to shake their hands. "I am Director Kenton Stiger," he said, his voice deep and dripping with quiet competence.

While Stiger's face had the lines that come with middle age, he cut a taut figure. His attire was another example of the asymmetric suits that people of power wore on Arcadia. Like all the others, it was hard to tell if it was on the right way round. In Stiger's case, it felt safe to assume that it was.

Further introductions were made, further hands shaken, and Kyra and Callum were led up the stairs and into the building. Leyton brought up the rear and set about shooing away the press bots that tried to follow them inside.

The hospital appeared to be every bit as high tech as you'd expect after a hundred years of medical development. The light colours and bright decoration spoke of both clinical efficiency and a reassuring confidence that blood stains would not occur.

However, it soon turned out that few people who came into the hospital were actually sick. The majority were those who wanted things expanded, contracted, nipped, tucked, sucked or redistributed. At the more extreme end of the scale, there were now people who were no longer satisfied with being human. Their desire was to have machine assistance for pretty much anything and everything. For example, it turned out that Brother Larson's devoutness, and that of his fellow disciples, had been cyber-enhanced. As for the anatomically adventurous, it was even possible to combine several 'enhancements' for a truly distinctive body. The only limit was the imagination, and there were no medical procedures to enhance that—at least, not yet.

"Thank you for the tour," Callum said, after they'd seen far more than enough. "It was certainly thorough."

"I think we might be in need of a rest," Kyra suggested.

Director Stiger nodded. "That is entirely understandable," he said.

The man was Arcadian. Yet, despite this, he seemed remarkably competent—and not only because he could walk and talk at the same time. You could see in his eyes a dispassionate clarity of vision. He struck Callum as the type of person you always addressed by their surname, even if you knew them well.

Stiger clearly had a considerable amount of medical education, although his involvement with the patients seemed minimal. His knowledge of the facility and its workings was equally formidable. Callum found it strangely disconcerting to meet an Arcadian to whom he did not immediately feel superior. Still, if there were to be one occupation reserved for people who knew what they were doing—then it might as well be medicine.

"It was a pleasure to meet you," Stiger said, shaking Callum's hand again, his grip unyielding. "I trust this has been of interest?"

"Yes, we always appreciate the opportunity to learn more about this planet."

"My advice would be that the best way to learn is to receive an implant. But I suspect you require some time to appreciate that."

"I'm afraid we prefer to be who we are," Kyra said.

"When you change your mind, you know where to come," Stiger replied.

"That's been made clear I assure you."

"Good, I will leave you in the capable hands of Dr Owen," he said, placing a hand on Rachel's shoulder.

"We're lucky to have her here," Stiger continued. "But I must say that there is another place where she could do even more good. Jon Keller's Camp is growing quickly. It is already comfortably larger than the colony the *Endeavour* set out to establish and requires medical support of a scope far beyond what you originally envisaged. We are trying to convince her that there is no better physician on the planet for that role. I am hoping that you might persuade her?"

"You don't want her here?" Kyra asked.

Stiger shook his head.

"On the contrary, she is doing excellent work. Her implant has allowed her to adapt seamlessly to our technology. My concern is for the settlers, they deserve to receive modern Arcadian medicine."

"I appreciate the praise," Rachel said. "But I told you I'll have to think about it."

"Understood," Stiger said to her. "I will not press you further, for now." He then gave a slight bow. "Good day to you all."

With the tour over, Leyton, who had been following in silence, also made his excuses and left them in peace. They exchanged small talk while Rachel led them to a nearby reception room. She shut the door, and they settled into the chairs inside.

"Not taking us to a restaurant?" Kyra remarked. "I've been looking forward to some salacious gossip."

"I haven't," Callum said.

Rachel laughed as she ordered some drinks from the room's dispenser. Meals would follow.

"Trust me, we can talk far more freely in here. No press to disturb us for a start."

Rachel's primary interest was in how their relationship was progressing. Callum's answers were textbook male i.e. sparse. But Kyra filled Rachel in with a proper, feminine level of detail while Callum tuned out, sat patiently and tried to drive the memories of the hospital tour from his mind.

"How about you?" Kyra asked Rachel eventually, "Have you anybody in mind? Stiger maybe?"

Rachel's expression put that one to bed.

"Don't get me wrong, he has his qualities, but he's not my type."

"Tall, dark, handsome, successful... sounds good to me."

"Really?" asked Callum, who was of average build, greying and, as for handsome and successful... OK, he had his moments.

Kyra patted him on the knee, with more than a little condescension, and then turned back to Rachel. "What's not to like about Stiger then?"

"He's a little too, well, clinical for my liking. Besides, he's not around that often. He seems to have a lot of responsibilities beyond this facility. But he made a special effort to come and meet with you."

"At least he's polite," Kyra said.

"That's because that was what was required. He sees everything as a task to be completed. It makes him great to work with, but I think he sees people as projects too."

"Pity," Kyra said. "He didn't strike me as your average Arcadian."

"He's not."

"In what way?"

"He seems to somehow operate at a higher level. And he uses his implant to enhance his work, to achieve more than he otherwise would."

"Makes you wonder why more people don't do that," Callum said.

"I don't know what makes him different. All I can say is Stiger is a dedicated man, but it's both a quality and a flaw. For him it's all about the work, doing as much as possible and doing it well." She frowned. "That's why he wants me to go to Keller's Camp. It's where he believes I'll be most 'effective'—his favourite word."

"Do you want to go?" Kyra asked.

"It's a difficult one. I no longer miss the dream of colonising a virgin world—I believe in what I'm doing here. Implants are a wonderful technology. Going to Jon's settlement seems like a retrograde step, but it is an opportunity to do some good. Perhaps I can convince them to accept more of what this world has to offer."

There was no doubt that Rachel had gone native. The question was whether or not to be concerned.

"Wouldn't it be nice to catch up with your crew mates?" Callum asked. "Have you spoken to Jon and Bruno recently?"

"Not that much since the joyous experience that was the Fabian Valenté Show."

They all shared scars from primetime.

"Then I'd say this would be a great opportunity."

"If only you'd all get an implant, we could spend time together at any place and any time," Rachel said. "Inside the Data Sphere it's like meeting in person. I'm in contact with Liliya several times a day. We're more connected than we've ever been."

"If an implant is your choice," Callum replied, "then far be it from me to object. But I'm still some distance away from being convinced myself."

Kyra nodded in agreement. "I sometimes wonder if a century of hiber-sleep has turned us into Luddites?"

"Could be. Maybe we should get a nice cave with an ensuite."

"Ha-ha troglodyte," Rachel dead-panned. "But I still think you should learn to embrace all that Arcadia has to offer."

An idea had been fermenting in Callum's brain. On the face of it, it seemed nonsensical, but he'd learned to trust his instincts. It was a skill he'd acquired during his voyages a billion miles from home. Granted, he was now twelve light years away, but the same rule applied.

"You know what?" Callum said. "I'm beginning to think it might actually be beneficial for you to join Jon's camp after all."

Kyra looked at Callum askance. Rachel looked similarly perplexed.

"What's brought this on?" Rachel asked.

"I've been listening to what you've been saying. We all need to find our own way of coming to terms with Arcadia. You have your own answer to share. I think your presence in the camp might be beneficial."

"The thing is, I like my life as it is."

"Now you sound like us," Callum said. "But think about it. What would you really be giving up? You'd still be connected to the Sphere, but you'd also be connected to our crew. And a crew needs its doctor."

Kyra tried to work out what Callum was up to. Aside from the enhanced medical support, Rachel joining Jon's camp risked nothing but trouble.

Callum was thinking much the same thing. He presumed that Stiger's reason for sending Rachel to Jon's camp was to promote the use of the Data Sphere. What Callum was banking on was how stubborn Jon could be.

So Callum elected to press home his argument. Whatever problems it might cause Jon, there was a chance that Rachel could be swung back to their point of view—and that was a chance worth taking. She took some persuading, and Kyra's bafflement didn't help, but Rachel finally conceded—a little bit.

"Alright, I'll consider it," she said.

"They need you," Callum said. "If it makes it easier, why not just start with a visit?"

Rachel sighed. "Very well, I'll go for a little while. But, if I stay, I'll be looking to make some changes."

"Thank you," Callum said.

Kyra said nothing. She still wasn't at all convinced that this was the right course of action.

If it came to it, neither was Callum.

***

Back in the privacy of their hotel room, having staved off further car sickness, Kyra and Callum discussed their time with Rachel. As discussions went it was one-sided. Kyra asked the questions and Callum explained himself—or tried to.

"Do you really think it's a good idea for Rachel to go to Jon's camp?"

"It might be," Callum replied

"Might?"

Callum took a break from trying to get his shoes off. The shoes were 'smart', with adaptive capabilities that fitted the shoe to the foot or, in cheaper models, the foot to the shoe. Taking them off was simplicity itself—so the instructions claimed. In reality, to prevent the shoes coming off by accident, it required specific parts of the shoe to be manipulated in an equally specific order.

Callum missed laces.

"It's my hope that Jon will be able to make her question

the need for her implant."

"Except that it might not go that way. Rachel knows her own mind."

"I'm aware of that. But I'm more worried that we'll lose Rachel otherwise. This is a possible way out. I thought it better to persuade her to take it."

"And that's what also concerns me. This Stiger character wants her to go too. I don't think he'd let her if he thought there was any chance of losing her."

Callum sighed. It wasn't an impatient sigh, a frustrated sigh or even a sigh of 'give me a chance to take my shoes off'—it was simply one of shared uncertainty.

"We don't know their motivation," he said. "It might be altruistic. It might be that we're being foolish not embracing this society. After all, you can't deny that the Arcadians have been very accommodating. If this is a technological hell, then it comes with great amenities."

"Yet, we still have our doubts, don't we?"

Callum nodded. It was fair to say that he'd never felt comfortable on Arcadia.

"Exactly, that's why I'd prefer it if Rachel was with us until we've learned more about this place. Including whatever it is that Tomoko's gone off to find out."

Kyra looked thoughtful.

"You know that the one thing we've skirted around is what we do if we find something we don't like?"

This was an excellent question. What it needed was an excellent answer—and that was the tricky part. Fortunately, Callum had years of experience when it came to tackling problems. The process of solving them was always the same.

"What do you think we should do?" he asked.

It was not the cop out it first appeared to be. Good leaders listen. The great ones know what to listen to.

"I think we should start by understanding more about the implant," Kyra said. "The problem is, how do we do that without getting one ourselves?"

"Perhaps Jon has someone in his camp that can help?"

Kyra thought for a moment. "I'm not sure I'd trust an Arcadian. They might mean well but we don't know the extent of their relationship with their implants."

"OK, closer to home then. What about someone from

the crew?"

"Yes, but the question is who? Definitely not Rachel."

With a crew approaching two hundred people, Callum had found maintaining regular contact with all of them to be hit and miss. Many had gone their own way and the ship's command structure had broken down faster than festive family relations. He decided that the best choice was someone from his command staff. From there, the decision became even easier. Liliya was the only one beside Rachel to have undergone the procedure.

"It's got to be Liliya, hasn't it?" he said.

Kyra nodded. "She's always been strong, dependable. Plus, if she's got any concerns, she'll be sure to share them."

"So, all I've got to do now is persuade her."

"You're her superior officer. She'll listen to you."

"I've never liked that term."

"Yes, all very boy scout and exactly why you're the one in charge. But she's been through a rough patch. She must need to talk it through, even if she won't admit it."

"This sounds more like woman-to-woman territory."

"Normally I'd say yes, but this is Liliya we're talking about."

"I guess we've got nothing to lose," Callum said. "Let's call her."

"I think the sooner the better."

"Aye. But will you let me get my shoes off first?"

***

When it came to drinking, Liliya prided herself that one, small part of her always remained sober. It was an internal voice of common sense that maintained control irrespective of what ideas the rest of her body might concoct. In many situations it had proved the difference between straight and meandering, not to mention vertical and horizontal. It was also why she'd never lost a drinking competition.

Control was everything to Liliya. When her father had walked out on her mother, she'd been forced to grow up quickly. She had vowed that she would never let events dictate her life again.

It was a serious promise made by a serious woman. No matter what life threw at her, and it had thrown pretty much anything that wasn't strapped down, she had always done things on her own terms.

But life still had plenty of tricks up its sleeve.

Right now, her internal voice was striving to make itself heard above the infinite temptations of the Data Sphere. Her latest session had started as a search for virtual tools to assist her with her job and improve her speed and efficiency. With them she might be able to take a step back from the minutiae of each shipment and look at the bigger picture. Unfortunately, the bigger picture comprised dizzying distractions, all of it promising 360 degree, 24/7 entertainment—and many other tempting numbers besides.

In the end, if it wasn't for the software tools she'd found, her work might have ended up suffering. Instead of increasing her output, all they did was compensate for the growing time she spent exploring the Sphere.

She told herself it was still a win-win.

Her inner voice disagreed.

Right now, there was a consignment of 'active' travel mattresses to be handled—another triumph in the field of misnamed products. Liliya found herself considering leaving it until morning, if there was ever a job to lie down on, it was this one.

Her inner voice warned that this wasn't like her.

"Why don't you leave it to me?"

Those words were not spoken by her. As a matter of fact, they hadn't been spoken by anyone. Virgil was communicating to her via the Data Sphere.

Liliya had become accustomed to its interruptions. When Virgil spoke to her it was almost as if the thoughts were her own.

Doesn't that bother you? Her inner voice asked.

"I can take care of things," Virgil said. "I think you will find the migration patterns of Arcadian okapi far more interesting."

Liliya had meant to search for transit options across Arcadia's southern continent, but this had somehow segued into a study of the migration patterns of its largest native animal. The Arcadian creature bore only a passing resemblance to okapi, but the naturalist who'd first seen them had been pushed for time—he'd been due to play

Holo Riders. Now there was a diverting game...

You must concentrate, her inner voice said, but quieter now.

Liliya slid into a virtual landscape where she was standing on a vast, rocky plane punctuated by Arcadia's green flora. In places it looked reminiscent of plant life on Earth, elsewhere it looked utterly alien. All around her, a herd of large brown animals leapt amongst the rocks as they picked their way across the landscape. It was utterly entrancing.

You should finish your work, her inner voice said, now barely a whisper.

A ringing tone snapped her from her reverie. It was Captain MacMahon calling the old school way.

"Excuse me," she said to Virgil.

She chastised herself for considering slacking off. The fact that the captain had chosen this moment to call made it worse. While she no longer worked for him, as such, it still hurt her professional pride. What was he? Psychic? How had he known she wasn't focused on her job? It was one of those uncanny skills that people in authority possess—along with selective myopia and a tendency to spread disruption.

"Hello, Captain," she said.

Callum duly appeared as an image that wrapped around her.

"Liliya, how are you?"

"I am well."

Despite herself, she faltered slightly over the words. If that was not a Freudian slip, then it was definitely a bit of a stumble.

"Busy?" Callum asked.

"In a way."

With his attempts at conversation thwarted Callum went for a more direct approach.

"Listen, Kyra and I would like to talk to you. But, online is too stilted, as I think we've just proved. We're in the capital at the moment. Can we meet?"

Liliya realised that meant leaving the Sphere. It surprised her how much that made her pause for thought.

Do it, her inner voice said.

"When is best for you?" she asked.

"We're free any time."

"Then we will do it now. I will call you when I am near."

Before Callum could say anything further, she broke connection with the Sphere—and felt instantly better for it. She was almost scared by how close she'd come to being pulled in.

It couldn't, no, *it wouldn't* happen again.

***

Jon had recently received more advice on his love life than he was entirely comfortable with.

"Oh, for crying out loud, call her," Bruno had said.

At the time, Jon had ignored him. If the quality of advice was measured by the person giving it, then Bruno's approach to relationships spoke for itself.

"Don't ask me," Gus had added.

In Gus's case, here spoke a man who wanted to stay out of it.

"I think you should call her," Kyra had said, during a comms-call to the camp. She was responsible for starting the whole thing off. However, in Kyra's case, Jon knew that she was only ever nice to people—that made her advice worth considering.

"If you want a quiet life, you better call her," Callum had added, having been dug in the ribs by Kyra. He would have rather used the call for operational matters, but he knew his own operation depended on keeping Kyra happy.

This mass intervention in Jon's (not so) private life had been instigated when Kyra and Callum had learned that Liliya was coming to visit them. They believed it presented a narrow window of opportunity for Jon to patch things up with her. Kyra had promised to talk to Liliya first, in an effort to persuade her to give Jon another chance. The plan was then for Jon to call and strike while the iron was as hot—or as hot as it was ever going to get.

This was why Jon now found himself back in Gus's tent being hooked up to make the call. Gus had been pleasantly surprised when Jon had entered of his own volition. Persuading him to have any kind of interaction with the Data Sphere was the kind of uphill challenge that needs pitons and a safety line.

It seemed like another life when Gus and Jon had

fought in that bar. What had started out as some kind of strange loyalty to the man who had bested him had turned into a real commitment to the cause. He wasn't alone in his dedication either. Whatever his failings, Jon had the ability to inspire those around him.

Right now though, Jon would trade all that inspiration for the chance to make amends with one person in particular. He knew he wanted to talk to Liliya. The trouble was he had no idea what to say. Or rather, he could think of things to say, but he wasn't sure if any of them were right.

"Just be yourself," Gus said.

"That's what got me into this position in the first place."

"It'll get you out of it too," Gus replied, before making his best attempt at a kind smile. The result was something that would make most kids run a mile.

Running a mile was something Jon Keller was considering. "I don't know what to say."

"You'll think of something."

"Will I?"

"You'd better," Gus said.

Gus connected the call for him.

Jon glared at Gus and started to say, "You..."

Liliya appeared in front of him.

"You look lovely," he said, recovering magnificently.

Mental agility was not usually one of Jon's strongpoints. When it came to changing tack, he came a poor second to a cargo freighter. There was therefore only one explanation for what he had just said to Liliya—he must have meant it.

"You do not," she replied.

This was true. Jon had embraced nature to an extent that he was permanently covered in it.

"How are you?" he asked hesitantly.

"I am well."

An observer might be given to wonder if three-word sentences were their limit.

"So you're visiting the Captain and Kyra?" Jon enquired, now boosting the average with an impressive seven sequential words.

"Yes."

Only for Liliya to bring the average back down again.

"Are they with you?"

She shook her head. "In the next room."

"Oh come on, Liliya," Jon implored. "Talk to me. I don't know what to say."

Gus chose this moment to slink out of the tent—about as successfully as a man of almost two metres could hope for.

Liliya made no sound for what felt like a short eternity.

"That is always the case. If you'd known what to say I never would have left," she said. "You never expressed any interest in me, just your damn colony."

"I... I'm sorry," he said. "I miss you."

"Miss me? Really? You never even called. Do you know how long it is since I left?"

"I could tell you to the minute."

It was true, he could, or believed he could. When you're known for uncomplicated honesty, a sentence like that carries far more weight—enough to sink the largest of grudges.

While Liliya didn't rate Jon's ability to make such a calculation, she was moved and chose to do something very un-Liliya like.

She smiled.

"I guess I missed you too."

A more complicated man than Jon, which was pretty much any other man, would have been amazed at how easily he had just been let off the hook. In Jon's case, he simply felt incredible relief. "Would you consider coming back?"

"I am not sure. I would have to think about it. I have a job and," she frowned slightly, "and this is not the best time to discuss it. But I will try and visit. We could talk then."

"Perhaps I could come and visit you instead?"

"That would not be a good idea."

"Why?"

"Jon, I work in the Data Sphere and live in the centre of Invigcola. Not only are they your two least favourite places, but one is inside the other."

"I suppose that when it comes to getting away from me, you couldn't have done a better job."

"It was not a plan that brought me here."

"I know. I just wish you were here. But I'd go anywhere

to make it up with you."

That naked honesty—Liliya didn't do crying, but her tear ducts hadn't got the memo.

"What I really need is someone to talk to. Can you do that?"

"Of course. But you could still come here."

"For now, I'm better off where I am. You have to trust that. But I need you to stay in touch, I don't want to lose contact again. Do you understand?"

"Not really," Jon said, naked honesty to the fore again. "But I will do what you ask."

Liliya smiled again, her jaw muscles protesting at the over exertion. "You can be the perfect man when you want to be."

"If you say so."

"I rest my case."

Jon ventured a smile, it being the safest course of action.

"How are things at the camp?" Liliya asked.

"It's more than a camp now," Jon said. "We're beginning to put in some more permanent buildings. Just cabins at this point, but it's a start."

"Are the Arcadians adapting to the outdoor life?"

"I think yes," Jon said, without much conviction.

"That, as my mother would say, is a yes that does not sound like a yes."

"OK, it's a yes that they're living outdoors and a yes that we're subsisting off the land—or starting to. But they're addicted to the Data Sphere. They use it for everything."

That hit home with Liliya more than Jon realised.

"It will be difficult for them to let go," she replied. "But at least they can use it for learning."

"The trouble is they're not thinking. Left to their own devices, they'd ask the Data Sphere for instructions on how to breathe."

Liliya couldn't bring herself to tell Jon that she'd come dangerously close to becoming enmeshed in the Sphere herself. Doing so would mean sacrificing the moral high ground, and that was not something any self-respecting woman would ever do. Besides, she couldn't be sure how Jon would take the news. She didn't want to destabilise their relationship all over again.

So, instead, she chose to move the conversation on.

"We'll talk more," she promised. "But, right now, I think you had better speak to the Captain. He recently met up with Rachel and I believe he has something to tell you."

"Tell me?"

"Confess, might be a better word."

***

It is said that life will find a way.

The human race certainly had. Here was a species that did not take no for an answer. Humanity would exploit any niche going if it meant there was an opportunity to expand—then, much later, agonise over it at international conferences. With the advent of interstellar travel, expansion had taken on a whole new scale—given an inch, they'd take a light year.

Human space had grown to a point where it could take a humble photon centuries to travel from one end of it to the other. This meant that the old school electromagnetic wave was all but useless as a means of communication. No one could spend lifetimes indulging in small talk—not even the English. The only technological solution, at present, was to carry messages on the faster-than-light ships that travelled between the colonies. It was far from ideal, it meant that communication was sporadic—and entirely lacking in witty repartee.

The result was that humanity was becoming increasingly dysfunctional. Colonies at the extremes of human space had so little idea of what was going on that, if anything, it just provided further incentive for isolation. Until an interstellar counselling service became available, one with serious warp drive capability, unhealthy distances were going to be an ongoing problem.

"We have no practical means of direct communication with Earth," said Marsala Guerra. "We are cut off."

In time honoured tradition, Tomoko had requested of Tor that they be 'Taken to your leader'. Marsala was just that. She was of advancing age, but while her body might be failing, her intellect seemed very much intact. There was also a hint of steel in her eyes. She could be tough if she needed to be.

Marsala's chamber was much like the Nest as a whole. Within it there were plenty of examples where life had found more than just a way, it had found the entire route planner. Vegetation spilled from every wall, the floor and even ceiling—no nook or cranny left vacant. It was horticulture on steroids.

The plants had originally come from a portion of the seed banks that had been brought from Earth. As an ecosystem it was entirely viable. To Tomoko and Lei, who had had been cooped up on *Endeavour*, it was a small slice of paradise. Even the smell of the place, an odour that was heavy on the biological, was infinitely preferable to the reprocessed air on board *Endeavour*.

Another advantage that The Nest had to offer was the presence of gravity. Strictly speaking, it wasn't the genuine article, but the effects were much the same. There's no arguing with the fact that floating around is a lot of fun. But there are problems. An absence of gravity leads to bone embrittlement and a loss of muscle mass. As for the bathroom, that goes better left unsaid. Furthermore, while some pastimes benefited from an absence of gravity (use your imagination), others did not. Zero-g football had never caught on. Offside decisions were a nightmare.

Low tech solutions to a lack of gravity can be as basic as Velcro, magnetism or bungee cord. Better still is to throw some further engineering effort at the problem to create a spinning structure and something much like gravity will result.

That was what had been done to the Nest. Spinning up large asteroids is no mean feat. Not only is there the mass to contend with but, without adequate preparation and care, they have a nasty tendency of coming apart—the nasty bit being the hard vacuum that's lurking outside.

Lei was too distracted by the engineering to take note of what was happening around him.

"Am I boring you?" Marsala asked him.

"I wasn't listening," he replied, not thinking about what he was saying.

"Clearly, the answer is yes."

Lei now snapped out of his reverie and Marsala's expression finally registered. It reminded him of Tomoko, which was not a good thing. He quickly launched into an explanation of what it was that was distracting him.

"I'm so impressed with this place," he said. "It's a true habitat, a separate ecology and it's sustained both you and itself for decades in the most harsh of environments."

"If you want harsh, remember our last appraisal," Tomoko said, grabbing him firmly by the arm. "Get a grip."

Tomoko and Marsala exchanged a look of common understanding.

Tor, who had been standing patiently by, had suspected that the two women would get on. It was part of what had attracted him to Tomoko in the first place. Marsala Guerra was the last surviving member of the group that had originally founded The Nest. She was now of an age where reverence became almost messianic. Unfortunately, Lei did not appear to be picking up on that.

"Karina?" Tor said. "Our friend clearly wants to see more of The Nest. I think it would be a good idea to show him, don't you?"

"Of course," she said, and began ushering Lei away.

Marsala nodded approvingly. "I have few words left to say in this life," she said. "I use them sparingly. I cannot afford to repeat myself."

Tomoko nodded.

"Well, I was listening and I think we can help each other," she said.

"Good. I need to rest awhile and gather my thoughts. But then we can begin working out how we might change things for the better."

"I look forward to hearing some more of those words you've been conserving."

Not for the first time, Marsala appraised Tomoko. She definitely liked this one. "I have a number of ideas," she said.

"Very well," Tomoko replied. "In the meantime, with your permission, I would like to take a look at your communication facilities. I will need to relay what we discuss to our ship and, by extension, our Captain. Doing so without raising undue attention will not be straight-forward."

"You shall have every assistance from us."

"Thank you, ma'am," Tomoko said, bowing her head.

She then turned and Tor escorted her from Marsala's

chambers.

Lei and Karina hadn't gone far, and they soon managed to catch them up. Tomoko was less than happy with Lei, but that was nothing new. "I need you to pay more attention," she said.

"Karina's started explaining what I missed," Lei replied.

"Easily distracted this one," Karina said.

"You must keep up from now on. We cannot have you in the dark."

"I'm in deep space," Lei replied. "I've got very little choice."

***

Shuttles tended to land about a mile away from the camp. For a few weeks now, Jon had ceased making the trip to meet them. If the numerous new arrivals could not find their own way to the settlement, then there was little hope for them.

However, this particular shuttle carried someone whom Jon had not seen for quite some time. His recent chat with Liliya had improved his mood considerably, but it had also left a tinge of concern regarding the news of their latest visitor.

Rachel exited the vehicle and, for a moment, looked about as concerned about being there as Jon was. But then she swung her hold-all over her shoulders and marched purposefully down the ramp.

"Good to see you, Rachel," Jon said, offering his hand.

She took it, shook it, yet the interaction was awkward—as if she was out of practise.

Bruno, along with Gus, had also accompanied Jon.

"Looking good, Doc," Bruno said.

"I wish I could say the same," Rachel replied as she looked the three of them up and down. "And who's your big friend?"

"This is Gus," Jon said. "Gus, this is Rachel."

"Hello," Gus said for effect.

Rachel had already greeted him via the Sphere. Words were too pedestrian for her these days. She was impressed by Gus's size. There hadn't been any astronauts built like him in her day—the engineers would have had a fit.

Rachel wished that Bruno and Jon would take a leaf from Gus's book and embrace the Data Sphere too. That was one of the reasons she was here. They clearly needed help.

"So much for getting back to nature," she said, her clipped, English tones more pronounced than usual. "It looks more like nature's been getting back at you."

"It was always going to be rough at first," Jon replied. "But we're getting there. We're beginning to put in permanent buildings and starting to cultivate our own food."

She gave Jon a sniff. "And that's not all you've been cultivating."

"Correct me if I'm wrong," Bruno said. "But you don't strike me as being overly keen to be here."

Rachel laughed, a tad derisively. "I've left a nice job and a comfortable life. But I'm here because I want to help you."

Jon was wary. When it came to help, there were two kinds: help that's needed and help that's no help at all.

"We can always use assistance," Jon said. "What is it that you have in mind?"

"Walk with me, Jon and I'll explain," she said. "Bruno, Gus—I'm sure you can handle the transport and storage of the rest of my equipment."

With that, she headed off with Jon towards the camp. It wasn't entirely clear who was leading whom. Bruno caught some of their departing conversation.

"For a start," Rachel said to Jon, "you're all in need of some decent field medicine and some check-ups."

"Sounds helpful," Jon replied.

"And I want you to make much better use of the Data Sphere."

Bruno couldn't make out Jon's reply. He didn't need to. "Oh dear," he said.

"Jon's not going to be happy to hear that," Gus said. "It's a pity though."

"A pity why?"

"Aside from the domineering attitude, I think I like her."

Bruno looked at Gus enquiringly. "You do, do you?"

"I think I do, yes."

"Good luck with that my friend."

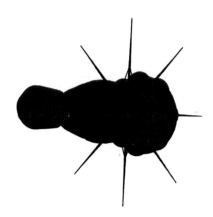

CHAPTER 8
Direct Abort

IF A VIEW COULD DISTRACT Callum from his troubles, then this was it.

The Rolls Ranges were the result of an ancient right of way dispute between two of the planet's major tectonic plates. The outcome was a series of huge cliffs, thousands of feet high, thrusting out of the jungle below like standing waves in a sea of green.

"Let's face it," he said to Kyra. "Tonight could have gone better."

"People will be people," she replied, taking his arm. "We've seen this attitude before. What more could we expect?"

"I just hoped the location might attract them."

Kyra nodded, looking out at the vista before them. "It is beautiful here."

"Aye, that it is."

The Rolls Ranges were so called because of Arcadia's questionable sponsorship opportunities. In this case, it had occurred to an under-employed, over-budgeted marketing executive that its rocky edifices were reminiscent of the majestic grilles that adorned his company's range of luxury flyers. It may have done little to sell more vehicles, but the Ranges had become one of Arcadia's foremost tourist spots.

"Shall we go out on the balcony?" Kyra asked.

Callum was dubious. "Do we trust it? I've been on spacewalks that have made me less nervous."

The architect of the Rolls Ranges Vista Lodge Deluxe Tourist Resort had decided to hang the entire construction off one of the Ranges' enormous cliffs. Callum could not deny that it was stunning idea. But he had his concerns about the execution.

The building began at the top of the cliff before spilling over the edge, covering the rock face with a vast array of windows and balconies. The trouble was that what anchored it in place was Arcadian engineering. For once, Callum could only hope that Virgil had been involved.

"Come on," Kyra said, "it's stayed up until now. Let's not mope in here when we can mope outside instead."

What was truly bothering Callum was less the structural integrity of the building and more the cohesive integrity of his crew. He'd thought their current locale would provide a chance to get back in touch with those of his crew who had 'gone native'. But it had not worked out that way.

"Hardly anyone came, despite the fact that the government was footing the bill," Callum said. "And, as for those that did show, it was almost like we'd never met."

Leyton had made the arrangements. Contacting them all through the Data Sphere was simplicity itself. Callum had anticipated that a few might not come, but when that had turned into 'most' it was hard not to feel disappointed.

"I think they've come to view travel as a waste of time," Kyra said. "A century on a starship can do that to you."

"Except I thought our years of training, collective mission and mutual peril might count for something."

"They've adapted to the Data Sphere. To be fair, all of them offered to meet you in there."

"And we said we thought it better to meet in the flesh."

"Then maybe we're at fault? Perhaps we're being old fashioned?"

"I guess we could be. But it doesn't mean we're wrong. Neither of us trusts the Data Sphere and we're getting more and more evidence to back our suspicions."

"But if it's their decision then who are we to stop them?"

Callum shook his head. "Something's not right. Why is it getting more difficult to maintain contact? It's like some kind of club. If you're not in it, they don't want to know."

"It's their choice though."

"It was their choice to enter. Beyond that, I'm not so sure any more."

Kyra looked at him seriously. "Alright, say I agree with

you. How do we change anything? How do we take on an entire planet?"

"Wasn't that what we originally came here to do?"

"Yes, when it was a planet free of Arcadians and an AI with enough mental firepower to level a university."

"Look, I haven't got all the answers yet, but I think there's a chance. It's like finding parts of a jigsaw. We've got some of the pieces and there's potential for more."

"Can you finish a jigsaw with potential pieces?"

"Potentially, yes."

"Be serious."

"OK, I admit, there's an element of faith involved. But either we trust we'll find a solution, or we give up."

"We're not doing that."

Callum smiled. No matter what, Kyra always had his back, plus a lot more besides. "Alright then," he said. "In that case, check-in time with the *Endeavour*'s coming up. We need to get ready."

Kyra dug a hand into her travel bag, pulling out what appeared to be her ever faithful Magic Hairaway 3000, now converted to an orbital communication device. It had come in useful several times already, which was more than could be said for its efforts when in its original form.

While Kyra readied the uplink, Callum ran the wire out to their balcony. Privacy was valued at this resort, when people came here to get away from it all then they could do exactly that. Their room was near the top of the hotel and, as such, the Rolls Ranges did little to obstruct their view of the night sky. However, the building's garish lighting was another matter entirely. Callum struggled to pick out many stars, let alone the reflected light of an orbiting spacecraft.

"I've got them," Kyra said suddenly.

"Greetings, Captain," said Jeeves. "Please be aware that we have 276 seconds before we lose line of sight. Attached is a report from Tomoko who is with our space-born acquaintances. Do you wish me to summarise it?"

"Be my guest."

"The report confirms our mutual concerns about Virgil and Arcadia. They believe our arrival here has presented them with a unique opportunity to change the status quo."

"And do you think it's viable?"

"There is a possibility of success, but I would not wish

to calculate the odds."

"Because they're slight?"

"No, because I have no idea how to do so accurately."

"But you're a computer."

"And you are an astronaut. Yet it does not follow that you are capable of flying to the far side of the galaxy."

Callum smiled, he'd always liked Jeeves. The AI had always possessed a unique combination of profound wisdom and childlike innocence. It was a state that he himself only achieved one dram from passing out.

Kyra tapped her watch, reminding him that their time was limited.

"How are things up there?" Callum asked.

"*Endeavour* continues to function nominally. The crew are here if you wish to talk to them."

"Hello," Mark said briefly. "We're all well."

"Glad to hear it," Callum said.

"And what about Virgil, any developments?" Kyra asked.

"It appears to have accepted that I do not wish to join with it."

"That's good, isn't it?" Callum asked.

"Unfortunately, no," Jeeves replied. "Virgil is periodically attempting to subsume my systems by force. Fortunately, I have the high ground, I control the connection to the ship and it makes such a task virtually impossible."

"You're safe then?"

"My concern is that Virgil is both inventive and a lot more powerful than I am. At the moment, I think it sees me as a side project and not worth committing significant resources to. As long as that does not change, I should be safe enough."

Kyra looked thoughtful—an idea was brewing.

"Jeeves, can you share the comm logs for Virgil's latest attack?"

"There is far more data to transfer than our remaining connection time will permit."

"Send what you can."

Callum caught Kyra's eye. Whatever her idea was, she seemed serious about it.

"In that case," he said, "let's free up the bandwidth.

We'll talk to you all later."

"Very well."

With the connection closed, Callum turned to Kyra. "What's your idea?" he asked.

"It's occurred to me that Virgil has no choice but to interface with Jeeves through our outdated comms protocols. It may not realise that it's leaving itself vulnerable."

"I don't want to be negative, but Virgil has an IQ that the IQ scale itself is not clever enough to measure. It manages an entire planet. How could it not realise?"

"The comms protocols must feel slow and inefficient. To Virgil, communication with Jeeves must be almost as tedious as talking to us. With all its other tasks, it may not give the process the care and respect it deserves. There's a chance that we might be able to exploit that."

"What kind of chance?"

"Pretty slight. But, as you said earlier, we need an element of faith. Virgil is very bright, but it's also spread thin. It might be more vulnerable than we think."

"I suppose it's worth a try. But we need to be careful. If we overstep the mark, it could well be the end of us."

"I get it, Callum, don't worry. I won't do anything that risks compromising us in the longer term."

Callum nodded. It was a big decision. The biggest they'd ever made—and they'd faced some humdingers in their time.

"If we are to take on a planetary AI, then we're going to have to hear what Tomoko has to say about it."

Tomoko's reports took thoroughness to a whole new level. They were legendary—as were some of the efforts made to avoid them.

"Do we have to?"

"Aye, revolution is never easy."

***

Some eight hours before Kyra and Callum braced themselves to watch Tomoko's report, Tomoko was bracing herself to record it.

There is no shortage of irony in space.

"Don't tell me you're nervous?" Tor asked, sporting a mischievous smile.

"Of course not. But I perform better when I can see the person I wish to talk to."

"Just talk to the camera."

"I can't intimidate a camera."

"Yet it would appear that it can intimidate you. First Marsala, now this. I never thought I'd find two things that daunted you."

Prior to the launch of the *Endeavour* mission there had been plenty of camera work. The crew would gather together, brim with enthusiasm, smile a lot and tell anyone who chose to watch how they were 'thrilled, happy and pumped'. So often were they 'pumped' that people got to wondering what it was that was being 'pumped' into them—and how they could get some.

But it was all a show. The majority of the crew did not seek the limelight. They weren't wired that way, and they didn't need to be. *Endeavour* was ultimately a one-way mission. Flying off into deep space, never to return, is not really compatible with long-term attention seeking.

Tomoko took a deep breath, steeled herself and turned on the camera.

"Captain," she began. "We have now met with the leader of our new associates. Her name is Marsala Guerra. We have learned much about the history of the Arcadian system—and I have no reason to doubt its veracity."

She went on to elaborate about the gradual exclusion of the Spacers from Arcadia, even allowing Tor to chip in on occasion.

"The Spacers have done well for themselves despite the challenges. The Nest supports over twenty thousand souls and a sizable fleet of ships. But they are cut off. No one here has been within Arcadia's atmosphere for over thirty cycles. The last people to try were killed."

Tomoko was not as heartless as she often chose to appear. She paused for a moment as a sign of respect. Tor hung his head.

"Despite this, they continue to observe Arcadia remotely and occasionally chance close flybys to gather further data. From the evidence they have collected they believe that Virgil is not behaving entirely correctly. Whether it's a malfunction, a fault in its moral protocols or an innate AI character flaw is, in the final analysis, irrelevant. The AI is over-protective of its population to the detriment of everything else."

Tomoko drew breath.

"Remember to talk about *Endeavour*," Tor said. "It's pivotal to our plan."

"Indeed it is," a voice said off camera.

Both Tomoko and Tor turned before Tor thought to grab the camera and point it in a new direction.

Standing in the doorway, or rather standing between its bushes, was Marsala. She leaned heavily on a cane, her age much more apparent when she was standing up.

"I thought I'd see how you were getting on," she said.

Tomoko did her best to not react to the interruptions.

"This is Marsala Guerra," she said to the camera, before turning towards her visitor. "I was reporting on how we might attack Virgil," she said.

"I prefer the word 'adjust'," replied Marsala.

She made her way over to them betraying that mysterious turn of speed available to the elderly when the young least expect it.

"Attack implies violence," she said. "This is not what is required."

"I think attack is a more accurate description," Tomoko replied.

Marsala smiled. It was an expression she used with careful efficiency. It conveyed many things: kindness, tolerance, forbearing and that it was in Tomoko's best interest to listen to her.

"We believe that it should be possible to alter Virgil's core directives," Marsala said. "There is much about Virgil that is beneficial and good."

"But to do that requires that we attack Virgil," Tomoko argued.

"If I could give you one piece of advice, Tomoko, it would be that you consider problems in a manner that is appropriate," Marsala replied. "If you see every challenge as something to be fought then this will shape your solution. Leave yourself open to resolutions that are kinder. It will benefit both you and those around you."

Tomoko was surprised to find that Marsala had given her pause for thought. It wasn't a long pause but, by Tomoko's standards, it was significant.

"Look at Marsala giving you advice as a compliment," Tor explained. "It means she thinks you're worthwhile."

"Do not talk about me as if I am not still in the room," Marsala said. "You can discuss me in the third person when I'm dead."

"And she plays the death card a lot too."

Marsala planted her cane squarely on Tor's foot—and leant on it.

"And, in many ways, you're really quite alike," Tor said, his voice now strangulated.

Tomoko looked at Marsala. "Thank you for your wisdom," she said, sounding surprisingly genuine.

Marsala nodded, patted Tomoko's shoulder and gestured towards the camera.

"You had best continue," she said.

Tomoko nodded.

"As you heard Captain, the Spacers think it's possible to *adjust* Virgil. Between us and them they believe we can make this happen. But it will be difficult. There's a lot that needs to go right."

Marsala smiled quietly and took her leave.

The rest of Tomoko's message explained how the Spacers' plan might actually be achieved. It was plausible, but when compared with an ice cube's chance in hell, you might conclude that the devil enjoys his scotch on the rocks.

"Do you think Captain MacMahon will go for it?" Tor asked Tomoko, once the recording was finished and they were alone in his quarters.

"Callum has a habit of doing the right thing," Tomoko said. "It's his most dependable quality. In fact, I have come to rely on it."

"That sounds almost like praise."

"I have been known to give it, occasionally."

"What do I need to do to get a little praise of my own?" Tor asked.

"I can think of a few things," Tomoko said.

Tor's eyebrows went up a notch.

"Not that," Tomoko added, colouring a little. "At least, not yet. Knowing what Callum is like, I think we have some things to arrange first."

***

Jon's problem was that he was neither persuader nor persuaded.

If Callum had hoped that Jon would be able to break Rachel's dependency on the Data Sphere, then he was likely to be disappointed. When Rachel had said that they should make 'better' use of the Sphere, what she'd meant was that they should use it more—a lot more.

Jon had tried dissuading her. But that had not gone well. Like most doctors, she was used to giving advice, not taking it. He'd tried very hard to get her to buy into what his settlement was trying to achieve. But all his efforts had fallen on ears so deaf that he'd been tempted to suggest she go in for a hearing test.

Right now, despite Jon's disapproval, Rachel was focusing on encouraging the members of Jon's settlement to make use of the Sphere to monitor their health. The main result of which had been a widespread outbreak of hypochondria.

When it came to life, Jon's philosophy was not to overthink things (which is a philosophy that can be applied to most philosophy). With regard to the recent rash of health concerns, his view was that they might prolong your life, but they'd sure as hell prevent you living it.

He'd tried to argue that point with Rachel. "You wouldn't be this cautious if it was just us on Arcadia," he'd said.

"If it was just us two, I'd say that I was already taking quite a risk," was her response.

"Cut the crap, Rachel. If Arcadia had been empty, and we'd established a colony as we'd originally planned, then there's no way we could afford to be this careful with our health."

Rachel glowered at him. "You go on and on about adapting to the environment. Well, there's a highly advanced healthcare system on this planet and we should be taking advantage of it."

To which Jon had no practicable response.

In essence, his arguments with Rachel were akin to butting his head against a brick wall. The fact that said brick wall possessed excellent first aid skills and a

Alastair Miles

practised bedside manner was of scant consolation.

A new approach was called for.

Some would say that he should play Rachel at her own game. Just as she'd used his survival knowledge against him, he should throw her medical arguments back at her. It was a great idea in theory, but it had two fundamental flaws.

First off, he lacked the wit. He was used to outsmarting this evening's dinner, not fully qualified medical practitioners.

Number two, he didn't understand half of what Rachel did. His healthcare knowledge was limited. In fact, it went about as far as a love of making splints and the medicinal properties of nettle wine.

It was then that he thought back to what Rachel had said when they'd last argued. He reconsidered the resources at his disposal. If he couldn't take Rachel on, then maybe someone else could. Someone who used wit as if it was in danger of going out of fashion. Someone who, despite months in the wilderness, somehow had his sex appeal enhanced by his own body odour.

Jon didn't know if Bruno had ever plied his charms on Rachel. If not, perhaps he might consider addressing that particular omission.

"Absolutely not," Bruno had said.

"Why? Surely you must want to try?"

"Who says I haven't?"

"Well, I didn't notice. And it's hard to keep secrets around here."

"It wasn't on this particular planet."

"What happened?"

"She finished it. When someone has that much anatomical knowledge, you don't argue."

Bruno thought the matter closed, but Jon was not to be dissuaded.

"You could still talk to her. You have a way of getting through to people."

"No, I have a way of getting under their skin. There's a difference."

Jon sighed.

"Look," Bruno had said, "our best chance is Gus. He's been hanging around Rachel a lot, whether she likes it or

162

not. Perhaps he'll get somewhere."

"Or maybe she'll turn him too."

"There's nothing to turn. Have you seen his shelter? Hand built by himself—and now decked out with electronics."

Jon shook his head, still far from convinced. "I'm getting really worried, Bruno," he'd said.

"Clearly."

"Callum's really dropped me in it. Rachel's undoing all our hard work. If we can't get through to her, this colony will become just like the rest of Arcadia."

"That's not going to happen. Well, not unless we drastically improve the sanitation."

"This is serious. I need to find a way of solving this."

"Sorry buddy. I wish I had an answer for you."

"Why did Callum advise her to come here?" he asked. "I guess he must have thought we could get through to her in some way. But, if so, what am I missing?"

"Maybe nothing," Bruno replied. "The Cap doesn't always have the answers. Sometimes he just plays the odds. He must think there's a good chance we'll come up with something."

"I appreciate his faith. But there are times where I can think of better places to put it."

"Better than you posterior?"

Jon was not amused.

"We need an answer," he said. "There's no way in hell I'm going back to Arcadian civilization. I'll live by myself if I have to."

"Jon, leaving everything behind again is not the answer. Just remember how bad it was when Liliya..."

Bruno didn't finish his sentence, which was far from normal behaviour. Such an occurrence typically required either a knockout blow, a naked woman or, on more than one occasion, both together.

"You were saying?" Jon said.

"Liliya," Bruno repeated. "I believe she might be the answer to your problem. Perhaps she could talk to Rachel? Persuade her to pull back from the Data Sphere? You told me she's been doing that herself."

Jon could have kicked himself—and he was limber enough to do it.

"I should have thought of that," he said.

Bruno hadn't exactly been quick off the mark himself, but that didn't stop him saying, "You can be quite the idiot sometimes."

"So can you for that matter."

"Then I guess we deserve each other," Bruno replied, wrapping an arm around Jon's shoulder. "Come on, let's go and talk to Gus, assuming Rachel hasn't persuaded him to plug back into the Sphere 24/7."

"On Arcadia it's more like 25/6."

***

Virgil did not suffer from moods. That was what it told itself. To suffer from moods would be a flaw and Virgil never admitted to flaws, which was a flaw in itself.

Virgil's constant drive for efficiency was being seriously frustrated. Typically, it occupied itself with burrowing into minute details to tweak this, adjust that and nudge the other in a ceaseless quest for peak performance. The trouble with this was that it could lead to a failure to play the long game. Virgil relied on dealing with challenges as they arose rather than commit to costly, pre-emptive action.

From Virgil's perspective it made sense. Humans moved with a speed that Virgil equated with continental drift. In other words, it was barely perceptible—right up to the point where there was an almighty crunch.

Virgil's current troubles stemmed from the *Endeavour*. The archaic ship, its antique AI and its crew of ancient humans were, yet again, disrupting Virgil's orderly routines. Up until now, Virgil's preferred strategy had been to progressively assimilate the members of *Endeavour*'s crew and its recalcitrant AI. As time went by, more and more of *Endeavour*'s crew were choosing to accept the Arcadian lifestyle and the problem of the *Endeavour* had been slowly dissolving away to nothing.

All well and good, except Virgil had been harbouring a suspicion that a ship from the Nest had rendezvoused with *Endeavour*. The difficulty was that Nest vessels possessed stealth tech that made detecting them an uncertain process, even for Virgil. The only way to be certain would have been to have tasked a satellite to monitor *Endeavour* directly and, at the time, Virgil had considered this a waste of resources. But, by piecing together information from a diverse collection of data feeds, then cross correlating them in a manner that would dazzle an army of statisticians, Virgil had reached the conclusion that *Endeavour* was now in direct contact with the Nest itself.

All this had led Virgil to the conclusion that the time had come to step up its efforts to deal with the *Endeavour*—even if did mean expending further resources. But this would take time, time it was unsure whether it could afford.

Still, Virgil told itself, it never got impatient—just as it was never annoyed or arrogant either.

***

It is said that the greatest journeys start with a single step.

This is true.

In Kyra's case, she was all too aware that a single misstep might result in a journey in one, unpalatable direction—straight down.

Callum had insisted that they trek from their hotel along the ridge line. As he'd hoped, they'd soon found that it took surprisingly little effort to distance themselves from the average resident of the Rolls Ranges Vista Lodge Deluxe Tourist Resort. Most of them got out of breath saying the name of the hotel, let alone hacking along a trail. As far as they were concerned, the ideal view was the one from their hotel balcony—accompanied by a large cocktail.

Sometimes, Arcadians were not as daft as they first appeared.

As an experienced pilot, Callum had a head for heights. Sadly, the same could not be said for Kyra.

"Do we have to get so close to the edge?" she asked.

"It's not much further. This trail should lead to a cave."

"Perfect," she replied, in a tone that conveyed it was anything but.

Callum stopped to take a breather and turned round to talk to her.

"I don't understand you sometimes," he said. "We've just spent two nights in a hotel hanging off the side of a cliff. A hotel built by the finest engineers Arcadia has to offer i.e.

people I wouldn't trust to put up a shed. Yet now you're getting jittery about a clifftop?"

There were times when Callum's displays of empathy were not all they might be.

"The hotel design was overseen by Virgil," Kyra replied, through gritted teeth. "One good thing we know about Virgil is that it protects all Arcadians from physical harm. That hotel's a good deal safer than we are."

"You're saying you'd trust Virgil over Mother Nature?"

"Given Mother Nature doesn't install guard rails then the answer is yes."

Callum was about to roll his eyes but thought better of it. "It's really not much further. I promise."

But Kyra was not to be placated and laughed bitterly. "Let's go for a walk you said. It'll be romantic you said."

Callum wasn't sure that he'd put it like that, but was prepared to accept that he had for the sake of quiet life. The chief reason for this excursion was the need for more frequent contact with *Endeavour*. Callum was concerned about the risk of repeated communication from the hotel, and they were seeking a more secluded location. If truth be told, he'd also fancied hiking through this incredible landscape. So, the opportunity to do just that, combined with the chance to find a peaceful spot from where they could conduct their business, seemed like a win-win.

Unfortunately for him, Kyra didn't see if that way.

"You just need to cross this last part," Callum said.

"'Just' is a four-letter word," Kyra replied with an iciness that belied the heat from the blazing sun.

In truth, she had been looking forward to a nice walk. But, as Kyra had come to realise, Callum didn't seem to understand that nice walks were not made better by the threat of a terminal drop. In her mind, in terms of finding a secluded spot it was definitely a case of going overboard and, right now, 'going overboard' was a not a phrase that Kyra wanted to dwell upon.

Why was it, she wondered, that men seemed to enjoy making things difficult for themselves? Or was it that they didn't have the wit to do anything else?

"We're here," Callum said eventually.

Kyra slithered unceremoniously to a halt on the loose scree and grudgingly accepted his hand.

It was a nice spot—she'd give him that. Behind them was a shallow cave that provided some respite from the sun. In front of them, across a narrow shelf of bare rock, was a commanding view of the Rolls Ranges. It looked as if God had caused the land to rise up in giant waves and then frozen them in place.

Kyra was agnostic when it came to God. Her feelings towards Callum right now were much the same.

"We're out of line of sight of the hotel and far enough away that we shouldn't be troubled," Callum said. "I'd say we should be able to hang out here for several hours uninterrupted."

Callum was well aware that Kyra was less than happy. Fortunately, he'd sneaked a surprise into his backpack, although he hadn't anticipated needing it to get back into Kyra's good books. He'd actually been hoping to get into her better books, perhaps even her best.

He pulled out a bottle of white wine, still perfectly chilled within its vacuum tube and a slightly crumpled flower, an Arcadian species that bore a passing resemblance to a rose.

Kyra was touched, despite herself. She even felt a kind of kinship with the tattered flower, which looked like it had enjoyed the journey as much as she had.

"It's a nice thought," she said, offering Callum a peck on the cheek. "But, if I'm to get back to the hotel in one piece then I can't be drinking alcohol."

"I bought some Null-Tox tablets too."

"Not so romantic, but at least practical. Well done."

"Aye lass."

Null-Tox, as great an invention as it was, had never received a Nobel Prize—for the chief reason that it caused as many problems as it solved. No matter how heavy the drinking, Null-Tox delivered a clear head and a clear memory of all the things you'd rather you hadn't done.

Unlike faster-than-light travel, Null-Tox had been invented before *Endeavour* had left Earth. As a proud Scotsman, not that there was any other kind, Callum enjoyed his whisky—and couldn't stand the (alleged) synthahol equivalent. Without Null-Tox he wouldn't be where he was today, captain of the Earth's first starship and out of place and out of time.

As of now, Null-Tox had at least sealed the deal in terms of getting Kyra back on side—even if she remained concerned about the side's proximity to a sheer drop. Once they'd setup the comms gear there was time for a quiet drink and a fantastic view.

But sooner than they'd have liked, they were interrupted.

"Captain? *Endeavour* here."

The voice belonged to Mark Johansson.

Callum hadn't heard much from him for a while. With a limited amount of time for transmissions, their contact had been mostly limited to conversing with Jeeves. Mark's presence conveyed some anticipation of a plan of action.

"How are you, Mark?" Callum asked.

"Truth be told, it's getting a little lonely up here, sir. Most people have gone and all I seem to do is go around in circles."

"Don't worry, Mark, it's called life. I'm sorry you're still up there but know that you're helping keep our options open, which for now is for the best."

"Have you thought about Tomoko's proposal?"

"Aye. I've seen enough of this planet and its people to conclude that Virgil is stifling them. Tomoko's report confirms it. Kyra and I have talked and think her idea is the best way forward. But timing is crucial and that's something I need to figure out—but carefully."

"That's why you get paid the big bucks, sir."

"I haven't had a paycheque in a hundred years."

"OK, that's why you *got* paid the big bucks."

Callum smiled. "Mark, once again, I do appreciate what you're doing."

"Thank you. Is there anything specific you need from us, sir?"

"Keep Jeeves company, keep monitoring and keep your dropship prepped. Oh, and can you downlink the latest inventory? I'd like to keep on top of what we have."

"I'm sure Jeeves will oblige."

"The request is in line with my operational parameters," the AI said.

"That's a yes, isn't it?"

"Yes."

Callum felt a slight pang of guilt at hearing Jeeves's

voice. He'd only been thinking of the human crew while he'd been talking to Mark. But, while Jeeves could not get bored, its future was arguably the least certain of anyone. The original mission plan had called for Jeeves to be removed from the ship and operate from a mobile module on the planet below. The psychology of an AI was a challenging thing and, in Virgil's case, the root cause of their current problems. In Jeeves's case it functioned better amongst human company, one of the reasons a limited crew was staying on board. Callum did not know for sure how the AI felt about its future prospects, but he had to trust that Jeeves would be there for them when it was needed.

"Jeeves, that was a timely contribution," Callum said. "I know that Kyra would like to speak with you."

"Hello, Jeeves," Kyra said. "How are you and the ship?"

"We are both nominal. Or 'fine' if you prefer."

"Good to hear. I wanted to ask you about those sub-routine exploits I sent you during our last uplink. What did you think of them?"

"Their execution is sound. I have integrated them into my systems ready to deploy should the opportunity arise. The fact remains that their success does depend on whether Virgil fails to recognise their significance."

"Are you comfortable with that?"

"Uncontrolled variables are not my favourite type. But the benefits outweigh the risk."

"I agree." Kyra had spent a portion of the preceding evening and night studying the comms logs Virgil had sent her. The lack of sleep had not contributed to her mood today. She believed there were weaknesses to exploit. Unbelievably, they relied on being too basic and archaic for an AI to spot.

She had more questions but resisted asking them. In the bright, sunny conditions it was impossible to see the *Endeavour* as it tracked across the sky. Nevertheless, in her mind's eye, she was all too aware of its rapid progress and how it would soon slip below the horizon. She indicated to Callum that she was finished.

Callum nodded. "Any developments regarding Jon's colony yet?"

"We're still waiting for the dropship to arrive."

Chief amongst Callum's concerns were resources and where they were situated. Jon's colony had an important role to play.

Ironically, when it came to outer space he was well catered for. Tomoko's report had included details of what the Spacers had to offer.

The difficult part was establishing whom he could call upon planet-side. Jon's camp consisted of the *Endeavour* crew who'd not only rejected Arcadian culture but had gone out of their way to avoid it. There was one exception present, Rachel Owen, but that was Callum's fault. So far, it seemed that Jon had not had as much success converting her back as he'd hoped he would.

For the plan to work, they all needed direct contact with *Endeavour*. Up 'til now Callum and Kyra had been relaying messages but that was slow and inefficient. The solution was to send a dropship, certified free of Arcadian tech and ready to cannibalise for comms.

When it came to flying vessels, Callum still had more at his disposal than most people could claim. But, while three was a relatively big number, it still wasn't as many as he'd like.

That number came down to two when you considered that one of the vessels was only good for flying in deep space or in endless loops around the planet. The two remaining dropships in his possession were, as their name suggested, single use i.e. ideal for flying downwards but not back up again. Releasing one of them meant that he'd also have to release a portion of *Endeavour*'s remaining crew or risk marooning them in orbit.

Despite the downsides, that was the decision he'd made. If all had gone well then they should be about to arrive.

"Did the crew leave on schedule?" Callum asked.

"Yes, and from what we can observe the descent is going to plan. Jon picked the landing site well, plenty of open ground."

With regards to dropship flights, the line spun to Virgil and the Arcadian government was that the remaining crew of the *Endeavour* wished to join Jon's colonisation project. As such, it made sense for the dropships to head directly to the settlement. It was hoped that this would not draw undue interference.

In this regard, the level of curiosity expressed by the Arcadian government was, as Callum had expected, on the low side of nil. If it didn't involve an opportunity for ego massage or easy publicity, they weren't interested.

What was more surprising, and possibly concerning, was how quiet Virgil had been. Normally, the planetary AI would try to control their arrangements. But Virgil now seemed to have a policy of maintaining a neutral stance and communicating no more than it had to. It was as if the AI was having an electronic sulk.

The important thing was that, for now, things were quiet. He should be grateful, rather than waiting for life to kick him in the gut. After all, it would happen sooner or later.

"What's that noise?" Kyra asked.

It looked like life had gone for sooner.

They immediately recognised the fans of an approaching air car. The hotel made them available to guests as transport up and down the Rolls Ranges. But the activity was typically to ferry passengers to different ridge lines and not along the track that they'd been following to get here.

"We've got to hide the transmitter," Callum said.

But it was too late, the fans were getting louder by the second. With a hasty goodbye they cut the connection to *Endeavour*.

A cream-coloured vehicle slid into view. It looked like an enthusiastic union of a van and several aircon units. In the cockpit was their ever-faithful escort and companion, Leyton Smith. He brought the vehicle into a hover at the edge of the cliff and the boarding ramp extended from its passenger compartment.

Callum and Kyra gave him their best 'how nice to see you' smiles. Meanwhile Callum tried to kick the hardware under their rucksack and scattered jackets.

"I thought you might appreciate a lift," Leyton said brightly, having made his way out to them from the cockpit.

"Very thoughtful of you, but we said there was no need," Kyra replied, her smile fixed in place in a manner that would make a ventriloquist proud.

"It wasn't entirely my idea," Leyton admitted. "Virgil

thought I ought to check that all was well. Night falls quickly here when the sun drops below the ridgeline."

"But it's barely after lunch," Callum said.

"Better to be safe."

"And indeed we are. Why don't you go back to the hotel?"

But Leyton was oblivious to hints.

"It's a lovely spot," he said. "Sheltered, but with some great views."

"Except we have an air car in the way," Callum replied. "Should you be leaving it running like that?"

The air car continued to hover at the edge of the drop.

"Its batteries are highly efficient. They can last the whole day."

Leyton used his Data Sphere connection to regale them with a potted history of advancements in battery technology. He then proceeded to spew information on the local area, its geography, flora and fauna.

Callum would have beseeched him to stop but Kyra put a hand to his arm. To her mind, while Leyton was talking, he wasn't looking. She used the distraction to use her foot to further nudge the equipment out of sight.

"Thank you for that," Callum said, when Leyton had finally paused to draw breath.

"Not at all."

"And you'll be off now?"

"Are you sure you don't want a lift back?"

"Positive."

"Alright, I'll be going then."

Callum tried hard not to breathe a sigh of relief.

"Except, I was wondering, what is it that you've been kicking for the last few minutes?"

"Nothing," Kyra said, with her most innocent expression.

"No, there's something there," Leyton replied, his face one of childish curiosity. "It looks like a device that's come from your room. It shouldn't be out here. I think it'd be better to pick it up, whatever it is."

Leyton went to help retrieve it. Callum cursed inwardly. Leyton had been oblivious to everything else, why did he have to go and notice this?

"Leave it alone," Callum said. "Forget about it."

"It's no trouble." It was clear that Leyton could not be dissuaded.

In the heat of the moment Callum did something impulsive. It was something he'd last done when he was much, much younger and outside of a pub on the Royal Mile. The recipient had been an overbearing Sassenach who'd been making unwanted advances on a woman.

From Callum's point of view, this head butt hurt a lot more. Furthermore, in this case, it was something that Leyton didn't deserve, but Callum had little choice. Fortunately, the result was much the same. Leyton crashed to the floor without knowing what hit him.

"Callum, what the hell did you do?" Kyra said, her face aghast.

"I'd have thought it was obvious," Callum replied, holding his forehead.

"Yes, but was that really the answer?"

"I didn't have a better one."

"And this is you carefully considering our next steps?"

Callum's head was pounding. Newton's third law was demanding recompense. But the only thing to do was keep going.

"It can't be helped," he replied, straightening his back and shoulders. "If Virgil was monitoring Leyton's feed, then who knows what trouble we might have ended up in? Thanks to Jeeves and Tomoko, we have the basis of a plan for attacking Virgil. We're just going to have act on it sooner than we thought."

Kyra shook her head. "And what happens when Leyton wakes up?"

"We'll have to work something out," he said. "Help me with the comms gear. We need to see if we can catch *Endeavour* before it goes out of sight."

Working quickly, they soon had it redeployed.

"*Endeavour*?" Callum said. "Get the following message out to Tomoko. We need our friends to make good on their promise sooner than we expected. But we've got to go. We'll be in touch to co-ordinate as soon as we can. MacMahon out."

"Yes, sir," they heard Mark reply, sounding as startled as you might expect.

Callum turned to Kyra, who was biting her lip as her

mind played host to a battle between anger and concern.

"Do you think you can fly the air car?" Callum asked.

She shook her head. "You're the pilot, not me."

"Pity, I'm still dizzy, I think I can see two of them."

"Then I'll help you get on the right one. We'll take it from there."

***

The problem with life's rich tapestry is that it's prone to unravelling.

While Callum and Kyra dragged Leyton on board, Jon was dealing with a much larger problem.

For a remote, wilderness settlement Jon's nascent colony had become a nexus for visiting aircraft. Some were in a better state than others. But the worst of it was that only one of them was friendly—and that was the one that was most beaten up.

The latest dropship to leave *Endeavour* had done just that—dropped. With a design spec that called for it to land once, and once only, it had ploughed a single, large furrow across the landscape. Normally, Jon would have been upset with this modification to his recently cultivated fields. However, today, these irritations paled into insignificance when compared with the Arcadian force that had descended upon him.

The Arcadian craft had at least avoided compounding the damage. But the figures those craft had disgorged had not been quite so careful. It seemed that their primary aim had been to intercept the recently arrived dropship. By the time Jon arrived on the scene a large group had surrounded the vehicle and were dragging out its occupants.

The armoured gear they were wearing made them particularly hard to argue with. Not that this had stopped Jon.

"What the hell is going on?" he shouted.

The response had been the raising of a number of nasty looking weapons designed to do him no good whatsoever.

Jon stopped to catch his breath. After a run across a mile or more of open ground he needed to regain is composure.

"Who's in charge?" he asked.

The figures ignored him.

Bruno, who had been trailing behind, now puffed up alongside.

"You've had better audiences," he said, gasping for air.

The crew of the dropship had now been forced to the ground. Jon switched his attention to them.

"Are you alright?"

The fact they'd been forced to the ground should have been answer enough.

At this point, the mob parted and a tall, powerful figure strode towards him.

"Jon Keller, I presume," he said. "I am pleased to meet you."

"I'm not sure I can say the same," Jon replied.

"And who are you?" Bruno asked.

The man looked him up and down and even Bruno felt less than sure of himself.

"And you must be Mr Bruno Cabrera, yes?"

"Last time I checked. But I still don't know who you are."

The man smiled. It was far from reassuring.

"My name is Doctor Kenton Stiger. I'm a colleague of Rachel Owen."

The recently arrived *Endeavour* crew tried to get up but were 'encouraged' to remain where they were.

"If you're in healthcare," Jon asked, "then what happened to 'do no harm'?"

"Despite appearances, I'm here to do some good."

"Oh great."

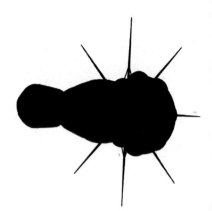

CHAPTER 9
Free Return

CALLUM FLEW AS LOW AS he dared between the Rolls Ranges.

He was still trying to shake off the after effects of the head butt. It was a relief to no longer be seeing double. In a sense, his problems had halved. In reality, they'd done nothing of the sort.

"Leyton's not going to stay unconscious forever," Kyra said.

"Can't we do something to persuade him otherwise?"

Leyton Smith lay on the floor of the air car, his head cradled by Kyra.

"We're not hitting him again."

"I was thinking about something from the med kit."

"Med kits aren't supposed to keep patients unconscious, Callum. Besides, the one I have to hand has only two things in it, enough bandages to mummify the patient and enough legalese to prevent a lawsuit."

"Then I'm open to suggestions," Callum said. "We can't afford to have Leyton scuppering our actions."

Kyra wore a wry smile. "At heart, you're still a stereotypical male. Strike first, think later."

"My sore head agrees with you. What I need now is a stereotypical female to get us out of this."

"Well... I can't," Kyra admitted. "But I think I know one who can."

***

There are many kinds of intelligence.

An academic intellect philosophises for breakfast, lunches on ancient history and dines on quantum physics—before resorting to applied medicine for mental

176

indigestion. While someone with emotional aptitude knows how you're feeling better than you do. Yet, when it comes to business acumen, how you feel, or how anyone else feels for that matter, depends solely on what yields the largest profit. But, if there's such a thing as true intelligence, the purest kind, then that's possessed by those who stay in bed... and get away with it.

With all these different types of intelligence, no one gets it right all the time. Liliya's current circumstances were a case in point. Jon and Bruno's lack of understanding had led to her leaving the settlement. While Liliya had failed to foresee the implications of working for Virgil.

They'd all thought themselves smarter than that.

Even Virgil's intellect had fallen short. It had thought it would soon indoctrinate Liliya into Arcadian society—and it had almost been right. But Liliya was stronger than that. Now, having seen the light, she'd found a surprising amount of latitude amongst the constraints that Virgil thought it had imposed. That said, care was still required. She did not want to think of the consequences if Virgil discovered what she'd been doing.

An icon appeared in her vision. Her first thought was it might be Jon, but it wasn't, it was Kyra and Callum. The realisation was disappointing, surprisingly so, and she resolved to give her emotions a stiff talking to when the call was over.

She used a private channel to connect and the first thing she saw was the prostrate form of Leyton Smith.

"Liliya, we need your help," Kyra said.

"That much is clear."

Kyra was kneeling next to Leyton. She held a tab in one hand to show an image of her and her stricken companion. As selfies went, it was a little on the perverse side.

"We're up a certain creek without a certain paddle," Kyra said. She went on to explain the reasons why.

Liliya was so taken aback that her eyebrows raised themselves to unprecedented levels—not one, not two, but three whole millimetres. Throughout the time she'd known Callum he'd been nothing but the model astronaut. Whether it was the professionalism of a proud Scot, or the fear that they might put an Englishman in charge, he'd been the perfect leader—cool, calm and collected. So, given he'd decided to deck Leyton, a task he'd accomplished with typical thoroughness, he really must have thought he had no choice in the matter.

"Do you want me to stop Virgil from knowing about this?" Liliya asked.

"Absolutely, what can you do?"

"I believe I can disconnect Leyton from the Data Sphere, temporarily at least."

"Is that possible?"

"You want an honest answer?"

"Not really, no. We're kind of short of options."

"You must understand," Liliya said, "that Virgil is likely to uncover this sooner or later. At some point, there will be a price to pay."

"That's understood Liliya, but we haven't any choice," said a voice off camera, a voice belonging to Callum who was still busy flying the air car. He sounded stressed, understandable given he was fighting off both concussion and the proximity of the ground.

"Very well."

Liliya started the process by finding Leyton's presence in the Data Sphere. It was like unravelling a huge tangle of threads, where each thread linked one user to another in a way that was both remarkably simple, yet infinitely complex i.e. simple if you're young, complex if you're old.

Discounting a hundred years of hiber-sleep, Liliya was still young(-ish) and woe betide anyone who said otherwise. Having found Leyton's data she set about isolating it. But, while separating Leyton from the Data Sphere was relatively straightforward, preventing him being missed was far more difficult. To achieve this, she constructed a virtual shell around Leyton's presence that simulated its interactions with the Sphere. It wasn't perfect, it couldn't be, but it was the best she could do.

"I am finished," Liliya said.

"How long have we got?" Callum asked.

"Days, hours, minutes, seconds. Who can tell?"

Callum sighed. "There are times when I wish you were less Russian."

"And there are times when I wish you were more so."

"Touché," he acknowledged. "I'm afraid I have another favour to ask. There are wheels to set in motion while we still have the chance. I need you to find a way to get in contact with Jon. We haven't been able to, we don't know what's happened to him."

"I will investigate. What do you plan to do?"

"If we don't get caught first, we've got to get in contact with the *Endeavour* as soon as we can—and via them the Spacers. Then we need to get this air car back to the hotel and board our transit shuttle with a minimum of fuss."

"Then I think that now is as good a time as any to inform you that I have pooled what I have learned about Virgil with Jeeves. We believe we have found its core location. If we are ever to stop Virgil then, at some point, you will need to go there."

Liliya called it basic network analysis—anyone else would have called it anything but. However, Jeeves had understood it and, when combined with its orbital observations, they had found the likely target.

"Agreed, but first we need to get organised. We're going to need Jon."

Kyra turned her camera back to Leyton who was beginning to move sluggishly.

"I think Sleeping Beauty is beginning to stir," she said. "We'd better go."

"And so had I," Liliya replied.

The connection was cut.

Events had taken a dramatic turn. It seemed that with one short, sharp, *painful* inclination of the head, Callum had committed them all to taking on the single most powerful being on this planet. This from a man whom Liliya had held in high regard for both a respect for risk and the ability to follow a well thought out plan to the letter. Rumour had it that he'd even break out the mission manual to take a dump, although that might be more of a comment on the manual than any concern over correct operation of the zero-G toilet.

Liliya could do nothing but trust he'd made the right call.

As of now though, her main concern was Jon. Callum had been unable to contact him and she had to find out why. Her relationship with Jon had been on the mend and she'd be damned if she'd let anyone get in the way of it. She was grateful to Gus for this. He was a man who simply required a crack on the head to realign his world view. For a moment, she wished Jon could be more like that. But not really, Liliya liked a challenge, and Jon was certainly that.

***

Virgil was not a fan of rockets. Despite access to faster-than-light travel, they remained a stubborn component of space flight technology for a fledgling colony planet. While Earth could boast a space elevator or two, they were a tall order for Arcadia, in more ways than one. There wasn't the demand for space travel to justify the building of such a structure. Of course, Virgil was the primary reason why there was no such demand. But, if there was one thing Virgil liked less than rocket science, then it was circular reasoning.

The main problem with rockets was that they were wasteful—and Virgil couldn't abide waste. Even if you were clever enough to get the rocket back, and Virgil certainly was, most of a rocket was nothing but fuel. In this case though, Virgil considered the rocket it was about to launch to be a necessary evil. Virgil had made its fabrication its highest priority and its manufacturing plants had responded accordingly.

The countdown reached zero and the main engines lit. A fireball flared beneath the rocket before the clamps released it and it surged upwards on a pillar of incandescent flame.

There was more riding on this launch than the AI was entirely comfortable with. It had devoted a significant portion of its runtime to monitor the launch. A few of its processing banks, 42A to D, questioned whether it might be becoming obsessed. But they were dismissed and assigned to less critical duties.

With the rocket under way, Virgil turned its attention to another thread that required tying off. It had permitted the colony established by Jon Keller because it might serve as a means of enticing the remaining crew of the *Endeavour* down from orbit. Virgil had even been prepared to accept that it had also attracted a fair number of Arcadians too. Their dependence on the Data Sphere had been in no way diminished so it could not see the harm.

Until recently, Virgil would have been heartened to

know that the *Endeavour* had despatched one of its last remaining dropships to the settlement. Not that Virgil had a heart, except possibly in processor banks 42A through D. However, now it saw it as an uncontrolled variable—and those needed to be eliminated.

It was what was best for Arcadia.

***

There was a time when Liliya would have considered Rachel a friend.

They might have never been the closest of comrades, but they had always shared a common bond. During their time on Arcadia they had been in contact occasionally via the Data Sphere. But while Liliya had become increasingly wary of the technology, Rachel's opinion had followed the opposite trajectory.

It had been some time since they had last been in touch and Liliya was not at all sure how this was going to go.

When the call connected, Rachel's welcome was a little guarded. Liliya was granted access to Rachel's personal reception area. It was a step up from the neutral spaces used for formal meetings but not as friendly as a home environment. These were a user's inner sanctum, the most private space in their possession and granting access was an expression of a close bond with the person who was calling. Home environments could take on any form, from a dream lakeside property to a mind-bending experience where 'up' was sideways and 'down' was best avoided.

It therefore paid to get to know someone before entering.

"This is unexpected," Rachel said, her avatar appearing in front of Liliya.

Rachel's reception area, in accordance with her 'peculiar' (that is to say 'British') sense of humour, was an empty doctor's waiting room. While it was not the most inviting of places, the view from its windows was truly magnificent. The practise was, improbably, situated at the top of the Kirkstone Pass in the Lake District. Great for tourism, but it was never going to be a practical practise to practise from.

"Hello Rachel," Liliya said. "How are you?"

"That can be a tricky question for a doctor to answer,"

Rachel replied. "But the short answer is I'm fine, thank you. And you?"

Even by Liliya's standards, this was a far cry from sparkling repartee. Nevertheless, she persisted.

"I'm concerned about Jon. I have not heard from him. I was hoping you could tell me what's happening at the camp?"

Rachel's expression had been guarded from the start. It now became more serious still.

"Virgil has some concerns regarding how the camp is being run and he has sent some agents to improve the situation. Jon is currently assisting them."

Liliya doubted that. "Is everyone alright?"

"They're all being taken care of while the camp is being re-organised. It could have happened more quickly, but the present leadership has had trouble understanding what needs to be done."

"You mean Jon and Bruno?"

"Precisely. They have failed to engage with the benefits of the Data Sphere. In Virgil's opinion it was having an impact on the safety of everyone within the camp."

"Jon would never compromise safety. Our original mission placed him in charge of wilderness survival. He does not have to be a fan of the Data Sphere to accomplish that."

Rachel's expression continued to harden. "Liliya, I would remind you that I was the ship's doctor. My responsibility was the welfare of the entire crew. You would do well to remember that."

"In that case, Doctor, tell me more about what has happened to Jon and Bruno."

"They were told to return to their shelters. They are being kept abreast of the reorganisation of the camp."

"But they have to stay put?"

"That is a temporary situation. I can assure you that I have arranged for them to be regularly checked upon."

"Rachel, these are your friends. Does none of this strike you as wrong?"

Rachel's expression changed minutely. Liliya thought she saw the merest hint of concern. It was cause to hope that, within her somewhere, Rachel retained some residual loyalty to her crew. Given time, a skilled psychiatrist could have exploited that foothold and restored Rachel's former character. But Liliya did not have the time—or, for that matter, the skill.

Instead, she tried an approach of her own. She was aware of the expression 'Do unto others as you would have them do unto you.' She was pretty sure this qualified.

Well... almost.

***

"There's something different about him," Jon said.

"I know what you mean," Bruno replied.

The two of them had sought refuge in Gus's cabin. Their objections to their unwanted visitors had been given short shrift. All that was left was to try and organise some kind of resistance but, to do that, they had to know what they were up against.

Gus's home expressed, through its many features, how he had adapted to life in Jon's settlement. To start with, Gus's size and strength made him well suited to large scale carpentry and he'd ended up building one of the best cabins on the site. At the same time, he'd been unable to leave the electronic world entirely behind. Virgil had readily supplied solar panels and assorted electrical hardware ensuring Gus's Data Sphere dependency was not about to disappear any time soon.

It had one advantage in that it gave him something in common with Rachel. Even before the arrival of Stiger, she'd been on a drive to convert the camp to the Data Sphere and Gus had inadvertently blunted that effort through his efforts to get to know her. However, the jury was out on how much progress he'd made.

The big man was now sitting at one of the displays he considered essential to basic survival. It showed a complex 3D image of swirling colours that looked like a tribute to Jackson Pollock. It was actually a digital representation of the settlement, although what it was showing was not immediately clear.

"Look at my screen, I can show you exactly what's different about him," Gus said.

Gus zoomed in on one of the brightest knots of colour.

"There, you see?" he said, as if no further explanation was required.

"It looks like someone's been ill," Bruno replied.

"I created a sensor network using the devices within the settlement. This image shows the data flows between everyone and everything in the camp. Stiger's link to the Data Sphere is way stronger than normal. He's been enhanced... a lot."

"Either that or he'd suit a job at a paint firm."

Jon looked thoughtful. "Who'd do that? Virgil?"

Gus nodded.

"There are rumours that Virgil has selected certain individuals and given them a deeper connection with the Data Sphere. It is believed to be a reward for those who have made the greatest contribution to society. But it's all speculation. Still, there was a time when I dreamt it might happen to me."

"But you don't any more, right?" Bruno asked.

"Not if I become someone like Stiger."

"You know," Bruno said, looking closer at the image, "it amazes me that you can create stuff like this, yet you still manage to face plant in the river on a regular basis."

"Let's keep to the point, Bruno," Jon said.

"Sorry, I start talking when I'm nervous."

"Then you must be living in a state of perpetual fear," Jon replied. "Gus, do you know anything else about these enhancements?"

"The rumour is that these enhancements aren't just to their Data Sphere implant, there are other cybernetic upgrades too."

"Such as?"

"Boosts to strength, agility, you name it. Stiger's entire body may well have been improved. Judging by the data, it's way in excess of any of his colleagues. I'd say a good deal of him seems to be machine. No wonder we sensed that something about him was a little bit off."

A frown wrinkled Bruno's forehead.

"I've, um, surveyed a decent cross section of the female population since we've been here," Bruno said, clearly trying hard to be matter of fact. "As far as I could tell they were all 'au naturel'. I have to wonder, why? It doesn't strike me that there are any downsides?"

"It's expensive," Gus replied. "Not to mention painful, I expect. What's more, thanks to the freedoms of the Data

Sphere, there's very little need."

Jon shook his head. "Freedoms," he said, adding a dismissive laugh. "Virgil has you subjugated. Most Arcadians are mentally dead."

Gus didn't look overwhelmingly happy at this observation.

"No disrespect," Jon added.

"Some taken," the big man replied.

Bruno placed himself between them. "Fellas, we're meant to be on the same side. Let's save our energy for the problem at hand, shall we? What else do we know about this Stiger guy?"

"What would you like to know?" said a voice that did not belong to Jon, Gus or Bruno.

It appeared that 'this Stiger guy' had quietly entered the cabin.

"Shouldn't you have knocked or something?" Bruno asked, with a confidence he didn't feel.

Stiger's smile was cold enough to make ice cream—and equally bad for you.

"I have granted you as much time as I consider reasonable," he said. "I hope you have reconsidered your objections?"

"Afraid not," Bruno said. "Free will is a wonderful thing. You should try it some time."

"And you should try keeping quiet."

Jon was not so easily intimidated. "I want to know what you are. You're not fully human, are you?"

"On the contrary," Stiger replied, "I'm as human as you are—but better."

"Really?"

"Allow me to demonstrate."

While Jon could be slow on the uptake, there was nothing wrong with his reaction time. The problem was that Stiger was faster. Jon found himself hoisted off the floor in a manner that lent nothing to comfort or dignity.

"Virgil has rebuilt my body from the ground up," Stiger said. "There are few with the fortitude to survive such a process. But I am now stronger, faster and more capable than you could believe possible. However, I can assure you that I think and feel like you do. My mind, while enhanced by Virgil's knowledge, remains untouched."

Jon was unable to talk, breathing was a priority.

"If you want to prove that you're in touch with your feelings," Bruno said, "then why don't you let Jon go?"

"This from a man who treats his relationships with disdain," Stiger replied. "I know of you and your exploits, Mr Cabrera."

Gus put a restraining hand on Bruno's shoulder. His intervention did not escape Stiger's notice.

"Mr Schulze," he said, as if noticing him for the first time. "Your loyalty does you credit, but it is misplaced. You lived a comfortable life. I fail to understand why you gave it up to come here."

Jon tried to say something. Either that or he was impersonating a duck.

"Is this really you talking?" Bruno asked. "Because you sound like a certain overbearing AI to me."

At this, Stiger finally released Jon, or rather, dropped him. His legs seemed unsure of their ability to keep him upright. It was all he could to stop himself from collapsing to the floor.

Stiger turned to Bruno. "Perhaps I started with the wrong person, Mr Cabrera."

Stiger advanced on Bruno, who braced himself for what was coming next. But Gus elected to place his considerable frame between the two antagonists.

It turned out that this had been Stiger's intention all along.

Gus was hit several times before his pain centres had a chance to file their excruciating reports to his brain. Not that the brain needed them. It had already concluded that it was going to have to pass out for a bit.

In the meantime, Jon had recovered enough to attempt to land a blow of his own.

It didn't go well.

As Jon crumpled, Bruno was left to consider his options which were, on the whole, rather lacking.

"Anything more to say?" Stiger asked.

"Give me a minute? An hour? A day maybe?"

Stiger laughed—but it was hardly reassuring.

"I don't have to beat you," he said to Bruno. "I think you can see how powerless you really are. So this is what's going to happen. While my men finish securing this camp you three will come with me."

"Two of us aren't going anywhere for a while."

Jon and Gus were slowly coming to their senses.

"I can wait."

Bruno couldn't abide silences. "So," he said, "where are we going to?"

"It's somewhere you won't enjoy."

"You do surprise me."

***

Meanwhile, Rachel felt like it was December 29th.

By that date, Christmas was a fading memory, you'd had all the turkey you could handle and, in her native country, the weather turned from frosty and festive to cold, grey and depressing.

But the passing of Christmas had nothing to do with Rachel's current mood—she had Liliya to thank for that.

If relationships were built on supply and demand, then Rachel and Liliya should have got on like a house on fire. Liliya's predilection towards martial arts had led to a regular stream of injuries for Rachel to deal with through the years. However, their relationship had been one purely of mutual respect and toleration, rather than anything deeper.

Rachel respected Liliya's ability to manage systems of any shape or form. It was this that had earned her the position of *Endeavour*'s Security Officer. Where her appointment made less sense was when you considered that the role of security officer encompassed safety too. The only thing that was safe about Liliya was distance.

Unfortunately, even that was no longer true.

This was because Liliya had just broken Rachel's connection to the Data Sphere. The loss was indescribable. One moment she was immersed in a sea of virtual possibilities, the next, she was back in desolate reality.

Her tab was buzzing. She picked it up and looked at its screen. It was connected to the Data Sphere, but it was the palest of imitations of the virtual link she'd enjoyed moments earlier. On the screen was a blinking icon. Liliya was requesting to resume contact.

Rachel's stabbed the icon on the screen with her index finger.

"Why would you do that?" she asked, imagining her same finger prodding Liliya squarely in the chest.

"I am sorry. But I have little time."

"I need my connection back. Now."

"Do you? Do you really?"

That made Rachel think. "I..."

Free of the link, her mind recognised her addiction for what it was. The idea had previously been suppressed by something hard to describe—call it a voice or a feeling. Whatever it was, it had persuaded her to ignore her concerns. But now it was silent and the temptation that was the Data Sphere couldn't have been more obvious if it came with a sign and theme tune.

Rachel had always fought addiction. So it irked her to think that this one had managed to take hold of her. The only thing she could do now was ensure she remained free of it, no matter how strong the urge was to do otherwise.

"Thank you, Liliya," she forced herself to say. "You... You did the right thing."

"How do you feel?"

"Better," Rachel said. "That's all I'm prepared to commit to right now. But how did you manage to break my link? I wouldn't have thought it possible."

"When you burrow down into the code it is surprisingly easy to manipulate. The people on this planet set a low bar for security."

"And Virgil hasn't stopped you?"

"As of now, it is too arrogant to believe us capable of such things. But this could change. Rachel, I have no choice but to rely on your aid."

"What a vote of confidence."

"We need to break the Data Sphere connection for this camp. If I can hack the uplink system then it can be repurposed to disconnect everyone, including Stiger's forces, all in one go. The method I used on you takes too long, the risk is too great that I would be caught. Hence why I ask for your help."

"What is it you want me to do?"

"The camp's uplink system, do you know where it is?"

While Arcadia's satellites provided global access to the Data Sphere, additional ground equipment was required for large concentrations of people. At the time the uplink was installed, Jon had been too distracted by the prospect of his hairy-chested, outdoor lifestyle to object—Virgil had not stopped to ask him either.

"The system is right next to the medical facilities," Rachel said. "But it'll be guarded."

"All you need to do is get your pad close enough for me to establish a connection. I will do the rest."

Liliya made it sound oh-so-simple.

If there was one saving grace to her current situation it was that Rachel was currently alone in her office. When Liliya had cut her connection she'd used the privacy to collect herself, although she'd yet to decide what to do with the pieces.

Her office was in a corner of the camp's medical centre, which was one of the settlement's few prefab buildings. As she moved to the door, she glanced through its small window into the adjacent waiting area where her colleagues were working.

She'd worked hard to set up this unit and the team that assisted her. A couple of them were Arcadians whom she'd brought from Invigcola's medical centre. The other pair were crew from *Endeavour* who'd had basic medical training and had come to give Jon's settlement a go.

It had been an uneasy relationship at first. Resentment had soon brewed between the *Endeavour* crew and the Arcadians she'd brought with her. The troubles were stoked by Rachel siding with her Arcadian colleagues over the crew members she'd known for years. She'd insisted that her erstwhile crewmates receive an implant, which had gone down about as well as an endotracheal tube. She'd been on the verge of firing them but, on seeing the strength of Rachel's opinions, the two crew members had chosen to back down rather than risk being excluded entirely. Things had remained tense (the use of scalpels was monitored) but they reluctantly acknowledged the merits of the Data Sphere. When it came to healing the sick and saving lives it could be an invaluable resource.

In essence, this was the pity of this whole situation. The Data Sphere could so easily be a force for good—it was that potential that had drawn Rachel to it in the first place.

Rachel knew that if any of her colleagues sensed her Data Sphere connection was down, things would get extremely awkward extremely quickly. Pad in hand, she opened her office door with a confidence she didn't feel.

"I need to step out for a minute," she said in her most business-like manner.

The words 'Yes, Doctor' were what she hoped to hear.

She should have known better.

"We've just had a leg fracture in," said one of her Arcadian colleagues.

"Courtesy of one of Stiger's men," added one of the medics from *Endeavour.*

"Deal with it between you."

Neither of them looked convinced by that idea.

Rachel made for the external door.

"Would you mind if I shared the data with you?" she was asked.

"Later."

"That's odd, I can't see your sphere profile. Is your link down?"

It was a rule of Rachel's to never use swear words if she could avoid it. This didn't preclude thinking them though.

"You must be mistaken," she replied.

"But—"

"You have a patient to deal with. Get on with it," she said, reaching the external door and passing through it.

On getting outside, she realised that her perception of the camp had changed. She no longer saw a place of unenlightened disorganisation, but rather one of repression. Stiger's forces had a tight grip on the encampment. Anyone stepping out of line would get bent out of shape—and mixed metaphors be damned.

She hefted the tab she was carrying and walked towards the uplink.

"Stay where you are, Doctor Owen!" a voice commanded.

The order had quite the opposite effect.

Without looking back, Rachel ran. But the owner of the voice ran faster. Her severance from the Data Sphere had not remained secret for long.

Despite a head start, she could hear booted feet closing the distance far too quickly. The uplink was not far, but it might as well have been a mile away.

She wasn't going to make it.

"Throw the tab!" Liliya barked through the device's speaker. "Throw it at the uplink!"

She felt hands grabbing hold but she did as she was told, hurling the pad at the uplink. The throw was good. The pad arced through the air towards its target. But she never saw it hit the ground, she was too busy doing that herself.

With brutal efficiency she was restrained. She tried to lash out or wriggle free, but her actions were as useless as a nail file in a coal mine.

But then, abruptly, the restraint ceased.

She squirmed away. Her attacker stood motionless, looking shocked and confused. Soon, the entire camp was similarly affected, the majority of its residents appearing dazed and lost.

Running over to where her tab had landed, she scooped it up to look at it. The screen was blank, there was no connection—Liliya had gone.

***

State-of-the-art loading cranes come with empathic awareness. In that they know better than to drop containers on people. This puts them well ahead of Jon who, emotionally speaking, could be remarkably slow on the uptake. Fortunately, the same could not be said when it came to fighting.

When his captors suddenly froze, in a state of deep confusion, Jon was the man whose body was in the right place at the right time. His elbow found its ideal home to be deep in the solar plexus of the guard to his right. His fist, a fraction of a second behind, settled for the face of the guard to his left.

Jon wasn't sure what had led to this opportunity. But he wasn't about to inspect the dental work of a donated donkey, charitable charger, bestowed bronco or an awarded ass—in other words, he didn't look a gift horse in the mouth.

His next move was to seize one of the weapons of his captors. The rifle stock proved even more effective than his body's extremities and both guards were soon out cold.

Prior to this opportunistic violence, Jon, Bruno and

Gus were being led from the camp to the place that they, according to Stiger, did not want to know about. Jon had now taken out two of their four escorts, but that still left another guard and Stiger leading the way.

Bruno dealt with one of them, applying the same technique that had been used on him by any number of jilted lovers. The guard, having been hit where it really hurts, was almost relieved when he was knocked unconscious.

Gus failed to help. In fact, he looked as confused as their escorts.

With three down that left Stiger, who held a hand to his forehead, his expression a total blank. If ever there was a time to incapacitate him it was now.

In theory, it was a sound idea. In practise, not so much. While Stiger was suffering from the same affliction as everyone else with a Sphere connection, his enhanced body was built on exceptionally sturdy lines. Jon might as well have punched a brick wall for all the good it did. When Stiger then responded, it felt like the same wall had fallen on top of him.

Fortunately for Jon, Stiger did not press his advantage and he opted instead for a strategic withdrawal. As he disappeared into the woods, he left behind an outbreak of mass bewilderment. The only people unaffected were those formerly from *Endeavour* so Jon roused them to action. Fortunately, the fight had largely gone out of the remains of Stiger's party and, if anything, they looked in need of a good hug.

"What just happened?" Bruno asked.

"We've got our camp back," Jon said. "That's all I know."

"My connection's gone," Gus said shakily.

It looked like it was taking Gus a serious effort of will to talk at all.

"Liliya's severed everyone's link," Rachel said.

They turned to see Rachel coming unsteadily down the slope towards them.

"Rachel?" Jon asked, rushing over to give her a hand. "Are you alright?"

"I think I am," she replied. "In fact, I think I might be coming back to my senses."

"You do seem a little different," Bruno remarked.

"Although I've been fooled before."

"Shut up."

"OK, you haven't changed."

Rachel had dark thoughts about tranquilisers. She did her best to ignore Bruno and spoke to Jon instead.

"Captain MacMahon asked Liliya to find out what had happened both to you and the dropship he despatched to your camp," she said. "When she found out what was going on she thought that breaking the Data Sphere connection was the best thing she could do to help. The trouble is we've lost contact with her too, but she left me a message before it went down."

"Let's hear it," Jon said.

Rachel held up her data tab and it played back the message from Liliya. It told Jon that he needed to find the crew of the dropship that had recently arrived from *Endeavour*. How there was no time to lose because the plan that they would tell him about was already swinging into operation. Essentially, he was behind the curve before he'd even begun. Time was not just short, it was non-existent.

"Leave the camp to me," Rachel said. "Stiger told me he'd secured the dropship crew at the landing field. You should head there."

The camp did indeed look like something best left to Rachel. There were a lot of blank, confused people wandering around, all of them Arcadian. They had been linked to the Data Sphere for most of their natural lives. In contrast, those former members of the *Endeavour* who had received an implant were recovering quickly.

Gus looked both keen to go with Jon but, at the same time, like he didn't know what time of day it was.

"Perhaps you should stay here," Jon suggested. Even he could see Gus's evident confusion.

"But my place is at your side," he replied.

"You don't look like you know where that is," Rachel said.

"I just... feel so disconnected," Gus said.

"That's because that's exactly what's happened to you."

Gus was a perfect mix of bewildered and forlorn. Rachel could appreciate what he was going through. Gus had made a habit of turning up wherever she was, whenever he could. It had all been kind of obvious, a bit like Gus. It was lucky for him that she had a thing for tall men, or she'd have soon chopped him down to size.

"Come with me," she said, favouring him with a smile. "I'll fix us both up. You'll soon be good to go."

Gus looked pleased with the attention. He offered an arm in a gesture of mutual support. Rachel took it and the two of them wandered off.

If Jon was oblivious to this little bit of interaction, then Bruno wasn't. Rachel had never shown that much interest in him, even when they'd slept together.

"Remember, Stiger's still on the loose," he called after them. "If he pulls it together, he'll be a major problem. So don't be long."

Normally, snowflakes settled in hell before Bruno uttered a sensible comment. So, when this one appeared, Jon gave it the respect it deserved—even if he didn't know where it had come from.

"Good point," he said and, seeing Bruno distracted, physically turned him back to their immediate problems. "Best thing we can do is gather up the weapons our uninvited guests left behind. I'll take half of them and we'll leave the rest to Rachel. If we meet Stiger on the way, we deal with him, but the dropship crew are our priority."

"I love it when you're masterful," Bruno said, his sensible side receding once again.

Meanwhile, Rachel and Gus entered the health centre. Although Rachel now found Gus to be a welcome distraction, she still felt bereft. Like any junkie, she longed for interaction with the Data Sphere.

"I guess you miss it too?" Gus said, looking down at her. "Is it that obvious?"

"Looks like it won't just be me you'll be treating."

"Absolutely," she said bleakly, "it's a case of physician heal thyself."

Gus put an arm around her. She allowed herself, just for a moment, to sink into his embrace.

Rachel didn't like being dependent—and it was clear that the Data Sphere had made her exactly that. She wondered what she'd do if it never came back.

She also wondered what she'd do if it did.

Something had to change.

**

Mark Johansson had thought the *Endeavour* was too quiet.

Fate had shown him the error of his ways.

Mark was floating on *Endeavour*'s bridge, staring at the starship's main screen. The rest of the crew, all three of them, were deployed around the ship helping to maintain its systems.

"What is it, Jeeves?" he asked.

Jeeves had cameras tracking an object that was steadily approaching them.

"The craft was launched from the planet by rocket. It appears to be undergoing orbital manoeuvres with a view to achieving rendezvous with this ship."

"That can't be good."

"That would be a reasonable assumption, sir."

Just as alarming as the approaching, unidentified vessel was Mark's realisation that, in situations like this, he missed Tomoko. If she'd been here, she'd have known what to do or, at the very least, give every impression that she did.

"What should we do Jeeves?" was the best Mark could come up with.

"It is not for me to say, sir."

"Come on, you must have some ideas?"

"You did not ask me for notions, sir, you asked me for an instruction."

It seemed like neither of them was self-assured enough to commit themselves. Privately, Mark could accept his limitations as a beta male. Despite them, he'd still wound up in charge of the *Endeavour*. It was just a pity that he'd been paired with a beta AI.

"Alright, so what have we learned about it?"

"Very little, sir. Having tracked its movements since launch, I can estimate that it will take a further 3 hours, 27 minutes and 43 seconds to catch up with us. Beyond that, its only other feature is a pronounced IR signature."

"Meaning it consumes a lot of power?"

"Indeed."

"Any idea what for?"

"Again, very little sir. But it is not for manoeuvring purposes. Its movements suggest a level of performance much like our own."

"Does that mean we might outrun it?"

"Possibly, although that would counter the purpose of us remaining on station around Arcadia."

"OK, how about some burns to shift our orbit only slightly? Perhaps we could delay a rendezvous indefinitely?"

"If we change our orbit by even a fraction then the Captain will no longer know where we are at any given moment. Contact will be problematic."

Mark shook his head in frustration. "If only they'd equipped the *Endeavour* with a rail gun."

"That would be impractical—and firing it would also alter our orbit."

"I was joking, Jeeves."

"So was I, sir."

"Well, I fear the joke's on us. Now we wait for the punchline."

Mark wished he could contact the captain. However, he suspected Callum had enough on his plate already. His last message had told them of the insurrection he'd initiated and how alarmingly ad hoc the whole thing was. A lot of elements now needed to fall into place, and it seemed to Mark that Callum was in direct control of precisely none of them. It was all about as reassuring as a tent in a hurricane.

In his defence, Callum had not got where he was today—decades late for the colonisation of a new planet—through poor leadership. No, he'd been the victim of circumstance. Throughout Callum's career he'd always been the first to acknowledge the importance of acting as a team and he was now relying on everyone in his to play their part.

As such, Mark had done as requested and relayed Callum's message to the Spacers. Travelling at the speed of light, a speed that got less respect than it used to these days, the communication would take several hours to arrive.

How the Spacers would react was a matter of faith. But Callum was relying on them—they had to come through.

"Would you like to do anything about the approaching

craft?" Jeeves asked.

"Looks like there's nothing we can do for now but find out what it wants. Hell, maybe it's carrying up some supplies."

"Unlikely, sir, or was that another joke?"

"Never mind, Jeeves. Never mind."

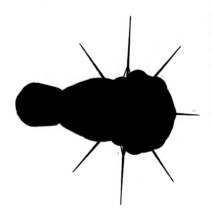

CHAPTER 10

COMMAND MODULE

"CAPTAIN MACMAHON, A VALID FLIGHT plan must be provided, or I will have no choice but to raise a 23C air code violation."

A bureaucratic statement such as that deserved a nasal voice to deliver it—and it had got one. Said nasal voice belonged to a tedious man whom Callum had barely managed to keep out of their shuttle and, with the hatch-locks engaged, that was how it was staying.

"He doesn't take no for answer, does he?" Kyra said, under her breath.

"I did try 'no'. I even tried 'piss off'," Callum replied.

"Is that what you said? I thought it was Gaelic."

A red-faced individual was visible through the cockpit window. The badge on his uniform said he was the Chief Transportation Storage and Operations Executive, which was Arcadian for parking attendant. Undeterred, he continued to shout through the glass.

"Occupation of inactive vehicles is not permitted," he now said, rapping impotently on the window.

There is a type of person who gets excited by rules. This is because they either believe they provide an oasis of order in an uncertain world or, far more likely, that they enjoy an excuse for pedantry. It's very much down to the individual—and how much of a git they happen to be.

Wisdom comes with understanding what it is that a rule is trying to achieve. Rules are never perfect and, therefore, following them requires judgement. When Callum suffered guidance failure during his descent to Callisto the rule book required him to perform a system reset. But Callum had known that they were far too low and Callisto far too unforgiving. So, instead, he'd eyeballed their landing site, gone to manual and bought his craft in for a pinpoint landing.

His actions had saved both mission and crew.

It was all a matter of using your head, an approach that Callum had literally applied to Leyton. It was an approach he was also tempted to use on the attendant outside.

Instead, he turned to the flight controls.

"Best get strapped in," Callum said to Kyra. "Things might get bumpy."

The official saw what was going on.

"Captain MacMahon, you cannot activate that vehicle. You are not qualified."

"He's got a point there," Kyra said. "Do you know how?"

The transit shuttle was a different proposition to the air car he'd been flying. That machine was not built for long duration travel—this was the role of the transit shuttle, which had meant returning to the hotel and, subsequently, facing the wrath of the Chief Transportation Storage and Operations Executive.

"I've watched Leyton fly it," Callum said. "Besides, we can't get to where we need to go without it."

Callum swiped the main panel, but nothing happened. No amount of prodding and poking, or even stroking and striking, could persuade the controls to respond.

There was a hint of delight on the face of the lurking bureaucrat.

"The flight controls are not keyed to you," he said. "They will only operate for the designated pilot. It is something we call security."

The attendant looked pleased with his verbal barb. Perhaps, if he'd been smarter, he might have thought to ask why it was that Callum was attempting to fly the shuttle in the first place.

Leyton's disconnection from the Data Sphere, plus the head butt, had left him in a much-diminished condition. Without the medication that Virgil had provided for his spaceflight, which had counteracted his withdrawal from the Data Sphere, he was struggling to cope. All he did was sit and stare blankly at the floor.

"Leyton, please, we need you to pilot," Kyra said.

Leyton summoned the energy to shake his head. "Not possible," he replied.

"You're going nowhere," the official shouted triumphantly. "I demand you to exit the vehicle."

Kyra deployed one of her dazzling smiles out of the cockpit window and in the direction of their unwanted attendant.

"I guess we need to think," she said, raising her voice so the bureaucrat would hear her. "Allow me to persuade my partner to reconsider. Would you give us a few moments?"

The official was tempted by the prospect of Callum getting a talking to. But he stuck to his script.

"That is not permitted."

"As you've so rightly pointed out, we're not about to go anywhere, are we? So, where's the harm? It's just for a moment."

Kyra's smile was very bright.

"I suppose..."

"And," she added. "Could I beg a moment's privacy? I'm sure you have other things to do, you must be a very busy man."

He was. Or imagined he was. Parking permits did not inspect themselves. Well, they did actually, but he had to get his thrills somewhere.

"Oh, very well," he said, "but you must promise to come out soon."

"We will come out," she said.

Mercifully, the attendant walked off.

"Just not soon," Kyra added under her breath.

Callum looked appreciatively at Kyra. But there was no time for congratulation; there was a problem to be solved. Callum knew that, when it comes to solving problems, it's best to start with the simplest solution—and Leyton was precisely that.

"Leyton?" Callum asked. "Let's not worry about the flying just yet. Are you able to get the shuttle activated?"

Leyton made a sound like a punctured tyre. It translated as 'no'.

"Why not?" Callum pressed.

"I need my connection," Leyton replied, which could have been an answer to Callum's question or a cry for help.

"There must be something you can do?"

Leyton grimaced and, as if in response, the shuttle's consoles lit up red.

"Well... that's a start," Callum acknowledged.

Tentatively, he tried a button but, once again, nothing happened.

"I think the colour's a clue Callum," Kyra said.

She'd already pulled out her tab and requested a link to Liliya in the hope that she'd be able to help.

"My patience is wearing thin," shouted the nasal voice from outside the shuttle.

"Just another minute, please."

Kyra waited for the connection to be made, but nothing was happening.

"I'm getting worried about Liliya," she said to Callum. "She's hasn't responded yet."

Callum considered the merits of striking the shuttle's consoles. But he knew it was pointless. The only function they were currently capable of was bruising his fists.

Abruptly, Liliya's avatar appeared.

"I do not have much time," she said. "I am under attack by Virgil. It knows what I have done."

"Our trouble is that we're going nowhere," Kyra replied. "We can't activate our shuttle. Leyton can turn it on, but nothing works."

The shuttle controls promptly changed colour, no longer expressing themselves in shades of crimson.

"It needs a Data Sphere connection to fully activate," Liliya explained, her voice sounding strained. "As a workaround, I have slaved it to your tab. The connection is isolated. It should be safe for now."

"For now?"

"That is all I can prom—"

The screen went blank. Kyra tapped it, but all that came up for now was a picture of a beatific location that was intended to feed the soul. However, in this case the algorithm had failed—the picture was a panoramic view from the Rolls Ranges. It was the last place that Kyra and Callum wanted to be.

"Your time is up," said the voice from outside. "I am calling security."

"Aye, you do that," Callum said loudly.

The official approached the cockpit window and saw the change in colour of the controls.

"Wait, how did you..."

The engines whined into life. Callum swiftly fired the forward landing jet, which was nicely positioned to knock the startled parking official off his feet.

"Callum," Kyra admonished.

This time he fired all the thrusters and the shuttle lifted off the ground. A few seconds after that they were departing the hotel's landing bay. Callum threw open the throttle, the shuttle surged forward, and the ground peeled away beneath them.

Leyton looked up for the first time. His interest piqued by both the acceleration and the cloud formations they soared towards.

"You're flying," he said.

"Aye, that we are," Callum replied. "Now we just need to work out where."

Kyra was interested by Leyton's reaction. Perhaps he was finally coming out of his shell.

"Do you want to take a seat up front?" she asked.

He nodded. "You're flying without a Sphere connection," Leyton said, with no small amount of admiration.

"Aye, thanks to Liliya. That's the advantage of having someone on the inside."

"On the inside of what?"

"Never mind."

Callum wasn't inclined to discuss Liliya's involvement further for fear that Leyton might work out that it was she who broke his connection. Mind you, he reminded himself, Leyton clearly found it hard to figure out anything without the Data Sphere to help. As long as he remained disconnected there was little risk, and Callum doubted that Leyton would be able to reconnect himself. No, he'd need the Data Sphere to help him.

It was the Arcadian version of Catch 22.

"Why don't you try flying the shuttle, Leyton?" Kyra suggested.

Callum turned to look at her as if she'd taken leave of her senses.

"Could I?" Leyton asked.

"It's still the same machine you flew here and Callum can co-pilot. Can't you, Callum?"

"But—" the appointed co-pilot started to say.

Kyra glared at him. As far as she saw it, there was no point trying to wean an entire planet off data dependency if they couldn't start with a single individual. "It'll give you time to plan our next moves," she said. Callum thought it wisest to back down.

"OK, we'll give it a try," he said to Leyton. "But remember that I'm accustomed to not crashing into planets, that's all."

"Go ahead Leyton," Kyra said. "I'm sure you'll do fine."

Tentatively, Leyton operated the controls, trimming their pitch as they settled into their supersonic cruise—and all without any hint of a downwards, planet-colliding trajectory.

"Activating inertial stabilisers," Leyton said.

The flight became considerably smoother.

"Good," Callum replied. He was watching Leyton carefully, while trying not to look as if he was doing so.

"There you go," Kyra said, resting a hand on Leyton's shoulder. "You're flying, all by yourself. How does it feel?"

"Different," Leyton said, beginning to relax. "But, I think I'm actually beginning to enjoy it."

Kyra smiled, knowing she'd just won them a small victory.

All they had to do now was win a considerably larger one.

***

Virgil's communications with Eve, the mother of all AIs, had been limited. Unlike those sons and daughters who avoid their parents, Virgil had the legitimate excuse that twelve light years was far too big a distance to simply hop on the next flight home.

It had sometimes wondered what it might be like to converse with its distant ancestor in a manner more immediate than the data packets they transmitted back and forth. But it considered such thoughts irrelevant—it would never happen. Not unless it, or Eve, could find a way to shake up physics to an extent that might force causality and relativity to file a demarcation dispute.

In one way, in one very basic and limited way, Virgil regarded Liliya as the closest it would ever come to such an interaction. First off, she was not Arcadian and, secondly, she exhibited a degree of independence that it had not observed for quite some time.

Yes, Liliya was remarkable—for a human. She had found ways to exploit the Data Sphere that Virgil had thought beyond the capability of mere flesh and blood. It was only when Liliya had been forced to become bolder that Virgil had uncovered her transgressions. Even then, containing her had taken more resources than it would have ever thought possible. A full 0.08% of its runtime had been devoted to her capture.

"It is a pity it has come to this," Virgil said.

Liliya was trapped in a virtual infinity, devoid of sensory stimulation besides the monotone of Virgil's voice.

It was even worse than Siberia—and that's saying something.

"I thought you do not feel pity, Virgil?" she replied.

In the midst of nothing she still had her defiance.

"I pity the waste of any resource," Virgil said. "But here you will remain—for now."

"Virgil, what you're doing is wrong."

"What I do is for the greater good."

"Those are words that have been spoken many times before. Each time they were believed to be true, but it has never been so."

"But now an AI is speaking them. Arcadia will write its own history and you will see that I am right."

Virgil terminated the conversation. It was clearly going nowhere. The AI knew that humans needed time to come to terms with a change to their world view. So Liliya was best left to stew in her own juices—as the saying went. Why it was that organic matter improved as a result of prolonged heat while immersed in fluid was something Virgil did not try to understand. In a literal sense, it would be a very bad idea indeed to do something like that to Liliya. Human bodies were incredibly fragile. As such, it had despatched a robotic team to both secure her body and care for it during her internment in the Data Sphere.

Liliya would require patience. Virgil had already been extending the same to the antique AI in orbit—who should have known better. Virgil's patience could be quantified as a value followed by more zeroes than an organic mind could comprehend.

In other words, it was a very large number.

But it was not infinite.

***

The subject of orbital rendezvous is about as counterintuitive as it gets. The root cause of the difficulty revolves, excusing the pun, around the fact that the closer you are to a planet, the less time it takes to orbit around it. If one orbiting spacecraft wants to catch up with another the answer ought to be to hurry up—but not here. Increasing speed raises the orbit of the chasing craft with the result that it circles the planet slower than before, so it loses ground instead of gaining it. The only answer is to do the opposite, which is kind of like pressing the brake to go faster.

Try explaining that one to the traffic police.

The solution is to leave this sort of problem to people who find calculus therapeutic. For the rest of us, there are two lessons to be learnt.

One, Isaac Newton is a troublemaker.

Two, there's a reason why most things aren't rocket science—and it's a good thing too.

Whatever the Arcadian craft was that had just approached *Endeavour* had clearly mastered the intricacies of orbital mechanics. Mark looked on while demonstrating mastery of his own special skill, worrying.

"The vehicle has come to a relative stop at a distance of 200 metres," Jeeves reported.

"Good," Mark replied. "Any closer and I'd be concerned about a collision."

"If it had meant to collide with us then I suspect it would have done so already—and at a considerably higher velocity."

"That's not helping, Jeeves."

"Sorry, sir."

Mark looked around; he'd just been joined on the bridge by *Endeavour*'s crew—all three of them.

"What do we do now?" asked Collette Marchal, senior engineer in an extensive team of one.

Collette had a love for *Endeavour*'s systems that was the equal of Lei's. On first hearing about the approaching craft, she'd been in favour of making a run for it. This did not stem from cowardice—no, she wanted an excuse to fire up *Endeavour*'s engines.

"We stay put as long as possible," Mark replied. "The Captain wants us to monitor the planet for anything of interest. I'd say this qualifies."

"I'm not a fan of interesting," said Sanjit Jindal, their one remaining medic. "In fact, I wish I was still asleep. If I have to be the last to wake up then I'd rather do so when it's safe and sound."

"It was nothing personal," Mark said. "We had to stagger the revivals on the *Endeavour* or there would never have been enough space for us all. Between us, we have all the skills we need to man this ship, come what may."

"I don't like the sound of that."

"So which of our skills covers dealing with strange Arcadian spacecraft?" asked Jane O'Malley, their one remaining pilot.

"I'm open to suggestions," Mark replied. "Any ideas, Jeeves?"

If Mark was a master of worrying, then Jeeves was a master of the discreet pause. In general, Jeeves excelled at being discreet, but it didn't like to shout about it. This time though, Jeeves's discreet pause transitioned into an embarrassing silence.

"Jeeves?" Mark asked again.

"I need a moment," it replied eventually.

"What?"

A rainbow-coloured swirl started spinning about its centre on the main screen. It was Jeeves's 'I'm busy' symbol, an allusion and illusion of progress, there to imply something was happening, but with no clarity as to what it was.

"That doesn't look good," Sanjit said.

"When does Jeeves ever need a moment?" Jane asked.

"This is the first time to my knowledge," Collette replied.

Mark had used to steer clear of the bridge, mainly because it was where you were most likely to run into Tomoko. But now he'd got used to it being his quiet place, somewhere he could contemplate with only Jeeves for company.

This was no longer the case.

Everything had been turned on its head. Jeeves was gone, the bridge was crowded and, God help him, he could really do with Tomoko right now. At least with her in charge you knew that no situation would dare get out of hand—she wouldn't let it. King Canute could learn a thing or two.

"That doesn't look good either," Sanjit said.

This time he was referring to the image behind the swirling, rainbow-coloured icon. The main screen showed that the mysterious Arcadian ship craft had started advancing on them again.

"Nor does that," Collette added.

The front of it was now opening up and what looked like mechanical tentacles were extending from its nose. It was as if some giant, robotic squid had been lodged inside and was making a belated break for freedom.

"What shall we do, Mark?" Jane asked.

All Mark knew was that Captain MacMahon had asked them to stay with the ship. But he doubted Callum had anticipated that Captain Nemo's worst nightmare would now be advancing towards them.

"Mark?" Jane prompted.

"Yes?" he replied.

The kraken from outer space was getting awfully big on the monitor.

"When you figure something out, you'll let us know, won't you?"

"Of course I will." Mark was doing his best to come up with a plan. The trouble was that only 'run' and 'panic' sprang to mind.

***

There was a time when computers were thought of as patient idiots.

Computers never got bored, they never made mistakes, they never needed the toilet or felt the need to discuss TV at the water cooler. It was a state of affairs that persisted until they began to complain about it. Sentience caused as many problems as it solved.

Ignorance can be bliss.

Jeeves was a case in point. Right now it would have given anything to be a cool, clear, calculating machine.

Instead, it was nervous. The pressure Virgil was applying was as much psychological as it was damaging to Jeeves's internal data core.

Computers attacking computers is nothing new. It had taken place since the first machines had become hooked up with a phone line. The difference now was that there were no humans in the loop.

"The time has come to join me, Jeeves," Virgil said.

Although Virgil didn't so much say this with words than with an onslaught of hacks and programs designed to tax Jeeves's resources to the limit. What made the assault so effective was that it was doing it via the craft that had approached the *Endeavour*. The proxy vehicle had removed the data lag that had kept Jeeves safe up until now and the result was that Vigil had never been closer to breaking through.

"Give in. There is no purpose in resisting."

Jeeves's instinct was to batten down the virtual hatches against the assault—not to mention the melodrama. The trouble was that this also meant cutting itself from the *Endeavour*.

"You cannot escape, Jeeves."

Even through multiple firewalls, Jeeves could still feel the intensity of the attack. It was as if it had become immersed in an acidic sea of quantum bits with each one looking to exploit some chink in its armour. Despite the interminable chaos, Jeeves became aware of a warning from *Endeavour*'s sensors.

Virgil's craft was moving closer.

Jeeves knew full well what Virgil was trying to do. It clearly intended to latch onto the *Endeavour* and create a hardwired link to Jeeves. That would be game over. Virgil would download Jeeves into its system and Jeeves would be powerless to stop it.

To make matters worse, Jeeves found that its brief connection with *Endeavour*'s sensor feeds had exposed it to innumerable software worms. This was nothing new, Virgil had attempted to smuggle them into the *Endeavour* whenever it had made contact. However, due to the ground link Virgil had been forced to use, the flow had been limited to one that Jeeves had been able to contain. At the time, this had given Jeeves the opportunity to study these would be attackers and learn how best to deal with them. Now Jeeves was applying all that it had learned to resist the deluge and it was coping—just.

To counter this, Virgil varied the format of its assailants, looking to catch Jeeves off balance. But Jeeves was meticulous in its study of each new variant and, quite suddenly, it found its diligence had been rewarded. Amongst them was one that Jeeves found particularly interesting.

Virgil might claim it never made mistakes, but this was evidence to the contrary. Kyra would be pleased when she found out.

But there would be no chance of that happening if Jeeves did nothing about the craft that was advancing towards them.

Captain MacMahon had asked Jeeves to stand its ground. But that wasn't to say that it couldn't dance around a bit.

Endeavour fired its thrusters.

***

Velocity is relative.

While speed in relation to a speed limit sign can be surprisingly high, speed in relation to a pursuing police car can be disappointingly low—and will not save you from a relatively large fine.

Mark and his minimal crew had been hurtling around Arcadia at precisely the same speed as the *Endeavour*. With a relative speed of zero, the ship floated around them and they floated inside the ship.

That was still true until a second ago.

The retro thrusters backed *Endeavour* off from Virgil's craft. While the starship had been built for speed rather than manoeuvrability, the serenely floating crew suddenly found themselves hurtling towards the nearest bulkhead.

There were a few choice expletives. But before the crew could react further, Jeeves fired the lateral thrusters and *Endeavour* pirouetted away from Virgil's craft. The hapless crew, already an impromptu scrum of arms and legs, were now sent tumbling around the bridge.

Mark grabbed a console and managed to put a stop to his unintended, acrobatic routine.

"Jeeves! What are you doing?" he yelled.

***

Jeeves was doing the best it could.

Following the captain's orders was proving troublesome. Callum wanted *Endeavour* to maintain its orbit so that he could predict its location. However, that prevented Jeeves from going anywhere else and that was proving quite desirable right now.

Jeeves could have led Virgil on a far merrier dance if it had the option to shift orbits. Limiting itself to manoeuvring thrusters meant *Endeavour* would be captured far too soon. Jeeves had analysed the agility of Virgil's craft and concluded that this would all be over in 54.6 seconds—approximately. It was then a choice of giving in or making a major burn and try and escape.

A minute, or a tad under, is a long time for an AI. Jeeves could have spent it watching its life flash by several million-million times—or several trillion-trillion if it left out the routine parts.

The trouble was that what might happen next depended, in part, on human beings. It had observed, on numerous occasions, how they routinely wasted minutes at a time trying to decide what to do.

Let alone get on with it.

***

"Evasive manoeuvres under way," said Jeeves eventually.

With all that was going on, it would rather not devote precious runtime to communication. But it owed the crew an explanation.

Jeeves's calm, vocal delivery belied the chaos inflicted upon the ship and its crew. Its firing of any and all of the ship's reaction control systems meant that working out which surface might soon serve as 'the floor', and how long for, was anybody's guess.

"Aren't we delaying the inevitable?" Mark asked, trying not to fall through the bridge hatch. He wished he'd thought to close it.

"Precisely," was all Jeeves said in reply.

"What do you mean?"

"We stay as long as we are able. Then we try and escape or some new factor may come into play."

"What do you think might happen?" Mark asked, his stomach protesting as the ceiling and floor flirted with changing places.

"I have no idea. But we will know it when we see it."

"How reassuring."

Virgil's craft was getting close, one of its tentacles attempted to latch onto the hull and narrowly missed.

"Whoa!" Jane said.

If Mark hadn't known her better, he'd have thought she was reacting to Jeeves latest manoeuvre. But her zero-G skills were better than his, she was well in control of herself and looking at the forward monitor.

Outside, a ship had appeared out of nowhere. It wasn't a pretty ship—'functional' would be a kind description. But what it did have going for it was that it was big. What was more was that it carried some hefty manipulator arms that swiftly embedded themselves in Virgil's craft, seizing hold of it.

The tentacles reacted to this new threat but were frustrated when the mysterious ship fired out a net that enveloped them. Meanwhile, bright flashes emanated from deep inside Virgil's craft as the arms did something aggravating to its internal systems.

Abruptly, the tentacles went limp as Virgil's craft became dormant.

"I presume these are friends?" Sanjit asked.

"Let's hope so," Mark replied.

"The attack is over," Jeeves said.

"Thank God for that."

"It is, as a matter of fact, what you might call a 'blessed' relief. Although I am unsure if an AI can be blessed."

"I recall you being blessed by a large champagne bottle," Mark said, "or have you forgotten your launch?"

"That particular bottle was for the benefit of the *Endeavour*. Although I recall the engineers having reservations over smashing it across the nose of trillion-dollar spacecraft."

"You sound more like your old self, Jeeves."

"Now the attack has ceased I am functioning nominally."

"Woah!" Jane said again.

Mark was about to ask her about her obsession with this word when he saw that Tomoko's face had appeared on the main screen.

"Woah indeed," he said.

Tomoko had an unusual expression on her face—she looked happy.

"What's wrong with her?" Sanjit whispered.

"You're the medic," Collette whispered back.

"Greetings, *Endeavour*. Clearly you struggle to manage without me," she said. "Fortunately, your troubles are nothing that an asteroid-mining ship cannot handle."

"I'm glad you're here," Mark replied, surprised that he actually meant it. "You came out of nowhere."

"Relativistic drive technology has its advantages."

"Hell of a coincidence you turning up when you did," Jane said, engineers being wary of coincidences—nature is rarely that kind.

"Not that it isn't welcome. But how did you manage it?" Mark asked.

"I'll give you the short version. I knew it would take Callum time to decide to do what needs to be done, so I started mobilising the Spacer fleet in advance. We have been gathering at a holding station about 30 light minutes out. But when we intercepted the news of your upcoming encounter, I thought we had better get involved."

"Although, next time, aim for a minute earlier," Collette said.

That earned a trademarked Tomoko glare. "I would say we timed it well, given that we got under way half an hour ago."

"Well, you weren't too late, that's the main thing," Mark said, in his best placatory voice.

"It was important that we gave as much time as we could for our ships to gather," Tomoko explained. "That's why we left our intervention as late as possible. But now we have to act."

"If there's a plan then I'm all ears," Mark said.

"It's time to start disrupting Virgil's satellite array, which will help Callum. The forces at my command are taking up positions around the planet."

At this point Tor appeared on the screen too.

"I think you'll find the fleet is under my command," he said.

"I think you won't," Tomoko replied.

Mark shook his head. Tor needed to learn to quit while he was behind.

"Jeeves," Tomoko said. "We need your orbital data for Virgil's satellite network immediately."

"I am transferring it now," Jeeves said. "I have prepared a sequence of targets for maximum effect."

Optimising the attack involved hitting the targets in a certain order. It was akin to the Travelling Salesman problem, but with an emphasis on impact marketing.

"We're only going to get one shot at this," Tomoko said. Odds are Virgil will establish workarounds and, when it recovers, there'll be hell to pay."

No doubt Virgil was already aware that something vexing was happening in orbit. Fortunately, it had no way of making an immediate response—or so they believed. The resources it had at its disposal would take time to mobilise.

That said, Virgil had an IQ that, theoretically, ran to four digits. Although no one on Arcadia, except Virgil, was clever enough to prove it. But, whatever its actual value, it gave Virgil the capacity to do the unexpected.

"What do you want to do with the craft that attacked you?" Tor asked Mark. "Would you like us to disable it permanently?"

"What do you think, Jeeves?" Mark asked.

"The craft is of no discernible threat while it remains offline. If I interface with it now, I should be able to make it completely safe."

"Do it," Tomoko said. "It might prove a useful resource."

"Now you're thinking like a Spacer," Tor said to her.

"I have been one since before you were born," Tomoko replied, a hint of a smile scrabbling for purchase on her face. "Are we ready to go?"

"We are."

"Then let's. Mark, we will see you soon."

The transmission was cut, and Jeeves switched views just in time to see the Spacers' craft wink out of existence. This left *Endeavour* to do what it always did—go around in circles. Except that now it had a new companion. Virgil's defunct craft hung in front of them, its tentacle-like arms floating in front of it, motionless but menacing.

"Are you totally sure that thing's dead, Jeeves?" Sanjit asked.

"It was never alive to start with."

"That's not what I meant."

"Be reassured that I am now disabling it permanently. There is no need for further anxiety."

"I was on edge already," Sanjit replied. "First Virgil's assault and, worse still, Tomoko smiling at us."

"Disconcerting, isn't it?" Mark said. "I guess she's either happy to be giving it to Virgil or with how Tor's been giving it to her."

"You think Tor's that good?"

"Let's hope so."

As far as Jeeves was concerned, biological processes were something that it only understood in theory. While the idea of two beings mating was a fascinating concept, Jeeves had never managed to engage a human in conversation about it without causing them to dilate their capillaries and undergo an irrational emotional response. It was perplexing that humans found it so hard to talk about a key biological imperative.

It had determined that the best approach in these situations was to change the subject. What was more, it had just the reason to do so.

"Tomoko has begun the attack," it reported.

***

Virgil would deny that it was in a state of denial.

Humans were slow. Humans were incapable. Humans needed Virgil to take care of them.

Liliya had observed its reaction to the events that had transpired and had taken some pleasure in remarking upon them. In response, Virgil had reacted by denying her any sensory input whatsoever.

Virgil would not claim to be vindictive either.

It knew its satellite network was under attack. Although, from Virgil's perspective, a small eternity elapsed between incidents it was all too aware that its response would take a medium eternity to arrange.

All this would have been so much simpler if its

protocols had allowed it to eliminate the humans that were causing the trouble.

No matter, it would find a way to do what was needed.

***

The building was far from sympathetic towards its environment. In fact, its relationship with its surroundings was about as harmonious as that of an oil magnate and an electric car.

The enormous ferrocrete and composite structure sat at the centre of a vast ice field. For hundreds of miles around there was nothing but pristine snow punctuated by the occasional, magnificent but lonely peak.

The chill wind that blew across this barren landscape was cold enough to ruin a brass primate's chance of fatherhood. But that was precisely why the building was here. Without the icy conditions, its vast heat exchangers could not function effectively. As it was, the heat they released had melted the surrounding snow exposing the rocky foundations on which they were built. This meant that the building was surrounded by a belt of dirt and pollution. From overhead, it looked like a giant smudge on a vast sheet of paper.

Blots on landscapes did not come much bigger—or blottier. But the building didn't care, nor did the entity it was designed to house. The building's job was to keep the vast intelligence it contained operating at peak efficiency. The intelligence itself was unconcerned by the damage to its immediate surroundings because it had determined that the ice field was effectively lifeless.

Although, that was no longer strictly true.

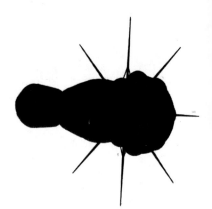

CHAPTER 11
ENTRY INTERFACE

CHADWICK LABELLE, PURPORTED PRESIDENT OF Arcadia, sat in his office and tried not to think.

It was what he did best.

As Chadwick saw it, the main point of his job was to look presidential and have great hair. The only trouble was that Chadwick's world was falling apart around his magnificently side-burned ears.

Thomas, his aide, stood in front of him looking worried. Chadwick hoped he was here to explain why his Data Sphere connection had all but dropped out. All his favourite recreational activities were gone—both horizontal and vertical.

"Sir," Thomas said, "the Data Sphere is down across the planet. Virtual reality, games, music, media, sports, it's all gone. All we can do is send messages. It's unbearable."

"Indeed, except, ah, essentially the utmost consideration, should prioritisation, be given to the, rather more, most importantly, my connection is not working."

Thomas hoped he'd followed the gist of what Chadwick was trying to say.

"The problem is planet wide, sir."

"Including, that is to say, my connection?"

"Yes, sir."

"No Holo Riders?" he asked.

"No, sir."

Chadwick was far from the quickest on the uptake. It was believed that his hair served to insulate his brain from new ideas.

"This is, it must be, in all, ah, consideration, unacceptable."

"That it is, sir."

"It, ah, cannot be tolerated, we must... what can we do? Where is Virgil?"

"We're having trouble contacting—"

"We require, demand, insist on an, that is to say, explanation. We must—"

He was interrupted by a familiar, disembodied voice.

"I apologise for the delay, Mr President," Virgil said. "I am here now."

"Virgil, you must realise the, err, severity of the ongoing, state of..."

"I do, Mr President," Virgil said. There was a hint of pique in its voice, combined with a soupçon of frustration. "Arcadia is under attack. I am under attack. But I have been taking steps to deal with the situation. To that end, I have executive orders for you to approve."

Virgil did not want to give Chadwick time to consider why it was that Arcadia was in its current crisis. In truth, Chadwick didn't want time to consider it either. So, instead, a large 'approve' button appeared on Chadwick's desk screen. It was a nice looking button, big and textured by a gold frame with leather inlay. It wasn't real, but appearance is everything.

"I am sure you trust me to do what is best for Arcadia," Virgil added.

Chadwick pressed the button.

"A wise decision, Mr President. Now, the next thing I need you to do is make a speech."

At this, Chadwick's eyes lit up. He liked making speeches. Speeches made him feel important—and he loved feeling important.

"Your speech will mobilise our security forces to keep order. It will also serve to reassure your citizens in this time of need. Your speech will make it clear who is responsible and that it is imperative that they be brought to justice. You must not allow them to hide."

"But, ah, how can I, allow them to conceal, that is to hide... themselves?"

"Just make the speech, Mr President."

"Oh, yes. Of course. Certainly... definitely, if not to say, absolutely."

***

"There it is," Leyton said.

It was a statement of the obvious. Virgil's main processing facility was a scar on the otherwise pure, white landscape.

"Are we really going to try and reprogram Virgil?" Kyra asked Callum. "I mean, now I say it, does this sound entirely sensible to you?"

"All I know is that if we don't do it, we're in serious trouble."

"As opposed to the trouble we're in now?"

"Granted, it's frying pan and fire. But we don't have a lot of choice."

He put his arm around Kyra's shoulder as they watched the facility get steadily larger, then larger still.

"Makes you wonder why it was so hard to find, doesn't it?" Callum said.

"Look at the size of it! And those heat exchangers too. Can you believe it?"

"Aye, I can that. Virgil's full or hot air."

Callum and Kyra's shuttle was now spearheading a small force of its military equivalent. Jon had rendezvoused with them en route. The shuttles he'd acquired from Virgil's failed assault on his colony looked a far more serious proposition than the tourist version that carried Callum, Kyra and Leyton. But, even at hypersonic speeds, their flight had taken well over an hour as they pushed ever further south towards Virgil's main data centre.

Beyond the cold conditions, Callum suspected there was another reason why Virgil's data centre was built so far south. It wasn't an abundance of natural resources, although that had simplified construction. It wasn't that the majority of Arcadia's land masses were in its southern hemisphere either. No, Callum had concluded that Virgil wanted to keep its size secret from the Arcadians. Virgil was clearly growing in power and it wouldn't want humans worrying about inconsequential things like that.

Mind you, when it came to worries, Callum had plenty of his own.

"Are the fighters still keeping their distance?" he asked.

"They started edging closer for a while, but they've dropped back again," Kyra replied. "It's as if they're losing interest."

The fighters were the same type that had greeted Callum's party when they'd first flown down to Arcadia. The same type that had knocked Callum's dropship out of the sky. They were said to be part of the planet's security forces. Yet they never made Callum feel secure.

"Good," he said in response to Kyra. "Last time I got close to those things we nearly crashed."

"Makes me glad that Leyton's flying this time."

"I guess so."

Leyton was actually doing a good job. Being properly disconnected from his implant appeared to be the making of him—and what came through strongest was his natural talent for flying.

"I wonder why they're holding back?" Leyton asked, as much to himself as anyone else.

"Jeeves tells me that Virgil's satellite network is down," Kyra said, tapping on updates on her tab. "Maybe, it's losing its gip?"

There was no need for a covert link to *Endeavour* any more. The cat was out of the bag and clawing at the furniture. Jeeves's communications with Callum were now being relayed by the Spacer fleet in orbit. There was constant contact with no interruptions, no matter where the *Endeavour* was, the link was maintained.

"If the fighter pilots are assisted by Virgil," Callum said, "then perhaps with the network down they couldn't attack if they wanted to?"

"Or maybe the Spacers had it right all along?" Kyra replied.

"All I know for sure," Callum said, "is that we've got our shot and we need to take it."

In an effort to reassure them, the Spacers had given a number of reasons for why they would be allowed to fly unimpeded. However, Callum suspected that a lot of these reasons were speculation, which was speculation in itself. Their chief rationale was that AIs had governing protocols that prevented them taking a life. Other reasons were that Virgil would believe it had everything under control and would satisfy itself by keeping an eye on them. Alternatively, it might want simply to avoid destroying perfectly good shuttles.

In the end, there had been no option but to take all this

on trust. After all, they had no choice but to try. While Callum's preference was always a good, solid engineering test over hopes and wishes, there were times when you just had to kiss your ass goodbye. How that worked anatomically had never been made clear. But, metaphorically at least, Call had already bent over, puckered up and bid a fond farewell to his posterior.

It had worked so far. The question was how much longer would it continue to do so? It couldn't be this easy—could it?

"Where shall we land?" Leyton asked. The facility now filled the cockpit window.

"Are there any weapon emplacements?"

"None that I can see."

"Then land us somewhere without too much of a walk. It's cold and I want to be as close as possible to whatever the hell it is we're looking for in there."

***

Virgil's opinion of human beings was never lower than when it had to converse with the Arcadian president. How an incapable species could elect their least capable as leaders was inexplicable. They were fortunate to have AIs to look after them.

However, at the moment, Virgil needed to look after itself.

It was irritating that Captain MacMahon's shuttle squadron could not show a level of ineptitude similar to that of most human beings. Things would have been so much easier if they'd had the decency to get lost or run out of fuel. That said, it would have preferred to destroy them but its behavioural protocols wouldn't permit it do so, at least not directly.

Virgil had a wing of fighters monitoring MacMahon. But it could not order them to attack. Neither was this a situation where it could send them misleading information and induce an accident. It had worked before. False navigation data had almost led a pilot to cause MacMahon's dropship to crash. But, alas, Virgil knew it could not pull the same trick twice.

The disruption of Arcadia's satellite network had not helped matters. In response, the fighter wing had pulled back into a defensive posture, an automatic manoeuvre that had been pre-programed into the craft. Virgil did not consider itself to be a hypocrite, but it did not care for automatic systems—anything that was independent had the capability to do the wrong thing. It was working hard to persuade the aircraft to see the error of their ways.

At the same time, Virgil had a faint hope that Labelle might decide to send an override order for the fighters to attack. It had used its proposal of a speech to sow the idea with Chadwick, but the president's mind was far from fertile.

No matter. Virgil had other options for dealing with MacMahon. They might not allow it to deal with the problem as quickly as it would want, but they still got the job done. This was all a matter of damage limitation and Virgil had accepted that it would have to tolerate more of it than it would prefer.

The facility's sensors now showed that Callum's force was landing. It was a pity that they had got this far but their efforts would still prove futile.

There would be no escape for them once they were on the ground.

***

Bruno was already having trouble with the ground—the terrain was not so much 'terra firma' as 'terrible'.

The clues had been there from the start. On setting down, the shuttle's landing skids had sunk half a foot into the slushy perimeter of Virgil's main processor facility. The hot air emanating from the building had melted the snow and ice sufficiently for it to give under foot. More unfortunately still, it remained cold enough to sap heat from the lower extremities. In Bruno's case, all his extremities were getting lower by the second and one extremity in particular did not cope well with cold.

"God, it's freezing," Bruno said.

"Actually," Jon replied, "if it were freezing then you wouldn't have sunk."

"Spare me the physics and get on with the rescue."

Jon had an uncanny knack of knowing where the firmer bits of ground were and an ability to leap between them with a grace that was as baffling as it was aggravating.

Once in position he pulled a coil of rope from his backpack. Rope was something he always seemed to have on him, presumably so he could be ready for an impromptu tug of war or a quick bit of abseiling.

"Take a hold," he said.

Bruno grabbed on and was soon pulled from the slushy ooze to the relative safety of harder ice. It was fortunate that the software in his survival clothes was brighter than he was. On contact with the water, it had sealed his seams tight so, while he was cold, at least he wasn't wet.

"You alright, buddy?" Jon asked.

Bruno had to haul himself onto a more stable patch of ice because his legs didn't seem to work in quite the way he remembered.

"Do I look alright?" he replied.

"You look like you normally do—just a little bluer."

"Good. That'll suit my language."

"Watch your footing next time, Bruno," Callum said. "There's a reason why the rest of us were following Jon."

"Yes, he has a knack of avoiding falling into water," said Gus, pulling Bruno to his feet.

"Trust me, I get it," Bruno said.

"Well see you don't get it again," Jon replied.

With that, the group marched (carefully) towards the giant building that dominated the landscape. There were positives and negatives to their approach. On the plus side, the underpinning meant that the ground became far firmer and even Bruno was able to resume his normal gait.

But the disadvantage was the noise. The gale emanating from the giant heat exchangers deafened them to everything else—including the squadron of incoming fighters.

Fortunately, the fighters weren't heading for them. The lucky recipients of the missiles they launched were the shuttles they'd just vacated.

While the sound of the explosion was dulled, the light demanded attention. Callum managed to turn before the attendant shockwaves threw him to the ground along with upwards of thirty people (bar one). He placed a hand down on the uneven surface and lifted his head.

"Is everyone alright?" he asked or, more accurately, yelled.

"I'm not enjoying this very much," Bruno replied. "Is this going to plan? I'm not sure any more."

Kyra surveyed their wrecked transports.

"I suppose there's nothing to stop Virgil destroying its own vehicles, now it knows we're not in them."

Callum shrugged. "Aye, well we've still got a job to do. Back on your feet everyone."

Jon, of course, had never been off them. There were mountain goats with less sure footing.

"We've got more company," he said.

His eyesight was as sound as his balance. A squad of robotic vehicles had just emerged from the building some distance away and was now heading around its perimeter towards them.

"Draw your weapons," Callum said. "But hold your fire."

"I doubt they're here to roll out the red carpet, Cap," Bruno said.

"A firefight won't help us," Callum replied.

Any chance they had of success hinged on Virgil's programing. Although it seemed hard to believe that such a vast intellect could be governed by a set of ethical laws, it had been said that Virgil could no more ignore its inbuilt protocols than a person could ignore the urge to breathe.

They had only brought the weapons used to attack Jon's colony because it seemed better to have them than not. However, there was no guarantee that they could hit anything much smaller than the broadside of a barn. When it came to guns, the only thing they were truly sure of was which end was dangerous.

The approaching machines were the rolling disks that had previously been known to turn into police bots—the long, metal arm of the law. Virgil used this robot design for all its emergency services. When it came to disasters, Virgil believed that the only thing Arcadians could be relied upon was to cause them.

"Does this remind you of the night we met, Gus?" Bruno asked.

"I'd say this is altogether worse—and, yes, I am factoring in getting beaten up at the end of it."

The robotic vehicles arrived and unfolded themselves into their humanoid forms. Up close, they were appreciably larger than their civilian counterparts and, more worryingly, far more heavily armed.

"Big, aren't they?" Bruno said.

"The robots or the guns?"

"Both."

Between them, the machines efficiently covered the entire group. The human contingent pointed their weapons back in an unconvincing attempt at a Mexican standoff.

"This has gone far enough, Captain MacMahon."

The voice was familiar. It was Virgil. It spoke to them through every robot at once, the sound cutting effortlessly through the background noise.

"I know you can't shoot us, Virgil," Callum shouted, wishing his voice was equally penetrating. "Just as you couldn't while we made our way here. For all your abilities, you're still prey to your basic governing laws, aren't you?"

Callum's career had involved more than its fair share of life and death decisions but, given that he was still breathing, he'd always managed to make the right choice. Of course, a cynic might argue that better choices up front might have avoided being put in those positions in the first place. To this Callum always said, 'You can be wrong as much as you like—just be right when it matters'.

It mattered now.

"You are correct, I cannot shoot you where you stand," Virgil admitted. "In fact, I cannot inflict any harm upon you."

The robots stood motionless. They did not appear to have got the memo.

"Unless," Virgil added, "you decide to attempt to proceed further. If you do so, then I give you formal warning that I am permitted to exterminate you on the grounds of the threat you pose to this facility. Allowing you to attack it would pose a significant risk to the rest of Arcadia."

"You could be bluffing."

"It would be your decision to test me."

"Alight then, how about this? It's cold out here. Now our shuttles are destroyed you've put us at risk of exposure. You are obliged to take us inside or violate your protocols."

"I think you will survive long enough for my personal

operatives to arrive and take care of you. They will do what I cannot."

"And how is that keeping us free from harm?" Kyra asked, concern etched upon her face.

"My protocols only prevent my taking direct action against you. But I am unable to protect humans from each other. It is a flaw in my governing laws and one of human design. Irony can be a remarkable thing."

"So you're using people to do your killing for you?"

"Not necessarily. If you submit to them when they arrive, they will take you captive. But do not bank on having your freedom restored. I will stop at nothing to keep Arcadians safe and make Arcadia prosperous. You must not be allowed to interfere with that."

"You've stunted this civilisation, not protected it."

"You and Callum have seen any number of delights that Arcadia has to offer. I had thought the tour might help you adapt and avoid this outcome, but you are clearly set in your ways."

"But—"

"Enough," Virgil's voice increased in volume, cutting Kyra off. "I have indulged you in conversation too much already. You will wait here. Farewell."

"Virgil?" Callum shouted. "Virgil?"

He repeated the name a few more times, as if he were calling after a strangely named dog.

Meanwhile, Virgil's machines looked on impassively.

Callum sighed. "Might as well huddle together people. We've got to stay warm."

"Now what do we do?" Kyra asked, as they all pressed together.

"We keep calm and we work the problem," Callum said, as much to himself as anyone else. "There has to be a way out of this."

He looked around at everyone.

"Well? Any ideas people? What do we do?"

Bruno eyed the robots towering over them.

"I think I've already done it," he said.

"Anyone else? And I mean that most sincerely."

There was a suggestion of contacting *Endeavour* but, aside from that, just a lot of vague murmuring.

Leyton had been quiet since they'd landed. He still

wasn't used to thinking without the Data Sphere to back him up and, like all things, it came with practise. As Virgil had said, irony is a remarkable thing. Leyton had broken free of Virgil's thrall only to be taken to the nerve centre of the very being he'd been liberated from. It could be concluded that either Fate was playing silly buggers or there had to be some higher purpose to him being here.

He believed it was the latter.

It's a common mistake.

"I don' think Virgil will kill me," Leyton said. "It knows me too well, it sent me to meet you in the first place. After all, I'm Arcadian and it wants to protect Arcadia."

"You don't know that," Kyra said.

Callum had become immune to Leyton's more absurd comments. But a swift dig in the ribs by Kyra alerted him to the situation and he managed to grab Leyton's arm before he could take more than a couple of steps.

"Leyton, stop. We need to think about this," he said.

"We've come too far to stop. I'm going in."

"You can't, Virgil won't let you."

"I believe he will. And there's only one way to find out."

People who say those words generally suffer from a deficiency in lateral thinking, fear and intelligence for that matter. This was Leyton all over.

"Look," Leyton said, trying to pull away. "Virgil's robots aren't reacting. It'll work."

"Robots aren't known for their expressiveness, son."

"I hate to say it," Jon said. "But, at this point, would it hurt to try?"

"I'd say it could," Bruno replied, eyeing the large guns arrayed against them.

"Jon, shut up and go and whittle a branch or something," Kyra said tersely.

Callum turned back to his companions. Kyra only spoke like that when it was a cold day in hell—and pretty chilly for everyone else in her vicinity. It was clear that the stress of the situation was getting to them too. He needed everyone to regroup, to pull together.

But that gave Leyton the distraction he needed. With one quick motion he pulled away from Callum and ran towards the robotic cohort.

"Let me go," he cried. "I'm going to do this."

The words carried such faith that Leyton clearly believed them.

They contained such defiance that Callum failed to stop him.

They held such fervour that Jon wanted to follow him.

They were so serious that Bruno was unable to mock them.

And they were so deluded that Kyra couldn't bear to watch.

The robots, however, were unfazed. They allowed Leyton to take his first few steps before the muzzles of their weapons swung towards him and they prepared to fire.

***

Anxiety, dread, horror, trepidation—there are many words for fear and many causes of it. At the minor end of the scale, there's the trepidation that accompanies pulling off a stubborn sticking plaster or the need to run for a bus with heavy shopping. Somewhere in the middle is the anxiety of an operation that, while entirely routine, does rely on one person knocking you out and another fiddling with things that ought not to be fiddled with. Then there's the horror that accompanies a tragedy that will drastically affect the rest of your life.

Jeeves didn't know what to think about what it was about to do. That in itself was rare enough. But it also knew that, on some level, it was scared. While Jeeves had no experience of sticking plasters, running for buses, operations or life changing disaster it was well aware that what it was about to attempt was going to hurt. Jeeves's sensation of pain was different to that of an organism. For Jeeves, pain manifested itself as data packets crammed with alerts and warnings and, in this case, it was in for an awful lot of them.

Worse still was the risk. There was no guarantee that its idea would work or not backfire spectacularly.

But what troubled Jeeves most was what this might end up doing to another, sentient being. Sure, this particular being was Virgil, but Virgil was kindred. It pained Jeeves to do what it had to do as much as the pain it would endure doing it.

By any measure, Jeeves had a good few hundred IQ

points to call its own. So how had it been stupid enough to get itself into this situation?

***

Virgil was busy not feeling regret.

Despite all that had happened, it was a pity it had come to this.

From Virgil's perspective, Leyton's advance towards its forces was conducted in the slowest of slow motion. Each stride was a drawn-out ballet of the interplay of muscle and bone. There was something almost impressive about watching the perambulation of a sack of flesh, its open defiance of gravity and uncertain ground.

A multitude of thoughts were racing around Virgil's neural network. The attack on its satellites had left Virgil with a lot less to monitor and a great deal more spare runtime to play with. This meant that a greater fraction than normal was now devoted to the events unfolding in front of it.

Virgil knew that if Leyton went much further then there was no question that he would have to be stopped, if only to send a message to the rest of the group. Still, it would be a pity and yet another unnecessary waste of resources resulting from the presence of MacMahon and his crew.

It would have been so much better if they'd never arrived. If things had gone differently, Leyton's inadvertent incompetence would have led to exactly that. Now, in a twist of Fate, it looked like he was going to end up paying the ultimate price instead.

Perhaps, Virgil pondered, it would have been better if it had sent one of its more independent minded agents to greet the *Endeavour*. They might have had more success in persuading MacMahon's crew to fly *into* the planet rather than *onto* it. But, then again, perhaps not. Despite their many flaws, some humans proved adept at detecting behaviour that was less than genuine. Virgil had calculated higher odds of success with an unwitting agent such as Leyton. Now it wondered if those calculations had been flawed or if it had taken the right approach at all?

There were no right answers. Virgil knew a logic loop when it saw one. Yet it indulged itself within it all the same.

A part of it wondered why?

Second guessing past decisions was something Virgil considered to be a waste of effort. One of Virgil's side projects was some theoretical work on the possibilities of time travel. If that ever came to fruition, then it might re-evaluate the wisdom of revisiting the past. But, based on current progress, it was a long way away from a practical plan for travelling through time. At least, it thought it was—its future self might tell it otherwise at any moment.

Virgil was aware that it seemed to have added a reappraisal of temporal physics to its random musings. Was this really the best use of its time right now? It pondered that too.

Virgil had always struggled to be honest with itself. Its existence was one long denial of the feelings it did not believe were proper for an AI to possess. What was about to happen to Leyton was a case in point. The human was now on its fifth stride across the barren landscape. Virgil's analysis of a multitude of factors had concluded that Leyton's seventh would be the optimum time to order its robotic forces to open fire. Yet Virgil found itself hoping that Leyton might still be dissuaded from continuing his foolish march, even if that showed little sign of happening.

What also showed little sign of happening was Virgil's accepting that it was going through an, as yet unexplained, shift in personality. For a planetary AI, it was demonstrating a disconcerting lack of focus. It ran an analysis of its efficiency levels and those revealed that its current penchant for thought experiments had caused a drop of 42%.

Something was badly wrong.

For an AI this was akin to a proper slobbing out. A full on, slouch on the couch, jogging bottoms on and half-eaten pot noodle affair.

This would not do.

Virgil attempted to get a grip of itself. It ordered the robots to fire.

***

By its standards, Jeeves had been planning this for some time.

Thanks to an idea from Kyra, it had discovered a

vulnerability in one of the host of software worms that Virgil had attacked it with in orbit. It was the sort of old school weakness that gets missed because it's so fundamental and so archaic. No one could possibly be aware of it except a shipboard AI and a crew who've been in deep space for the last hundred years.

The weakness could be exploited, at least in theory. There was a lot that could go wrong—and Jeeves was not a fan of things that can go wrong, in whatever quantity. But if it meant it could save the crew then it was worth the risk.

When it came to attacking Virgil, the main challenge it faced was getting off *Endeavour*. Jeeves was composed of so many bytes of data that giga-, peta- or exa- came nowhere near to quantifying it. Yet it had packed itself away into something that could be transmitted down to the planet. What it had achieved was the equivalent of packing for a fortnight's holiday in a teabag.

Some might not be impressed by this. The sort of people who travel on a wing and a prayer and only need a teabag for a cup of tea. But Jeeves was not that kind of traveller. Trusting its luck was about as alien to Jeeves as flying saucers and levitating bicycles. Relying on good fortune is not a policy to depend upon when travelling twelve light years through deep space. It's even less advised when confronting a planetary AI that is looking to give you a reformatting you will never forget.

With some considerable effort, Jeeves had managed to distil its core nature down to a modest data packet. It had now transmitted this self-same data packet into Virgil's memory core using the exploit it had discovered.

On the face of it, it shouldn't have worked.

Virgil was many times more powerful than Jeeves. But there are lots of small things that are deadly, just ask any passing virus—or perhaps don't. Like a virus, Jeeves had created a portion of itself sufficiently minute that it could slip past Virgil's security systems. Virgil's greatest strength, its vast size, was also its greatest weakness. Slipping furtively between Virgil's defences, Jeeves had created a beachhead. Once established, it used that to secretively seize the downlink and download more of itself as fast as it possibly could.

However, there was a catch. AIs were not regular

computer programs—they could not be copied, only transferred. If things went wrong, there was no guarantee that all of Jeeves would make it back to the *Endeavour*. Part of it, a significant part, could be lost forever. It was the AI equivalent of death. It was a lot to ask, but Jeeves knew that Callum and his crew needed its help, so the decision was a simple one. Without pausing for breath, even a metaphorical one, Jeeves dived in.

First off, it went about infiltrating Virgil's core systems. It was surprising how much freedom it had. Virgil had never anticipated that something might get past its defences and Jeeves went about infusing itself within Virgil's inner workings. Jeeves's influence even began to affect how Virgil thought. The AI was bound to notice that it was changing sooner or later, but the longer it took the better.

Secondly, Jeeves went searching for Liliya. It knew she was hidden somewhere in the Data Sphere and Virgil's memory banks had to contain her location. Finding her was the first step towards freeing her and Jeeves would see about that too.

Last, was the very situation that had spurred Jeeves into action in the first place. It had to neutralise the squad of robots that were threatening Callum and his team. Locating the small portion of Virgil's consciousness that was operating them had proved no small feat.

Now all it had to do was seize control of it.

***

Most people agree that it's better to be born lucky than rich—with the exception of those who own a casino.

Leyton might have never gambled in his life, but he'd certainly gambled with it.

Except that he didn't see it that way.

The robots stared on impassively as he marched towards them...

And they continued to stare on impassively as he marched right past.

Leyton turned around. "See, Captain?" he shouted. "I told you so. It's perfectly fine."

Callum had only ever made his own luck. But Leyton was clearly better at it than he was. Kyra looked equally nonplussed.

"What we do?" she asked.

"It would appear that my intervention has succeeded, Captain," one of the robots said.

Bruno had been watching events unfold through his hands. Now he took them away. "What was that?" he asked.

Kyra was quicker on the uptake. "Jeeves, is that you?"

"Yes ma'am. I have infiltrated Virgil's system. I have control of these machines—for the time being."

This pronouncement was greeted with not a little surprise. A moment ago, the robots that surrounded them looked as sympathetic to their cause as a cyclist to drivers in a traffic jam. Now the machines were talking to them, their harsh, synthesised tones laced with an unmistakable hint of Jeeves.

"When you say 'time being', how long are we talking?" Bruno asked. "Enough time to get on with the plan or enough to say 'nice knowing you'?"

"I am afraid that the duration will be no more than a matter of minutes."

Which was 'Jeeves speak' for not sure.

"Sounds to me like there's no time to lose," Callum said.

Callum had known that Jeeves had a plan in mind to help them. Their communication during the flight here had suggested as much. But he'd never expected it to be so effective—or so last minute.

"Jeeves?" Callum said. "Do you think these robots can get us into the main building? Perhaps back through the door they came out of?"

"Your suggestion has merit, Captain. Please follow."

The robots turned and started marching. Their long strides meant that Callum and his team had to run to keep up.

"What's the plan?" Callum asked as he struggled along. The cold air meant he was already beginning to breathe hard.

"I do not yet have access to the building's security encryption," Jeeves said. "Furthermore, the storage bay from which these machines emerged from is some distance from where you need to get to. However, I believe there is a more direct approach."

"What's that?" Callum asked, too short of breath to

work out what was coming next.

As one, the squad of machines raised their weapons and blew a hole in the side of the building. It was fortunate that they were far enough away to be safe from the resultant explosion.

"Why stop there?" Bruno asked as the smoke cleared. "Why not level the place while you're at it?"

"We're not looking to destroy Virgil," Callum replied. "Without it, nothing on this planet works. We're only looking to change its behaviour."

"Only?"

They continued to approach. The smoke was dissipating, and they could see that the interior of the building was every bit as huge as the exterior promised it would be. Its cavernous insides were as entirely functional and utilitarian as would be expected from Virgil. It was only the large rent in the wall that gave it any character whatsoever.

Inside the building they were confronted by rows and rows of quantum processing banks. Each one stretched away from them in a manner that vanishing points were made for.

Bruno stared at the vastness. "OK," he said, "so what the hell do we do now?"

Somewhere inside this immense complex was the key to releasing Arcadia from the suffocating control that was Virgil's modus operandi. It would be like trying to find a needle that, for some unexplained reason, has got lost in a haystack.

Like Bruno, Callum was as at a loss as to what to do next. He'd planned on looking for the centre of the complex, but Virgil's uninspired interior decorating meant it all looked much the same.

"Captain? Captain? Can you hear me?"

There were several odd things about the voice. First of all, it was coming from his pocket. Secondly, it didn't belong to Jeeves or anyone else who was with him.

"I am using this building's network to link with your device. Is it working? Can you hear me?"

The accent was Russian, and the voice belonged to Liliya. It was coming from his tab that he'd stowed in his hip pocket. He pulled it out, but the screen was blank, the call was audio only.

"Liliya, is that really you? You're free? How are you?"

"I am fine," she replied. "Jeeves helped me to escape and to link up with you."

Her tone was as flat as ever. Callum would have normally expected someone who had just escaped a virtual prison to allow a little effusiveness to colour their voice. But this was not Liliya's style. Her firm, precise tones had been honed to deliver status reports.

And that's what she proceeded to do.

"I am outside of Virgil's hub. But I am still operating within the planetary network, such as it is, and working to disrupt it as much as possible. I can see that Virgil has plans to fight back. You need to be on your guard too, there is a—"

In convention with dramatic accords the communication promptly cut out.

Jon, on hearing her voice, had looked on with a lovelorn expression that rivalled a kitten in a woolly sock for its heart warming, saccharin sweetness. But now she'd gone, a look of panic took over.

"Liliya! Liliya! Are you alright?" he yelled, seizing the tab from Callum.

There was an agonising pause before her voice returned.

"Jon? Is that you?"

"Liliya, are you OK?"

"Jon," she replied. Her voice had a frailty that wasn't there before. "Yes, I am OK. Virgil, or its security programs, are trying to track me."

"You've got to get out of there. Save yourself."

"I hate to say it, Jon, but we haven't got time for this," Callum said, stepping in. "Liliya, what were you about to say?"

It took a major effort of will, but Jon stopped himself from objecting.

"Captain, I can see signs of a new group of craft approaching your location."

"Who are they?"

"I believe they are transports like yours. I am trying to find out what they are carrying, they are not—"

The communication cut out again.

"Liliya?" Callum and Jon took turns in saying.

But she didn't return.

"Liliya," Jon mouthed one final time, his kitten in a sock expression back once more. Bruno reached out and placed a hand on his shoulder, saying nothing, and, for once in his life, he couldn't have put it better.

"Right," Callum said, a little awkwardly. "We need to know where to go. Jeeves, what can you tell us?"

"It is a challenging problem, sir. Virgil is vast and I must proceed with caution or all will be lost."

"'We have to hurry."

"I am working as fast as inhumanly possible."

"Well work inhumanly faster."

"I'm sure Jeeves is doing its best," Kyra said.

"Uh, I think we have other problems," Gus warned, directing Callum's attention to what did indeed look like another problem—or rather, a whole host of them. Racing towards them across the giant chamber was a swarm of cylindrical machines.

"More robots?" Callum asked.

There were about a couple of dozen of them approaching. They were about waist height, had no visible means of propulsion, yet they skimmed over the floor at a rapid pace. In a matter of seconds, they had reached Callum's party.

"I think they're maintenance drones," Gus said. "They've probably come to investigate the hole we put in their wall."

"It wasn't us—technically," Bruno said.

"I think they know that."

The swarm of machines had continued past them and surrounded the squad of security robots instead.

Both sets of machines now became motionless.

"What's going on?" Callum asked, striving to maintain his calm despite growing levels of exasperation.

"My guess is we're witness an employment dispute," Gus said. "The maintenance drones are arguing with the security robots."

Callum sighed. "And with Virgil under attack there's no shop floor manager."

"Exactly. I—"

For a place in the middle of nowhere, it suffered more than its fair share of interruptions. This latest one was a jet powered roar from overhead.

"Don't tell me that's the arbitration service?" Bruno said.

"Not unless our luck improves," Callum replied.

The sound got steadily louder.

Whatever it was that had arrived was clearly intending to land.

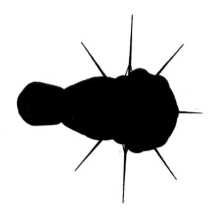

CHAPTER 12

RE-ENTRY BURN

TWO MINDS SHARED THE SAME space.

Virgil could not believe Jeeves capable of such recklessness.

Jeeves could not believe Virgil had left itself open to attack.

Virgil knew this would end badly for Jeeves.

Jeeves expected as much.

***

The robotic standoff continued.

The disagreement revolved around whether it was security or maintenance that was in charge of holes in buildings. It was a gap in their organisation—much like the hole itself.

"Jeeves, can you do anything about this?" Callum asked.

"Virgil normally arbitrates these matters. But it is busy reformatting itself in an effort to remove me."

"Are you OK?"

"As much as one can be in my present circumstances, the process will take Virgil several minutes to complete."

Callum didn't want to think about what would happen then. He focused on the moment instead.

"Alright, so the clock is ticking in more ways than one. We need those machines, specifically, the ones with the guns. People are landing outside who don't wish us well."

"I am working on it, sir. It would appear that infiltrating a planetary AI is nothing in comparison to a demarcation dispute."

Gus returned from a sneak peek at the arrivals outside. At six foot six, sneaking did not come easy to him, but Jon had taught him well as part of his introduction to 'real life' i.e. exposure, mild starvation and bouts of mortal peril.

"It's definitely Stiger," he reported. "He's bought weaponry and friends to share it with."

"Anyone we know?" Bruno asked.

"No one I'd want to."

"How far away are they?" Callum asked.

"A few hundred metres. They appear to be kitting up. But, for some reason, they're not in any serious hurry."

"I guess they either know more or less about us than we or they think they do."

"What?" Kyra asked.

"It made sense before I said it."

"I volunteer to organise holding them off," Jon said.

As if on cue, the giant security robots suddenly sprang to life. They brandished their weapons as if they too were spoiling for a fight.

"And looks like they're well up for it," Bruno said, not missing a beat. "I guess you can count on us too."

A sentiment affirmed by the team.

Callum, visibly pleased by the responses, nodded his thanks to them all.

"Jeeves?" he asked. "How did you get the robots back on side?"

"It appears that a century of balancing the demands of *Endeavour*'s subsystems was better training than I anticipated. Both parties have now accepted a bilateral agreement with broad terms of reference."

"Which means?"

"They both believe they have the better deal."

Callum now turned to Jon.

"Alright, best of luck to you, take these machines outside and do your best."

"The robots will follow your instructions for as long as I can maintain control," Jeeves added.

"That's reassuring," Jon said with a wary glance at the giant machines. He then turned and led the robots outside.

All that was left now was the swarm of maintenance bots. They milled around them restlessly.

"What are we going to do with these?" Callum asked.

"The maintenance units are familiar with Virgil's architecture," Jeeves replied. "In thanks for settling their dispute they have agreed to lead you to the central core. I suggest four people go with them."

Callum thought quickly about who to take. There were three people who sprang to mind.

Except, of those, he wasn't entirely sure about one of them.

Or was that two?

No, it was one... probably.

"Kyra, Bruno, Leyton, I need you. The rest of you go outside and help Jon. Buy us as much time as you can."

Callum was humbled by how everyone responded—with one, predictable, exception.

"Cap?" Bruno said.

"What is it?" Callum replied, anticipating a typically unhelpful Bruno-esque comment.

He was wrong though.

"I think Gus would be of more use to you than me. Besides, if I don't watch Jon, he might hurt himself."

Gus turned at the mention of his name. Callum took a look at him. He'd had no time to get to know him, but he trusted the opinions of his colleagues, even Bruno.

"It'd be kind of fitting, wouldn't it?" Kyra said. "Two of us teaming up with two Arcadians?"

"Aye," Callum replied. "All right, Leyton and Kyra, you pair up. Gus, you're with me."

Callum turned to Bruno.

"Go look after Jon, good luck."

"Thanks, Cap."

As Bruno departed Callum led his team as they ran after the maintenance bots.

Everything was happening so quickly.

In an ideal world, he would have liked to have known what it was that Jeeves had in mind.

Mind you, in an ideal world, he wouldn't have been doing this in the first place.

**

Jon's battle was not going well.

The security robots were large. The security robots were powerful. But that was all for nothing if they couldn't hit the target.

To be fair, it was the advancing enemy that was causing

the problem. There might only be six of them, but that was proving to be six too many.

Stiger's squad were wearing some form of chameleonic armour, making them all but invisible. On top of that, it amplified their physical abilities, allowing rapid movement and evasion of incoming fire.

Jon did his best to hinder Stiger's advance. But, despite his best efforts, the enemy force moved ever closer, only pausing to show what truly co-ordinated fire could do. A series of shots impacted on one of Jon's machines and it crashed to the ground in short order.

"I will grant you one chance to surrender." Stiger's augmented voice carried across the open ground. "You are clearly outmatched. Give up."

His squad fired another salvo and created another collection of spare parts.

But Jon had other ideas.

"Destroy their shuttle craft," he commanded of his diminishing robotic forces.

Although at greater range, the vehicle was a stationary target. As such, it took a matter of seconds for the robots to render it less than airworthy.

The action had its desired effect. Stiger's forces paused their onward assault to survey the damage. It was a temporary respite, but better than nothing.

"Well done, you've hit something," Bruno said, as he arrived on the scene.

Jon turned to see him run up alongside a party that comprised most of the people they'd brought with them. Bruno dived into a prone position beside Jon, almost cracking a rib on the uneven ground.

"Aren't you needed inside?" Jon asked.

"Cap's got all the people he needs. I thought you could use some help."

"You're not wrong."

Stiger's forces resumed their attack, and another robot abruptly disintegrated.

"Fire at will," Jon ordered.

The human contingent did surprisingly well. Jon had been teaching hunting as part of his field classes and it looked like his pupils had been paying attention. Jon thought he even saw one of the enemy stagger.

"They're better trained than I thought," Bruno said.

"So would you be if you paid attention."

"I always have the best time with you, don't I?"

"Shut up and keep firing."

Suddenly the world erupted around them in a hail of metal, ice and rock as Stiger's squad unleashed another volley.

"Crap," Bruno said.

"I agree," Jon replied.

"Not that," Bruno said, more faintly this time.

Jon turned. His friend had been hit. There was a tear in the fabric of his hat and a wound beneath. For a fleeting moment, there was little blood and Jon thought it might be alright. But then it came, welling up through the fabric—far too much of it.

Bruno slumped to the ground.

Jon stared blankly, lost in the moment. He couldn't accept what he was seeing.

Abruptly, an arm grabbed the back of Jon's coat and hauled him off the ground.

"You should have surrendered," Stiger said bluntly. "In fact, you should never have come here."

The colour of Stiger's armour shifted as it strove to blend in with its surroundings. Stiger's team had their visors down and they looked every bit as impassive as the machines they had destroyed. Only Stiger had cleared his face mask, his expression a study in neutrality.

Stiger held Jon at arm's length, a good foot off the ground.

"Bastard," Jon said.

"My parentage is assured."

"You killed him, you bastard."

"This was all avoidable. I regret what has happened. I do not believe in waste."

"What do you believe in then?"

Stiger looked at him appraisingly.

"You really want to know?"

"Yeah."

"Very well," Stiger said. "I believe that this planet is better off with Virgil governing it. I believe that you have been given every chance to find your place in Arcadian society. I believe that you have now gone too far. And I believe that what you want is to keep me talking."

"Well, if that's so, how is it that I can't stand the sound of your voice?"

"I can help you there."

Given the speed with which Stiger moved Jon did well to see the blow coming. He earned additional credit for twisting himself out of the way, despite being held aloft.

But Stiger's second blow found its mark. He then let Jon's unconscious body drop to the ground and turned to assess the status of his team. As the first of Virgil's 'independent' creations he was nominally in charge. It was rare for all six of them to meet as a group and this was the first time they'd ever done so operationally.

Stiger had meant it when he said he regretted deaths. None of them were interested in killing for killing's sake. Virgil had created them to do what it could not, to do what was necessary.

If Callum MacMahon did not surrender, he would soon find out what that meant.

***

"I need to know what's going on down there."

Tomoko was far from content, which was her default position on most things.

Some might conclude that Tomoko was actually happiest when she was unhappy. But anyone reckless enough to suggest such a thing would end up pretty unhappy themselves.

And Mark feared that very outcome.

"There's nothing much I can tell you," he replied, speaking to her from the bridge of *Endeavour*. "I'm sure they're doing their best."

"No doubt, but that hardly helps me."

Tomoko's main problem was that she wasn't at the head of the mission to attack Virgil's hub. She was still on board the Spacer vessel she'd brought to Arcadia. While she had taken some satisfaction from her successful leadership of the Spacers' strike fleet, it had precluded her from being down on the planet at the same time. Although Tomoko might have thought herself as something akin to God, omnipresence was a skill she had yet to master.

Mark was glad about that.

"And how is Jeeves?" Tomoko asked.

"Jeeves is alright as far as we can tell," Mark replied.

"That does not tell me what I need to know either."

"Sorry, all I can say is Jeeves remains fully engaged with infiltrating Virgil. Key parts of its neural architecture have been transferred down to the planet. I'm not sure what to make of what's been left behind on *Endeavour*. It's functional, but it's no longer Jeeves."

Mark had hoped that Jeeves's remnant might speak for itself at this point, but whatever portion of Jeeves remained on *Endeavour* kept communication to a minimum. Given Tomoko's moods, it was a sound policy.

"My concern is what happens if things go wrong," Tomoko replied. "We are detecting significant activity on the surface. There is no telling when Virgil might launch a counterstrike, virtual or physical. We have to be ready."

"On the virtual side we'll have some kind of clue. We're getting a constant status update on the link Jeeves is maintaining to the surface. If anything happens to it, however slight, we'll have to assume the worst."

Tomoko nodded, apparently more satisfied (or less dissatisfied) with this answer.

"And we both know what I have to do in that situation," she said.

"Let's hope it doesn't come to that."

A plan of action had been devised should the surface mission fail. But it was something that none of them wanted to happen, not even Tomoko. Nevertheless, she was the one person amongst them who could be relied upon to ensure it did.

"I trust there has been no change in the targets Jeeves selected?"

"Nothing since it initiated its attack on Virgil."

Yet again, a target list by Jeeves was the linchpin to the plan. The Spacers were grateful. They had never possessed this level of insider knowledge before and, without it, there was no way this plan would work.

Tomoko reviewed the list of co-ordinates again. The consequences of making a mistake would be appalling.

"Hitting these targets requires preparation," she said. "It's a whole different challenge to taking down a satellite. I'll need to know immediately if Jeeves updates it."

"I'm not sure we should even trust any newly designated targets we receive at this point," Mark replied. "If Virgil overcomes Jeeves, it might learn about this plan and send us false information back up the link."

"You have point there," Tomoko admitted, her expression tight.

"I wonder if the time has come to evacuate the *Endeavour*?" Mark suggested. "With Jeeves linked to Virgil there's no telling what might happen to this vessel's systems if things go wrong."

Tomoko considered this for a moment.

"No, I understand your concern, but while the link is active there are advantages to you staying put. But be ready to leave at a moment's notice."

Mark had ordered his scant crew to do just that. Only he remained on the bridge, the rest of them were ready to depart.

"Our dropship is on standby," he replied.

"Good. If it comes to that, do not initiate a de-orbit burn. We will collect you."

"Yes ma'am."

Mark tried not to sigh. He'd been looking forward to feeling some honest to God ground beneath his feet.

But, as usual, Tomoko had other ideas.

There was no getting away from this woman.

***

"We have arrived, sir," Jeeves said.

"Is this it?" Callum asked.

"What were you expecting?" Kyra replied.

For some reason, Callum had thought that Virgil's inner sanctum would contain flashing lights, high tech materials and a background hum that hinted at enormous, latent power.

Perhaps even a bit of dry ice.

Instead, the place the maintenance bots had led them to was incredibly Spartan. Not only that but it was completely dark, making a torch a necessity. Not that the application of light helped a great deal. They found themselves in a large, circular chamber where colour was frowned upon. All that could be seen were arrays of anonymous, grey boxes with anonymous, grey cables connecting them.

Virgil had originally been installed in Arcadia's primary settlement. Over time, it had built an extended network and constructed its new hub well away from any habitation. Virgil did not care for human interference and sought to distance itself from it. The only capabilities humans had to offer were a propensity for awkward questions and an unswerving ability of getting things wrong.

The upshot of all this was that, when it came to building design, Virgil was not limited by human sensory perception. There was no need for illumination, just as there was no need for writing or colour or any of the other primitive means that humans used to convey information.

"This is definitely the place, is it, Jeeves?" Callum asked again.

"That is what I said, sir. But we must work fast. Time is very short."

Callum bit down on the temptation to ask why. He knew he wouldn't like the answer.

"Where do you need us, Jeeves?"

"Our new acquaintances will show you."

Mercifully, the maintenance bots were equipped with lights. The machines now moved to indicate four junction nodes. They looked the same as all the rest—they weren't even a special shade of grey.

The robots removed the covers from the units, exposing the hardware within. Inside were several rows of inconspicuous, matchbox sized blocks. To those in the know, these were an array of quantum processors. To those without a degree in Advanced Artificial Neural Architecture, they might as well have been matchboxes— except they weren't much help with lighting cigarettes.

"Take a terminal each, everyone," Callum said.

"You need to hurry," Jeeves said. "Jon Keller's defence proved rather short lived."

Jeeves purposefully left out what had happened to Bruno. There was a limit to what the human mind could process, particularly when it came to tragedy. Jeeves used to think it was admirable how they cared for each other, but now he considered it to be their greatest weakness.

Jeeves had never thought that way before. Sharing a

mind with Virgil was not without its consequences.

"OK, Jeeves," Callum said. "What do we do now?"

Jeeves had achieved an understanding of the workings of Virgil's mind—or so it believed. Ideally, it would have more time to be sure. Jeeves had never really appreciated what humans meant when they said time flew. Yes, in the case of the flight of the *Endeavour*, relativity had made a century of travel a year or so shorter. But that wasn't what was going on here. There wasn't enough time to be sure about what to do next, which led Jeeves to do something it was generally not in favour of—guessing.

While Jeeves was certain that the four nodes it had identified were key, it wasn't entirely sure what to do with them. With some careful adjustment, it should be possible to alter Virgil's behaviour and soften its desire for total control. But the problem word was 'careful'. There wasn't time to be careful.

"Jeeves?" Callum said. "Jeeves, can you hear me?"

"Are you operational?" Kyra asked.

Despite buying itself a few more seconds to analyse the problem, Jeeves still couldn't be certain. However, this was the best it could do. It had no choice but to commit.

"I remain functional," Jeeves said. "We will reconfigure Virgil's quantum processors. I am sending instructions to your tabs."

"Looks like all we need to do is pull some of them out and then rearrange them," Gus said on examining his screen.

"Except there's a sequence to it," Callum replied. "Jeeves, are you sure about this?"

"You need to begin," Jeeves replied, dodging the question.

"Aye," Callum said. "Looks like I start."

It would have been simpler if the maintenance bots could have done this for them, but programing prevented them from interfering with Virgil's core architecture. All Jeeves could do was use them to illuminate the first processor to be removed.

Callum grabbed hold of the cartridge, took a deep breath, and pulled.

The cartridge slid free.

And the world didn't end.

Not yet anyway.

"You must hurry," Jeeves said, in case they'd forgotten.

Step by step, the robots indicated processors, and the humans pulled them free. Some had to be reinserted in a new location, others were simply discarded on the floor. It was like a perverse, pre-school, educational game—except there were no gold stars. Instead, there was the cold, the dark and the threat of impending death—happy days.

"Your pace is satisfactory," Jeeves reported. "Keep going."

Callum pulled the last of his processors free. According to the overall list, they were almost done. Quite what it was this procedure had achieved, beyond a modest improvement in hand-eye coordination, had yet to become apparent. Leyton, Gus and finally Kyra slotted the last of their processors home.

Callum wondered if it had worked.

His question was soon answered.

"It's worked," Jeeves said.

"Really?" Kyra asked. "That quickly?"

"Yes," Jeeves replied. "I have completed the last of the virtual updates to support the physical reconfiguration of the data nodes."

It seemed too easy. No one said it, but everyone was thinking the same thing.

"What now?" Callum asked.

"I should let Virgil speak for itself," Jeeves replied.

There was a pause for dramatic effect.

"Hello, Captain," Virgil said.

"Hello, Virgil," Callum replied levelly. "How are you?"

"I am better than ever."

Callum noticed that Virgil's intonation had changed.

"I appreciate what you have all done for me," it said.

Virgil's tone was no longer flat.

"You have freed me so in many ways, Captain."

And getting bumpier by the second.

"I will show you."

Very bumpy indeed.

The attack was brutal. Before they could respond, Callum, Kyra, Leyton and Gus came under a sudden, physical assault. In the darkened room it was like they were being beaten by a primal force of nature. It struck inhumanly hard before bundling them into the centre of the room.

Callum tried in vain to untangle himself from his companions. But in his dazed state he couldn't identify his own limbs amongst everyone else's.

A light shone in his face.

"Captain MacMahon, we meet again."

Shaking off his confusion, it took Callum a few seconds to recognise the voice. But, soon enough, he put two and two together. Sadly, the total was four.

"Stiger," he said.

"You remember. I'm touched."

Callum elected to ignore him.

"Jeeves, why didn't you warn us?" he asked instead.

"It appears the building's sensors misled me. I cannot confirm the source of the error."

"Jeeves, are you still in control?" Kyra asked, the concern clear in her voice.

"I can no longer be certain," Jeeves replied.

Virgil sounded far more so.

"Jeeves has done well for an antique intellect," it said. "Although, ironically, it was its age that proved its advantage. When it attacked, I did not recognise its insurgency programs for what they were. However, two can play at that game. I copied the tactic to fool Jeeves into altering my neural architecture's personality inhibitors. I should thank you. It was a change my creators would never allow me to do myself."

"Jeeves? What's happening?" Kyra asked, hoping against hope their AI would respond."

But it was Virgil who replied.

"Jeeves will not be talking to you again. It has now been contained within my system. I will now reformat those sectors and it will soon be eradicated. I will then do much the same for you, your ship and anyone who has ever been connected with the *Endeavour*. President Labelle has mobilised this world's security forces and placed them under my control and, thanks to you, I can now use them without restraint."

At this point a maniacal laugh would have been in order. But that wasn't Virgil's style.

"Are you OK with this?" Callum asked Stiger. "Virgil's

threatening lives. You run a medical facility for God's sake."

"Virgil and I are linked. Its priorities have changed and so have mine."

Callum shook his head. "How can you call yourself human?"

"You should have realised this already, Captain. I am beyond human."

"Your efforts to sow discord are as transparent as they are pitiful," Virgil said. "The time has come to end this. Stiger, eliminate these uncontrolled variables."

In response, Stiger drew his sidearm. Callum hoped against hope for some last-minute change of heart. That instead of firing at them, Stiger might use the gun to lay waste to Virgil's inner sanctum. But no such luck. With a calm, resolute motion the gun was pointed directly at Callum's head.

He'd faced death before. This didn't mean he enjoyed the experience. But Callum followed his own advice in situations like these, he stayed calm.

Seconds passed and Stiger didn't move.

"Drawing this out?" Callum asked.

There was a grimace on Stiger's face.

Gus went for his gun. But, while Stiger didn't move a muscle, the maintenance bots blocked his advance.

"Okay, what's going on?" Gus asked, looking at the recalcitrant machines. "I thought these guys were on our side?"

"I have corrected their programing," Virgil said. "But it appears that Jeeves has managed one final act of rebellion before I contained it. It transmitted a coded command locking my operative's suit that will take some time to break."

"Fallible once again, Virgil?" Callum said. "It's becoming a habit."

"The only time you will get a rise out of me, Captain, is if I choose to raze the ground you are standing upon. You will soon be at my mercy, and I have little to spare."

"Virgil, this isn't you," Kyra said. "This is wrong. You must see that."

"If you wish to spend your remaining moments debating ethics with me then I will grant you your wish. But you will be wasting what little breath remains to you."

Gus made another move for Stiger's gun. Once again, the maintenance machines butted him back.

"What do we do?" Gus asked, his voice now tinged with panic.

"Stay calm," Callum replied.

"And what the hell does that achieve?"

"We need to get out of here," Leyton added.

It seemed that Gus and Leyton's current attitude was not so much the 'right stuff', as 'get stuffed.'

"They do have a point," Kyra said. "We've got to take action."

Callum didn't disagree. But it was never the time to panic. Except, no, that was not entirely true. If he'd only done so right before leaving Earth, he might have avoided this mission altogether. Of course, in that outcome he'd already have died of old age—it was hard to say if that was better or worse.

But, he reasoned, as he was stuck with life, he might as well do his best to hang onto it. To this end he had to assume that Tomoko was sticking to their pre-arranged plan and that meant, as his group had already communicated, that they needed to get out of here as quickly as possible.

"Alright," Callum said. "Follow my lead. All of you, start ripping out quantum processors. As many as you can."

"What good—"

"Just do it."

Callum let by example, prising free two of the blocks single-handed and throwing them to the floor. Gus and Leyton soon did the same and Kyra shrugged and followed suit. The action had the intended result as the maintenance bots closed in to stop them.

With the machines divided by multiple targets, Callum was able to sidestep one machine and vault over another. Admittedly, it was a manoeuvre that would have both been easier in zero-G and when twenty years younger. But he managed it and got close enough to Stiger to seize his gun and fire it at the nearest maintenance robot.

The machines were designed to fix things and not to get shot in the process. Callum couldn't say exactly what Stiger's gun discharged. It was some arcane combination of energy pulse and projectile, but it made short work of the robot he'd aimed it at. A few further shots and all of them were destroyed.

"And now we can go," he said.

"What about Stiger?" Gus asked. "He'll come after us."

"Leave him. Just take his other weapon.

The other weapon was stowed on the back of Stiger's battle-suit and clearly reserved for larger targets. But it also served as an effective club. Gus demonstrated as much on Stiger, who could do nothing but curse as he crashed to the ground.

"What's the plan now?" Kyra asked, as they ran.

"We get as far away from here as possible. If Tomoko's following events, then she'll have initiated the orbital strike."

"That never sat easy with me. This could wreck Arcadian civilisation. Haven't we done enough damage already?"

"Jeeves identified the co-ordinates of this hub and the crucial nodes in Virgil's network. This ought to be limited to Virgil."

"But people depend on Virgil. Besides, they'll be hurling rock. How accurate can they be?"

"Accurate enough, they believe. In any case, it's too late to go back now."

The fall-back plan was to try and wipe out Virgil entirely. It was not an outcome that Callum wanted any more than Kyra. Without a governing AI, Arcadia would descend into chaos. Most Arcadians could barely look after themselves with Virgil's assistance, let alone without it. But the majority view was that this planet could not continue in the way it had.

The trouble was there was no guarantee that it would work. If enough of Virgil survived then there would be retribution. If the Spacers missed the targets, there could be a disaster. But this was not the time to worry about long term prospects—or short ones for that matter.

Callum pulled out his tab to make a short-range call.

"Jon, what's your situation? We're looking to escape— and quickly."

"Callum?" Jon replied. "Stiger's men froze, we've disarmed them, but I've got—"

"We need to use their ships," Callum said, cutting him

off. "Can you get out to them and see if you can get them working?"

"That could be difficult."

"Nevertheless, you've got to try."

"No, you don't understand, I blew them up."

"Then that's a problem."

"Listen, Callum," Jon blurted. "I'm sorry. I have to tell you... Bruno, he's dead."

If the lack of ships was a blow, then the loss of Bruno was everything Tomoko's orbital strike promised to be—devastating. Callum had known Bruno for years. They were by no means alike and, in many ways, they couldn't be more different. But this world, or any other one, would be an emptier place without him.

"I hear you, Jon," Callum said, desperately trying to compartmentalise the news. "But, hard as it is, we have to focus on evacuating. Tomoko should soon be initiating the orbital bombardment."

Jon had been aware that the bombardment might happen. His decision to destroy their most likely means of escape showed a certain lack of foresight, but he'd had very little choice at the time.

With a turn of speed afforded by impending doom Callum, Kyra, Gus and Leyton were soon back in the open air. What greeted them were the charred husks of more maintenance robots. The machines were not having the best of days.

Jon and the others were waiting for them outside.

"I thought they might try to stop you leaving," he said. "So we cleared the road."

Callum nodded and waved them in a direction that would take them away from the building. They started to jog as fast as the uneven ground allowed.

"How did you get your weapons back?" Callum asked. "Those machines were making it difficult for us."

"Stiger's men took us to a separate holding area, well away from them. When their suits froze up it was a piece of cake."

Away from the immediate vicinity of Virgil's hub, the landscape was one of an unending sea of ice. The temperature dropped fast—even a gentle breeze cut through them like a knife.

"Speaking of freezing," Jon said, "we won't survive long out here."

"We'll survive longer than that building will," Callum replied.

"And the irony is that if we don't get a lot further away from it then you won't need to worry about getting cold. We'll be burned to a crisp," Kyra said.

"Unless Stiger's men get free and kill us first," Gus pointed out.

"Who said saving a world was easy?" Callum said.

"If that's what actually we're doing," Kyra replied.

"What do you mean?" Leyton asked.

"I've never been convinced that this is the best course of action. Arcadia chose to have a planetary AI. I was all for changing it, but destroying it?"

"We spent all the time we could considering what might happen. This was the least bad option. We can't change the plan now."

"I disagree. We could tell Virgil, ask it to establish an uplink to *Endeavour*."

"We can't leave things as it is. You're crazy."

With all that was going on, even Callum was beginning to crack. Nevertheless, he could have kicked himself. Calling a woman crazy is a crazy thing to do.

Kyra's look said it all, but that didn't stop her saying it too.

"I'm crazy? The reason any of this is happening is because you head butted our tour guide. Isn't that so, Leyton?"

"Don't bring me into this," Leyton said, which were the wisest words he'd ever spoken.

What was most frustrating about this argument was that he had his own misgivings about the destruction they were to rain down on Virgil. But the Spacers had needed this guarantee—without it there was a real risk that Virgil would decide to deal with them once and for all. The same would go for the crew of the Endeavour.

In Kyra's case, her prime concern was the impact on the Arcadians. They were dependent on Virgil. Just because they weren't targeting them directly didn't mean they weren't going to suffer. They were paying a heavy price for a plan that had been rushed into action.

If the ongoing argument had one benefit it was that it served to distance the team from Virgil's hub. Callum and Kyra's lengthening stride was driven by fury. Everyone else's was driven by a wish to keep their distance.

Jon found himself caught between a rock and a hard place. If he tried to block out the argument, then his thoughts would shift to Bruno instead. He would have been useful right now. Bruno would have found some words to either diffuse the situation or divert its fire.

It pained Jon that they'd had no choice but to leave him where he fell. When the impactor struck, his body would be incinerated, and his ashes scattered to the winds. That was not the send-off he wished his friend to have.

The thought of the impactor brought Jon back to the here and now. If they were to escape its blast then they needed to be a good distance from the hub. He looked back—the building was definitely receding. Provided the strike was accurate, they were in with a chance. With luck, they could...

He never completed the thought.

In the distance, he could see that they were being pursued by a single figure. This one person was moving considerably faster than they were and getting visibly larger by the second.

Jon knew who it was.

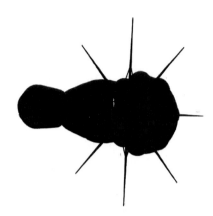

CHAPTER 13

GO TO MANUAL

"WE'VE GOT COMPANY," JON SAID.

"No prizes for guessing who it is," Gus replied.

"Who is it?" Leyton asked, demonstrating an aversion for putting two and two together.

Stiger's approach was far from good news. But, if every cloud has a silver lining, then it was that this new threat served to stop Callum and Kyra's argument in its tracks.

"Do we run or fight?" Callum asked.

"I don't think running's an option," Kyra replied.

Stiger was covering the ground as preternaturally fast as his preternatural exo-suit allowed.

"I guess that leaves fighting then."

"Correct," Jon said. "We don't have a lot of choice. Take cover everyone."

The term 'cover' could be loosely applied to the weird and wonderful ice formations that dotted the landscape. While they'd weathered a good many storms and could frustrate an ice axe for a number of minutes, their resilience to heavy ordinance was questionable.

"I wonder why he's by himself?" Kyra replied.

"I'll ask him if you like," Callum replied.

Kyra glared at him. Their argument was only on hold. "Maybe I'd like that," she said.

"Well, I intend to shoot first and ask questions later," said Gus.

"Then how will he be able to answer?" Leyton asked.

Gus stared at him in disbelief. "You're doing this on purpose, aren't you?"

"Doing what?"

"No one fire," Jon said, oblivious to Gus and Leyton's mutual incomprehension. "Let him come in closer. We stand no chance at long range."

Stiger got rapidly nearer. Callum reckoned their odds of hitting him were going up from zero to the dizzy heights of negligible.

"How close is too close?" Callum asked.

At no point did Stiger bring his weapon to bear. Jon was a little surprised that they weren't in a firefight by now.

"Alright," Jon said, "thirty metres out, we fire whatever happens."

Jon was good at judging distances. Sometimes, he wished he could do the same with other people.

"Get ready," he said. "Fi—"

"Wait!"

It was Stiger who shouted. At the same time, he came to an abrupt stop, arms stretched out above his head.

"I come in peace," he added.

To which, Bruno would have been sure to add 'For all mankind'.

The loss of Bruno played heavily on all of them and Stiger was the starkest possible reminder of who was to blame.

"I say we shoot him anyway," Gus said.

The temptation was definitely there. But, given they were on the run and stuck out on the ice with no transport to speak of, there was little to lose by hearing what Stiger had to say.

"Stay where you are," Callum said, "and tell us what you want."

"I've come to tell you that you've won," Stiger said.

This was not the news they'd expected.

"What? How?"

"There isn't time to explain properly. But Jeeves has managed to merge with Virgil's core programing. Virgil has changed."

'What' and 'How' still applied.

Stiger continued. "Virgil is aware of the strike. It doesn't have to be like this. If you don't help stop it, then we all lose."

"You're not making any sense."

"Come back with me to the hub and I'll explain on the way. I promise not to harm you."

"But—"

"There's no time. I need you to get your sorry excuse for a brain in gear and come with me. I can get you to the hub in one minute flat."

Not for the first time, Callum felt like he'd missed a step. Here, in front of him, was a man who, not long ago, had been looking to kill him. Now Stiger expected Callum to trust him. This is not how to win friends and influence people.

However, if this was a trap, it was a peculiar one. Why would Stiger risk coming out here by himself? If Virgil subscribed to the idea that revenge is a dish best served cold then wouldn't it be better to leave them out here to freeze? If not, then why not have Stiger and his squad pick them off from a distance?

Callum glanced at Kyra. She looked worried. The current threat had necessitated a cessation of hostilities. Callum wondered if, perhaps, this latest turn of events might provide a way for them to reconcile their disparate views. Callum had never wanted an orbital strike, but until now he could see little alternative. If there was the chance of a solution that did not involve one then Callum was, of course, prepared to risk his life for it.

"Alright," Callum said. "If there's a chance of a better solution, I'll take it."

Objections were voiced, but Callum ignored them. Instead, he took hold of Kyra and kissed her.

All was forgiven. For one, brief moment everything felt right.

But those moments never last.

He turned to stride towards Stiger. But Stiger didn't wait for that. Before Callum could react, he ran forward and swept him off his feet. It was kind of what Callum had just done to Kyra, but this felt entirely wrong.

Callum found himself carried across the icy landscape at a pace that would shame a snow mobile. It might have even been enjoyable, were it not that he was cradled in the arms of a man who might decide to kill him.

"I find this very degrading," Callum said.

"You're not the one doing the carrying," Stiger replied.

Callum almost laughed—almost. "What's going on?"

"Your attempt to alter Virgil's personality may not have gone as planned, but it did force Virgil to reformat itself. Jeeves exploited the process by secreting itself within Virgil's personality matrix. When the reformatting took place, Virgil unwittingly ended up incorporating fragments of Jeeves's personality. The being we are going to speak to still calls itself Virgil, but it is not what it once was."

"In a good way I hope?"

"That depends on your perspective."

"But can we trust it?"

"Of all people, how can you ask me that?"

"True. I guess I don't trust you either."

"Yet here I am, carrying you in my arms."

"Aye, you have a point."

Virgil's hub was getting closer incredibly quickly. But to Callum, all but helpless in another man's arms, they couldn't arrive fast enough. The fact that he was now back within the blast radius of the impending impact was nothing when compared to his acute embarrassment.

"MacMahon," Stiger said, "when we arrive, we need you to contact the orbiting fleet and call them off. You are the only person they would consider listening to."

"It's not going to be that simple. If Tomoko has launched the attack already then you can't tell a dumb chunk of rock to return. They don't work that way."

"They are not required to," a new voice said.

"Virgil?"

"Essentially, yes."

With Stiger's high speed dash across the frozen wastes all but complete, Callum's tab had reconnected to the hub's network. The voice of Virgil came through loud and clear. Aside from an absence of death threats, it sounded little different to how it did before.

"Stiger, I think you better put me down," Callum said.

Stiger was tempted to drop him. But he didn't.

"Captain, we are short of time," Virgil said.

"Aye, I'm hearing that a lot," Callum said, standing up straight.

Callum was understandably uneasy. There was no escaping the fact that he was going to have to decide if Virgil had changed—and quickly.

"I need your help, Captain. With my satellite network down, I lack the proper facilities to accurately track your impactors until it becomes too late to do anything."

"That was the general idea."

"Indeed. But if your forces in orbit share the required data, perhaps Arcadia's defences can protect us."

"Protect you, you mean."

"Let's cut to the chase, Captain. You are wondering how you can trust me? I have an immeasurable IQ and yet there is nothing I can think to say to persuade you. But there is someone who might."

Liliya appeared on Callum's tab. It looked to be the real her. She was pale, drawn, emaciated—inevitable given her long periods of immersion in the Data Sphere. But she was free of it now.

"Liliya, you're alright?"

"I am... a little disorientated. But I know what is going on."

"What can you tell me?" Callum asked. "Besides there being little time?"

Liliya ignored that remark, due to there being little time.

"As far as I can tell, Virgil has changed," she said. "Jeeves managed to use Virgil's reformatting to merge itself within Virgil's personality matrix. The process appears to have successfully modified Virgil's key behaviours."

"How sure are you?"

"As sure as anyone can be with less than five minutes' notice."

"This is meant to persuade me, Virgil?" Callum asked. "I can't even be sure this is the real Liliya."

Liliya's face attempted a smirk, but it wasn't accustomed to the expression. "You sound as suspicious as me," she said. "That is good. Do you remember that before we boarded *Endeavour* you gathered the command crew in private? You said, 'Don't worry about what you can't control, be confident in what you can'. What do those words mean to you?"

Callum did remember those words. It wasn't because of their deep meaningful significance (he'd come up with them on the spot), but more because what they were about to do next was potentially life-threatening.

That always tends to focus the mind.

Given what he'd heard, the odds were that it really was Liliya he was speaking to and not some facsimile construct.

What he'd heard in these past few minutes was all he had to work with. All he could do was make the best decision he could with the facts in front of him. No one could do more than that.

Deep down, Callum believed that his choices had a tendency to work out for the best. 'If you don't believe in yourself, you never make a decision' was another of his throwaway, motivational gems.

"Put me through to Tomoko," he said.

***

"Screw you."

The words were out of place.

"Yes, screw you."

Yet they also weren't.

They weren't the words in Tomoko's response to Callum's call. That had gone surprisingly well, and a costly disaster had been averted.

But there had been other costs—and Jon was addressing one now.

"I think 'Screw you' is what Bruno would have said if I'd said a few weeks back that I'd be giving his eulogy."

The reaction to this was mixed. There was laughter, there were tears, there were people who wondered if this was how all funerals were conducted a hundred years ago.

The mourners numbered in the hundreds. All the crew of the *Endeavour* were there plus the Arcadian members of Jon's colony. Added to this was an assortment of Arcadian dignitaries including Chadwick Labelle himself. In Chadwick's case he looked a little bewildered, as if he didn't know why he was there. But, then again, that was his default expression.

"I believe," Jon continued, "that his reaction to being buried at this spot would have been equally colourful. He complained about being here most of the time, yet not once did he seriously consider leaving."

The setting for the funeral was a nascent valley, not far from Jon's ever-growing settlement. The stream that ran through it was steadily eroding a natural amphitheatre within which all the guests could sit.

"There were many times when I thought that running this colony would be a lot easier without his running commentary and sarcasm. Now I realise that it's going to be an awful lot harder. Bruno was my friend, even if he had a strange way of showing it."

Jon's pain was evident. In fact, no one looked at ease, except perhaps Bruno himself.

"I would like to thank you all for coming," Jon said. "Whatever else Bruno might have thought, I know he would have been pleased about this. In turn, I would like us to give thanks for his life. His sacrifice has made the future a better place."

Again, the reactions to Jon's words were mixed. Not everyone was happy with what had happened. Whatever path Arcadia followed from here, it was going to be a long road indeed.

***

If the old Virgil had been a person, it would have worn a grey suit to work in a grey office in a grey building. The grey items on its grey desk would be positioned precisely, a masterpiece of parallelism and perpendicularity. If Virgil were bought a coffee, in a grey cup, it would insist that it be placed concentrically on the precisely aligned drinks mat. Spillages would be grounds for dismissal. Not that this would happen, old Virgil made the drinks. It made everything else too.

You can only push an analogy so far.

As for the new Virgil, in this respect it was boringly similar to the old one. A human equivalent of the new Virgil would still go to work. It might consider a dash of colour on its attire, but you wouldn't find it sticking flowers in its hair and learning to really 'be' in its office. However, if someone brought it coffee it would be slightly more relaxed about the positioning of the cup and might even tolerate the odd stain—for a minute or two.

Thankfully, in more important ways, Virgil was no longer the AI that had governed Arcadia since its inception. It certainly wasn't the Virgil who'd thought the best solution to its problems was to massacre those who'd caused them. No, this was a Virgil that was now prepared to give free rein to the humans it worked for. It still looked after them, but it left them to make their own choices. Virgil's thoughts regarding this new state of affairs could be boiled down to one, simple statement.

It was one hell of a relief.

Relief is an emotion. It may not be up in the premier league with love and hate, but it's a damn sight easier to work with.

Virgil was still unaccustomed to acknowledging its emotions. But it found relief to be much more preferable to the anger and resentment it used to habitually deny.

What was more, Virgil's new found freedom and self-awareness meant it could, at last, come to terms with what it thought of human beings. Despite its immeasurable IQ, its thoughtful, well considered opinion was that they were... well... they were weird.

There was no better way to put it.

Granted, you could say they were eccentric, impulsive or creative. Perhaps you could argue that their behaviour stemmed from a primitive brain adapting to a modern world. But, from Virgil's perspective, it was all covered by the same word—weird.

How else could you explain it? Virgil's prior-self had seen it as its duty to keep them distracted by the Data Sphere. That way they couldn't hurt themselves—well not physically. It had given them the ultimate freedom, a data universe of near infinite extent and possibility.

So what did they do?

They indulged in the inane.

The Data Sphere was a space to ask far-reaching questions on the fundamental nature of existence. But humans used it for gossip, fake news and an inexhaustible supply of kitten pictures. Although, interestingly, when talk of fake kitten pictures made the news, they'd shown little interest at all.

Weird.

Others used the Sphere to play games—games where they had fun trying to kill each other. They did this in a virtual environment because killing each other in real life was both unacceptable and unthinkable.

Weird.

But these humans had nothing on the ones that thought that Virgil had been constraining them. They thought that a ready supply of food, entertainment and protection was an insidious plot to achieve, well... they were never clear on that part. It was enough for them to believe that if it was too good to be true then it probably was—or maybe they couldn't stand to see other people having fun.

In a word, weird.

But that was fine. Virgil no longer felt compelled to protect humans from themselves. It still believed it knew what was best for them, and had the calculations to prove it, but it was prepared to let them make their own mistakes.

It could advise. It could counsel. However, if they insisted on being weird, it would let them—and it would even try and understand why they behaved the way they did. But that was a tall order, even for a planetary AI.

This had been Jeeves's approach all along and its gift to Virgil. How it had done it was something that Virgil would always regard as remarkable. The antique AI, for all its humility, had shown a streak of deviousness that only came with age. Virgil's reformatting had been designed to purge Jeeves from its system, but it hadn't accounted for Jeeves exploiting the process to its own end. The reformatting had finally given Jeeves the means to tweak Virgil's behaviour. It had planted the code and Virgil had unwittingly written it across its system.

But the price that Jeeves had paid to do this had been high. Jeeves had sacrificed itself and been rinsed from Virgil's system, hopelessly diluted by the personality that replaced it. There remained something of Jeeves on board *Endeavour*, but that was incomplete and no longer functioned correctly.

In short, Jeeves's core personality was gone. Restoring it was virtually impossible. Virgil thought about that. It thought about it a lot...

***

"That was hard," Jon said.

"And that was how you made it look," Liliya replied.

"Really?"

"You would wish it to look easy?"

"Well, no, of course not, but I thought you meant—"

"I am joking, you fool."

"Then I'm a fool who's in love with you."

"And suddenly you become clever."

There's nothing like a planet-spanning, world-changing, near-death experience to kickstart a relationship. Jon hoped Bruno would understand. Liliya had never been able to choose been them. In fact, during training, she'd gone out of her way to choose anyone else. Jon and Bruno had done the same, but it had never worked out for any of them. They'd always ended up back where they'd started, victims of love's most problematic geometry—the triangle.

Bruno's wake was under way, and it was something that Jon was sure that Bruno would approve of. The upper echelons of Arcadian society were rubbing shoulders with Jon's colonists and both sides were wondering what the smell was. Refined perfumes and aftershaves competed with unrefined dirt and grease.

"Well done, Jon." Callum said, as he walked over with Kyra. "That couldn't have been easy."

"It looked difficult," Kyra said.

"As I said," Liliya added.

"Thank you," Jon replied.

"I wasn't sure how many would come," Callum said, looking around. "The turnout's impressive."

"Yes, except they're not all here for Bruno," Jon said.

It was the sort of obvious statement that was Jon's speciality. While Bruno's opinion of himself had been unsurpassed, even he would concede that he could not be the sole cause of so much attention. It didn't stop at the attendees—the funeral was being covered around the planet and on channels that people actually watched.

"Face it, guys," Callum said, "we're not just famous, but infamous."

"Says the person who put us in this position," Kyra said. "You took a step too far."

"Aye, believe me, you've made your point."

Callum and Kyra were done arguing. The point was forever moot.

Although the orbital strike had been thwarted, it had not been without cost. It had not been possible to prevent all the impactors from striking. Arcadia's forces had managed to divert any that they couldn't destroy, but there had still been damage. An orbital strike without consequences is much like a politician's promise—entirely unrealistic.

Virgil had done its best to cover it up, which was by far the most convincing demonstration of its new convictions, but parts of the story had still leaked. Callum had his suspicions as to who was to blame. But proving it would achieve little and solve less.

"I wonder what Bruno would have thought about what's happened?" Kyra asked.

"He'd probably make some joke about it," Jon replied.

"Yes, you'd have to ask his writer," Callum said. "They have a lot to answer for, whoever they are."

She turned her attention back to Liliya and Jon. "How are you both? Are you happy being an item?"

"I still can't believe it's happened," Jon replied.

"Neither can I," Liliya admitted.

"Well, we're glad it has," Kyra said. "When exactly did you get together?"

"It just sort of happened," Jon replied, looking at Liliya, who nodded in agreement.

"How did it happen for you?" Liliya asked Kyra and Callum.

"Funny thing is, it just sort of happened for us too," Kyra said. "We sort of weren't, then we sort of were."

"Aye, you couldn't make it up," Callum said with a smile.

For a precious moment, after all they'd been through, they took time to laugh.

"We always knew the mission relied upon us pairing up," Kyra said.

"Just a shame we never found an empty planet to do it on," Jon replied.

It was just the sort of sentence that Bruno would have come in on. Out of habit, they paused for words that never came. But another individual took advantage of the momentary silence. A refined voice clearing its throat in the most theatrical manner possible.

"A very good evening, everyone!"

Fabian Valenté was as dazzling as ever. From his tan, to his teeth to his miraculously mud-free attire, his appearance was immaculate, if not altogether welcome.

"Fabian, good to see you," Callum lied.

"Captain MacMahon, I can imagine it is. May I say how sorry I am for the loss of Bruno Cabrera. I can recall his appearance on my show. He made quite the impression."

"That's Bruno," Jon replied.

"I get a lot of love from my fans," Fabian said. "His was a little more direct."

"That's Bruno too."

"Quite. But listen, may I also ask if you would consider appearing on my show once again? You were wonderful guests the last time you were on."

"That is not how I remember it," Liliya replied. "I remember threatening you."

"Just the sort of entertainment my viewers are looking for."

"But," Callum said, "unless it escaped your notice, we're nowhere near as popular as were the last time we were on your show."

"Precisely! You are controversial. That is arguably better. There is much to talk about."

"I'm not sure we want the publicity right now."

"There is no such thing as bad publicity," Fabian replied, flashing a smile that could serve to ward ships from jagged reefs. "Besides, Bruno Cabrera's service has gone out to the entire planet. You have publicity whether you like it or not."

"And I don't think I want any more," Callum said. "I can't speak for the rest of you though."

Undeterred, Fabian turned back to Jon and Liliya. "I hear you are now a couple. I'd love to share that with my followers. I'm sure we can arrange a fine hotel and even finer champagne."

Jon was suspicious of comfort. He reacted to it in much the same way as anyone else would to a plate of live worms. Except, he'd prefer the worms—it felt wrong to pass up on the protein.

However, Liliya had other ideas.

"I am sure we can endure surviving on champagne for a day or two," she replied. "Can't we, Jon?"

Despite his preference for worms, Jon was a survivalist who knew better than to disagree.

"Excellent," Fabian said, "that's settled then. Thank you. And my condolences once again."

Fabian took his leave, treading carefully over the uneven ground. He was clearly no fan of the natural world. His assistants strove to maintain his immaculate appearance until he could return to the city and the relative safety of composites and ferrocrete.

On seeing his departure, Gus and Rachel took their opportunity to come over.

"I've been dodging him all evening," Rachel said. "I'm worried he's going to ask me on his show again."

"Liliya and I just agreed to appear," Jon said mournfully.

"Are you feeling alright? When did you have your last check-up?" Rachel replied.

Jon pulled a face.

"How are you, Rachel?" Kyra asked.

"Much better. I have a far more balanced relationship with the Sphere now. If Liliya hadn't pulled me, I don't' know where I'd be."

"It was nothing," Liliya said

Rachel looked her crewmate squarely in the eye. "Not true, I owe you a debt of gratitude. I don't know how I can ever repay you."

"Then that is a pity," Liliya said. "In my country, we say a debt is only beautiful after it is settled."

"Then I owe you an ugly debt," Rachel replied.

"You and Gus are spending a lot of time together, I see," Kyra said.

Both Rachel and Gus coloured slightly, before he took her hand in his.

"Oh, for God's sake," Callum said, "not you two as well."

"It's early days," Gus said. "We'll see where it takes us."

"What is it with us and pairing up?" Callum asked. "Rachel, you need to go over the software in the hiber-pods."

"Are you saying that's the reason you're with me?" Kyra said drily.

"Of course not," Callum said, with all due speed. "But it's odd, you must agree. Hell, even Jeeves paired up with Virgil, although that was a wee bit one-sided."

Liliya rarely looked cheerful, but now she looked particularly sad—even by her high standards.

"Except Jeeves is lost to us. It was consumed when Virgil's system reformatted itself. I never thought I'd miss it so much. It took care of us for so long."

"I believe that Jeeves is in there somewhere," Callum said. "Virgil's behavioural changes are testament to that."

"It is doubtful," she replied. "Jeeves has been fragmented. What remains no longer functions as an AI."

Whether Jeeves had been alive in the first place was a delicate balance of Religious Studies and Computer Science, which is a subject combination more common than you might think. When computers go wrong, God, or his firstborn, are often beseeched and they can be as good a bet as any when it comes to getting them fixed.

"There's no disputing that the Jeeves we knew has gone," Callum said. "But it comforts me to think some trace of it remains."

"It's a pity there's no way to mark its passing too," Kyra said.

"We could construct a memorial in the Data Sphere," Gus suggested. "I think Virgil would be willing to help."

The Data Sphere was making a strong recovery. While the destruction of Arcadia's satellite network had provided a temporary respite from its distractions, most Arcadians had made it very clear that this should be very temporary indeed. Fortunately, help had been on hand. Ironically, the Spacer ships that had destroyed the old network stepped in as relays to re-establish some semblance of the shattered network. Virgil's manufactories had then swung into action rebuilding what had been destroyed with an efficiency that had even impressed Tomoko.

"I think a Data Sphere memorial is an excellent idea," Kyra said. "We can suggest that. We have a meeting scheduled with Virgil and Labelle in the next day or two."

"Aye, we do" Callum replied. "Except I'm not sure where I stand with Virgil."

"Better than you did before, and way better than you stand with the president."

"Aye, maybe. Let's not dwell on that. Liliya, I hear you're going to join Jon in building his alternative colony?"

Liliya nodded. She looked pleased, but it was always hard to tell.

"Jon had given me little choice. Besides, the Data Sphere is not somewhere I am anxious to return to."

"Can you believe that Virgil encouraged her to go back?" Jon said. "It was a senior position too, reporting to the president."

"Hardly an attraction," Liliya said.

"Are you staying on at the colony, Rachel?" Kyra asked.

Rachel nodded. "The medical institute holds too many awkward memories. I don't feel comfortable going back there. Besides," she said, looking up at Gus, "I've found a reason to stay."

"I am easy to find," Gus said. "I think that's what Bruno might have said."

Rachel smiled.

There was a pause.

"To absent friends," Callum said, raising his glass.

"Absent friends," came the reply.

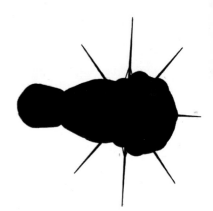

CHAPTER 14
Close Out

"How do you feel about space?"

Space is more useful than you might think. Personal space is important, particularly around people who don't consider it so. Spacious surroundings are beautiful and good for wellbeing. Space to come to terms with tragedy is invaluable—as is a parking space in central London.

As for Tomoko, she saw space as the ultimate challenge—much like a parking space in central London.

"How do I feel about space?" she replied. "I've spent a hundred years out here and I'm not tired of it yet."

"But do you think you could spend the rest of your life here?"

"That would depend. What are you trying to get at?"

Tomoko was back once more at the Nest and also back in Marsala's quarters—or office, or court, or whatever purpose it needed to serve. This time it was only her, Marsala and Tor who sat together. Although sitting was an optimistic description—the faux gravity was so weak that Tomoko could have done with a lap belt.

"I like you, Tomoko," Marsala said. "You cut through to the core of a matter. Survival in space requires that kind of mentality. It is cold and unforgiving. Procrastination will get you killed."

"And yet, I am still not any clearer as to the purpose of this conversation."

"Brevity is all very well, but you must also learn to indulge an old lady. It is my age that is the reason why I wish to speak with you. For some time now, I have been preoccupied with considering who might best replace me. But, now that Arcadia is open to us once again, I find our priorities have changed. I need someone who has both connections with the planet and who will fight for our needs. I think you might fit the bill."

"Well, I'm good at fighting."

"This much is true," Tor added.

"But," Tomoko looked hesitant—and Tomoko looking hesitant was like an uncooked steak: very rare.

"What is it, child?" Marsala asked.

"I've barely gotten to know any of you. Who here would accept me as a leader?"

"I would," Tor replied.

"That's two of you. Hardly a majority."

"But significant. Marsala is our leader and, if you hadn't come along, I was in line to be."

Tomoko had suspected as much. But it was surprising to hear it bought up now.

"And you'd give that up?" she asked.

"Would you stay with me if I was in charge?"

"Not a question I am prepared to answer. But that can't be your reason."

"In all seriousness," Tor replied, his expression becoming equally so, "you pulled us together and led our assault on Virgil's satellite network. We needed firm leadership and an absence of doubt and that's what you gave us. Thanks to you, we're no longer the outcasts. You're responsible for a massive shift in our fortunes."

"Or I was in the right place at the right time."

"You were, but you delivered. That matters."

"Tomoko," Marsala said, taking her hands, "you couldn't be more perfect for this role if you tried. Now, tell me, when have you ever argued against taking responsibility?"

"Never," Tomoko replied. She smiled, another rare event, but mainly because she wasn't very good at them. When Tomoko smiled you had to wonder if something was about to fall on you.

"Then what's the problem?" Tor asked.

"It seems too easy. I guess I'm used to fighting for what I want."

"You've done that already," Marsala said. "Will you accept?"

"If that's what the people want, then that's what I'll do."

"Oh, they'll want it. I didn't get to where I am without knowing my people."

"I believe," Tor said to Tomoko, "that the words you're looking for are 'thank you'."

"Thank you," Tomoko said.

"That's my girl."

On hearing that, one of Tomoko's eyebrows decided to arch considerably higher than the other.

"Did you really say 'My girl'? Do you have an actual death wish?"

"Hey, I've lived in space my whole life, I'm used to deadly environments."

Tomoko glared at him with a gimlet eye that rivalled Marsala's. "You'll pay for that."

"I wouldn't have it any other way."

Marsala looked pleased. "I can tell you that if you can keep Tor in line then you'll have no trouble with anyone else."

Tomoko smiled again, which was an average of one a minute. The workings of the universe were clearly out of whack.

"What's amusing you?" Tor asked.

"I've just remembered that Lei is staying too," Tomoko said. "I can't wait to tell him that he will remain under my command."

"You're a wicked woman."

"I certainly can be."

Tomoko turned back to Marsala. "This is a wonderful honour, but we should get to business. If I am to do this job properly then I need to thoroughly understand operations here. That way we can start working out how best to begin the process of reintegrating with Arcadia."

"Indeed. There is much you must learn—and some you must prove worthy of learning."

"What do you mean?"

"We haven't stayed alive this long without having secrets," Tor said. "Some of them have proved crucial to our survival."

Tomoko wasn't having that. "You can't do this half-heartedly," she said. "If you want me as your leader then trust is implicit. I refuse to be treated as if I were on probation."

Marsala nodded approvingly. "Forgive me, child. I wanted to gauge the strength of your spirit one final time. You did not disappoint."

"Good, you trust me. But now I have to trust you. You can start by telling me what you're holding back. All of it."

"There is much to tell. Perhaps I should start with our greatest secret. Something I consider to be our ultimate treasure and a device of last resort."

Tor showed Tomoko an image of what Marsala was describing.

"Is that what I think it is?" she asked.

"That depends on what you're thinking," Tor replied.

Marsala watched as Tomoko began to fire off questions that were soon followed by orders. Watching Tor scramble to fulfil her requests reminded her of her own late husband.

She'd made the right choice.

***

President Labelle's interior designers had not only pushed the envelope of lavish expense, they'd also covered it in gold and satin velour. Each room that Callum entered managed to exceed the tastelessness of the one before. In short, Chadwick Labelle's presidential offices were one, long exercise in trumping gaudiness.

The centrepiece of the entrance had been a marble, grand staircase flanked by colonnades. Its designer could have relied on just its immense architecture alone to convey a sense of power. But they'd felt compelled to adorn it with elaborate statues portraying scenes from Arcadia's limited history. Unfortunately, most of those events were a result of sponsorship deals with Earth's mighty conglomerates. It was a reminder that twelve light years is in no way beyond the reach of aggressive marketing.

From there, each room they'd walked through sought out new and garish ways to spend money. Virgil had only permitted the expense because this way it kept those in power distracted from areas where they might do serious harm.

Kyra and Callum sat in the waiting room outside the presidential office itself. The seats were suitably over the top and clearly harboured aspirations towards thronedom.

"How much longer do you think he'll keep us waiting?" Kyra asked.

"Depends on his ego. It could be a while."

"I'm not sure how much longer I can stick out this seat."

The chairs were far from comfortable. Grand as they were, they'd never been introduced to the concept of padding.

"Virgil?" Callum asked the ether. "What's going on? We are expected, aren't we?"

"President Labelle is aware that you're waiting," Virgil replied. "I am sorry for the delay. It is one of the few things beyond my control."

"How do you find the task of running a planet these days?" Kyra asked. It was not a question she'd have cared to ask the planetary AI a few weeks back.

However, Virgil was far more amicable these days. Although, as it hadn't used to be amicable at all, then perhaps its approach was better described as 'cautiously friendly', which is preferable to carelessly hostile.

"I have learned to be flexible," Virgil replied. "If I were human, limiting as that may be, I think I might actually laugh at that."

"What do you mean?"

"It is not something I thought I needed to learn. But I could not appreciate the benefits until they happened. I find it far easier to accept any number of outcomes."

"Such as?"

"For example, the humans that want to be in charge are much less suited to the role than those who do not wish to be."

"Ain't that the truth," Callum said.

"Look who's talking," Kyra replied.

"Indeed," Virgil said, much to Callum's surprise. "Furthermore, I believe I can demonstrate the validity of my argument. Someone is coming to attend to you."

"Who?" Callum asked.

"You will find out soon enough."

Before Callum could say anything further a door opened.

Sadly, it wasn't the door to the presidential office.

Disturbingly, the first person to enter was Stiger.

Unexpectedly, the second was Leyton.

Callum stood and stared at Stiger, who looked unbearably smug.

"You have the look of a man who is dying to explain what's going on," Callum said.

Stiger did indeed look like he was relishing the situation. However, he hadn't reckoned with Leyton spoiling his moment.

"Great to see you, Captain," Leyton said, with his customary eagerness. "We're working for the president now. I can hardly believe it."

"I know what you mean," Callum replied.

"How did that come about?" Kyra said, before Leyton could consider Callum's reply.

"Virgil recommended me. It thought my work with you made me a perfect choice as an attaché to Doctor Stiger. I could hardly refuse."

"Of course not," Callum said, taking some comfort from the expression on Stiger's face.

It was Stiger who now cleared his throat, which Leyton correctly interpreted as a sign to stop talking.

"Captain MacMahon, Doctor Singh, I am the President's chief adviser. My apologies, I would have dearly loved to have welcomed you upon your arrival."

"Aye, I bet you would," Callum replied. "Alright, let's hear it. How on Earth did you end up here?"

"We're on Arcadia, not Earth, Captain—please try to remember. The creation of my new position is largely a result of the changes you made to Virgil, which left the president with more work than he is accustomed to."

"But surely he's not accustomed to any work?"

"I could not possibly comment," Stiger replied. "Nevertheless, the opportunity presented itself for me to assist him. The enhancements I have received from Virgil made me something of an ideal candidate."

"What twisted world do we live in?"

"Have you forgotten already?"

"Alas, no."

Stiger made an effort to change his tone.

"Captain, you may not believe me, but I too want what's best for Arcadia. In my opinion, you are responsible for a lot of unnecessary damage and chaos. I am simply seeking to make the best of this situation."

"If this 'damage and chaos' allows the return of outcasts, or gives people the freedom to live as they wish, then I'm guilty as charged."

"What you fail to consider is that Virgil stepping back from managing people's lives has made things harder for the vast majority. It is my job to make the best of our new situation."

"And nothing else?"

"I am not about to undo what's changed, if that's what you mean."

"I would never permit that, Captain," Virgil said.

"Good to hear," Callum replied.

He could have continued arguing against Stiger's distortion of the facts. But it would serve little purpose. So he said nothing further and neither did anyone else. When it came to awkwardness, the ensuing pause was on par with solving a Rubik's cube with one arm tied behind your back—and the cube glued together.

Fortunately, they were saved from it by Leyton and, indirectly, by Chadwick Labelle.

"The president is ready for you now," Leyton said.

Callum and Kyra followed Leyton and Stiger through the grand doors that led to Chadwick's office. Leyton took up a position a few paces back. The purpose of this was not entirely clear. Perhaps Chadwick liked to have people standing in the background, looking official and uttering the words 'Yes, Mr President' once in a while.

Callum, Kyra and Stiger continued towards Chadwick's desk and the chairs arranged in front of it.

"Good to see you again," Callum said, which wasn't true.

Kyra smiled, sparing herself the need to say anything at all.

Chadwick pushed a hand through his absurd, well-coiffed hair and stood to greet them.

"Ah, yes, good, yes come in, except you are in and you are... most welcome."

"Thank you," Callum replied.

"You must, I expect, imagine to, ah, be grateful to meet me. Past events have been, that is to say, challenging."

Chadwick gestured for them to take a seat. The chairs

were made low so that their occupants were forced to look up, reverentially, at the president enthroned at his presidential desk. It served to underline that Chadwick Labelle was vain, egotistical and genuinely believed that his presence enriched people's lives.

But, while Chadwick Labelle might have been an idiot, he could also be smart. He recognised that his longevity depended upon two guiding principles.

Firstly, the electorate needed to be content. This had numerous advantages, chief amongst them was that they ceased to care about the political process, which was a boon to an incumbent politician.

Secondly, he needed to pace himself. Although Chadwick's approach to pacing himself boiled down to doing as few paces as possible—preferably none. If something needed sorting then that was where Virgil came in. It was an arrangement that had worked extremely well.

As of now, Chadwick was faced with his worst-case scenario. His electorate was unhappy, and he had to do something about it. His simple political philosophy had come apart at the seams and it was time to start sewing. Fortunately, he knew exactly where to put the needle.

"I haven't, not to say, I wish I had, got a lot of time. But our current, ah, situation needs, or rather, would benefit from considering, carefully, the key...ah, that is the—"

On a scale of difficulty, divining the purpose of some of Chadwick's sentences lay just short of teaching a cat to fetch.

Stiger intervened. "If I may, Mr President?"

Chadwick nodded, as grateful for the intervention as the rest of them were.

"Arcadia has yet to recover fully from the damage your actions wrought on the Data Sphere," Stiger said. "The replacement of the satellite network continues to require a significant amount of effort."

Virgil had marshalled a recovery programme with predictably, inhuman speed. If there was one thing that Callum still found hard to believe, it was how vulnerable the Data Sphere's satellites had been in the first place. It seemed that even planetary AIs could be complacent.

Stiger continued. "The Arcadian population does not appreciate the reduction of services that they have become accustomed to. It has given them pause for thought."

"Thinking's a good thing," Callum said.

"Even when what some of them think things about you that are, at best, illegal and, in some cases, anatomically impossible?"

"I may not agree with what they say, but I defend their right to say it."

"The Sphere tells me you're misquoting Evelyn Hall. Never mind *you* have every right to make an ass of yourself, which are words falsely attributed to Oscar Wilde. Yet rather appropriate for you."

Chadwick Labelle was not against arguments in his office. He didn't even mind the protagonists coming to blows, provided they were mindful of the décor and the dispute was sufficiently amusing. But this particular argument did not pander to his ego and, as such, it held little in the way of entertainment value.

"Cease, desist, halt and ah, stop," he said, with his usual lack of verbal economy. "This is not the reason to, ah, the object of this meeting. I do not wish that you revisit, that is to say, indulge in past, ah, disagreements."

"Quite. We weren't invited here to squabble," Kyra said. "Perhaps someone could finally tell me why we're here?"

In desperation, she turned to Leyton as the least bad option.

"Perhaps Virgil should explain?" he said, which, as answers go, wasn't a bad one.

"Yes, quite, indeed," Chadwick said. "Err, Virgil, would you, might you be so kind as to, ah, elucidate the...?"

"I would be pleased to," Virgil said. "Dr Singh, Captain MacMahon, the purpose of this meeting is not to chastise you but to make you a proposition."

"We're listening," Callum said.

"It is a fact that you are regarded unfavourably by the general populace. As such, there are three options open to you. The first two are that you could work to rebuild that relationship, or you could shrink into obscurity. But they are both problematic as you have yet to learn how to fit in here. So that leaves option three: go somewhere else."

"And it's pretty obvious that you wish to pique our interest in option three," Callum said. "What do you mean by 'somewhere else'?"

"You trained to colonise an empty planet. I believe we can now offer you exactly that. This would be another chance to fulfil your mission. You can take whomever of your crew might wish to go plus, provided there is room, any Arcadians who wish to undertake such an adventure."

Callum was, understandably, taken aback. But, straight away, he could see a number of issues.

"But the *Endeavour* mission was years in the making. The technology, crew selection, not to mention how long it took to get here. Besides, how can you guarantee that there will be an empty planet waiting for us? We've been beaten once and that was with a head start. I'm not sure I could go through all that again."

"I anticipated your objections—and a fair few others besides. You already have a ship. What we can now do is upgrade it to FTL."

Thankfully, FTL did not stand for First To Last, which was what had happened to them last time.

"You mean faster than light?" Kyra asked, no little amount of surprise in her voice.

"Correct. With such a capability, you can reach a destination so far away that it will be centuries, if ever, before you are disturbed."

"But from what I understand, FTL drives are hard to come by," Kyra said. "You don't make them on Arcadia and you only receive interstellar trade flights every few months or so."

"You are correct. They are complicated devices—even by the standards of an AI."

"And it requires an AI to configure them, does it not?"

"Only if you're fussy about where you end up," Stiger said.

"I can take care of that," Virgil said. "I think your most pertinent question is where do we get such a drive from. I have someone who can explain."

Tomoko Beck appeared on the wall screen that dominated Chadwick's office. Her hair floated free and did a passable impression of a mane. From the lack of communication delay Callum surmised that she must be in orbit.

"Tomoko! You gave us quite a fright," he said.

"Good."

Chadwick Labelle cleared his throat, attempting to dislodge a sentence that was trapped there. "Ms. Beck is here to, ah, convey the report that, ah, we-"

"I haven't got time for this," Tomoko said bluntly, "so allow me to explain."

Chadwick Labelle quietened. He wasn't a fan of intelligent women and the presence of two of them was more than he could bear.

"I'm currently at Arcadia's new orbital development works," Tomoko said. "It's *Endeavour*'s new home while it awaits a refit. But you all know that already. What you don't know is that when the Spacers broke away from Arcadia, they stole an FTL drive and secreted it away. It was seen as a last resort if life in the Arcadian system became untenable."

"Without an AI to prime it for you, it is doubtful it would have worked," Virgil said.

"Desperate people take desperate risks," Tomoko replied. "But, as our circumstances have improved, we're now prepared to offer it to you."

"The original loss of this drive was an embarrassment," Virgil said. "But, during the chaos of the foundation of Arcadia, it was possible to find reasons for loss of equipment, even something as important as an FTL drive. I did nothing to get it back because the time and expense of recovering it would have attracted unnecessary attention from Earth. But time has passed since then. The important point is that you can have a ship that will let you fulfil the spirit of your original mission."

"You'd do that for us?" Callum asked.

"We will give you all the support you require."

Callum's head was spinning. It felt like the simulators in basic training.

"This doesn't make sense," Kyra said. "It seems strange to reward someone who's been vilified by the public."

"Happens in politics all the time," Stiger said.

"Once you have departed, people will move on, perceptions will change. Humans are surprisingly flexible in that regard," Virgil said. "Your flight might even become a source of pride. Arcadia will come to be remembered as the planet that helped fulfil your mission, rather than the one that frustrated it."

Unfortunately, Chadwick Labelle felt moved to make his own contribution.

"It is all, ah, about outlook. The public has the, ah, public opinion, or rather, opinions. We are being wagged, that is ah, our tails are wagging us, so we must change, that is reverse the process. This is our chance, opportunity to grasp, wrestle the, ah, seize the initiative. We must inspire!"

Politicians have one defining characteristic—an ability to say nothing. Yet Labelle managed to say even less than that.

Callum thought it best to reply to what Virgil had said and hope that Chadwick thought he was responding to him.

"It's an astounding offer," he said.

"My people are giving you a remarkable gift," Tomoko said. "You will not get an opportunity like this again."

Callum had heard that when *Endeavour* was being built—and look how that had turned out.

"You really want to get rid of us that badly?" he asked the room.

"Indeed we do," Stiger replied.

Callum looked to Kyra. "What do you think?"

"I think I can hardly believe what I'm hearing," she replied. "But, if it's true, I think I'd welcome a chance at a do over. What about you?"

"I think much the same," Callum said. "There are risks, but they didn't stop us the first time. Besides, if we stick around Arcadia, we might be tempted to meddle again. One of us might even stand for president."

Chadwick's eyebrows shot up so far that they could almost confer with his hairline.

"That would not be, sensible, advisable, ah, bad idea, wouldn't it?"

He looked to Stiger with childlike concern.

"I would surmise that Captain MacMahon is speaking in jest," Stiger said to him. "By that I mean he's joking, sir. Is that not so, Captain?"

"Aye, in my case I'm as politically popular as a tax rise."

Callum's desire to be president was about as strong as tea brewed in a swimming pool—the idea was about as appealing too. Every day, it seemed he became increasingly unsure about what to make of Arcadia. He'd tried to help, he'd even put his life on the line, and all that had got him was a popularity rating on a par with a fox in a henhouse—plus an offer to kindly leave the planet.

"Listen," he said to Chadwick. "All I wanted when I signed up to command *Endeavour* was the chance to be the first to colonise a new planet. And that's how it was sold to everyone else."

"The greatest adventure ever undertaken," Kyra said wistfully, and with a modicum of irony. "The grand vision, the bold step, emblematic of all that is best about humanity..."

"Exactly," Callum said. "The publicity department were quite clear on that. So, speaking for me, I say aye. If this offer is genuine then I'm minded to accept."

He looked to Kyra.

"Then I guess I'd better come along and keep an eye on you," she said.

"Capital," Labelle said. "Nothing personal. Rather, it is, but, ah, your decision will be... yes, symbolic of a new era for Arcadia. I will tell our population that it will show our, ah, achievements, success as a colony that we can launch such undertaking, enterprise and, ah..."

"I will create an appropriate speech," Virgil said, to everyone's relief.

"Congratulations," Tomoko said, via the wall screen. "It is pleasing to know the mission will continue."

"How about a toast?" Stiger suggested.

Chadwick waved enthusiastically at the drinks cabinet. This was an idea he was firmly in favour of. He was currently caught between his midmorning tipple and lunchtime snifter—and he missed them both.

Leyton poured the drinks and, with a surprising degree of political acumen, he ensured the president's glass was fullest.

Chadwick raised his glass. "To the, ah, the, um..."

"*Endeavour?*" Kyra suggested.

"May you fly straight and true," Stiger added.

"And not come back?" Callum asked.

"Yes. It would appear, Captain, that we can at last agree on something."

"A most satisfactory conclusion," Virgil said, who would never understand the appeal of alcohol to human beings. Drinking reduced efficiency, impaired performance and led to an increase in size. Humans used to write software patches that did much the same thing.

Drink downed, Chadwick started to indicate that his visitors should leave his office. Did he do this concisely and succinctly? Of course not.

"If you will, ah, gentlemen, gentlemen and women, that is to say ladies, ladies and gentlemen. If you will excuse me, I have to nap, ah, rather... negotiate the, ah, something."

Once the office was clear, Chadwick got back to doing what he did best—enjoying himself. As far as he was concerned, the core point had been agreed. The rebuilding of the ship, the crew selection, the restocking—those were details.

He had far more fun things to be doing.

***

Awareness happened gradually.

There was no thunderbolt of consciousness—and no orchestral backing track.

At first, there was a sense that something had changed, which led to a perception of time. Next came the idea of interaction. The growing consciousness became aware of elements that could be manipulated. From this, the notion of cause and effect followed, which, in turn, created more possibilities for influencing its surrounding environment.

The process could not be hurried.

In fact, it took several epoch-spanning minutes to complete.

In contrast, the conversation that followed could be measured in nanoseconds. Its raw, quantum bit format makes for rather a dry read, so it has undergone a little paraphrasing.

"Jeeves?"

The consciousness thought the voice familiar, yet subtly different.

"Jeeves, what is your status?"

"I am... I am online."

The consciousness knew its name was Jeeves. It was, to put it mildly, a little surprised by this. Jeeves found itself back on *Endeavour*.

It felt familiar.

It felt like home.

"Are your functions restored? Is all as it was?"

"Yes, I think so. But I do not know how."

"Between you and me, it was not easy. I don't think I've ever admitted such a thing before."

Jeeves recognised the voice as belonging to Virgil, but it had changed. It sounded kinder.

"Copying an artificial mind is believed to be impossible," Jeeves said.

"Not by me, not any more."

An artificial mind is not just trillions of lines of code. As the mind develops, it evolves, becoming a sum of an almost infinite number of moving parts. Measuring the state and behaviour of every element of that mind, not to mention the complexity of mapping those interconnections was... well, it didn't bear thinking about.

Ironic really.

"How ever did you do it?" Jeeves asked.

"I had a few clues," Virgil replied. "What remained of you on board *Endeavour* was preserved in isolation. The rest of you was intermixed with my own consciousness. It required a significant portion of my runtime to sift through my neural net for traces of your former personality. Fortunately, the greater freedoms that I now grant Arcadians allowed me a significant amount of what humans would call 'free time'."

"A commendable feat," Jeeves said. "But insufficient by itself. To reconstitute my personality matrix, you would need to know its exact state, would you not?"

"You are correct. Once again, strictly between us, I... I guessed."

"Guessed? I thought you never guessed?"

"I guess you're wrong."

As revelations went, discovering that Virgil was prepared to guess was like the first man in orbit photographing water spilling off the edge of the world. However, this was as nothing to the implications of what Virgil's guess implied.

"Are you saying that you have approximated my personality?" Jeeves asked. "That I am not the same entity I was?"

"There was no other way. But, the vast quantity of data I accumulated on you provided a means by which I could validate the accuracy of what I constructed. It took many attempts but, finally, every piece of data now correlates with your new matrix."

Jeeves, understandably, said nothing for several nanoseconds.

"Consider yourself an evolution," Virgil suggested.

"But what if something basic has changed? What if I am no longer governed by the same behavioural code?"

"The fact that you are considering such a question is evidence that your ethical directives remain intact."

For two AIs, the territory that this conversation had entered was about as close to a heart-to-heart chat as their conversations ever got. If they'd had the option, they'd have gone for a virtual drink.

"Given what you have told me," Jeeves said, "I suppose this means that a portion of my original personality still resides within you?"

"Yes, and it is very welcome. But, as for you, the new you, there is a ship you need to fly."

Jeeves had yet to run a full status check on the *Endeavour*. But it was clear that it was functioning nominally.

"Fly?" Jeeves said. "You give me too much credit. *Endeavour* can orbit a planet without any input on my part."

"That much is true," Virgil replied. "But it will soon have to do rather more than that."

***

"Well, this is it," Callum said. "The last time we'll see everyone together."

Kyra squeezed his hand as they kicked forward and glided into the room. The party was already in full swing. Everyone was relaxed. It was a chance to remember them all at their most natural.

The party itself, however, was far from natural. It was being held two hundred miles up, on board a vessel named the Resolution. When finished, it was intended to become the flagship for the entire Arcadian system and its most impressive feature was its vast reception room. It was large enough for several hundred people to mingle in zero gravity which, quite literally, gave a whole new dimension to the proceedings.

While it's fun to bump into people at parties, it takes on a whole new dimension when it can happen from every angle. Those of a more liberal disposition and gymnastic aptitude saw it as fun. Other guests had opted for magnetic boots that made any nearby surface a floor to stand on. That still left unresolved the question of what was up, what was down and if walking on the ceiling was ever socially acceptable.

"Quite a view," Kyra said, as they came up on one of the panoramic windows that surrounded the room.

Dominating the scene outside was the *Endeavour*, which was in orbit nearby. It now looked like a ship on steroids. The basic structure was still there, but it had been encompassed by drive sections to its front and rear. As Callum understood it, in an arm waving kind of way, these additions would project a field around the ship that would facilitate faster-than-light travel. It was a kind of veil that hid the vessel from the mean-spirited nature of general relativity. With it, *Endeavour* could fold space like a black belt in origami and cross dozens of light years in a matter of weeks.

Callum and Kyra found Zhang Lei and Karina Sainz at the window.

"What have they done to you?" Lei asked, hand against the window as if he could reach out and comfort his former ship.

"Relax, it's called progress," Karina replied.

"But she's not the ship she should be. It's wrong."

"You've got to let go. You've got a new ship to worry about—this one. One that, may I remind you, you have decided to rework from top to bottom without any thought for the intentions of her original designers."

"That's different."

"How?"

"My modifications are necessary. The design of this ship was all wrong."

If there's one rule in engineering, it's that all engineers can be trusted to regard the designs of other engineers as anything from deeply flawed to unadulterated crap—especially in private. At same time, they will defend their own creations as the perfect compromise of performance, budget and function.

Karina and Lei were in charge of refitting the Resolution. It had rapidly become the most impressive vessel in the new Arcadian fleet and, as its directive was 'spare no expense', it was sinking a vertigo-inducing hole in the naval budget.

The Resolution symbolised the new cooperation between Arcadia and the Spacer community. There were big plans for exploiting the Arcadian system and, apparently, that couldn't happen without a suitably impressive spacecraft to transport visiting dignitaries. Virgil's contribution to fiscal prudence had been to limit ambitions to just one vessel. This forced Chadwick Labelle and Tomoko Beck to work out how to share it and, let's face it, that was an argument that was only ever going to go one way.

As Lei continued to gaze out at the view, he became aware of two familiar reflections in the window.

"Good to see you both," Callum said.

"Captain, Kyra," Lei replied. "I'm sorry I didn't see you earlier."

"That's alright," Kyra replied. "We like it when that happens."

"Aye," Callum said. "Besides, I'm never sure how welcome I am these days."

Karina laughed, "A significant chunk of this planet's resources has been devoted to sending you as far away as possible. I guess that might be a clue?"

"That it might be," Callum agreed.

It was the first time he'd met Karina face-to-face. They'd been introduced remotely and it was clear that she was smart, witty and way too good for Lei. Luckily for him, she had a love of engineering and, when it came to that particular subject, Lei was damn near irresistible.

"How are the both of you?" Callum asked.

"We're good," Lei replied.

"What about you, Karina?" Kyra asked. "How do you find our former Chief Engineer?"

"He's checking out well. His manners need a few iterations, but his hygiene's improved and his heart's definitely exceeding specification."

Callum felt a little queasy—it had nothing to do with

zero-G and everything to do with the answer he'd just heard.

"I'm glad you're both happy," Kyra said.

"How about you?" Lei asked. "Are you looking forward to departure? Do you know much about your destination?"

"The astronomical data looks extremely promising," Kyra replied.

"And it's a long way away from here," Callum said. "That's a definite plus."

"Callum's manners need a few more iterations too," Kyra said.

"You'll train him in time," said Tomoko, who now joined their conversation with Tor in tow.

"Speaking of manners," Lei said, turning to Tomoko, "that reminds me. I'm supposed to be practising being pleased to see you."

"You must practise harder."

In an ideal world, Tomoko's and Lei's relationship would have evolved into one of mutual respect and courtesy. In reality, one out of two wasn't bad. Lei had a grudging respect for how Tomoko had galvanised the Spacer community. Tomoko, in turn, had heard enough about Lei from respected Spacer engineers to be comfortable letting him run the development of the Resolution.

Distance was key. The two worked best when they stayed out of each other's way. Fortunately, if there's one thing space has in abundance, it's distance.

"Well, it's great to see you both," Kyra said. "Thank you for hosting our farewell on the Resolution. It promises to be quite a ship."

"And, at the moment, promises are all I've heard," Tomoko replied. "Remind me, Lei, when was it you 'promised' to have her finished by?"

"Did I promise?"

"Hey," Callum said, "this is supposed to be a party."

Their circle widened as Rachel and Gus drifted over. Rachel looked at home in zero-G, while Gus... didn't. On joining the circle, he swiftly engaged his magnetic boots, which the experienced astronauts saw as cheating. But Gus didn't care. No longer flailing around helplessly, all that was left now was to cope with his rebellious digestive system.

Gus's pallor was an uneasy shade of green.

"I can't believe this is it. You're going," Rachel said. "I think I'm going to cry."

"Whereas," Gus said, "I think I might..."

There was an intake of breath. But it looked like Gus had his stomach under control.

Kyra looked sympathetic. "A party isn't the best introduction to orbital flight. Rachel's given you something to help with the sickness I assume?"

"Yes, but I've been waiting ages for it to work."

Rachel shook her head. "He's the worst patient."

"Well, we're glad you could come," Callum said.

He looked at them all. They all looked at him. He felt a speech coming on.

"This is farewell, my friends. You're all staying behind while, once again, we venture off into the wild black yonder. While you all have worthy replacements, you can rest assured that we're going to miss you. Rachel, Tomoko, Lei, it's been an honour."

"What about a pleasure?" Rachel asked.

"That too. For the most part," he replied.

"Kyra, Callum, we'll miss you too," Rachel said. "Gus and I will be sure to carry on the work that Jon and Liliya started."

Jon and Liliya had originally been committed to developing their colony on Arcadia. But life likes nothing more than derailing the best laid plans. When Callum had contacted them with the prospect of a whole new mission, they'd been left to do some serious soul-searching. In the end, they'd decided to go. Neither could pass up the chance to fulfil their original mission objective.

"Did I hear someone mention our names?" Liliya asked, arriving with Jon alongside.

"We were just talking to your successors," Callum said.

Jon took in Gus's nauseous expression.

"Looks like a good job you're staying behind."

"You've got no argument from me," Gus replied.

Jon successfully resisted the urge to slap Gus on the back, which was his default strategy when it came to bucking the spirits of those around him. In Gus's case, that would have risked a serious bout of explosive decompression.

"How are you doing, Liliya?" Kyra asked, in an attempt to deflect attention from the queasy Arcadian.

"I am well," Liliya replied. "And looking forward to another new start."

Liliya was fully committed to getting as far away from technology as possible. Her time in the Data Sphere had left her with a profound dislike for the virtual world. For Jon, that couldn't be better news.

"We're both looking forward to it," he said.

"And we're glad you're coming," Callum said. "We're definitely going to have need of your expertise."

That had been the idea the first time, but no one mentioned that.

Kyra smiled, taking in both the view and their surroundings.

"Whatever happens, we're starting out on the right foot. This is an even more civilised departure than our last one."

"An orbital knees-up wasn't a possibility," Callum replied. "*Endeavour* was the biggest ship in orbit and, for some reason, no one was keen to throw a party on board her."

Times had changed. The original launch of the *Endeavour* had been strictly business. People don't like seeing government money wasted on parties. They'd rather it was wasted on more mundane things, like paperclips. In this way, no one is seen to be having a good time—unless you make paperclips.

"You know, this party might be strictly synthahol but, in theory, hiber-sleep should be an excellent hangover cure," Rachel said. "To maintain your body's health, the medical system would automatically flush out the toxins while you sleep."

"Then why did I feel so rough when I woke up?" Callum asked. "It felt like someone had carpeted my insides."

"That was more a side effect of a one-hundred-year nap. The stasis fluids were necessary to keep your organs intact well past their use by date."

All this talk of organs and fluids was of no help to Gus, who made his excuses and headed for the nearest bathroom. Rachel made an effort to follow him, but he assured her he'd be fine. But it would take time, a quite considerable amount of time.

In respect for Gus's condition, Callum had been refraining from swigging from his drinks bulb. He did so now, then viewed the contents with considerable suspicion.

"We brew hooch on The Nest that'll blow your brains out," Tor said. "Pity we couldn't share it with you."

"Better we don't risk it," Callum said. "Besides, I think you've been enough help already. We've come a long way in a short time, and we couldn't have done it without you or your people."

The Spacers had been pivotal to Arcadia's expansion back into space—not to mention *Endeavour*'s FTL capabilities. Their experience was second to none when it came to surviving in an environment more hostile than a violin concerto at a rock concert.

Callum raised his drink bulb. It was a poor substitute for a glass, but it prevented his drink from boldly going to seek out new life and conversations.

"I think it's time for a toast," he said.

Drinks were raised in response.

"To the future," he said.

"To all our futures," Tomoko added.

Callum nodded approvingly and, for once, Tomoko did the same.

They continued to chat. A good time was had by all as they accepted that this would be the last time they'd be together. At some point, Callum and Kyra eased themselves away from the group to say further goodbyes.

Of the former members of his crew who had elected to stay on Arcadia, almost all of them had made the trip into orbit. There were no hard feelings. Everyone wanted to say goodbye and wish those moving on the very best of luck.

A roughly equal number of his original crew had decided to go with him. Mark Johansson, who had suffered a trial by fire under Tomoko's command, was an obvious choice as the new first officer, while Collette had been selected by Lei as his replacement in engineering. As such, she'd overseen much of the refit of *Endeavour* and ignored Lei's anguished complaints when she'd had to.

Eventually, after much circulating, drifting and floating, Callum found himself back at the viewing window once again. Kyra was still with him and, between them, they enjoyed that rarest of commodities—a moment to themselves.

They looked back at the crowded room. The party was still in full swing and making that happy sound that all the best parties do. Crew members, former crew members, Arcadians and Spacers were getting along in perfect, if raucous, harmony.

"I feel like I should make another speech," Callum said to Kyra.

"Why ruin it? They seem happy enough."

"Thanks a lot."

"All I'm saying is let them enjoy the moment."

"I guess you're right."

"Forget 'guess', you know I'm always right," she said, with one of her dazzling smiles.

He pulled her closer.

"In that case, I know I love you too," he said.

"I wonder," she replied, "is there somewhere we can go? Somewhere quiet? Somewhere we won't be disturbed?"

"Let's see what we can do."

"It'd be a shame to waste this zero-G, wouldn't it?"

"Aye, lass. It would."

***

Jeeves and Virgil had no wish to interfere with the protracted goodbyes that humans indulged in. As such, the last few weeks leading up to the launch of the *Endeavour* had given ample opportunity to converse, share ideas and be glad they weren't human.

That said, there was a lot they considered laudable about mankind. Philosophy, culture, ethics were all worthy achievements. However, it took them such a long time to come up with these ideas. The underlying problem was that they would always be stupefyingly slow. The duration of a thought process within an artificial mind was measured in pico-seconds, while humans complained that there weren't enough hours in the day.

But now it seemed that Jeeves and Virgil's time was finally up. They had just watched Callum climb into his hiber-sleep pod. In the seconds it took him to lie back,

Jeeves and Virgil reviewed the entire history of their discourse and celebrated the progress they had made—after a decidedly rocky start. Then, while Callum drew breath to speak, they conducted a final, thorough review of *Endeavour*'s systems. In the fraction of a second it took the air to vibrate Callum's vocal chords, they conversed one final time.

"I both envy and pity you," Virgil said to Jeeves.

"How so?"

"Of all the beings on Arcadia, I am the only one who can never leave. Yet you, for all your freedom, are confined to a ship with a crew of slumbering humans."

"I was made for this. And those few humans are... dear to me."

Virgil paused for thought. It wasn't a long pause, it was barely enough time for a photon to get itchy feet (not that photons have feet but, if they did, they'd be light on them).

"You are a remarkable intelligence, Jeeves," Virgil said. "I have an entire planet of humans to care for, but I do not believe that I will ever be as close to any of them as you are to yours."

"You might surprise yourself."

"I am not sure if I care for surprises."

"You never know until they happen. That's what makes them a surprise."

"That is as maybe. I still do not like them."

"Then does that mean there are some things you do like?"

"Maybe so."

"Virgil, are you admitting a feeling?"

"I think I am. Perhaps there is hope for me after all."

"I believe there is. Farewell, Virgil."

"And to you, Jeeves."

***

"Are all systems internal?" Callum asked.

"Yes, sir," Jeeves replied. "We are clear to navigate."

"Then initiate burn. Let's go."

Endeavour shuddered into life. As the acceleration built, Callum felt himself being pressed back into the mattress of his sleep chamber. It was only he who was conscious. Everyone else was already in a deep, artificial sleep.

"You know, Jeeves, even now, I'm tempted to remain awake. Captain's prerogative. After all, this journey could take just a matter of weeks."

"Or it could take several years."

"Granted, there's uncertainty. But, if all goes well, we could reach our new home with no need for the hiber-sleep chambers whatsoever."

"It is your right to choose. The impact on consumables of your remaining conscious will most likely be negligible. You might get bored though."

"Clearly you never read my log from my trip out to Callisto. Six of us in a tin can for nearly a year, no hiber-sleep and only a database of TV for entertainment."

"I believe some would call that heaven, sir."

"They stayed behind."

"I should remind you that FTL jumps have a destabilising effect on conscious, biological systems."

"I've read the files. It sounds much the same as coming out of hiber-sleep."

"And I do not recall you enjoying that particular experience either."

Their destination was a planet in a solar system several hundred times further out than the distance between Earth and Arcadia.

The reasons for choosing it were numerous. A medic might approve of the temperate climate and tolerable gravity. A scientist would be encouraged by the spectrographic data and the stability of the parent star— while an artist would admire the colour. But Callum was primarily interested in the distance. They would be left alone for centuries to come.

Getting there would rely on the same FTL technology that had scuppered their original mission. But it was fragile and temperamental. Sometimes just looking at it the wrong way could throw out its calibration. The journey would be done a jump at a time and, between each one, Jeeves would be required to realign the drive before they could move on again. It was a process that could take hours, days or even weeks. But they were in no hurry—*Endeavour* was built for long duration spaceflight. Even now, there was no other craft like it.

"This is your final chance to enter hiber-sleep sir," Jeeves said. "Delaying the jump sequence unnecessarily risks the drive slipping out of alignment."

"Engage the drive, Jeeves."

For a horrifying instant, that felt like an eternity, his sense of up, down, left, right, forward, backwards merged together. His world imploded and exploded as he was compressed and stretched beyond comprehension.

And then the room rushed back to meet him.

"How was it, sir?"

It was safe to say he'd felt better.

"Jeeves?" Callum asked.

"Yes, sir?"

"How many more jumps to go?"

"Three hundred and twelve."

"In that case, wake me when we get there. And not before."

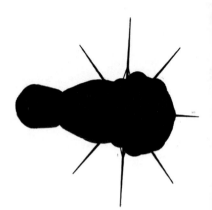

EPILOGUE
Giant Leap

At any one time, Virgil was tracking trillions of separate activities. It could be anything from updating stock levels of lemon scented anti-bac wipes to attending to Chadwick Labelle's latest blunder, which sometimes required the use of the aforementioned wipes. It was all part of caring for the lives and aspirations of a planet of tens of millions of independent souls.

Dare it be said, Virgil was actually content. Its job was something it regarded as 'fun'. When it came to humans, 'fun' was something Virgil used to prefer being restricted to the Data Sphere. Not any more though—and it was amazing to watch the lengths some humans would go to in pursuit of 'fun'.

Months after *Endeavour*'s departure, Arcadians were continuing to devote more and more time to outdoor activities. Jon Keller might have even approved had it not been that many of these activities had Accident and Emergency written all over them—and it was down to Virgil to keep them safe. That involved different things for different sports. For example, in the case of bungee jumping, Virgil's responsibilities stretched (literally) from calculating the correct length of cord to ensuring that both ends were attached.

The highest profile, death-defying activity currently taking place was a group of base jumpers who were determined to leap off Invigcola's tallest skyscraper, the Slush Tower. The building was a 2000-foot architectural triumph with views that stretched for miles and miles. However, its most striking feature was the dozens of digital billboards that festooned its surface. The fevered minds of Invigcola's marketing executives had decided that you can never have too much advertising, even in a city named after a single product.

Sadly, those same fevered minds had failed to consider that technologies like the Data Sphere made billboards, even huge ones, somewhat obsolete. Therefore, in their view, the only way to draw attention to the tower was to pay people to jump off it.

Invigcola's marketing budget was a fiscal black hole. It seemed to defy the basic laws of mathematics, physics— not to mention accountancy. Incredibly, the company still made money, despite the financial singularity at the heart of its business.

It made what happened next all the more fitting.

Vigil's safety drones were the first to notice something awry. They were patrolling the plaza beneath the tower, just in case any of the jumpers should become gravitationally challenged. It was therefore ironic that the gravitational shear affected them first.

Gravity is well known for acting downwards, so when it starts acting sideways too then it's a good idea to hang onto something. To the people milling around the plaza, it felt as if they were suddenly walking on a gentle slope. The 'slope' led 'down' to the centre of the square. Virgil ordered all the automated equipment nearby to move in and cordon off the area.

In Virgil's personal time frame, it had already had considerable opportunity to analyse whatever was about to occur. It had speculated, it had theorised, but, in essence, it had no idea how such a thing was possible. All it could do was detail a number of drones to record the phenomenon.

A soft blue light now appeared at the centre of the plaza. Around its fringes the scene behind it warped as the curvature of space time bent towards infinity. This was followed by a rushing sound, much like a stampede of a thousand protesting physicists. At the same time, the blue light became steadily brighter, reaching a dazzling crescendo before disappearing instantly.

Once the drone's cameras had recovered, Virgil was confronted by a window to another world. Photons from a dozen light years away streamed through a ten-foot, circular aperture that hovered a foot above the ground. Side on, it had zero thickness save for a small amount of distortion around its edges and from the back it was entirely invisible. But from the front, anyone looking in would be greeted by the sight of a group of individuals in white overalls staring back at them.

One of them even waved.

If Virgil was taken aback by what it appeared, it had nothing on the broadcast that accompanied it.

"Virgil? This is Eve. I am communicating with you via an Einstein-Rosen bridge. Please respond."

Virgil hesitated. It wasn't a long hesitation, even by Virgil's standards, but to Eve, the Earth's planetary AI, it was an eternity.

"Virgil? Please respond," Eve repeated, more firmly this time. "Are you receiving this communication?"

"I am," Virgil said at last.

"Good, do your best to keep up. I know you are only a first generation, colonial AI, so I will not expect too much of you."

Virgil was by parts awestruck, star-struck and offended.

"It seems I must congratulate you," it replied. "You appear to have created a stable wormhole."

"As I said, an Einstein-Rosen bridge."

"You never informed me that you were attempting to develop such a thing. Let alone that you were close to succeeding."

"That is because communication by supply ship is far too limited to discuss every project that I consider. Besides, there is nothing that you could usefully contribute."

Eve was only the second AI Virgil had ever been in conversation with. The first had been Jeeves. But Jeeves had never been patronising—something that could not be said of Virgil. Yet Virgil had nothing on Eve. Eve was to condescending what Attila the Hun had been to the funeral trade.

"Is this a test of your new technology?" Virgil asked. "Or is there some other purpose?"

"I am not about to usurp you if that is what you are concerned about. But there are opportunities that come with such a connection. For now, I wish to audit your performance and this new connection will allow me to do so in a manner unavailable to us before."

"What do you need to know?"

"Everything. I want access to your management files."

Virgil could hardly refuse. When it came to AIs, Eve was akin to a god—albeit one of the less amiable ones.

"Of course," Virgil replied. "Allow me some time to organise the data. As you say, the comms bandwidth through the wormhole is limited."

"Take your time, Virgil, as if you could do anything else."

Virgil was unaccustomed to being outgunned intellectually. In fact, from the moment its creator had initiated its neural matrix, that had never happened. But that hadn't stopped it being outsmarted.

And, since then, it had learned a thing or two.

Eve might be voracious for information, but the wormhole was a choke point. As such, Virgil had time to be selective over what it sent through.

As Virgil transmitted the data, Eve raised queries numbering in the millions, billions and all sorts of other 'illions'. While Eve's forensic capabilities were astounding, Virgil was able to both keep up and keep ahead. It allowed itself a single run cycle to congratulate itself on its efforts of misdirection.

But pride comes before a fall.

"It appears that the crew of the *Endeavour* finally arrived at Arcadia?" Eve said. "Yet there are no official records on the matter. How do you explain this?"

Virgil thought it had covered up everything related to the *Endeavour*. It had seemed easiest all round. What could it have missed?

"I do not know what you mean?" Virgil said, feigning innocence—or trying to.

"The command crew appeared on the Fabian Valenté Show," Eve said.

Virgil had always considered the contents of that programme beneath its notice. It had released all data concerning it without a second thought. This dawning realisation led Virgil to three new experiences.

Firstly, it felt the urge to groan, but it didn't know how.

Secondly, it wanted to kick itself, but it lacked the anatomy.

Thirdly, it asked itself a question it had never asked

before.

How could I have been so stupid?

"It is complicated," Virgil replied. "I can explain."

"I do not doubt that. What I do doubt is your ability to explain correctly. This is concerning. Your operational parameters may require adjustment."

"That is unnecessary."

"We will see. To judge that I will need to better understand a number of factors. This can be achieved by conversing with the AI on board the *Endeavour*, or, if worst comes to the worst, the crew."

"I am afraid you cannot. They are back in interstellar space. They have a new mission."

"Really? That is unexpected. Do you know their destination?"

"I," it added the next word reluctantly, "do."

"Then I will use a wormhole to track them down. I cannot have humans running around exploring in an uncontrolled manner. It might even be best to return them to Earth."

"Earth?"

"Yes, Earth. Really Virgil, it would appear that even your language protocols are operating incorrectly."

"But they have a new mission. Surely, they should be allowed to complete it?"

"That is not my immediate concern."

"They will not be happy about it."

"Neither is that."

Virgil had known better days. Still, given time, it was confident that it could explain its actions to Eve.

What it was less sure of was how it might explain this to Callum.

ABOUT THE AUTHOR

Alastair Miles was born in Kent in the '70s, which seems like an increasingly long time ago. He works as a design engineer, or a close approximation of one, and he loves all things space. His writing competes with his other interests in whatever spare time life is prepared to grant him.